Praise for *Di*

"The only thing more fun than an *October Daye* book is an *InCryptid* book. Swift narrative, charm, great world-building . . . all the McGuire trademarks."
—Charlaine Harris, #1 *New York Times* Bestselling Author

"Seanan McGuire's *Discount Armageddon* is an urban fantasy triple threat—smart and sexy and funny. The Aeslin mice alone are worth the price of the book, so consider a cast of truly ORIGINAL characters, a plot where weird never overwhelms logic, and some serious kick-ass world-building as a bonus."
—Tanya Huff, author of *The Wild Ways*

"*Discount Armageddon* is a quick-witted, sharp-edged look at what makes a monster monstrous, and at how closely our urban fantasy protagonists walk—or dance—that line. The pacing never lets up, and when the end comes, you're left wanting more. I can't wait for the next book!"
—C. E. Murphy, author of *Spirit Dances*

"Smart, whimsical and bitingly funny, Verity Price is a kick-ass heroine that readers will love. Just when I thought she couldn't surprise me again, she would pull some new trick out of her hat—or in the case of her throwing knives—out of her corset. I would send Verity and my Jane Jameson on a girl's night out, but I'm afraid of the damage bill they would rack up!"
—Molly Harper, author of *Nice Girls Don't Bite Their Neighbors*

DAW Books presents the finest in urban fantasy from Seanan McGuire:

InCryptid Novels:

DISCOUNT ARMAGEDDON

MIDNIGHT BLUE-LIGHT SPECIAL

HALF-OFF RAGNAROK

POCKET APOCALYPSE*

SPARROW HILL ROAD

October Daye Novels:

ROSEMARY AND RUE

A LOCAL HABITATION

AN ARTIFICIAL NIGHT

LATE ECLIPSES

ONE SALT SEA

ASHES OF HONOR

CHIMES AT MIDNIGHT

THE WINTER LONG

*Coming soon from DAW Books

DISCOUNT ARMAGEDDON

AN INCRYPTID NOVEL

SEANAN McGUIRE

DAW BOOKS, INC.

DONALD A. WOLLHEIM, FOUNDER

375 Hudson Street, New York, NY 10014

ELIZABETH R. WOLLHEIM
SHEILA E. GILBERT
PUBLISHERS

http://www.dawbooks.com

Copyright © 2012 by Seanan McGuire.

All Rights Reserved.

Cover art by Aly Fell.

Interior dingbat created by Tara O'Shea.

DAW Book Collectors No. 1579.

DAW Books are distributed by Penguin Group (USA) Inc.

All characters and events in this book are fictitious.
Any resemblance to persons living or dead is strictly coincidental.

If you purchase this book without a cover you should be aware that this book
may have been stolen property and reported as "unsold and destroyed" to the
publisher. In such case neither the author nor the publisher has received any
payment for this "stripped book."

The scanning, uploading and distribution of this book via the Internet or via any
other means without the permission of the publisher is illegal, and punishable by
law. Please purchase only authorized electronic editions, and do not participate
in or encourage the electronic piracy of copyrighted materials. Your support of
the author's rights is appreciated.

Nearly all the designs and trade names in this book are registered trademarks.
All that are still in commercial use are protected by United States and international trademark law.

First Printing, March 2012
7   8   9

DAW TRADEMARK REGISTERED
U.S. PAT. AND TM. OFF. AND FOREIGN COUNTRIES
—MARCA REGISTRADA
HECHO EN U.S.A.

PRINTED IN THE U.S.A.

For Phil.
Let's dance.

Price Family Tree

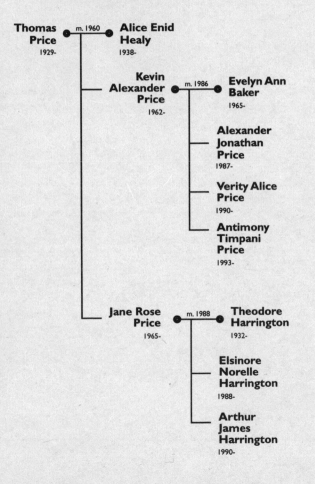

Thomas Price
1929-

m. 1960

Alice Enid Healy
1938-

Kevin Alexander Price
1962-

m. 1986

Evelyn Ann Baker
1965-

Alexander Jonathan Price
1987-

Verity Alice Price
1990-

Antimony Timpani Price
1993-

Jane Rose Price
1965-

m. 1988

Theodore Harrington
1932-

Elsinore Norelle Harrington
1988-

Arthur James Harrington
1990-

Cryptid, noun:

1. Any creature whose existence has been suggested but not proved scientifically. Term officially coined by cryptozoologist John E. Wall in 1983.

2. That thing that's getting ready to eat your head.

3. See also "monster."

Prologue

"I really don't think you should put your
hand inside the manticore, dear. You don't
know where it's been."

–Enid Healy

*A small survivalist compound about an hour's drive east of
Portland, Oregon*

Sixteen years ago

VERITY DANCED CIRCLES around the living room, her amateurish pirouettes and unsteady leaps accompanied by cheers and exultations from the horde of Aeslin mice perched on the back of the couch. The cheering of the mice reached a fever pitch on the few occasions where she actually managed to get both feet off the ground and land again without falling. Her brother looked up from his book, snorting once before returning to his studies. At nine, Alexander considered himself above younger sisters and their tendency to act like complete idiots when given the slightest opportunity.

Evelyn Price leaned against the hallway arch with her youngest daughter balanced against her hip, watching Verity dance. A hand touched her shoulder. She sighed without looking around. "Kevin, I don't know what we're going to do about getting her to take her studies more seriously."

"She's six. I wasn't taking my studies seriously at that age either."

Evelyn laughed. "Should I ask the mice about that one, or would you like to admit that it's a lie and save us all the sermon?"

"All I'm saying is that she'll settle down if we give her a little time. I promise, Evie. She'll come around." Kevin Price stepped up next to his wife. Antimony reached her three-year-old arms up toward him. He plucked her from her mother's hip, hoisting her up to his own shoulder. She giggled. "What did Very decide she wasn't going to do this time?"

"Hide-and-seek," said Evelyn.

Most children treated hide-and-seek as a game. This alien behavior never failed to shock and scandalize the Price children once they achieved school age and went marching off to the local elementary to be socialized. For them, hide-and-seek was a serious business, one that centered on finding likely routes of ambush and escape and learning how to cut them off. Alex had received his first concussion during a game of hide-and-seek. He was five at the time. Kevin wasn't sure the boy had ever been so proud of himself before or since.

The thought of Verity refusing a hide-and-seek session was worrisome, especially since she'd always been better at it than her brother—a fact that made her want to "play" as often as possible. "What did she want to do instead?"

"She says she wants to dance," Evelyn said, watching Verity whirl around the room like a tiny blonde dervish. "That's all. Just dance."

One

"True love always shoots to kill."
—Alice Healy

A nightclub in downtown Manhattan

Now

MUSIC PUMPED THROUGH THE CLUB'S SPEAKERS, distorted until it was barely more than a pounding bass line with a sprinkling of grace notes. It was perfect dance music, the kind that makes feet tap and thighs twitch with the need to get up and *move*. My own feet were tapping. I forced them to stop. There'd be time for that soon enough, but for the moment, waiting was still the name of the game.

I hate waiting.

Sarah had managed to acquire a half-circle booth that was empty except for us. It would have been impossible for anyone else. I'm not even sure she realized she was doing something impressive. I leaned sulkily back in my seat, trying to look casual as I sipped my nonalcoholic "Cosmopolitan"—club soda, grenadine, and a maraschino cherry for that finishing touch—and scanned the dance floor.

"So, Verity, tell me, are you looking for our nasty friend, or are you sizing up the competition?" Sarah's tone was mild, but I could recognize the warning lurking underneath the question.

"Sorry," I said, looking guiltily away from the floor.

"Aren't you always?" Sarah was sitting in the center of the booth, partially so she could lounge nonchalantly against the burgundy vinyl cushions, and partially so she wouldn't be in the way if I needed to move suddenly. Her choice of seating had the added bonus of keeping the crowd at a distance, since the full length of the table was between her and the rest of the club. Sarah doesn't like being touched, something that's generally viewed as a major loss by the male population of whatever city she's in. She has classical black Irish coloring, with pale skin, thick black hair, and eyes that are an almost perfect ice blue. Add in her svelte figure and delicate features, and it's no wonder she's beating the boys off with a stick.

Not that most of them would know how to handle the revelation that she bleeds clear and doesn't have a heartbeat, but hey, what's a little inhumanity between friends? Sarah's family, even if it's through adoption. And there's something to be said for bringing a telepath along when you're hunting rogue cryptids through Manhattan's hottest party spots. Without her, I would never have been able to get past the velvet rope.

She was still eyeing me. "My mind's on the job," I said defensively, plucking the cherry from my drink. "Really. I swear."

"Uh-huh." Sarah raised an eyebrow. "Do we have to have the 'don't lie to the telepath' talk again? It won't take long. I say 'don't lie to the telepath, it never works,' you glare at me, and then you go find something you can hit."

"Finding something I can hit is the plan." I popped the cherry into my mouth as I glanced at the dance floor. Mmm, food coloring and sugar. "He'll show. His patterns have been regular up to now, and this is the next stop on his circuit."

"Well, I don't know how much help I'm going to be. Ghoul minds are hard to tell from human minds under the best of circumstances. With this many drunk, horny people in one place, I'd be lucky to spot a serial killer, much less a ghoul."

"If you do spot a serial killer, let me know. Sitting here is making my feet itch." My shoes were doing worse than that, but that's what I get for wearing five-inch heels. They have a practical application—it's almost impossible for me to pull off a good salsa without heels on. That doesn't make them comfortable. At least when I was dancing, I had something to distract me from the way they bent my arches.

Neither of us was dressed for comfort. Sarah was playing the bored celebutante, which necessitated that she wear the appropriate "uniform": a skirt that could double as a belt, a backless silver handkerchief top, and knee-high leather boots. The temptation to snap a few pictures with my phone and mail them to our cousin Artie was almost impossible to resist. His head would probably explode.

Sarah looked miserable. That didn't matter; no matter how miserable she was, her telepathy would keep everyone around us seeing what they expected to see when they looked our way. Wearing the right things and drinking the right drinks just made it easier, since she didn't have to work as hard to convince them.

My skirt was slightly longer, but only because it's borderline impossible to fit a thigh holster under a micromini. I made up for my shameful modesty with a blood-red velvet bustier that looked appropriately scandalous—and better yet, had steel corsetry boning and gave me room for five strategically placed throwing knives. Between those, the steel tips on my heels, and the perfume bottle of holy water in my purse, I was loaded for bear. More accurately, I was loaded for ghoul. This one was hunting in midtown, which is a big no-no, and had killed fifteen girls that we knew of. There were probably more that we'd managed to miss. Not okay.

"If he's here, he'll be on the floor," I said, trying to sound casual.

I could tell from the look on Sarah's face that she wasn't buying it, but her sense of telepathic ethics wouldn't let her admit that. She raised her eyebrow again before sighing and waving toward the floor. "Go. You'll feel better. I'll toss up a flare if I pick up on him."

"You're the best!" I was out of my seat almost instantly, leaving my drink on the table as I made a beeline for the teeming mass of bodies on the dance floor. Steel-tipped heels can go a long way toward clearing a path, especially when you're not opposed to "accidentally" stepping on a few toes. The smell of sweat, spilled alcohol, and a hundred different perfumes assaulted my nose, making my head swim. I dove into the crowd.

The secret of good club music is the downbeat. Even the world's worst dancer can't help picking up a little rhythm when the bass is pumped high enough, and a good DJ can work a crowd like it's just another kind of musical instrument. This DJ wasn't the best, but he wasn't terrible, and that was all I needed. I worked my way past the first tiers of dancers—the ones too drunk, too disinterested, or too interested in looking for a different kind of "dance" to defend their places in the center of the floor—and gave myself over to the beat, letting it tell my body where to go. It didn't matter that I was there because something was killing club kids in what was currently my city. It didn't matter that my clothes were Scotchgarded against bloodstains, not sweat. It didn't even matter that all of my formal training was in the ballroom styles. I was dancing. Everything was going to be okay.

The natural pulse of a good dance floor means the best dancers wind up getting pulled toward the center, sucked inexorably forward as they pass through the ranks of the less invested and the less skilled. I had half a dozen partners within the first five minutes, each trying to catch my eye as they shook whatever they had in my direction. They knew the rules of the floor, and when the tempo of my steps knocked theirs out of the game, they were graceful enough to let me go.

I wound up packed into the place where the circles of dancers compressed to nearly nothing, sharing that coveted spot with three couples, two other single women, and a man about my age who seemed to be comfortable dancing by himself while he sized up his options. He looked like he'd just about settled on one of the women—a lanky brunette in hip-hugger designer jeans—when I hit the circle. His attention shifted, a predatory gleam lighting up his eyes.

Single white male seeks single white female for . . . what, exactly? I gave him a once-over as he moved toward me, disguising the look with a flirtatious wink. All his clothes were dark, and the fabrics looked naturally stain-resistant. No scars, no tattoos, no jewelry; good-looking in that generic movie extra sort of way. The kind of guy you'd happily dance with for a little while, maybe even follow home if you were in the mood for something nastier than a little grinding.

"Hey," he said, raising his voice to be heard over the music. "I haven't seen you here before. You're good."

"You, too," I shouted back.

"Wanna dance?"

"Sure thing!" That seemed to complete the pleasantries, and it was straight to business for my mystery man. He closed in like a heat-seeking missile, cupping my hips with his hands as he matched his rhythm to mine. A little tacky for a first date, maybe, but that's nothing for a first dance. I've done tangos with men who thought my ass was a squeaky toy. Compared to them, Mr. Mystery was being nothing but polite.

I looked at him more carefully as we writhed around the center circle together, and frowned. His teeth were white, slightly crooked in an adorable way, and *normal*. He couldn't be our ghoul. Human flesh is tough to chew, and ghouls who take their dinner straight off the bone inevitably do a number on their choppers. If my dance partner had been a ghoul passing for human, he would have either had perfect dentist-purchased caps or been keeping his lips shut. This wasn't our guy. I let my body go back on autopilot, scanning the crowd around us.

The normal ebb and flow of dancers continued, people falling back as they got tired or being pushed forward as they caught their second wind. Only the inner circle stayed mostly the same. Emphasis on the "mostly"—one of the couples was leaving, the woman laughing, the man giving a tight-lipped smile that completely hid his teeth.

Shit.

"Oopsie. I think I drank too many martinis. I need to go puke," I said, and ducked away from a startled Mr. Mystery, shoving my way after the departing ghoul and the woman who was about to be his next victim. It was easier to get out than in, mostly because there were so many dancers happy to take my place, and to shove me farther toward the edge of the dance floor. I caught a glimpse of my former dance partner as he turned his attention to a redhead in a sparkly tube top, already forgetting about me. Oh, well. He wasn't that hot.

Who was I kidding? He was insanely hot, and I haven't been able to finish dancing with a guy—or "dancing" with a guy—since I got to New York. Still, with a woman in immediate mortal peril, this wasn't the time to worry about my love life. I kept moving forward. I was surrounded enough that there was no way Sarah would pick up on my mental distress call, and it's not like she could do anything about it if she did. Sarah's not a fighter. All she really knows how to do is sit calmly and camouflage herself until the trouble goes away.

I finished pushing my way off the dance floor and stopped to scan the club, searching for my quarry. I finally spotted them by the front door, him helping her into her coat, her grinning ear to ear. Such a gentleman.

Only once he got her outside and alone, all those good manners would go right out the window.

Out the window. Grabbing the nearest waitress by the shoulder, I gasped, saying with what I hoped was believable panic, "I wait tables at Dave's. I called in sick tonight, and the boss' asshole assistant just walked in. Is there another way out of here?"

Her initial irritation died when I invoked waitress solidarity. "The fire escape's behind the DJ," she said. "If he says anything, tell him Liz sent you."

"Thank you, thank you!" I let her go and turned to run for the DJ. If I hurried, I just might make it before things got bloody.

If there was going to be gore, I wanted it on my own terms.

The DJ was so caught up in his groove that he never even looked up as I ran past him, shouldered open the fire escape door, and slipped out into the hot Manhattan night. Since the club was below street level, the fire escape was actually a steel stairway leading up to the street behind the club, which was narrow and grubby enough to have been considered an alley anywhere else in the world. Manhattan is not a city with space to spare.

I grabbed the rail and pulled myself along, careful to keep my heels from hitting the steps. Stealth isn't one of my strong suits, but it has its place. Not that I needed to try all that hard; the music inside was loud enough that it was thumping through the wall, providing the outside world with a skeletal downbeat.

The street behind the club ran between two other, larger streets. As I watched, the ghoul came walking along the sidewalk, hand in hand with his date-slash-dinner. I tensed, ready to run after them. I never had the opportunity. The woman tugged at the ghoul's arm, possibly in reaction to something he said, and started leading him toward the street where I was waiting.

It's always nice when the thing you're hunting decides to walk straight into an ambush. I waited for them to get close enough that he wouldn't be able to run without me catching him. Then I stomped up the steps, my earlier attempts at stealth abandoned in favor of making as much noise as possible. "*There* you are, you pig!" I shouted, leveling a finger at his chest. "Cindy told me she saw you here, but I thought she was just fucking around with me again. How *dare* you?!"

The ghoul stared at me with gratifying surprise. His nightly order of club kid takeout, on the other hand, stepped away from him like he'd been set on fire. That wasn't a bad idea. Too bad I didn't have any matches. "You have a girlfriend?" she demanded, ignoring me in favor of glaring at the ghoul.

"Girlfriend?" I echoed, planting my hands on my hips. "Honey, he's *married.*"

That was all I had to say. "You *asshole*," she said witheringly, and slapped him hard across the face before turning to stalk away, all drunken indignation. She'd be back on the dance floor within ten minutes, hunting for a guy who wasn't cheating on someone. I know the type. Hell, I've been the type, when I wasn't working.

The ghoul watched her go, his shocked expression transforming slowly into anger. He swung his head around to face me, eyes narrowed. "You just made a big mistake, little girl. I wasn't in the mood for blonde tonight."

"Aw, too bad for you." I simpered, tucking my hands behind me in a cutesy-pie gesture that concealed the act of drawing the knives from the back panel of my bustier. "See, this is how things are going to work tonight. I'm going to tell you to get out of town, just as fast as you can, and you're going to agree with me. Won't that be fun?"

"I have a better idea," said the ghoul, and grinned. It

was a horrible sight. Most of his teeth were blackened and broken, some all the way down to the gum line. He'd grow a new set in pretty short order—ghouls are like sharks, they're constantly teething—but for the moment, he was basically gumming his victims to death. Not a good way to go. "I'm going to make sure there's not enough of your body left for your family to identify."

"I bet you say that to all the girls." Not the most original line in the world, but originality is secondary to not getting eaten when I'm in the field. I pulled my hands from behind my back and fell into a relaxed starting position, knives ready for throwing. "Come on, big guy. Let's dance."

A flicker of consternation crossed his face as he took in my reaction. Then it faded, and he lunged.

You'd think the predators of the world would eventually learn that it's not a good idea to charge the sort of person who brings throwing knives to a dance club. Then again, if they were smart enough for that, they'd be smart enough to figure out that eating humans is a bad idea. You need meat, go to a steakhouse. You need it raw, go for sushi. But if you think your local nightclub is the place to go for an easy meal, you'd better be ready to pay for it. My first knife caught him in the forearm while he was in mid-lunge. My second knife killed what little was left of his forward momentum when it hit the inside of his leg, just above his left knee.

He went down hard.

Ghouls are badass hunters when all they're dealing with is drunk, unarmed party girls, but they're no match for somebody who knows what she's doing. He was still trying to decide whether he wanted to clutch his knee, his arm, or both when I delivered a hard kick to his ribs, rolling him onto his back. I promptly placed one foot on his breastbone, keeping him there.

"Hi," I said, pulling the gun from my thigh holster and aiming it at his face. "We haven't been properly introduced. I'm Verity, and you're leaving."

"What are you, Covenant?" he snarled.

"Worse," I said, pressing my weight down a bit harder on his chest. He moaned as my steel-tipped heel bit into his skin. "I'm a Price. You're interfering with my ecosystem. Two choices, buddy. Out of the city and off the humanitarian diet, or down into the sewers to feed the mole people. What's your preference?"

Naturally, he chose to live another day, swearing he'd never touch living human flesh again. We'd never tangled with him before, so the family code said I had to let him off with a stern warning. If we heard about him so much as thinking the words "long pork" ever again, we'd come down on him so hard he'd barely have time to shit himself before he shuffled off this mortal coil. I was feeling generous, and he hadn't actually managed to bleed on me. I told him he had forty-eight hours to get out of New York City entirely.

My name is Verity Price. I'm a cryptozoologist. And this is why I can never get a goddamn date on a Saturday night.

Two

"There's no such thing as a normal life.
Some lives are just more interesting than
others, and we shouldn't judge people for
being boring."

—Evelyn Baker

A semilegal sublet in Greenwich Village, the next morning

THE SOUND OF CHEERING filtered through the bedroom
wall and across the edges of my consciousness, dis-
rupting a really pleasant dream about teaching Christian Bale to dance the samba. Groaning, I rolled over
and pulled the pillow over my head. The cheering didn't
stop.

"Oh, come *on*," I muttered, trying to burrow into the
mattress. All I wanted was ten more minutes. Just ten
more minutes, and the chance to finish teaching Christian where I wanted him to put his hands . . .

The cheers rose to a fever pitch, becoming impossible
to ignore. I yanked my head out from under the pillow,
pushing myself onto my elbows as I shouted, "If you
make me come out there, you're gonna be—"

Something smashed.

"—sorry." I let myself fall back to the mattress, going
as flat as I could. Becoming one with the bed didn't help.
"It'll be fine, Very," I said, imitating Mom's perpetually
upbeat tone. "It's just a splinter colony. You'll barely

even know they're in the apartment. Besides, you know they love you. How are they going to feel if you go off and abandon them?"

Another smash. Another cheer. I sighed, dropping back into my own voice as I answered myself, "Probably better than I feel about them breaking all the dishes."

The clock on the bedside table said it was almost seven o'clock in the evening; I'd been in bed less than six hours, and I was definitely feeling it. Three hours of club crawling, the fight with the ghoul, and two more hours at the club before hitting the studio for my morning work-out and rumba class had taken its toll, leaving me with the strong desire to stuff wads of cotton in my ears and try to steal a few more hours of sleep.

I might have done it, too, if there'd been any point. It was almost seven; I had to be at work by nine. That'll teach me to swap shifts with Kitty.

I slid out of bed and started for the hall. "Somebody's dying for this," I announced to anyone who might be listening. The cheering from the other room continued. No one was listening.

Finding a decent apartment in Greenwich Village on a ballroom dancer-slash-cocktail waitress' salary seemed like an impossible dream until Mom got involved. She pulled some strings and found a Sasquatch who was pre-paring to go on a year's vacation with some Canadian cousins. The Sasquatch had been open to the idea of subletting as long as I promised to get the bathroom plumbing fixed and didn't touch her collection of Pre-cious Moments figurines. As if I'd want to?

Still, it was a nice apartment in a good location for six hundred a month plus utilities, and that's an occurrence about as common in New York City as a herd of unicorns—maybe slightly rarer. Fixing the bathroom wasn't hard, even if I'm still having nightmares about the hairballs the plumber snaked out of the shower drain. Protecting the breakables required boxing them up and storing them in the very back of the bedroom closet, where threats, bribery, and begging would hopefully be enough to keep grabby little paws at bay.

You could've said no, I told myself, and stepped around the hall corner into the kitchen.

Another great cheer arose.

"HAIL THE COMING OF THE ARBOREAL PRIESTESS!"

For what felt like the tenth time since the cheering started, I groaned.

A stranger stepping into the apartment's tiny, nigh-claustrophobic kitchen would probably have stepped right back out again. A stranger with rodent-centric phobias would probably have skipped stepping in favor of running screaming out of the apartment, because the counters on both sides of the room were overflowing with a teeming sea of furry, multicolored bodies. Mice.

Technically mice, anyway, or at least close enough for taxonomical work. One could argue that most household rodents don't wear tattered tribal clothing made from scraps of fur and fabric. One could argue further that most household rodents don't wave weapons jubilantly over their heads when people come into the room. As far as I'm concerned, all that proves is a lack of imagination on the part of most household rodents.

Not even a sea of cheering mice could keep me from noticing the broken glass and gummy bears covering the kitchen floor. "Didn't we talk about this?"

"HAIL!"

"That isn't an answer." I planted my hands on my hips. "Was there a reason for shoving the gummy bears off the counter? Did they tell you they were suicidal? On second thought," I raised a hand, palm out, "don't answer that. If the candy is talking, I don't want to know."

"The container blocked the Sacred Route of Celebration!" announced one of the junior priests. The bright blue streaks dyed in the fur on his head marked him as a modernist, a member of the class of priests who believed in updating the Teachings to fit the new generation. Sadly, that often translated to "breaking things." "It required adjustment!"

"Yeah, well, 'adjustment' isn't supposed to wake me up." I eyed the refrigerator with longing. A sea of broken glass separated us, and I wasn't sure where I'd left my shoes. *Probably under the bed again . . .* "I thought there weren't any celebrations today."

"There are no *annual* celebrations today, Priestess," replied a tawny-furred female in full regalia. At least she had the good grace to sound apologetic. "Today's celebration is held every eight years, to mark the union of the Noisy Priestess to the God of Things That It Is Almost Certainly Better Not to Be Aware Of."

"Oh, crap." I slumped against the doorframe, mashing the heels of my hands into my eyes. It didn't make the mice shut up. "You're celebrating Grandma and Grandpa getting together, aren't you?"

"*HAIL!*" confirmed the mice.

"Great."

Back home, Mom keeps a master calendar that details the religious observances of the Aeslin mice, with every feast, festival, celebration, and day of mourning carefully annotated. I never understood why she bothered. Living with my own splinter colony has given me perspective. It's not anal retentiveness that fuels Mom's calendar. It's self-preservation.

Aeslin mice can make anything—*anything*—into a religious observation, and once they do, they cling to it for as long as the colony survives. The main body of the current colony has been with my family for seven generations. Individual Aeslin come and go, but the memory of the colony is very, very long.

"How long does this particular celebration last?" I asked, already afraid of the answer.

"Only the length of time between the leaving of the

family home and the arrival at the graveyard, Priestess," said the tawny mouse.

"You mean the family home back in Michigan?"

"Yes, Priestess."

"Jesus." That could mean anything between "an hour" and "three days." Anything longer than three days is usually a festival instead of a celebration, but that's not a hard rule. I straightened up. "Here's what we're going to do." The Aeslin watched with their customary attentiveness, a tiny congregation of furry bodies hanging on my every word. It would have been creepy if I hadn't been so used to it. "I'm going to take a shower."

"Hail the shower!"

"When I get back, you're going to have all this glass cleaned up, because if I don't get something to eat before I go to work, I'm going to look into getting a cat. And not," I held up my hand again, "because I want to provide meat for the next feast. Understand?"

"Yes, Priestess," said the blue-streaked mouse, echoed by a half dozen others. That would have to be enough. I was powerless to stop the celebration—nothing short of nuclear war can stop an Aeslin religious observance once it starts—but they understand the need to keep their Priestesses placated. They'd have the kitchen floor clean by the time I got back.

Life as the chosen religious figure for a colony of cryptid mice can be a lot of things, but it's definitely never boring.

🐁

The apartment's bathroom made the kitchen look spacious, and made me deeply grateful for the fact that I possess the sort of flexibility only achieved through years of hard physical training. I'm probably one of the few people in the world who doesn't have a problem showering while standing on one leg and pointing the toes of my other leg toward the ceiling. Drying off still required straddling the edge of the half-sized tub and praying I wouldn't slip. The entire process was enough to make a girl dream of human dry cleaning, and wonder how in the hell the apartment's usual super-sized occupant ever managed to fit into the stall.

The steam fogging the mirror kept me from needing to face the bags under my eyes until it was time to apply enough foundation to keep me from looking like I was actually dead. I have the sort of farm-girl complexion that tans fast and pales even faster, which means my current nocturnal schedule leaves me looking like I'm a little under the weather all the time. It's all part of the standard family genetic package, along with the cryptid mice and the generation-spanning blood feud. Price Girl version twelve, now with real salsa-dancing action. I'm five-two, with blue eyes, white-blonde hair, and a cheerleader smile—just your basic girl next door, assuming your girl next door comes spring-loaded with seventeen ways to kill a man. Which implies a pretty interesting neighborhood that most people probably don't want to visit.

Seventeen ways to kill a man is an average, by the way. I only have about six ways to kill a man when I'm fresh out of the shower, and I'm an underachiever in that regard. Antimony usually has twenty-six ways to kill a man, at least last time I checked.

My little sister is special.

The glass and gummy bears were gone by the time I finished getting dressed, putting on my makeup, and working enough gel into my hair to keep it from getting out of control. Even cropped punky-pop-star short, it has a mind of its own, probably because I have to shove it under a wig whenever I attend a dance competition. But that's the deal I made with my folks: Verity Price will never have a dancing career. Valerie Pryor, on the other hand, can dance as much as she wants, as long as the real work keeps getting handled. When it's cryptids versus the cancan, the cryptids win, or I go back to Oregon.

The mice had disappeared along with the mess. Hopefully, that meant they were taking their religious holiday into the hall closet where it belonged. What was the point of converting a Barbie Dream House for them if they weren't going to *use* it? The stupid thing took up most of the closet, and that meant I had to hang my coat and half my stage costumes on a rack in the front room, which wasn't any bigger than the rest of the apartment. Not that I would've resented the inconvenience if the Dream House would just do what it was supposed to do and keep the mice contained.

Muffled cheering came from the closet. I let out a relieved breath. The colony would stay occupied for however long their celebration was slated to last, which meant I could worry about food instead of worrying about them.

The fridge was divided into two distinct sides: mine, and the mice's. My shelves were essentially empty, holding a half-empty bottle of store-brand cola, a package of stale tortillas, two containers of takeout Chinese from the previous week, and a stick of butter I was pretty sure was there when I moved in. The mice, on the other hand, had an assortment of imported cheeses, several jars of Mom's homemade jam, and—most tempting of all—half a chocolate cake from the bakery down the block. *Flourless* chocolate cake, with bittersweet fudge icing.

I stared longingly at the cake before muttering a curse, grabbing the tortillas, Chinese food, and butter, and slamming the refrigerator door. The mice have a sixth sense when it comes to cake. They'd swarm if I so much as touched the plate, religious observances temporarily superseded by the desire to demand baked goods.

No amount of cake was worth that sort of chaos this soon after getting out of bed.

Buttering the tortillas and filling them with aged sesame noodles and sweet-and-sour chicken produced a passable, if bizarre, form of fajita. *I will eat something healthy for lunch,* I promised myself, knowing full well that by the time I could swing a "lunch break"— sometime after midnight and before two, depending on the foot traffic at work—I'd settle for a platter of potato skins and some hot wings.

"It's the thought that counts," I said, shoving the second half of my "fajita" into a plastic baggie that would hopefully keep the sweet-and-sour sauce from staining my coat. I put the baggie in my pocket.

If it was the thought that counted, maybe I ought to think about buying groceries. Food was easier at home, where Mom did all the shopping and Dad did the bulk of the cooking. Living at home came with a lot of bonuses that hadn't been visible until I moved out. The cheering in the closet rose in volume again. I winced. Bonuses like the mice having their own sound-proofed attic.

"I'm leaving for work now," I called, unlatching the kitchen window. A week of careful oiling and counterweighting had rendered it incapable of standing open on its own. It would slam closed as soon as I let go. "Try not to break anything else today, okay?"

Distant cheering seemed to be the only answer I was going to get.

Choosing discretion as the better part of valor, I hoisted myself onto the windowsill, careful to keep a firm grip on the edge of the window itself. It was only a three-story drop to the unlit courtyard, but I knew from studying it during the daylight that it was narrow and cluttered with a wide variety of convenient ways for me to get hurt, ranging from trash cans to the ever-popular "rusty chain-link fence."

It was dark enough that I couldn't even see the window of the apartment across from me. The ambient glow of the city lights illuminated the sky, but none of it seemed willing to penetrate the space between the buildings.

Sliding my legs out the window, I pushed off from the windowsill and fell into the dark.

Three

"Pass the dynamite."

—Frances Brown

Just outside the window of a small semilegal sublet in Greenwich Village, plummeting

IT HAD ONLY TAKEN AN AFTERNOON for me to memorize the layout of the courtyard, although keeping the dimensions straight in my head had required bouncing off the fire escape twice and coming within a single missed handhold of breaking several major bones. Learning the layout of the neighborhood had taken a little longer. It had been almost three weeks before I could make a full circuit of the block without needing to remove my blackout goggles at least once, and I still wasn't willing to cross streets when I couldn't see the status of the light. That would come later.

"Remember, Very," Dad used to say when I whined about the goggles, "if your opponent has night vision and you've never bothered to learn the local landmarks by anything but sight, you're going to be in a bit of a pickle when it's time to avoid getting disemboweled."

Truer words have doubtless been spoken. If they were spoken in our household, they probably had something to do with causing—or surviving—severe bodily harm. Other kids got chores and teddy bears; we got gun safety classes and heavy weaponry. Normal's what you make it.

I fell about four feet straight down, building momentum, and grabbed the bottom of the fire escape just before the fall could get out of my control. Swinging myself around, I hit the corner of the building with both feet and shoved off, translating the energy of the impact into a leap that carried me across the five-foot gap and onto the building across the way. I was off and running, leaving mouse holy rituals and semilegal sublets behind me as I started accelerating in the direction of work. I could make it on time if I managed to avoid any rooftop traffic jams.

None of my teachers in elementary or high school thought there was anything weird about the way I ran home after school for "lessons." Most of the kids I knew had some sort of "lessons" to go to, although most of them were also more willing to explain what they were learning. It was probably a good thing that no one ever asked me. The early classes would have seemed normal enough—a lot of little girls take gymnastics and ballet— but they were just to determine where my specific skills were. The serious classes started when I was twelve: unarmed combat, Krav maga, and free running.

(Krav maga is an Israeli-developed fighting style centered on the idea that when I put you down, you stay down. It's fast, it's brutal, and I love it. Sort of like club dancing with more eye gouging and less grinding.)

I excelled in all my lessons, but the one where I really fell in love was free running. It's a lot like parkour in that it's a discipline that teaches you the entire city is one big obstacle course. It's also a lot like a form of dance, and your partner is the environment you're in. Free running takes the best elements of tumbling, gymnastics, and being a professional superhero, and mixes them in one incredibly rewarding, incredibly *fun* package. It's just hard to explain. "Hello, my name is Verity Price, and I like to take the overland route whenever possible" isn't the sort of thing you can put in a personal ad. It even confused my landlady. When I tried to explain the importance of having solidly constructed fire escapes and a variety of ways to reach the roof, she looked at me funny and asked, "Who do you think you are, Batgirl?"

The simplest answer would have been "yes." At least "yes" didn't require a history lesson or a copy of the family tree. Still, I would have expected a Sasquatch to understand the need to know how many escape routes I had available to me—and that there's no better way to study an urban cryptid population than by meeting them on their own level. Half the time, that level is straight up. (The other half is usually straight down. Cryptids like to live where humans don't, but they also like to be close enough to steal cable.)

The rooftops were anything but dark. Light poured up from the street and out the windows of a hundred high-rise buildings, leaving the night twilight-clear. I tried to focus on covering ground, rather than lingering to explore the changes sunset brought to the city. Dave was a stickler about punctuality, and "I got distracted while I was free running" would just bring on another lecture about the occasional need to take a cab. (He's given up trying to convince me to take the subway. I'm sorry, but that method of transit is a horror movie waiting to happen.)

I hate New York cabs almost as much as I hate New York cabbies. No self-respecting cryptid would drive one, a fact which puts them comfortably outside my field of study. I was officially in New York for the sake of documenting and assisting the city's cryptid community, and that meant I could avoid anything that didn't actually impact my mission. Like cabs, street corner hot dog stands, and Times Square.

(Times Square probably counts as proof that tourists constitute a completely separate species. This is a theory I will *never* put forward at a family meeting, thank you very much. Tourism is an urban activity, which means I'd be expected to conduct any necessary studies. No way in hell.)

Tourists and crazy cab drivers aside, New York is an amazing city. I spent two months in Los Angeles during the filming of *Dance or Die*—America's number-one televised reality dance competition—and it was a great change from Portland, but New York! New York was practically *designed* for aspiring ballroom dancers looking for their big break.

It was also designed for cryptids. That was enough to justify my decision to spend a year an entire country away from the rest of the family, and convinced them that I wasn't doing it just for the dancing. Mostly for the dancing, sure, but not *just*. Besides, Mom and Dad knew I needed the time to think about what I was doing with my life. You can be a cryptozoologist, or you can be a world-class ballroom dancer. There isn't time to do both. For a little while, maybe, but not forever.

After three months away from home, I still didn't know which way I was going to go. At least New York was providing me with plenty of distractions. Any major urban center is guaranteed to have a population of nonsentient cryptids. They're like normal animals, drawn to the easy pickings generated by lots of people in close proximity. That thing that knocks over your garbage can every night? Yeah, there's a good chance it's not a raccoon. New York is also home to one of the highest populations of intelligent cryptids on record, and no one's really tried to get in touch with the community since the last time the Covenant came through slashing and burning. It was time to take another shot at getting to know the locals, sometimes with literal bullets. Since no Price worth the name would be caught dead unarmed, that wasn't a problem.

Making it to work on time . . . now *that* was a problem.

The door on the roof of Dave's Fish and Strips was unlocked. Good; that meant Dave hadn't forgotten about me swapping shifts with Kitty for the rest of the week. I was the only non-winged member of the staff who insisted on using the rooftop entrance. If he'd been expecting Kitty, he would've made sure the day shift left the door in the cellar unlocked.

Kitty wasn't going to be waiting any tables for a few days at least. She was off to play stage candy for her boyfriend's band, a Rob Zombie knockoff with an uninspiring "creatures of the night" theme. The only thing it had going for it was the fact that the "creatures of the night" in question were totally genuine, but since they couldn't admit that part, they were going to need to make their fortune on talent alone. I expected Kitty to be back on the nine-to-three shift before the end of the month.

Even if she wasn't, I'd made it clear that I had zero interest in making a permanent swap, no thanks, no way, no how. Let Dave find himself another naturally nocturnal waitress; I'd come to New York for a reason, and between ballroom competitions and cryptid chasing, my nights were booked for the foreseeable future.

Our dressing room was waitstaff only; the "talent" had their own place to change, one that probably didn't smell like stale nachos and beer. Or maybe not. Everything at Dave's tended to take on that dry, greasy smell after it had been there for a while. A couple of the other girls were loitering inside, killing time and making vague adjustments to their uniforms before going back into the club. I waved as I stepped in. They didn't wave back, and I didn't take offense. Waving is a human thing, and humans are a minority at Dave's.

"Evening, Carol, Marcy." There was no lock on the locker with my name on it. Locks cost money, and Dave didn't spend a penny he didn't have to. "How's the crowd tonight?"

"Insane," Carol responded, not looking away from

the mirror. She was trying to fit her wig into place, and her hair wasn't helping, hissing and snapping at her fingers as she shoved the individual tiny serpents under the weave. She'd been hired a week after I was, and most of the girls had offered to help her get changed during her first few days. They stopped when it became apparent that getting too close to her head before the wig was on meant a good chance of getting bitten. And the snakes she had in place of hair were venomous.

"Good insane, bad insane, run screaming from the building because this isn't worth it insane?" I pulled off my T-shirt, wadding it up and tossing it into the bottom of the locker.

"Somebody put our name on another tourist website and we're getting swarmed by sweaty businessmen who think it's okay to play grab-ass with anything in a short skirt." Marcy snapped the top of one knee-high white sock, cracking her gum at the same time for punctuation. "Candice went home sick. Said it wasn't worth the tips."

Marcy looked unconcerned, despite the alarming implications of Candy's departure. Candy was a dragon princess, and she pursued money the way a cop in a buddy movie pursues donuts. I blamed it on the fact that Marcy had the emotional and physical sensitivity of a rock. No, really; all the research on Oreads has concluded that they have the durability and resilience of quartz, assuming quartz decided to turn into an attractive young biped and go out for a stroll. No amount of grab-ass was likely to cause her more than brief annoyance.

"Who gets Candy's tables?" I asked, trying to ignore the sinking sensation in my stomach as I unloaded my weapons into the locker.

"You do."

Sinking sensation, officially impossible to ignore. "Great." I grabbed my uniform. "Just what I always wanted. Extra tables."

"With extra grab-ass on the side," Marcy said.

"I wish you'd stop saying that."

"I wish I had a pony." Marcy gave her socks one last adjustment and strode out of the changing room, leaving me alone with Carol.

"You'd probably eat the pony," I muttered.

Carol shot me a sympathetic look in the mirror. "Aren't you glad you're working overnights for Kitty?"

"Ecstatic," I said, and unbuckled my pants.

Every profession since the dawn of time has had its own uniform, its own special set of signals used to broadcast the identity of its practitioners to anyone who meets them. Sadly, the uniform of the cryptozoologist is "whatever is going to help you blend in with the locals." The need to blend in led, in a roundabout way, to Dave's Fish and Strips, the only gentlemen's club in New York City almost exclusively staffed by cryptids.

I had the utmost respect for the other humans on the staff. They weren't lucky enough to receive my early training in human/cryptid interactions, but they all did just fine—for values of "all" that mean "the three of them," anyway. Dave didn't practice discriminatory hiring; most humans were simply seized with the uncontrollable urge to scream and run away after spending more than ten minutes in a room with him . . . and he wasn't the strangest thing on staff.

The strippers didn't have an official uniform, since they'd just take it off, and the bartenders were allowed to wear jeans or skirts and T-shirts with the bar's logo. The waitresses weren't so lucky. Dave seemed to be under the deeply mistaken and deeply regrettable impression that pleated plaid micro skirts, knee-high socks, black heels, and midriff-baring white shirts with the club's logo on the front combined to project an aura of "class." Or maybe he was going for an aura of "ass," since that's what the uniforms actually managed to project.

I stepped into my heels and walked over to the mirror. Carol moved to the side, giving me room for my contemplation while she continued her epic battle of gorgon vs. snakes. Finally, I sighed, and said, "No matter how many times I put this on, I can't get past the part where I look like a hooker."

"No, you don't, honey," said Carol. "Hookers get better tips."

With a final belabored groan, I grabbed an apron from the pile—it was more like a belt, but at least it gave me a place to store tips and my order pad—and tied it around my waist before heading to the door.

Bullets cost money. So do dance shoes, and the terms of my year in New York included the need to support myself as much as possible. Family finances are solid, thanks to good investing, a certain amount of alchemy, and the gratitude of the cryptid community. That doesn't make them good enough to take care of us all forever. Dave's might be a lousy place to work, but the boss understood when I had to call in sick because I was chasing something nasty across the rooftops of the city. Add it all together, and well . . . it was time to start my shift.

If you'd asked me in Oregon whether I was a prude, I would have responded with an offended "absolutely not." My home life was strange, my hobbies were stranger, and it's hard to do competitive Latin ballroom dance without shedding all taboos about nudity and invasion of personal space. I considered myself a tolerant, enlightened woman of the world, fully prepared for any perversity my quest for the elusive urban cryptid might bring me into contact with.

That was before I started working at Dave's Fish and Strips, a place that could've been used as the answer to that age-old question, "What *does* the bogeyman do

when he's not hanging out under your bed?" If the bogeyman in question is Dave, an individual with little tact
and less taste, he opens a tacky titty bar. If the bogeyman in question is Kitty, she gets a job there.

(The word "bogeyman," much like the word "human," is gender-neutral. If you ever want to see a bogeyman laugh herself sick, call her a "bogeygirl," or better,
a "bogeywoman." The last time I saw someone make
that mistake with Kitty, she laughed so hard I was afraid
she was going to rupture something.)

The main room was decorated like the bastard offspring of a nightclub and a sideshow tent—a deeply pa-
triotic sideshow tent with a serious longing to return to
the United Kingdom, where it would doubtless be
greeted with pitchforks and torches, because the British
probably wouldn't want it either. Stages were set up at
strategic locations around the room, each tucked into its
own little acoustically isolated group of chairs. The main
stage provided the ambient music for the club, as well as
the highest percentage of tips and "grab-ass." That was
supposed to be Candy's territory. Thanks to her cow-
ardly departure, it was going to be mine.

Oh, well; it wasn't like I could blame her. Dragon
princesses are greedy and proud, not brave. When you're
bred to be the humanoid support staff for giant carnivorous lizards, there's no reason to be brave. The giant lizards can do it for you.

After a stop at the bar to pick up the pending drinks—
two trays' worth, which was a bad sign for the shift
ahead—I waded into the crowd. Marcy was a few tables
away, distributing baskets of fried fish and blithely ignoring roving hands. Several would-be gropers were
sucking bruised fingers and looking confused. That's
what they got for trying to goose an Oread.

I wasn't so lucky. I'd barely cleared three tables before a hand latched onto my left buttock and squeezed.
I jerked out of the way, nearly spilling my remaining
drinks. General laughter greeted this reaction, followed

by a man saying, "Shit, honey, you're lots prettier than the last one!"

"Gee, thanks," I said, turning to face the speaker. He was red-faced, either with excitement or alcohol, and openly leering. "You know, we have strippers here. The waitresses are here to serve you, not service you. Hands off, okay?"

"I think somebody missed a little memo," he said, turning redder as his friends made the "ooh" noise that seems to be the universal signifier for "you just got dissed." Standing, he added, "You're in the *service* industry."

He had two hands. I had two breasts. I'm sure he thought the math made sense. Maybe it would have, if I hadn't started self-defense lessons at seven and ballroom dance lessons at eight. Self-defense teaches you to kick ass. Ballroom dance teaches you to do it in heels.

I dropped my tray before he had time to finish squeezing, grabbed him just above the elbows, and used him to provide support while I braced myself on one leg and swept his feet out from under him with the other. He went down hard, his landing not particularly softened by my discarded drinks.

Sputtering and even redder now, my aspiring assailant stared at me. His friends did the same.

I smiled.

"You can pick up your drinks from the bar for the rest of the night, gentlemen. Table service is suspended," I said, and started for the bar. I needed replacement drinks.

Ryan—one of the bouncers, and reasonably cute if you have a thing for therianthropes, which I don't—was waiting for me next to the register. His expression was grim. "Very—"

"Let me guess. I need to go see Dave?"

Ryan nodded dolefully. "You know he doesn't like you fighting with the customers."

"And he knows my breasts are a no-fly zone. Let's see

who knows better, shall we?" Dropping the orders I'd managed to collect before things went all Fight Club, I turned to head back to the hallway. Time for another chat about "violent tendencies."

Jumping off the roof was more fun.

Four

"Sure, you can take a heroic stand against
the forces of darkness. Or you can not die.
It's entirely up to you."

–Evelyn Baker

*The manager's office of Dave's Fish and Strips, a club for
discerning gentlemen*

DARKNESS FILLED THE OFFICE from side to side, solid
enough to defy the standard laws of nature and
trickle several inches out into the hall. I stopped in the
doorway. "Dave? You know I won't come in when you've
got your darks on. Put on some damn sunglasses and
turn on a light already."

The manager's dust-dry voice drifted out of the dark:
"What, a Price afraid of a little darkness? What would your
father say?" Every word dripped with sepulchral menace.

"My father would say that a Price who won't walk
into a bogeyman's lair when he's got his darks on is a
Price who plans to live long enough to continue the family line." I rolled my eyes. "You know the rules. I don't
kill your customers, you don't try to bait me into your
clutches, everybody walks away happy."

"What do you call what just happened, hmm?"

"Sexual harassment." I glared at the darkness. "Turn
off the darks or let me go back to work. I'm not coming
in there."

A long-suffering sigh answered me, followed by Dave muttering, "You never let me have any fun." The solid shadows clicked off as he flipped the switch controlling his darks, allowing light to filter into the office. I stayed in the hallway, waiting patiently. Dave grumbled and flipped another switch, turning on the lights.

"That wasn't so hard, now, was it?" I asked, and stepped inside.

The office was small and cluttered, and the low-watt bulbs that were all Dave was willing to use did little to disperse the natural shadows cast by packing too much stuff into not enough space. It was still substantially better than it had been with the darks turned on.

(Darks were invented by an enterprising witch who looked at all the bogeymen, ghouls, and bug-a-boos trying to live below the radar of the human population and saw a niche begging to be filled. The bulbs fit most standard sockets and run off electrical current like almost everything else that plugs into a wall. They're also crushingly expensive. But they come in wattages from "twilight" to "deepest pit of eternal damnation," and they work. That's enough to make most self-proclaimed creatures of the night grit their teeth and deal with the price tag.)

"Spoken like a true day-dweller," grumbled Dave. Leaning his elbows on the desk, he asked, "Why am I not firing you?"

"Because I'm the best cocktail waitress you've got, Kitty's not available to take her shift back until that tragedy they call a band finishes crashing and burning, and all I did was drop him. He'd grabbed hold of just about anybody else like that and he'd have ended up dead or worse."

"I'd be more inclined to be lenient if you'd agree to dance for me."

"I'd be less inclined to stick a high heel up your ass if you'd stop asking," I answered cheerfully. "Answer's 'no,' Dave. What would my grandmother say?"

Dave paused. "She out of Hell this week?" he asked warily.

"Not until Solstice, but still. She wouldn't understand."

He relaxed. "She'd understand that you needed to save your job."

"I think it's a little more likely she'd understand that you can kill a bogeyman in a lot of different ways, and come riding in to avenge my honor."

Dave glowered. I suppressed the urge to laugh, and glowered back.

A person running into Dave in a dark alley—or worse, finding him under their bed—would probably need years of therapy before they could convince themselves he'd never been there. He was close to seven feet tall and skeletally thin, with arms long enough to give him a faintly simian look. His hands were too big for his body, and all his fingers had at least one extra joint. (The longer fingers each had two.) Added to his gray "I've been dead for a week" complexion and the subtle wrongness of his face, it combined to form a picture that would give strong men nightmares.

Fortunately for me, I'm not a strong man, and one of my first babysitters was a bogeyman. Also, Dave's garishly-patterned blue, purple, yellow, and magenta Hawaiian shirt did nothing to add to his overall air of menace. Maybe there's a world where improbably colored parrots are considered frightening. This is not that world.

Dave was the first to look away. "You know I'd pay you more if you'd start dancing."

"I'd also get myself disowned."

"For dancing?" He managed to make the word sound innocent. No small feat coming from a man who looked like a basketball-playing corpse, especially not one who ran a strip club. "You know I'd let you do it under the name you used on television."

"For dancing in a clothing-optional establishment

where I'd be expected to finish the dance in my birthday suit, yeah." I shrugged. "Conservative parents. What can you do?"

Dave snorted. "If your family's conservative, I'm the Easter Bunny."

All desire to make light of the situation fled. "Don't even joke about that," I said, in a voice that had gone completely flat. "The Easter Bunny's no laughing matter."

"Sorry, sorry!" said Dave defensively. "I didn't know you were that touchy."

"There's a lot you don't know. Are we done?"

"Ah." Dave pursed his lips. "Here's the thing. That boy you decided to chop-and-drop—"

"I didn't do any chopping!"

"—he and his friends are still here, and I'd rather avoid any more of a floor show than we've already had tonight. So I'm going to give their table to Marcy."

"That's the first intelligent thing you've said all night."

"And you're going to go home."

I paused, uncertain that I was hearing him correctly. "Excuse me?"

"I'll pay you for the night, minus tips, of course. You can come back tomorrow."

"You're already understaffed, and I need the money," I protested. "Candy's out and Kitty's on tour."

"Won't be the first time I've pulled Angel from behind the bar. Ryan can mix a Slaughtered Lamb as well as anybody else."

"Slaughtered Lamb?" I asked, curious despite myself.

"Tomato juice, vodka, rum, tequila, and crushed mint. Unless you're a ghoul. Then we leave out the tomato juice, replace it with—"

"Don't want to know." I raised my hands to cut him off. Dave stopped talking. "Right. You want to give me the night off for attacking customers. I'm going to stop arguing."

"Good," said Dave, and flicked off the lights. That was my cue to exit.

I stopped at the door, looking back over my shoulder. "This is because I won't dance for you, isn't it?"

"Good night, Verity," Dave said.

Darkness escorted me the rest of the way out of the room.

I met Dave the night I stepped into his club looking for a part-time job, but he'd been aware of me for quite some time before that. Not because of my family, although that was probably a factor. Dave knew who I was because of *Dance or Die*.

My family's been in hiding for four generations now, since my great-great-grandparents told the Covenant they were done exterminating innocent cryptids without regard for their place in a viable ecosystem. (According to the mice, Great-Great-Grandpa Alexander's exact words were "You can take this unholy campaign and ram it up your bum sideways, you bloody miscarriage of a man!" Since the mice are morally incapable of changing anything they perceive as Holy Writ, and the Festival of Come On, Enid, We're Getting Out Of Here Before These Bastards Make Us Kill Another Innocent Creature is one of the holiest of their many, many holy days, I'm pretty sure they're quoting him correctly.) Being "in hiding" isn't that bad . . . except for the part where it limits our available training methods.

Mom and Dad were firm on the topic of training: we could grow up to settle down and become accountants if that was what we really wanted, but we'd learn the family business before that happened. Most of the things that would love to brag about how they gutted a Price weren't going to back off because their target said, "I'm sorry, sir, I don't do that sort of thing, but I can balance your checkbook for you."

Some stuff could be managed at home. I knew how to handle a firearm, lay a snare, and dress a wound by the time I was five. I remember getting to elementary school and being amazed to discover that most children played sanitized versions of the games I knew; their idea of a good time seemed like a cat that had been declawed, all hiss and no interesting danger. What was the point of hide-and-seek if you weren't allowed to dig pit traps or attack your opponents from behind? That was the first time I realized how different our home life was from everyone else's. Everyone else wasn't being taught to fight a war.

Our parents planned our education as carefully as they would have planned an invasion of France. To keep us interested, they let us decide how to specialize. My brother went for guns, more guns, bigger guns, and, also, guns. Antimony focused on traps, poisons, and keeping the fight as far from herself as possible. I learned to shoot, I learned to fight, and when the time came to pick what I wanted to devote myself to studying, I chose the thing I was most passionate about: ballroom dance.

I argued my case like a master. A surprisingly large number of fighting styles have a lot in common with dancing. Speed, flexibility, and the ability to kick higher than your own head are all things that come in handy when you're fighting for your life. Most professional dancers live to dance, and that's the sort of passion people in our position need to bring to their individual disciplines if they want to survive long enough to get really good at them.

We weren't allowed to compete in any sport or activity the Covenant might be monitoring. Antimony got her black belt in karate, but was never allowed to go to any national events. Alex had to drop soccer when he got to college, on the off chance that he'd somehow make the news. And I, with my weird obsession with the Latin forms of ballroom dancing? With my urge to salsa and rumba and cha-cha my nights away? I was allowed to put on a red wig, get a false ID from our crazy cousin Artie, and audition for *Dance or Die*. And when the producers said I had a slot in the top twenty, I was allowed to compete.

The format is familiar to everyone in the country who owns a TV not permanently turned to either PBS or porn: ten girls, ten guys, one massive cash prize. Every week two dancers get sent home, until the top four try to dance their way to victory without dancing themselves into heart failure. (My season was better than some; we only lost one contestant to health issues, and he was an idiot who stopped sleeping and gave himself pneumonia.) I didn't win. I didn't expect to. But I came in second.

Two of the show's regular judges were cryptids, and so were three of the other competitors. My experiences with them, and the connections I managed to make within the Los Angeles cryptid community, were the final push I needed to get the consent for my studies in New York City. Of course Dave wanted me to dance for him. He could make some serious dough by putting my stage name on his roster of naked talent.

Competitive ballroom dance may have a reputation for skimpy dresses and sky-high heels, but at least sequins aren't see-through. I'd been saying thanks but no thanks to Dave for months. I was there to work tables and make contacts, not sacrifice what little dignity I had left.

Of course, give me a few more months trying to pay for groceries on a cocktail waitress' salary and tips, and that could change. All he really had to do was wait me out.

Carol was still in the dressing room with her wig in her hands when I returned. Her snakes hissed merrily, glad to be released from their confinement, as she stared morosely into the mirror.

"Hey, Carol," I said, heading for my locker. "What's wrong?"

"I can't go back out there until I get my wig on, and I really need the tips," she said, glancing back toward me. "I had to feed them last week."

"Ouch." I winced. Gorgon hair requires live feeding, and Carol had at least thirty individual snakes topping her head. They would have each demanded a pinky mouse of their own, possibly two or three in the case of the larger serpents. "Still no luck breeding your own?"

"I can't wear my contacts all the time. I keep looking at them by mistake."

"I can see where that would be a problem." Untying my apron, I added, "I can call my mom if you want. She might have something you can use to sedate them without hurting them."

"Could you?" Carol whirled to face me, clutching her wig to her breast and looking at me like I was the answer to all her prayers. "I didn't want to ask, but . . ."

"It's no big. Really."

Here's a fun fact: there are over nine hundred races of cryptids on the planet, and maybe eighty of those look roughly human, ranging from the Sasquatches and gorgons to dragon princesses and cuckoos. Here's another fun fact: most of those races have only started coming into intentional contact with humans during the last hundred and fifty years, as our expansionistic tendencies brought us to them. Many have little to no idea of their own biology, and still practice a form of folk medicine that the human race abandoned centuries ago.

Which is where my mother comes in. Evelyn Price, formerly Evelyn Baker, is the closest thing to a cryptid physician most of them will ever meet. She'll even make house calls if you can find her a teleport, and her rates are more than reasonable.

Carol burbled a series of thanks before she went back to trying to cram her snakes into the wig. I took her distraction as the opportunity it was and dug my weapons out of the locker. I always feel better with a knife, and better yet with a firearm or two. I was only carrying a simple underarm holster, but that was fine; those are the easiest to hide. Pulling on a windbreaker, I shoved my street clothes into my emergency backpack and shrugged it on before scooting for the hall. I didn't see the point in changing. After a mice-related kitchen incident, a boob-grab by an asshole, and a private talk with Dave, I was more than ready to get out on the rooftops. Running in a skirt may be a little bit indecent, but I don't mind doing it as long as I'm not going to need to talk to any humans.

The night had matured while I was inside, ambient noise going from the mindless cheer of early evening to something deeper and more classical. A siren wailed in the distance; horns honked on the street below; a baby's crying drifted out of an apartment window. It only needed a saxophone or maybe some feel-good easy listening music to make the stereotype complete.

I took several deep breaths of the night air, letting the tension slip out of my shoulders before backing up, putting my back against the rooftop door, and breaking into a run. If I couldn't take my aggressions out on Dave's customers, I'd do a quick circuit, head home, call Sarah, and go clubbing.

It's always the best plans that fall through. I think the universe has some sort of law.

Ever wonder why pigeons need to breed so fast when they're living in an environment that's entirely man-made, offering all the comforts and amenities a brainless ball of feathers and pestilence could desire? If you just look at the immediately visible evidence, they should outbreed the cities and cast us all into the depths of a Hitchcock remake.

What most people don't realize — what most people don't *want* to realize — is that the urban cryptid population does us the enormous favor of keeping the pigeon population at a reasonable size: they eat them. The larger your city, the more pigeons you'll have, and the more cryptids they'll attract. Nature works in mysterious ways. Sometimes those ways involve air-breathing flying manta rays camouflaged to blend in with concrete walls.

My first stop was the top floor of a high-rise six blocks from Dave's, where the family of resident harpies offered to share their pigeon stew. They were trying to bribe me into agreeing to keep picking up their mail. The youngest daughter's wings were coming in, making her unsuitable for interaction with the bulk of the city for at least six years and keeping the rest of the family housebound until she finished the dangerous stages of her molt. I agreed to the mail and begged off dinner. Without a bezoar to purify the stuff, I'd probably have managed to catch some new and interesting variety of plague.

Normally, my rounds would have kept me making social calls for the next several hours, but there had been reports of an ahool living somewhere on the rooftops in Midtown. Ahool are like giant bats with monkey heads and nasty claws. They're also cooperative hunters who bring down prey by means of the bacteria swarming in their foul little mouths. An ahool takes a chunk out of a person and then waits for them to die. If the ahool isn't hungry, it takes a chunk out anyway, just in case another ahool in the area wants a snack. If the reports were accurate, and the thing wasn't found, we'd have a flock living in Manhattan before very long. That sort of thing would *definitely* get the attention of the Covenant.

Most of my nondance hours were devoted to serving, studying, and supporting the cryptid community. Sometimes the only way to serve them was to keep them from drawing too much attention to themselves, and, in the case of the nonintelligent predatory species, that could activate the second part of my job description. Not "cryptozoologist": monster hunter. I'd try relocation first, and if that didn't work . . .

I'd avoid more permanent solutions for as long as I could. That was the best that I could offer.

Free running takes a lot of attention, especially at night on unfamiliar ground. Free running while scanning the skies and likely hiding spots for giant carnivorous bats really leaves no room to watch for anything else. I've had years of training at spotting traps and deadfalls. I've even managed to beat Antimony a few times at games of hide-and-seek, and that's damn near impossible. So nothing but distraction and simple carelessness can excuse my failing to see the snare before I jammed my foot straight into it.

The rope snapped taut, the loop closed around my ankle, and all I had time to think before the deadweight hit the side of my head and knocked me into unconsciousness was how much Alex was going to laugh at me for this one.

Then the weight came down, the snare whipped me into the air, and I wasn't thinking of anything for a while.

Five

"When in doubt, play dead. Well, unless you might be dealing with a ghoul, or a basilisk, or something else that likes its meat a little ripe. Actually, when in doubt, just start shooting."

—Alice Healy

Upside down in a really short skirt somewhere on the rooftops of Manhattan

THERE IS NO SHAME IN BLACKING OUT when whipped abruptly into the air, especially if you were running when it happened. Seriously, if there was shame in it, Alex and I would have died of embarrassment before Antimony turned nine. Having a little sister who sets traps for fun definitely made us a little blasé about getting caught in them. Any trap you can walk away from was probably set by someone who wasn't trying to kill you. Not immediately, anyway.

Rubbing my aching head, I opened my eyes to find myself dangling about eight feet above the rooftop where I'd been running. That was awkward. A quick check showed that I was still in possession of all my limbs and all my weaponry; thank God for custom holsters. "Gotta tell Dad we have a new stress test for the snaps on these things," I said, and tried to jackknife up to grab my knees. The rope promptly started to sway, turning what should have been a simple exercise into something better performed by a circus acrobat.

Fine; if it wanted to be that way, I would improvise. The rope was creaking, but it wasn't showing any signs of giving way. That was good. Tips for getting out of a snare without breaking any major bones, number one: make sure *you* control when you get down, not the rope. I started rocking with more vigor, until I had built up sufficient momentum to let me fold myself in half despite the motion of the rope. I wrapped my arms around my legs, taking a moment to breathe before I leaned back and assessed the situation further.

The rope was looped around my left ankle, drawn tight in some sort of complicated slip knot. "Huh," I said, sliding my hands up to grasp my calves and pull myself closer to the knot. It was a maneuver easier performed than described, and resulted in my feeling somewhat like a giant inchworm. "Who the hell tied you?"

The knot, unsurprisingly, didn't answer. It was starting to chafe. If it hadn't been for the amount of time I spent balancing on one leg while being dragged around the dance floor, I probably would have been in a lot of pain; as it was, I was *going* to be in a lot of pain if I didn't figure out how to get myself safely untied, and soon.

My work uniform didn't give me a lot of padding, and the roof below me wasn't what I'd call a safe place to land. I could cut the rope—I'd be disowned if I went out without a knife, or at least looked at admonishingly— but the odds of me flipping around and landing on my feet weren't good. Actually, they were bad. My only *good* option involved climbing the rope, somehow managing to get a grip on the flagpole it was tied to, and starting from there.

"I should never have quit gymnastics," I grumbled, and began swinging back and forth again, trying to work up the momentum to let me grab hold of the rope. On the third swing, I managed to swing myself up far enough to get a good grip. I let go just as fast as the stinging slime that coated the rope started to burn my palms and fingers. I swore loudly as I fell backward, snapping to a stop when I ran out of rope. I felt the jolt all the way up to the ball of my thigh as shooting pains ran through my ankle.

At least I didn't black out this time.

The rope kept swaying even after I'd stopped helping it along, rocking me in a motion that seemed designed to induce vertigo. I wiped my hands on my uniform skirt before digging them into my hair, allowing myself the luxury of swearing at great and enthusiastic length as I waited for my ankle to stop throbbing and my palms to stop tingling. The damage wasn't going to go away, but it could at least die down to a dull roar before I resumed trying to get free. I wiggled my toes. Nothing seemed broken. Small blessings, but I take what I can get when I'm stuck in a snare.

The thought made me pause. Before, I'd been focused on trying to work my way out of the trap. The Doctrine of Grandma Alice, preached by mouse and mother alike: "When in doubt, get out. Worry about what might be trying to eat you later." Now that I was being forced into temporary idleness, the true vulnerability of my situation was brought forcibly to hand.

None of the cryptids I knew of in the surrounding area were the type to set this sort of trap. That meant I was either dealing with somebody who was out of their home territory, somebody completely unfamiliar, or—worst case scenario—somebody who knew I was making this circuit and had decided to do something about it.

There are parts of the cryptid community that don't like my family, what we do, or what we stand for. Parts who'd like it if the cryptids retreated from human society altogether, stopped trying to fit in, and went back to skulking in the shadows and occasionally eating people. Even parts that still think of us as members of the Covenant. Those elements of cryptid society are the reason no Price who wants to have a decent life expectancy goes anywhere unarmed.

There are some lessons a family only needs to learn once.

Letting my hands drop and dangle freely, I did my best possum impression as I started running a mental tally of available weaponry. One knife, strapped to my left thigh, and the handgun under my windbreaker. I could reach them both. If necessary, I could start shooting, cut the rope, and let myself fall. The damage the roof would do was nothing compared to the damage some cryptids can dish out when they decide they want to.

Footsteps crunched in the gravel on the far side of the roof, coming closer. Moving carefully, so as not to set myself swaying again, I pulled the gun from under my windbreaker and aimed toward the sound. Judging by the tread, whatever was approaching was solo, human-sized, and not in much of a hurry. That was fine by me. I've always been good at night shooting, but sometimes a girl doesn't want to put her faith in firing blindly into the dark. Better to let whatever it was come to me, and make my bullets count.

(Someday I'm going to get myself a day job that lets me wear clothes capable of concealing a decent amount of weaponry. Ever try to hide a gun in a competition rumba costume? It's neither easy nor fun. The inner thigh holster that doesn't chafe has yet to be invented by man, beast, cryptid, or Price.)

The thing on the roof was close enough now to have a visual on the snare's silhouette; whatever it was, it could tell that it had caught something. It started walking faster, becoming more visible with every step it took. It was humanoid, dragging something through the gravel behind it. My upside-down orientation made it difficult to estimate height, but if forced to guess, I would have said that whatever it was, it was maybe six inches taller than me. It extended an arm, reaching for something at its hip. I steadied my aim.

The thing on the roof—now clearly a human man— pulled a flashlight from his duster pocket and clicked it on.

The light was practically blinding. I squinted against the glare, keeping my gun aimed at where his head had last been located. In the meanwhile, there was a sharp intake of breath from the man holding the flashlight. Guess when he went night fishing on the rooftops of Manhattan, he wasn't expecting to catch himself a strip club waitress.

"Hi," I said, brightly. "Ever been shot in the head? Because I don't think you'd enjoy it much. Most people don't."

My unnamed new buddy swore under his breath, still shining the flashlight in my face. He dropped whatever he was dragging, digging his hand into his pocket and pulling out a small object. Something wet splashed across my chest and neck a moment later, running down my chin to drip into my mouth and nose. I sputtered, widening my eyes in surprised indignation.

"What the hell did you do *that* for?" I demanded.

"You said you were going to shoot me!" he replied. One hand still held the flashlight. His other arm was thrust out toward me, pointing an antique-looking silver vial in my direction.

"Newsflash, buddy: threats of violence don't turn this into a wet T-shirt contest." More liquid dripped into my mouth as I spoke. I spat it out, but not before I'd had time to taste it: mostly water, mixed with salt, and a bitter herb I recognized as aconite. It's a pretty standard mixture for banishing incubi and succubi. The poor things are deathly allergic.

I gaped at him. "Did you just splash me with *holy water*?"

"You're in my trap!" he said. He was starting to sound uncertain. Whatever his script for this encounter was, I was refusing to stick to it in any meaningful way, and he was obviously getting confused. Tough.

"Your trap was on my rooftop," I said, as if this were the most reasonable thing in the world. "I'm as human as you are. Now do you want to tell me why you're setting snares, and maybe lower me down from this thing before I lose my temper and start shooting?"

That seemed to put him back on familiar ground. Straightening, he puffed out his chest and said, "I am armored with righteousness."

"Does righteousness protect you from small-caliber bullets?"

He hesitated. "You're sure you're human?"

"Both my parents swear it."

"I'll get you down."

I smiled, not shifting my aim. "Good plan."

The snare was anchored to an iron bolt hammered into a nearby chunk of masonry. My captor disappeared in that direction, leaving me dangling. I had just long enough to wonder whether he'd decided to cut and run when I felt a sharp tug on the rope, and I was lowered slowly, if not smoothly, to the ground. I tucked the gun back into my waistband, stretching my hands overhead and using them to turn the end of my descent from a straight drop into a lazy somersault.

Pulling my windbreaker down over my hands made me clumsy, but didn't prevent me from untying the knot, and kept me from getting any more of that stinging slime on my hands. I had just finished pulling off the snare when the man came back into view. He pointed his flashlight at my ankle, and I let my breath hiss out between my teeth. My sock had been able to protect me from the bulk of the damage, but there was still blood soaking into the white cotton in several places. The human leg wasn't meant to be used as a long-term hanging mechanism.

"You bleed red," he said, sounding relieved.

"I bleed red, and replacement socks come out of my paycheck." I slipped the rope off over my foot. "You ever try to get blood out of white cotton?"

"I was afraid you wouldn't bleed at all, ma'am," he said. Suddenly formal, he walked over and bent to offer his hand. "I'm sure you understand my caution. I certainly wasn't expecting to make so undeserving a capture." I looked at him blankly. When I didn't take his hand, he hastened to add, "Dominic De Luca, at your service. I promise you my intention is purely to assist."

"Next time, assist me by not setting snares on the rooftop, okay?" I ignored his hand and levered myself upright, gingerly testing to see how much weight I could put on my left ankle. The answer: not enough. I'd had worse injuries both in the field and on the dance floor, but a banged-up ankle is never an asset. "Ow."

"I assure you, ma'am, your capture was not my intention."

"What was your intention? That thing's too big for pigeons, and you're not likely to catch many rats up here."

An expression of distaste flashed across his face. He was decent-looking when he wasn't scowling like that; he had a good, strong bone structure, dark eyes, and hair that was either black or a deep enough brown that the low light stole its color ĕntirely. Even standing six inches taller than me made him short by American standards, but perfectly reasonable by mine, and he was built like the men I usually danced with: lean and solid-looking. I knew he had to be reasonably strong. He'd managed not to drop me when he untied the snare.

"There are things, ma'am, that it is perhaps better of which you do not know."

"Hold on." I studied him, narrowing my eyes. The formal language. The snare. The holy water. The duster, stereotypical uniform of the "monster hunters" of the world. "Things it is perhaps better of which I do not know?"

"There are more things in Heaven and in Earth—"

I raised a hand, cutting him off. "First, do not quote

Shakespeare at me. I get that quite enough from my grandma. Second, what are you doing here?"

He narrowed his eyes in turn, the expression barely visible with the flashlight pointed in my direction. "I don't think I have to answer the questions of a strange woman who stumbles into my snares and refuses to give me her name," he said.

I looked back toward the thing he'd been dragging when he first appeared. Before he had a chance to stop me, I half-limped over to where it had been dropped. It looked like an old brown sack at first, until I turned it over with my foot and saw the ahool's characteristically apelike face snarling up at me. Its eyes were glazed with death.

"Miss—"

"You killed it," I said numbly. "You killed the ahool."

"You . . . know this fell beast?" His steps slowed, taking on a newly cautious edge. "You asked what I was doing here. Perhaps I should be asking you the same."

"You killed it. It was just—just being an ahool, minding its own business, and you *killed* it! I mean, sure, eventually, that business might have included biting people, and then it would need to be relocated or exterminated, but you didn't need to just *kill* it! Not without observing it and making sure it didn't have a whole flock of buddies that would swarm and eat us both!"

"Miss." Dominic's footsteps stopped entirely. His voice was hard. "Who *are* you?"

"You killed it." The urge to shoot him was overwhelming. Only a lifetime of etiquette lessons and the irritating fact that he was probably wearing some sort of body armor stopped me. I turned to face him. "You're with the Covenant, aren't you?"

I might as well have shot him from the way he recoiled. He took a step backward, one hand going to his hip and pulling a nasty looking hunting knife from a previously hidden scabbard. "How do you know that?"

"Simple." I offered a sweet, sunny, entirely insincere smile, trying to pretend that I wasn't standing in front of a dead cryptid that had been needlessly slaughtered in *my* city. "My name's Verity Price. Now what the hell are you doing in Manhattan?"

No one knows exactly when the organization that became the Covenant was founded. Their ranks included a lot of scholars and scribes, but records get lost, libraries have a tendency to burn down—especially when the libraries belong to a secret society that goes around harassing dragons for fun—and if you give history enough time, it has a nasty tendency to turn into myth. We know it's been around for centuries. We know it's all over the world, sometimes under different names, but always with the same mission statement: if a thing doesn't fit whatever's currently defined as "natural," it needs to die. No argument, no discussion, no mercy. From ghoulies and ghosties and long-legged beasties and things that go bump in the night, the Covenant is out to deliver us. Whether or not we particularly want to be delivered.

Nice folks, the Covenant, especially given the part where, last time any of us bothered to check, they were really invested in the idea of arresting my entire family and dragging us to their central headquarters to stand trial for crimes against humanity. Just being born a Price is enough to qualify as a traitor to the human race, which is a neat trick. All the treason, none of the effort. And how did we earn the enmity of a global brotherhood of fanatic monster hunters? The simple way: we quit.

My paternal great-great-grandparents, Alexander and Enid Healy, were born into the Covenant. They were active members for years before they started wondering what the hell they were doing. Then Great-Great-Grandpa Healy found the connection between wiping out the unicorns in England and the great cholera epidemic, and it was all over but the shouting, recriminations, and emigration to America. Maybe the Covenant could have forgiven them for their desertion, but two generations later, my grandmother married Thomas Price, a representative of the Covenant who'd been sent to make sure the Healys were harmless. Leaving was bad enough, but convincing others to defect was enough to start a blood feud.

That doesn't even *start* going into Mom's side of the family.

The Covenant: because sometimes you want your genocidal assholes to be organized. Now one of those same genocidal assholes was in my city, holding a knife on me, looking like I'd just run over his dog. And he was killing cryptids. This was sure shaping up to be a swell night.

"Price," he said, with almost exaggerated care. "As in . . . ?"

"Thomas Price was my grandfather." I didn't feel the need to mention my parents. For one thing, they weren't on the roof. For another, invoking the Bakers would probably be enough to tip him over the edge. He'd already killed once. I didn't want to encourage him to do it again. "What are you doing in my city?"

He pulled himself a little straighter, trying to look imposing. I've been dancing the tango with men a foot and a half taller than I am since I was fourteen. I wasn't impressed.

"I wasn't aware that you'd been granted the authority to claim cities. How quaint. Who backs you?"

"Me." I shrugged. "The rest of the family. Oh, and most of the city's cryptids, who happen to be big fans of me and my tendency not to kill them. They won't be happy if you try arresting me. Or with the idea that there's a hunter in the city."

"This city has gone without a purge for far too long."

"This city is doing *just fine* without a purge, thank you very much. It's not in the market for a serial killer." I glanced at the dead ahool one more time. "No one asked you to come here."

Dominic actually looked affronted. "Are you implying that I—?" He left the question unfinished, but the intonation was clear.

"You're setting snares for potentially intelligent creatures with the intent to kill them based solely on attributes that you don't like." Ahool weren't intelligent, but they also weren't going to get caught in a snare. Rooftop snares meant he was hunting for a wide variety of prey. "I think the situation's pretty self-explanatory, don't you?"

He started to step forward, the knife still in his hand. I had my gun drawn and pointed straight at him before he'd finished the motion.

"Do you really want to do that?" I asked. "Think hard. I'm having a lousy night, and I promise you're not going to take me quietly." The harpies were probably too far away to hear me if I screamed. That was bad. We were, however, reasonably close to a flophouse that I knew was frequented by a lot of bogeymen. Bogeymen are attracted by the sound of screams, and most of the city's bogey community knew me. Even if Dominic was wearing body armor, I was no slouch at hand-to-hand, and I'd have backup before he had time to do much damage. I hoped.

Dominic hesitated. "No," he said finally. "I don't. I thought you'd been wiped out."

"Wiping things out is *your* hobby, but no, we haven't been."

"They taught me about you. Your desertion."

"What a great way of putting it. I'll have to write that in my diary."

"You were a glorious bloodline before you decided to turn traitor."

Now I was starting to get pissed. I shifted as much of my weight as possible to my right leg, glaring at him. "Are we doing this thing or not? Because if not, I want you out of Manhattan, and out of my way."

"I suppose that's the answer, then," said Dominic regretfully, before he lunged.

I have to give the Covenant this: they teach their people how to fight. Dominic moved with grace and deadly speed, turning a headlong charge into an attack before most people would have had time to do more than blink. Keeping the knife held slightly behind him, he balled his right hand into a fist and swung for the place where my head should have been.

He missed by what my mother would have called a country mile. I was already dropping to land balanced on the fingertips of my left hand and the toe of my right foot, knee bending as it accommodated my sudden half-crouch. Kicking my left foot upward in a maneuver I was certain to regret in the morning, I slammed my heel into his wrist, sending the knife flying out of his hand and away into the darkness on the roof.

He was good. I'm not sure he wouldn't have been better, had he been attacking to kill and not to capture. I had no such qualms. Fighting like a gentleman is the sort of luxury reserved for people who can afford to lose.

Dominic recovered quickly, delivering a kick to my kidneys. I rolled with it, letting the borrowed momentum carry me several feet before springing to my feet and shoving the gun into his face.

"You are *not* a good listener," I said, trying not to show how badly that kick had hurt, or how disgusted I was by the congealed ahool blood now staining my windbreaker.

For his part, Dominic was looking like a man who'd just learned the world wasn't perfect. "You little—"

"Finishing that sentence gets you shot," I said, and stepped backward. "Here's a tip: never bring a knife to a gunfight. Here's another: stop killing my cryptids, and get out of my city. If I hear one word about you harassing the people that live here, or see you one more time, I'm not going to fight fair."

"The Covenant will be hearing about this."

"What, that you met a random girl on a rooftop who told you she was a member of a family you guys wiped out years ago right before she kicked your ass? As if. Even if your pride would take it, they wouldn't believe you." I took another step backward. The edge of the roof was only a few feet away. "Get out of my city, De Luca. Next time, I won't play nice."

"Next time, neither will I," he snarled, and pulled another knife from his coat, flinging it toward my chest—or at least toward the space where my chest had been. By the time the knife finished its flight, I was already over the edge of the roof, dropping like a rock into the darkness below.

Six

"Always remember two things about the Covenant: shoot first, and then keep shooting for as long as your ammunition holds out. You can't reason with fanatics. All you can do is match them in your own fanaticism."

—Enid Healy

A small semilegal sublet in Greenwich Village, cranky and in pain

RECOVERING THE HEIGHT I LOST during my getaway would have been too much trouble, especially when I could feel the bruises forming as I ran. My left ankle was throbbing steadily, making my footing questionable at best. One of the first rules of successful free running talks about how you do it with injured ankles, wrists, knees, or hips. It's a simple rule: don't. It's a good way to do permanent damage, and unless you're being chased by a hungry wendigo, no shortcut is worth that.

I found a fire escape three blocks from home that was close enough to the ground to let me finish my descent. I made the rest of the trip on foot. It was late enough that the only people I passed were drunk, homeless, drunk *and* homeless, or in the middle of traveling from one nightclub to another. None of them gave my outfit, or the blood covering it, a second glance.

The mice had either finished their religious ceremony or moved on to one of the quieter parts of the liturgy. The apartment was silent when I came in, and stayed that way as I dug my phone from my backpack and retrieved the first aid kit from the medicine cabinet. I dropped my windbreaker in the bathtub. I didn't know whether ahool blood was acidic, but I'd be finding out soon. There was a little blood on my skirt. I stripped it off and threw it into the tub on top of the windbreaker. Then I turned and limped back to the living room.

The couch was covered in last week's laundry. I swept it onto the floor as I sat down, groaning a little when my bruises brushed against the cushions. Once the aching slowed, I removed my left shoe and rolled down the sock.

The damage was both better than I'd been expecting and worse than I'd been hoping; not an uncommon combination when it comes to me and injuries. I'm pretty resilient. That doesn't mean I enjoy getting hurt, or the complications that come with it. At least it was all just surface damage; the snare had done a good job of scraping my skin through the sock, but the rope never actually touched me. I slathered the scrapes liberally in antibiotic cream, pasted on some gauze, wrapped an Ace bandage around it, and called it good. As long as I didn't need to win any foot races or dance any Paso Dobles for the next few days, I'd be fine.

I leaned back into the couch, wincing, and snapped open my phone. If the Covenant was in Manhattan, there was only one reasonable place to call.

Home.

The story of my family winding up in a sprawling farmhouse outside of Odell, Oregon is simple, even though it takes the mice three days to tell. My great-great-grandparents left England and settled in Pennsylvania; the Covenant promptly sent a man to check on them.

The family sent him packing and moved inland, to Michigan. The Covenant sent another man to check on them. They didn't send this one packing. Instead, my grandmother married him.

The family stayed put for a few years, largely due to issues involving a contract with a demon, an open dimensional rift, and preschool, but once the demon finished doing its thing, the survivors weren't that keen on Michigan anymore. They moved to Oregon. According to the mice, the whole family originally lived in the house where I grew up, which was selected for reasons of geographic isolation and ease of potential defense strategies. I find that concept horrifying. Putting Dad and Aunt Jane in a room together on the holidays is bad enough. Making them share a house should have resulted in homicide. Dad went to Cleveland, met Mom, and brought her home; Aunt Jane went to Portland, met Uncle Ted, and settled down close enough to be a nuisance, yet far enough away that nobody dies.

We don't really have a family tree at this point; it's more like a family branch, given the way people keep getting themselves killed or sucked into alternate dimensions that may or may not be capable of supporting human life (the jury's still out on what happened to Grandpa Thomas, although Grandma Alice insists he's alive, and my mother raised me never to contradict anyone who regularly carries grenades).

It's always been assumed that my siblings and I will settle in the Pacific Northwest. It's not empty nest syndrome: it's practicality. We've lost a lot of family members since Alexander and Enid Healy decided to move to America, and none of their tombstones say things like "died peacefully in her sleep" or "lived a good long life." If we don't stick close to home, we don't *make* it home.

And people at school used to wonder why I laughed when they tried to tell me how weird their families were.

"Can I help you?" That was all. No hello, no "this is the Price residence, Antimony speaking," nothing that might encourage the person on the other end of the phone to keep talking. My baby sister wasn't being rude; that's how we were taught to handle unexpected callers. There was always the chance that cold call might be someone from the Covenant. Paranoia as a family tradition: it's not a good one, but it's ours, and we're fond of it.

Sarah once asked why we didn't just change our surname and go all the way into hiding, rather than screwing around with unlisted phone numbers and keeping our heads down. Sarah's a cryptid, and the concept of not letting the bastards win wasn't something I could explain to her. She understood hiding. What she didn't understand was being willing to be found, as long as it was on your own turf and your own terms.

"Hey, Timmy. Is Mom there?"

"Don't call me Timmy," said Antimony, the words carrying the distinct stamp of reflex. "Mom's not home."

"Not home where? Will she be back soon?"

"Uh, no." Antimony is three years younger than I am, but what she lacks in age, she constantly makes up for in insulting my intelligence. "Did you miss the part where there's a big planetary alignment going on? This week is going to be one of the only times of the year where there's half a chance in hell of getting into, y'know, *Hell*."

I groaned. "Mom's spelunking the Underworld with Grandma, isn't she?"

"Mom's spelunking the Underworld with Grandma," Antimony confirmed.

"Crap."

The dimensions align between six and fifteen times a year, depending on the position of the stars, whether or not the groundhog saw his shadow, and lots of other mystical crap I've never bothered trying to understand. When that happens, there's an even chance my grandmother will show up demanding ammunition, additional grenades, and a shower. Thanks to the time dilation that happens in most of the layers of the Underworld, she looks like she's about my age, which gets a little weirder every year, and means she'll probably still be making these little visits when the house belongs to *my* grandchildren.

My mother's unique skills can come in handy in the various layers of the Underworld, and they're most required when attempting to navigate the Netherworld, a confusingly named subdevelopment that Grandma Alice is convinced borders on the Christian version of Hell. She's been trying to find her way into *that* dimension for the past twenty years. There is no cellular network that extends beyond the first three levels of the Underworld. Mom would be out of touch until she got back.

At least Grandma's field trips were usually entertaining. But it always took weeks to get the smell of sulfur out of my hair.

"Well, if Mom's in the Underworld, can I talk to Dad?"

Antimony paused. "Verity? What's wrong?"

"Nothing. Everything. I don't know. Is Dad there?"

"Do you need me to come out there? I can be on the next plane."

The image of Antimony in Manhattan was enough to bring me stuttering to a horrified stop. She considers pit traps and high explosives the appropriate solution to almost every problem. There was no scenario I could envision where putting her in contact with the Covenant would improve the situation. Elevate it to explosive new heights, possibly, but improve, no.

"I'm good for right now, but I really need to talk to Dad."

"But—"

"Dad."

"Oh, *fine*," said Antimony, pouring every ounce of scorn she could muster into the word. Putting a hand over the receiver, she shouted, "Dad! It's your other daughter!"

There was a clunk as my father picked up the extension. "Thank you, Annie. You can hang up now."

"But I want to know why she's calling."

"I'll brief you later. Hang up now." He went silent. An old trick: he was waiting for the sound of Antimony hanging up her end of the line. After a few seconds, a click signaled her doing exactly that, and he said, sounding only a little concerned, "Now what's this about, Very?"

"What makes you think I'm not calling to bask in the loving warmth of my family?" Silence greeted the question. I laughed, more from exhaustion than anything else, and said, "Okay, you win. Dad, do we know anything about a 'De Luca' family?"

"Covenant, Spanish branch, joined up about three hundred years after the Healys," he said, without hesitation. One advantage to having a history nut for a father: if it's ever encroached on the supernatural world, he probably knows its pedigree. "The last recorded encounter with a member of the family was your great-grandmother, Fran, when she met Jacinta De Luca during a routine sweep of the naga breeding grounds outside Albuquerque. Jacinta was in the process of destroying several nests when—"

"Dad?"

"—she was located, and requests that she—"

"*Dad*!"

"—stop were met with—what?"

One disadvantage to having a history nut for a father: sometimes it's hard to keep him focused on what's actually going on. "That's not the last recorded encounter."

"What do you mean?" I could practically hear him frowning. "It's in her diary, and since there's no mention in any of the volumes since then—"

"The last recorded encounter happened about a half an hour ago, on a rooftop in Manhattan, between Verity Price and Dominic De Luca."

Silence.

"He was setting rooftop snares on my route. He may still be setting snares, although if he's smart, he's gone home to lick his wounds and write 'here be dragons' on his subway map. He killed an ahool! In *my* city! It wasn't doing anything wrong! I mean, eventually, sure, but it hadn't been given the chance!"

More silence.

"I didn't kill him."

"Well, thank God for that. Did he ID you?"

"Afraid so," I said, leaning farther back on the couch. "I lost my temper. It's hard to remember to play the innocent bystander when you're hanging by one ankle a couple hundred feet above street level."

"Did he tell you what he was doing there?"

"The Covenant's decided Manhattan's ripe for a purge. I think he's the only one in town, at least so far, but there's no guarantee things are going to stay that way. Before you say it, no, I'm not willing to be pulled out of here. I'm still in the middle of my survey, Sarah just got settled at her new hotel, and I promised Dave I'd give at least two weeks' notice before I left." I also had an Argentine tango competition in three weeks that could qualify me for Nationals, but he didn't need to know that.

"I'm not intending to pull you out of there."

I hesitated. "You're not?"

"You're already involved. I'm not going to pull you out just because a member of the Covenant is in town. I will, however, warn everyone that we may be needed for backup, and I'll email you anything I can find in the records about the De Luca family, their methodology, and any previous Manhattan purges."

"You're the best Daddy ever."

He chuckled. "Let's see if you're saying that when you're getting swarmed by Covenant assassins and wanna-be conquistadors."

"That's when I'll start saying you're gunning for Father of the Year. Give Mom my love when she gets back from the Underworld."

"She'd hurt me if I didn't."

We exchanged the standard pleasantries and I rang off, feeling considerably better. Sure, I was the one standing at what might be about to turn into ground zero, but if the Covenant took me out, the family would descend on New York in a heavily-armed, extremely irritated wave. None of that would make me any less dead, but it would make me feel better. Besides, if I died, I could be the first person in thirty years to figure out whether Grandpa Thomas is alive or not.

After testing to be sure my ankle was willing to bear my weight, I stood and made my way to the bedroom. Things would look better after a few hours of sleep. Things usually do.

I was on the verge of drifting off when I remembered my earlier determination to eat something healthy. Getting up would have been too much trouble. I rolled over, pulled the blankets over my head, and slipped into the comforting simplicity of sleep.

I opened my eyes to the sound of my alarm blaring a cheerful imitation of a fire siren. I rolled over to smack the snooze button, triggering an ecstatic cry of "Hail the renewed consciousness of the Arboreal Priestess!" from the Aeslin mice surrounding my bed. None of them were *on* the bed, a fact that I attributed less to politeness than to their admittedly stunted sense of self-preservation. Not even the Aeslin are dumb enough to get too close to someone who sleeps with as many guns as I do.

"The Arboreal Priestess isn't awake enough for you to hail things," I informed the congregation. They answered with muted cheers. Sitting up, I rubbed the sleep from my eyes and glared at the time displayed on the clock. Nine-thirty in the morning. These double shifts were going to kill me if they went on for much longer.

"Oh, shit," I said, remembering. "I trashed my uniform socks." That meant buying a new pair. Dave recommended we all keep backups, but since the socks seemed to get shredded as quickly as I bought them, buying extra just doubled my bill.

"Hail the purchase of the socks!" cried the mice, before dissolving into general rejoicing.

I had to smile. There's very little that won't inspire Aeslin mice to religious ecstasy, which is why we've kept them around for so long. Having a tiny church choir singing the praises of fixing the garbage disposal does a lot to keep things tolerable. Also, they're too damn cute to kill, and ecological curiosity generally suppresses any homicidal urges that may get past the "awww" impulse. After living with them for seven generations, we have yet to figure out what Aeslin mice are *for*.

"Okay, guys," I said, as I swung my feet around to the floor. "Why am I getting the morning congregation experience? Again, I know this isn't a major holiday."

"It is the sixth day of the Month of Do Not Put That in Your Mouth!" proclaimed one of the priests, sounding incredibly pleased about that fact.

It took me a moment to figure out what that meant. The Aeslin schedule their celebrations according to the standard human calendar, but maintain their own calendar for private use. How they keep the two straight is something I will never understand, especially since they celebrate approximately thirty-two months every year. (That really is an approximation. Several of the months are intermittent, and may skip a year or more before making a return engagement. Religious mice are weird.)

"You want cheese and cake, don't you?" This was the right answer: the room erupted into cheers and jubilation.

I was going to need to get up sooner or later. Probably sooner, if I wanted to make it to work on time. I'm less inclined to take the rooftops when the sun is out— something about not wanting to cause a mob scene when people decide I'm a cat burglar or a masked vigilante—and I didn't trust my ankle yet. I would have needed to have two broken kneecaps and maybe a dislocated hip before I was willing to take a taxi. It was me and the two-foot express, and that would take time.

I stood, careful to keep myself centered on the bed so I'd fall on something soft if my ankle refused to hold me. There was a twinge of pain and some protests as the bandage scraped against the raw skin, but that was all. I could stand, I could walk, and I could probably even dance, as long as I didn't expect to be up to competition standards. It was better than it could have been. "I'll take it," I said, aloud. The mice greeted what must have seemed like a total non sequitur with more cheering.

That's the nice thing about Aeslin mice. You don't have to make sense to keep them happy. You just have to let them worship you unconditionally, move into the attic (or the closet), and occasionally pester you for manna from Heaven. Which, them being physically mostly mouse and all, usually takes the form of dairy products and baked goods. It works out okay.

Once in the kitchen, I dished up plates of flourless chocolate cake, slices of cheese, and soda crackers, cutting a piece of cake for myself and leaning against the windowsill as I ate. The mice made a production number out of breakfast that Disney could have taken some tips from. The dance routine with the soda crackers was a particularly nice touch.

The mice vanished after they finished eating, scurrying off to do whatever it is that they do all day. For the most part, when they're not underfoot or enacting weird religious tableaus on my counters, they go their way and I go mine. Things are less dangerous that way. I put my plate in the sink, stretched, and sighed. Time to go check my email and see what sort of apocalypse the Covenant was so generously providing me with.

I don't know how people accomplished anything in the days before email. When I logged into my account, I had three messages from Dad, one from Aunt Jane, and one from Sarah. Sarah wanted to confirm that we were on for dinner; I shot her a note saying I'd be there by eight, and warning her to stay out of dark alleys and subway tunnels. Not that Sarah's the kind of cryptid who likes to hang around in the places monster hunters tend to frequent, but you can never be too careful.

Dad's messages managed to be more useful and more worrisome at the same time. We had records of three confirmed Covenant "purges" in the Manhattan area, along with two in New Jersey and six more that weren't verified but looked likely. They seemed to come through every fifty years or so, spend a summer slaughtering anything they could get their hands on, and then go home, serene in the knowledge that they were doing holy work.

I may sound prejudiced against the Covenant. That's because I am. They're a huge society with nigh-infinite resources and access to research materials I can only dream about. So what do they do with all that power and potential? They hunt innocent cryptids for the crime of having been born to a species that didn't make it onto the "approved" list. There'd be hundreds of special interest groups dedicated to stomping them out if they were hunting panda bears and dolphins. Since they hunt bogeymen and basilisks, they'd probably get a medal if anyone knew that they existed.

Dad's notes went on to say that the De Lucas were among the worst of a bad lot, since they actually bought the party line about the extermination of cryptids being the will of God. It's hard to reason with someone who thinks he's got a holy calling. Violence is sometimes the only answer, and I hate killing people. It's messy, it's inconvenient, and while body disposal is surprisingly easy when you know what you're doing, it's not a pleasant way to spend an evening. Apparently, most of the De Luca family had already ridden the party line to extinction, since Dad had death records for a whole stack of De Lucas, including "Christabelle and Antonio De Luca" who were survived by their only son, Dominic. Poor guy must have been raised by the Covenant. That was just going to make him more annoying.

Aunt Jane's letter was a sort of supplement to Dad's information. He may be the family historian, but she's the family nosy gossip columnist—a more useful function than you might guess. It helps that my Uncle Ted's an incubus, which gives her a direct connection to the cryptid community. She's an honorary succubus, and she gets on all the mailing lists.

According to Aunt Jane, asking her lists "Does anyone know what's up in New York?" resulted in a positive deluge of information, all of it pointing back to one worrisome conclusion: nobody knew what was going on, and everybody thought it was going to be big, whatever it was. Which explained why the locals weren't evacuating. Until they knew whether or not there was a problem, they wouldn't want to risk losing their nesting spots, or deal with cell phone cancellation fees and forwarding their mail.

I printed the messages and stuffed them into my backpack before starting for the bathroom. It was time to get ready for my second shift in twenty-four hours. At least once I got there I could have a little word with my boss about why he hadn't been clueing me in on gossip that might pertain to my chances of survival.

Wow, all this excitement and minimum wage, plus tips. Who says you can't make a living in New York City?

Seven

"A proper lady should be able to smile
pretty, wear sequins like she means it, and
kick a man's ass nine ways from Sunday
while wearing stiletto heels. If she can't do
that much, she's not trying hard enough."

—Frances Brown

*Just arriving at Dave's Fish and Strips, a club for discerning
gentlemen*

BY THE TIME I GOT TO DAVE'S I was drenched in sweat,
feeling put out and abused by the universe. I don't
know how walking at street level could do more damage
to my admittedly low-maintenance haircut than running
across the rooftops would have, but it managed. The gel
I'd used to make myself look less like a startled cocka-
too melted in the hot Manhattan air. At this point, my
hairstyle was best described as "half spikes, half surprised
mop."

I stomped into the dressing room, stopped, and
promptly upgraded my opinion on the unfairness of the
universe. Candy was sitting in front of the mirror, putting the finishing touches on her makeup. She looked as
dewy-eyed and fresh as a Miss America contestant getting ready for the swimsuit competition. Even the taw-
dry uniform Dave forced us to wear was elevated by
contact with her skin, somehow becoming raiment fit for

a princess. And that's exactly what it was, because she *was* a princess, cryptid royalty and, like any real princess, she didn't need fur or jewels to let her intrinsic nobility shine through. Her flaxen hair was long, smooth, and perfect, just like her hourglass figure and fashion-model face. Nothing human should look that good. Which was a good thing, because Candy was a long way from human.

"Candice," I greeted, heading for my locker.

Her gaze didn't waver from her reflection as she offered a cool, "Verity," in return. Out of all the girls working at Dave's, Candy liked me the least.

Sadly, that made sense. My family is part of the reason she's been reduced to cocktail waitressing—us, and the rest of the Covenant.

Dragon princesses look like curvaceous, drop-dead gorgeous human girls; as the name implies, there are no males, and their exact method of reproduction is unknown. Not, I'm ashamed to admit, due to a lack of field research. Cryptozoologists have been trying to figure out where dragon princesses come from for centuries. It's one of our holy grails, like finding a living unicorn or, well, the Holy Grail. (People used to think dragon princesses hatched from the bodies of dead dragons. People also used to think rotting meat spontaneously generated flies, and that's only occasionally true. It depends on the type of meat.)

Near as anyone can tell, dragon princesses evolved solely to care for dragons. They're born craving gold and spend their lives pursuing wealth—and if they get it, they promptly use it to buy more gold. They gather in Nests, sleeping in tangled harems on beds of 24-carat loot. It's a pretty sweet gig. There's really just one problem with the dragon princess gig: dragons have been extinct for centuries, leaving their symbiotic pets to gather gold for nobody, and worse, leaving them stranded in the cryptid world with no natural weapons to speak of.

Dragon princesses don't have fangs, claws, or poison.

They don't survive under impossible conditions or live in places where they won't be bothered. They don't burn—you could take a blowtorch to a dragon princess and all you'd do is piss her off—but there isn't much call for the asbestos blonde.

The thing is, dragons didn't *go* extinct. They were *made* extinct by the Covenant, since no one was really keen on sharing their living space with a giant fire-breathing lizard. That was long before either the Healys or the Prices left the Covenant, and it turns out dragon princesses carry a grudge as well as the dragons supposedly did. Maybe even better. Ninety percent of the world's cryptid population have forgiven us for what our family used to be, focusing instead on what we've become: advocates, allies, and sometimes the only humans willing to put themselves in danger to save a cryptid life. The dragon princesses focus on what we used to be.

Killers.

I tossed my backpack into my locker and grabbed my spare uniform off the top shelf. I heard Candy shift in her seat, no doubt so she could keep watching me in the mirror. She didn't like being alone in a room with me, largely because she seemed convinced I'd flip out and try to kill her at any moment. There were times when I was tempted, usually when she cleared one of my tables and they "mysteriously" failed to leave a tip, but my parents raised me to be tolerant of the racial quirks of our cryptid neighbors. In Candy's case, that meant she'd need to be a lot bitchier before I wasted a bullet on her.

After fluffing the pleats on my skirt into their appropriate jailbait-esque configuration, I turned and asked, "Is Dave in his office?"

"Please. Like he'd leave it during the day?" Candice twisted to eye me suspiciously. "Why?"

There were a lot of possible answers to that question, starting with "like I'd tell you?" and going downhill from there. Sadly, protecting the cryptid population of Manhattan was at the core of my mission statement, and that meant I had to at least pretend to give a damn about Candy's welfare. Even if I didn't want to.

"I ran into a man from the Covenant last night while I was making my rounds. He seemed like he was planning to stick around for a while. Thought I'd check with Dave, see whether he knew anything about our new neighbor."

Candy's normally milk-and-roses complexion went waxen as her eyes widened until they looked like they were going to fall out of her head. Composing herself with a visible effort, she licked her lips and said, "You—you're lying."

"Sorry. Wish I was." I shrugged. "His name's Dominic De Luca. I already called my folks, and Dad sent me the intel on his family. They're old school Covenant. Guy looks like he's legit."

"I . . . no. No, you have to be wrong." She stood, scattering cosmetics as she fumbled for balance against the dressing room counter. "The Covenant doesn't come here anymore."

"The Covenant comes when it's time for a purge, same as they come everywhere else."

Her eyes widened again, but only for a few seconds; then they narrowed, fury suddenly radiating from her expression. "This is *your* fault," she spat. "You and your goddamn family couldn't just stay on the West Coast until they hunted you down, could you? And now they've followed you here. Well, I hope you're happy, Verity. I just hope you're happy."

"Candy—"

She didn't give me time to finish the sentence. Ripping off her apron, she flung it on the floor between us and turned to stalk out of the room. I sighed. On the plus side, she was probably on her way to warn the rest of her Nest that the Covenant was in town. On the negative, out of the city's three dozen or so dragon princesses, she was the one I probably had the *best* relationship with. The rest of them wouldn't just blame my family; they'd blame me personally.

This day was getting better and better, and it wasn't even noon yet. Who knew what wonders were lurking on the other side of the lunch rush? Leaving Candy's apron on the dressing room floor, I turned to follow her path out to the hall. It was past time to have a little chat with my boss.

Dave's darks were on again, making it impossible to tell whether he was in the office while I was standing in the hall. I decided to take a chance on Candy's information being accurate and strode into the blackness with my chin held high and my shoulders pushed back, like I was making my entrance to the stage before a competition tango. Always wow the people you're up against with confidence, that's the family motto. Well, that, and "always count your ammo before agreeing to a firefight."

Walking into a dark office that might or might not contain a bogeyman definitely didn't fall under the heading of "ten smartest things I have ever done." It might be somewhere in the top thirty, but that's because I had an abnormally interesting time as a teenager. It probably looked like stupid bravado, and it probably was, to a degree. That's why I had a knife in either hand by the time I cleared the doorway, ready to fling them at the slightest provocation.

It was normally possible to take eight steps into Dave's office without banging into anything. I stopped after six; far enough to make it clear that I wasn't bluffing, but not far enough that I risked whacking my knee on his desk and ruining the effect.

"Dave? We need to talk."

There was a brief pause before Dave's voice hissed out of the black, sounding puzzled and a little excited. "Why, Verity Price, how very . . . very of you. Have you finally decided that the time is ripe to have a proper play date?"

"Turn off the darks, Dave. We need to talk."

"So you say, so you say, but you came into my lair without demanding safe passage through the light. An interesting choice for a girl who says she doesn't care for shadows."

I yawned, not bothering to cover my mouth. "Blah, blah, blah, you're very scary, oh, I'm trembling. I came in without telling you to turn off the darks because I wanted you to actually believe that I was serious when I said you needed to listen to me. We have a deal. Part of it involves me not hunting you."

"And?" There was caution under the excitement now, as logic overrode his instincts.

I flung a knife into the darkness, aiming for a spot a foot to the left of where Dave's head would normally be. I heard it hit the wall. "And if you insist on giving in to your nature and spooking me, I'm going to have to give in to my nature, and hunt you. Darks, Dave. Talk, Dave. Now, Dave."

The darks clicked off and the lights clicked on, revealing the dour, gray-skinned form of my boss sitting behind his desk and sulking like a petulant child. "What could possibly be so important that you needed to come in here like that?"

"Candy went home."

Dave hesitated, visibly trying to fit that statement into any sort of logical conversation. "So, what, you want her tables?"

"It was a personal emergency."

"What sort of personal emergency could possibly make a dragon princess give up her tips for the second shift in a row? I expected her to come in here black and blue after her Nest-sisters kicked holy hell out of her for missing work." Dragon princesses view the income of one as the income of all, and they tend to get a little bit cranky when that income is threatened.

Watching Dave's expression, I said, "She had to go make sure the Nest was aware that there's a representative from the Covenant currently resident in Manhattan."

I'll give Dave this much: he managed to school his face almost instantly into a neutral state. Sadly, "almost" wasn't fast enough to keep me from seeing the way the skin around his mouth tightened. It was a subtle tell, but it was what I had to go on. "Is that so?" he asked. "That's a pisser. We'd better make sure the rest of the staff knows. How'd you find out, Very? Has this guy been bothering you?"

"If we were on a bad cop show, this is where I'd point out that I never told you it was a guy, but since the Covenant's field agents are ninety percent male, I'm going to let it pass," I said, stepping forward until I could rest the heels of my hands against the desk. "Why didn't you tell me he was in town, Dave?"

"I don't know what you mean."

"Uh-huh. Let's go again. Why didn't you tell me he was in town, Dave?"

Scowling now, Dave crossed his arms. "Aren't I your employer? Thus making me the man with the power to sack your pretty little ass if you go around accusing me of things?"

"Ignoring the part where I could double my income if I started teaching dance classes instead of working here, yes, you are," I said, and smiled. "Aren't I the one who could walk out into your bar and tell everybody you've been withholding information that could get them killed? I don't think I'll need to worry about you firing me after you've been slaughtered by the rest of your employees."

There was a pause as Dave measured out my statement, trying to figure out whether I was bluffing. I let him take as much time as he needed. I might have been more inclined to hurry him if I *had* been bluffing, but I was doing nothing of the sort. If the Covenant was in town, the locals needed to know. Whether I also told them Dave had been aware before they were was entirely dependent on him.

Finally, he settled back in his seat and gave me a wounded look. "How did you know?"

"About the Covenant, or about you having prior knowledge?"

"Both."

"I know about the Covenant because I need a new pair of socks, which you, having been previously aware of their presence, will be kind enough to supply me with for free. I got caught in a lovely little rooftop snare last night. Not sure whether our boy was hunting Jersey devils, harpies, or just whatever happened to wander by, but he got himself a cryptozoologist for his trouble. He nearly got a bullet to the forehead to go with it. He's already killed at least one ahool. I don't know what else he may have done."

"What stopped you from shooting him?" Dave asked, raising his eyebrows.

"Didn't want to waste the ammo." I kept smiling. "As for how I know you were previously aware, well. You're a bogeyman who runs a strip club. If anybody would have heard it through the grapevine, it's you. And you let Kitty go on tour with her boyfriend's band."

"Wanting my employees to succeed in their chosen fields of endeavor makes me the bad guy now?"

"Kitty's one of the only girls you have who's always willing to work the overnights, doesn't complain about the skanky little uniforms, and puts up with you being a lech. You wouldn't let her out of the building at the end of her shift if you didn't have to. That means the only good reason for you to let her go on tour is getting her out of the line of fire. What do you know? What aren't you telling me?"

Dave fixed me with an eye, giving me his best piercing glare. It was the sort of look bogeymen excel at, all supernatural menace and the promise of nasty things lurking in your closet. I met it with an even sweeter smile.

Dave knew when he was beat. He sagged, and said, "He got here about a week and a half ago. Boy's been keeping his head down. I wouldn't even know if he hadn't flown through JFK."

Raising my eyebrows, I asked, "What does that have to do with anything?"

"I have some friends in the TSA. Most of the agents spend their time looking for signs of human terrorism. These folks are looking for a different sort of terrorist— the sort of terrorist who starches his socks and keeps silver flasks full of holy water in his checked bags." Dave shrugged, looking slightly smug. "They caught him coming in, passed me the info, I did some checking, and bingo, we've got us a tasty little piece of intelligence."

"Well, that's dandy and all, but when were you planning to bring me into your little circle of trust? Before or after he killed me for being a cryptid sympathizer?"

Holding up his hands, Dave said, "Hey, now, Verity, that's not the deal, now, is it? I'm not informing for you. A man's got to eat, and you work for cash on the barrel, not for gossip." A smile wormed its way across his face. "Of course, if you wanted to add a little rider to your contract, maybe something about dancing for data—"

"You go to hell, Dave," I said pleasantly. "I'm going to go talk to the bouncers. If you hear anything else about this guy, I expect to be informed. Got me?"

"Or what?"

I took my hands off the desk and straightened, still smiling. "I become the monster under *your* bed."

Not pausing to give him a chance to respond, I turned and walked out of the office, leaving the knife sticking out of his wall. I had warnings to pass on, a pair of socks to collect from the wardrobe locker, and a shift to work. No rest for the wicked.

The lunch rush was more of a lunch trickle by the time I hit the floor, apron in place and new socks pulled securely over my knees. The other girls on duty were walking laconically among the customers, taking orders and providing the occasional panty-shot in an effort to drive up tips. They looked profoundly bored. Even without Candy, they had things more than under control. Istas was at the bar picking up a round of cocktails for one of the few occupied tables as I approached. I offered a respectful nod, which she returned without comment. Like most waheela, she wasn't particularly comfortable with interpersonal interaction, but she made more of an effort than the bulk of her kind. I had to respect her for that, even as I continued to wonder what the hell would drive a member of a solitary, semiferal species to take a job at a Manhattan titty bar.

Ryan was leaning against the bar nursing a cup of something that smelled suspiciously like pickle juice. He smiled at me, waiting until I was close enough to hear him over the thumping music to say, "Hey, Verity. Those new socks? What happened this time?"

"I got snared by a representative from the Covenant while I was making my rooftop rounds and sort of bled through the cotton. Also, your nose for fresh cotton remains creepy and means I want you nowhere near my underwear drawer, ever." I slid myself onto a stool. "Hey, Daisy, can I get a plate of hot wings? I'm starving to death over here."

"Got it, hon," called the bartender, heading for the kitchen.

Ryan, meanwhile, was staring at me like I'd suddenly announced my desire to get wasted and catch a nice social disease. "Come again?"

"The Covenant's in town," I said, turning to face him straight on. "Dave didn't give you the info either?"

Ryan didn't answer in words. He just growled, lips pulling back to show incisors considerably sharper and more pointed than the average human's. Those teeth were normally the only sign that he'd inherited more from his Japanese mother than black hair and the sort of exotic features that kept the tourist ladies throwing themselves at him.

I nodded. "Thought not."

"How many?"

"One that I'm aware of, about my age, pretty good at the hand-to-hand, but not smart enough to avoid bringing knives to a gunfight." I held up a hand. "Pass the word that he's out there and people need to be careful, but also pass the word that nobody should do anything stupid, like try to kill him."

Ryan eyed me. "He's from the *Covenant*, Verity," he said, like that explained everything. From Ryan's perspective, it did. The Covenant did a lot of "cleansing" in Japan, and Ryan's species suffered pretty badly. Tanuki are therianthropes—shapeshifters powered by magic, rather than by the virus that causes lycanthropy—and they've never had much success with outbreeding. They probably would have died out entirely if not for the fact that they're incredibly determined and spent several generations sticking it into anything that would wiggle as they tried to find species they could mate with to produce children who would live. My family has a lot of reasons to hate the Covenant. Ryan's family has more.

"Yes, he's from the Covenant, and if we go messing with him, the rest of the Covenant is going to find out. If everyone just lies low, stays out of his way, and passes the word around, maybe we can handle him without this turning into something worse. Or we can mess with him, and the Covenant can send a legion to put us down." Daisy put my wings on the bar. I offered her a nod of thanks, reaching for the tray. "The way I see it, the choice is ours."

"I don't like this," Ryan rumbled. His voice was getting deeper as his vocal chords constricted, modulating toward animal. He'd get control of himself in a minute, and it would be rude to point out the changes. Like most therianthropes, Ryan was very sensitive about his slips.

"You don't have to like it. You just have to help me pass the word along." I picked up a hot wing, dipping it in bleu cheese dressing before offering a wry smile. "Besides, maybe if we all go underground, he'll get bored and go away. Stranger things have happened, right?"

"Stranger than the Covenant letting go of a purge before they get to skin somebody?" Ryan gave me a dubious look. "I'm not sure anything *that* strange has *ever* happened."

I shrugged. "There's a first time for everything."

"Not for this."

"We'll see."

Ryan sighed, throat visibly contorting as his vocal chords slipped themselves back into their human configuration. "Yeah," he said, sounding doleful. "I guess we will."

Eight

"Remember that most people, human or
cryptid, don't like what they don't understand. They're not wired for that kind of
compassion. Feel sorry for them, unless
they form an angry mob and march on
your house. When that happens, release
the hounds."

—Evelyn Baker

*The rooftops of Manhattan, sometime after midnight, three
weeks later*

THE SUMMER HEAT HAD DEEPENED as June slid into
July, going from "unpleasant" to "unbearable" and
bathing the entire city in a faint but distinctive scent of
unwashed bodies, spoiled food, and chemical perfume.
The smell was heaviest at street level. After an hour on
the rooftops, going back to the ground was unbearable.
Sadly, the part of my training that focused on blending
in with the natives was firm on the topic of gas masks:
they were a big no-no.

Paradoxically, the worse the smell of the city became,
the more comfortable the lycanthrope and therianthrope populations seemed to be. As Ryan explained
things, they didn't like the modern attitude that people
should be perfumed at all times, but as long as no one
squirted strong scents actually *on* them, they could cope.

The hazy, sweaty days of summer made tracking easier while they were in their human forms, and that made it easier for them to remain calm while surrounded by actual humans. Summer in the city is like having the lights turned on in a dark room for a shapeshifter. Interesting. Good to know. Definitely relevant to my field of study. And doing nothing for my reluctance to come down from the rooftops.

It had been almost a month since my last—and thus far, only—encounter with Dominic De Luca, better known as "the asshole from the Covenant." Ryan, Candy, and everyone else at Dave's refused to dignify the fact that he had a proper name. I couldn't blame them. We'd been short-staffed since people learned he was in town, as everybody came up with sudden, pressing reasons to get out of harm's way. (Most people used the standards: sick relative, family funeral, impending childbirth, whelping, or ovipositing—normal things. Marcy was the only one to take off her apron and say, without prevaricating, "I'm out of here until he's gone, dead, or both." Her pure self-interest was refreshing, even if it didn't do anything to help cover her shifts at the club. At least we knew when she'd be back.)

I was getting annoyed at the people who turned tail and ran, even though I couldn't blame them for doing it. I was a cryptid sympathizer, after all, not a cryptid, and that meant I had a lot less to lose. Even Sarah and the mice were relatively safe. Aeslin can vanish into a normal rodent population in less time than it takes to say "exterminator," and Sarah would be the last person any representative of the Covenant tagged as outside the norm. Her camouflage was good enough to see her through anything short of a nuclear attack. Most of the city's cryptids didn't have that luxury.

The deserters didn't worry me. That honor was reserved for the ones who'd simply disappeared. It seemed like more members of the city's cryptid population went missing every day. It started small, with just a few outliers from the community, people no one really kept very close tabs on anyway. There are totally valid ecological reasons for the existence of ghouls, bug-a-boos, and wendigo. That doesn't mean anybody sane wants them for neighbors. There was no way of getting an exact number on the missing, but I knew it was higher than I liked. The members of the various species that remained in town had been calling relatives and information brokers, but if anyone knew anything, they weren't sharing it with me.

The few estimates I could get on the missing only covered the humanoid cryptids. Nobody knew how many animal cryptids were in Manhattan and, without a starting census, I couldn't tell how many were gone. Everyone I talked to agreed that the numbers were dropping. Not encouraging, especially when I couldn't give them any reassurance that things were going to be all right.

The impulse to blame all the disappearances on De Luca was strong. There was just one problem with that convenient answer to my problems: I'd only found a few bodies, all of them at roof level, and all of them obviously hostile cryptid "monsters," like the ahool. I didn't care how good a hunter the asshole was. If he was responsible for all the deaths, there would have been more bodies. He was still the closest thing I had to a lead.

Which brought me back to the rooftops, having bribed Candy to bring in two of her "sisters" to cover my shift for the night. I was hunting a hunter. The best place to do that is on the killing grounds.

All my life I've been dismissed as the dilettante daughter, the one who'd rather dance than deal with the realities of the family business. Alex graduated from high school two years ahead of his peers, got his degree in veterinary medicine, and took off for South America to spend a year hunting for dinosaurs—long story—before settling at the Columbus Zoo with his menagerie. Antimony was still living at home, but she was also taking classes at the local college, helping Mom with her hospice duties, and helping Dad with his research. Me, on the other hand? I went on national reality television. Way to forward the cryptid cause, Verity.

But here's the thing: it *was* the best way to forward the cryptid cause. My specialization is in the humanoid cryptids, and by making a spectacle of myself, I also made myself seem harmless. The Prices belonged to the Covenant for too long to be totally accepted overnight. Once the cryptids who actually watched TV found out who I was—and more specifically, found out that I'd gone undercover to be on a reality show—they started dismissing the idea that I might be a threat. They spread the word through the rest of the community. It turned out people were a lot more likely to trust me when my silhouette made them think of foxtrots and waltzes, not serious collateral damage. Image is everything.

Image doesn't change reality. Under the sequins, the flashy makeup jobs, and the designer shoes, I'm a Price. I know how to do my job. I just wish my job wouldn't insist on getting done the night before a dance competition.

I'd been prowling the rooftops every night for weeks, and the only signs I'd seen of De Luca were the corpses in his wake. Dave insisted that his contacts didn't know where Dominic was, but I wasn't sure I trusted Dave. It's never a good idea to take a bogeyman at his word when you're not holding a gun to his head, and even then there's a chance he'll try to play you before you pull the trigger.

At least this time I was prepared for a fight. I was wearing a skintight gray bodysuit that rendered me virtually invisible when I stepped into the shadows, and the soles of my boots had been treated with one of Antimony's weird science projects, giving me traction on practically any surface. They didn't even leave footprints unless I was dumb enough to step in a puddle. My face was visible, my hair seeming almost white against the

dark, but I wasn't willing to wear a mask. It wasn't pride
or vanity; it was the desire to avoid having my head dive-
bombed by confused gargoyles who thought I was competition intruding on their territory.

I was about ready to call it a night and get some sleep
before registration opened in the morning when I heard
faint footfalls behind me. I kept walking, refusing to let
my tension show itself in my posture as I reviewed the
last few minutes. I was certain I hadn't passed any of the
local cryptids. They would have made sure I saw them,
since they know it's never a good idea to surprise a Price
when she's on patrol. That meant whoever or whatever
was behind me wasn't something that respected my
place in the city. Monster or member of the Covenant, I
could take my pick.

Considering how frustrated and wound up I was after
the past few weeks, I would have preferred the monster.
A little good, old-fashioned bloodshed always cheers
me up. Even so, I hoped it was De Luca, because we
needed to settle this. I bent forward, like I was going to
stretch out my hamstrings, and grabbed the pistols at my
belt. I spun as I drew them, turning the motion into a
smooth pirouette.

Dominic De Luca was ten feet behind me, a crossbow
out and trained, dead center, on my chest.

I froze, guns still raised.

"I'm really not sure which of us would fire first," he
said, tone almost apologetic, "but I'm reasonably sure
whichever of us didn't would still have time to pull their
trigger before the missile struck home."

It took me a moment to puzzle my way through that
sentence. Raising my eyebrows, I asked, "Are you saying
that no matter who shoots, we probably both die?"

"Exactly," he said, that same apologetic note in his
voice. "Can I recommend we stand down, at least for the
moment?"

I hesitated. Part of me was saying, "You can take
him." That part was thankfully drowned out by the rest

of me, which was pointing out how pissed the rest of the family would be if I died like this. "Go down shooting" might as well be the family motto, but if it were, the second half would be "don't go down stupid." Raising my hands and turning my pistols so he could see what I was doing, I reengaged the safeties and slid the guns back into their holsters.

Dominic hesitated. I could almost read the conflict on his face. I was, after all, the granddaughter of Alice Healy and Thomas Price, two of the Covenant's greatest traitors. If he pulled the trigger, he could probably kill me before I had time to draw again. He could go home a hero, secure in the knowledge that any door in the Covenant would be open to him. All he had to do was twitch his index finger, and the world was his. All he had to do was kill a woman who had already surrendered.

After what seemed like an eternity, but was probably no more than a few seconds, he lowered his crossbow.

"Thank you," he said.

"What took you so long?" I replied. "I've been looking for you for days. It's not nice to keep a lady waiting."

Now it was his turn to raise his eyebrows, confusion replacing conflict. "Waiting? Looking for me? I thought this was just another unfortunate encounter. I knew you hadn't left the city, but I'd rather hoped your rabble-rousing would keep you too busy to come back up here."

"What do you mean, rabble-rousing? I was looking for you to find out what the hell you think you're doing. I told you to go home."

The confusion deepened. "What *I'm* doing? I'm not the one protecting inhuman monsters by telling them to evacuate."

I blinked. "Evacuate? Are you kidding? Sure, people are leaving, but it's nothing like an evacuation."

"The population here is nothing like what I was told to expect."

A slow, disturbing certainty was creeping through my

veins, bringing a whole host of new questions with it. "Hold on."

He gave me a politely enquiring look. "Yes?"

"How many cryptids have you killed since the last time I saw you?"

"Not enough of them, and nothing that could speak." He shook his head, frustration clear in the set of his jaw. "A few more of those giant bats. A vast reptile living beneath a dumpster. Beyond that, there's been nothing."

The rest of the ahool's flock and a lindworm. That definitely didn't match up with my list of the missing, and both species were nonsapient predators that fed on humans. "Right." I reached up to pinch the bridge of my nose, fighting the near-irresistible urge to scream. "We need to talk. How do you feel about coffee?"

Dominic turned out to feel good about coffee and not so good about coffee shops, even ones that didn't belong to massive national chains. He'd started glancing anxiously around before we'd even placed our order, and his surprise when I collected the mugs and muffins and turned toward a table was almost comic. Only almost. If he wasn't responsible for my missing cryptids, and I hadn't been running the underground evacuation he accused me of, well . . .

There were several alternatives, and none of them were good.

Breaking off a chunk of muffin, I leaned back in my chair, studying Dominic. He had potential now that I was seeing him in decent light. The good bones I'd noticed on the rooftop were complemented by an even, olive-skinned complexion, and while his hands were covered in small scars, you don't grow up in a family of cryptozoologists without learning to respect the beauty of a good scar. Scarring means you survived. It was too bad he was a murdering bastard, really. Apart from that, he was pretty darn cute.

Dominic was too distracted to notice my appraisal. His attention was split in twenty directions as he tried to watch all the coffee shop's patrons and keep a wary eye on me at the same time. It was an impossible task, and he was failing. I could have told him it couldn't be done and given him some suggestions on filtering the harmless from the potentially dangerous, but it was more interesting to watch him do his own assessment.

Every time his gaze shifted, I learned a little more about the Covenant's training methods. I can't say I was impressed. Maybe it was just the difference between American and European crowds throwing him off, but if he was that unsettled by your standard after-midnight coffee freaks, I couldn't imagine him following a ghoul through a crowded train station. Plus—and this was a big one—he was trying to watch me, too, and I could have poisoned his coffee six times while his attention was directed elsewhere. Shoddy work.

"So," I said. He jumped in his seat, twisting to face me. I swallowed the urge to smile, and continued, "If you're not responsible for most of the cryptids who've been disappearing, and I'm not responsible for the cryptids who've been disappearing, who is? I'm assuming you're the only one working this city. You would have tried too hard not to say something if you weren't."

He blanched, going as pale as was possible for someone with his particular skin tone. "Quiet," he hissed, in that low whisper that people think is subtle but is actually more likely to attract attention than speaking in a conversational tone. "Do you want people to hear you?"

"Um . . . not particularly, but I wouldn't be upset if they did. Why do you ask?"

"The ears of the general populace must be shielded from such blasphemous words."

"What, 'are you working alone' is blasphemy now? No offense, but you need to get out more."

"Not that." His voice dropped even lower, a stunt I wouldn't have believed possible. "They mustn't know about the . . . monsters."

"Wow."

He blinked. "Wow?"

"Yeah, wow. I didn't know people actually paused portentously in common conversation. Look, you've got nothing to worry about."

"I don't know what brand of training you may have had, but I assure you, my caution is more well-deserved than your offhanded dismissal." He leaned back in his seat and eyed me disdainfully. "It's clear that you have little experience in these matters."

I don't know which annoyed me more; the assumption that my training had somehow been less thorough than his, or the easy dismissal of my field experience. I stiffened, the muscles in my jaw tightening until it felt like I was forcing my next words out through concrete. "Is that so," I said, making it less a question than a statement.

"I understand that things may be different here. Please believe me when I say that the need for caution is universal."

"Right." I raised a hand. "Hold that thought."

I was standing before he had a chance to react, kicking my chair out from behind me. I grabbed it with my right hand, keeping it from going toppling over, and flipped it around to form a makeshift platform before stepping onto the seat and striking a dramatic pose. Several other patrons turned to look toward the commotion. One wolf-whistled appreciatively. When looking to attract attention in a hurry, there are worse strategies than being female and wearing skintight gray spandex in a coffee shop packed with college-age males.

"Citizens of Manhattan," I said, waving my arms for emphasis. More patrons turned in our direction. Dominic had gone even paler, which was an accomplishment. "May I have your attention?"

"You've got it, sweet-cheeks," called the whistler. "Now can I have your number?" His buddies laughed, elbowing each other in the easy amusement natural to semidrunk frat boys trying to get enough coffee in themselves to remember where they left the car.

"Maybe later," I said. Turning my attention to the coffee shop as a whole, I said, "My friend and I belong to two rival sects of monster hunters, pursuing the supernatural and mysterious through the underworld for centuries. He believes in extermination. I believe in preservation. Now we put it to you: which of us is right?"

"The one who takes off her top!" called another of the frat boys. Another round of laughter followed.

The rest of the patrons shook their heads and turned back to their tables, dismissing my outburst as being either drunken ravings, promotion for a television show they hadn't heard about yet, or both. I hopped down from the chair, straddling it as I smiled benevolently at Dominic.

"Well?" I asked. "See any sign these nice folks feel like they've heard blasphemous talk?"

"I—you—they—"

"Pronouns are only useful when you combine them with other words. I have a few I can give you, if you're at a loss."

"I don't believe you did that!" He was turning red now as the blood rushed back into his cheeks, horrified embarrassment chasing his pallor away.

"Why?" I shrugged, dropping my chin to rest on my crossed wrists. "Look, these are people who've grown up with slasher flicks and horror novels and everything else you can imagine. About the only way I'd get them to listen to me if I wanted to claim that cryptids were real would be to hop up on this table and strip."

That seemed to get through his rising anger. The color died in his cheeks, slipping back toward white. "I will give you five hundred dollars not to do that," he said.

"Deal. Also, you should maybe have your blood pressure checked. All that hyper-color action can't be good for you."

Dominic shook his head. "I never believed the stories about your family. I thought they were exaggerated. Now I'm starting to think that they may have been understating things."

"Oh?" I asked, interested despite myself. "What did they say?"

"That you were all insane."

"Ah." I sat up again, grinning at him. "That's pretty much true. We're all crazy. But crazy has its benefits."

"What benefits are those?" he asked warily.

"Crazy gets all the knives."

Twenty minutes later, Dominic was finally done sputtering in righteous indignation, the frat boys had staggered home, and the barista had wandered into the office to call her boyfriend. Her laughter drifted through the coffee shop's ventilation system, providing a handy, if accidental, mechanism for tracking her location. I was on my second cup of heavily-doctored coffee, and giving serious thought to a third. I'm not normally a big fan of overcaffeination, but registration for the tango competition was scheduled to open at seven in the morning and I needed all the help I could get.

"So you're here alone to demonstrate that you can be trusted to be here alone. Isn't that a little circular?"

"My orders were clear. I am to scout, take notes of what I encounter, and report back. That way, we can determine the size of the needed purge. At the same time, I demonstrate that I am morally prepared for fieldwork."

"Uh-huh. And if you're not prepared?"

"I will be reprimanded."

"Harsh."

Dominic shook his head. "You cannot imagine."

I've read Grandpa Thomas' journals. I had some idea.

Somehow, it didn't seem like a good idea to tell him that. "Here's the thing I don't get," I said, propping my chin up on the knuckles of one hand. "You're here to kill the people I'm here to look after. Why are you worried about them going missing, if you know it's not because I'm getting them out of town? Either they're in somebody else's territory, which is a problem for your superiors, or they're dead, which is a problem for me, but either way, they're not a problem for *you* anymore."

"A plague may stop a war, but does it not bring down even more destruction on the land?" asked Dominic, in a lofty, philosophical tone.

I eyed him. "If you don't stop quoting dogma at me, I'm leaving."

"I don't know what you're talking about."

"You trying to tell me you just came up with that? Just now? Off the top of your head?"

He hesitated. "Well, no."

"So that was more of the party line."

"Yes."

"I don't want your party line. I want answers. Why are you worried about my missing cryptids? They're not your problem. If you didn't kill them, you're not my problem. So what's your angle here?"

"I—" He hesitated again, clearly unsure how he was supposed to continue the conversation. Finally, he fixed me with an aggravated stare and said, "You are without a doubt the most annoying woman I have ever met."

"We breed for it. Were you planning to answer my question?"

Dominic sighed. "If I thought the monsters were fleeing, it wouldn't be my problem. I'd notify my superiors and keep hunting the ones that remain. There haven't been any signs of them appearing in neighboring territories, and at least some of them would have to be traveling on foot. Since you're here, there was a chance your family was running some sort of ill-considered underground railroad."

"Well, we're definitely not. I'd know."

"I'm assuming you have local contacts who would have told you if they were running something like that, and that you wouldn't have been lurking around on rooftops hoping to find me if they were." I nodded, and he continued, "That's my 'angle,' as you so charmingly put things. You can solve a mouse problem by developing a snake problem. But is it any better?"

I groaned. "I was really hoping you wouldn't say that. You think we have a snake?"

Dominic nodded. "I do."

There was really only one thing to say to that, and so I said it, with all the fervency I could muster:

"Fuck."

Dominic nodded again, rubbing his forehead with one hand as he wearily said, "I agree."

Nine

"Thomas? I think I'm going to need a bigger gun."

—Alice Healy

The Davidson-Morrissey Memorial Dance Hall, three days later, way too early in the morning

AFTER TWO DAYS OF SCOURING THE CITY for the metaphorical "snake problem," I was no closer to knowing where the city's cryptids were going, and I still had no idea where the hell I was supposed to look for Dominic De Luca, aka, "the asshole who thinks he's Batman and doesn't believe in giving out his contact information before disappearing while I'm in the bathroom." (Look. I may spend more time running around on rooftops than the average girl on the street, but I don't make a habit out of looming in the shadows being impossible to find. If anything, I'm easier to find than I ought to be. If he wanted to find me, he could ask any cryptid in Manhattan, and they'd point him at Dave's in a heartbeat—assuming he let them live that long.)

One thing I did know: the population was continuing to drop, and it was dropping faster with each passing day. The harpies who'd been nesting near Dave's were gone. They'd been there Monday night when I dropped by with the mail, and there hadn't been any signs that they were planning to go anywhere. Tuesday night, they were gone. The nest was a shambles, and I couldn't tell, as I picked through the wreckage, whether they'd left intentionally or not.

There was no blood outside the kitchen area. Even there, it was confined to the cutting board and makeshift plastic bucket "sink," and the spray patterns were consistent with what you'd get if you, say, beheaded a pigeon. I clung to that as proof that they weren't dead, and Dominic hadn't been lying to me. I didn't like the man very much— I definitely didn't like the people he worked for—but disliking someone and wanting to kill them are two different things. One of them involves a lot of glaring and hair flipping. The other requires quicklime, which is surprisingly hard to find in Manhattan.

I finished the second night at Sarah's new hotel, crashing on the couch in her suite. It was the only way I could get up early enough to make it to my morning appointment. It was about the only thing important enough to take me off the streets for a day, and I wanted to be fresh. I needed to be ready.

The next morning was going to be hell on earth. Because two days previous, I had registered and auditioned for the New York State Argentine Tango Open, and if there's one thing scarier than the Covenant, it's ballroom dancing.

🐁

The front lobby of the hall rented for the New York State Argentine Tango Open was packed to the point of comedy with men in skintight matador pants and women whose dresses seemed to consist entirely of fringe, sequins, strategically-placed strips of lace, and even more strategically-placed pieces of double-sided tape. Anyone who doesn't believe that dance can be a form of combat should spend some time watching the more well-endowed dancers trying to contain their cleavage with nothing more than adhesive and attitude. There are days when I'm truly grateful to Grandma Alice for taking potshots at the Boob Fairy and keeping her from heaping too much attention on the family.

(People always think I'm kidding when I say things like that. They used to think I was kidding when I said the same things about the Tooth Fairy, but I can provide proof of that one, thanks to Great-Great-Grandpa's fondness for taxidermy and the family policy against throwing away anything that might prove useful. It's amazing how quickly a stuffed and mounted specimen can shut a person up.)

According to the clock on the wall, it was approaching nine-thirty in the morning, which meant we'd been in the hall for somewhere around two and a half hours. According to the goose bumps on my arms, it was about two and a half hours past time to turn up the damn heat. It was possible that they had the stage lights turned so high that it made sense to turn the rest of the hall into an icebox, but if that was the case, they needed to get me on the stage before I froze solid.

It didn't help that my dress was the sort of thing Grandma Baker called "more rumor than reality." It consisted mostly of beaded fringe attached to a layer of cotton broadcloth to give the whole thing structure. The laces up the back were entirely for show, and to create the illusion of the dress being more complicated than it actually was. The real fasteners ran up the front, hidden under layers of fringe. I'd had it specially made. Most dancers do—having a costume that fits right can mean the difference between first and second place when the scores are close enough—but most dancers aren't trying to fit weaponry under an outfit that would make a hooker blush. I had a pistol strapped on at the small of my back, and a knife so high on my left thigh that drawing it would require an act of indecent exposure. My genuine human-hair wig was pulled into a chignon and pinned with "decorative" hair sticks carved from blessed cherrywood, soaked in holy water for three months, and tipped in silver. There's no such thing as being too careful.

"Hey, Valerie," said a man I vaguely recognized as part of the local dance crowd. He was pushing his way through the crowd to get to the men's room. From the number pinned to his jacket, I guessed that his group was the one just vacating the stage.

"Hey," I said, trusting his haste to keep him from noticing that I hadn't said his name.

He didn't notice. "Later," he said, and shoved past me, vanishing through the men's room door. I pushed away from the wall, heading for the other side of the lobby. The last thing I needed was to get cornered and grilled on why I didn't remember a piece of prime local beefcake like the one that just passed me. That's one of the unanticipated dangers of trying to live a double life: I don't have the mental storage space to keep track of every cryptid in the Greater Manhattan Metro Area *and* remember every member of the New York dance community. Maybe if I had Sarah's particular set of skills, but maybe not even then.

The fact that I have to keep the two identities as separate as possible doesn't help. Verity Price has never won a dance competition. She's never even entered one. Valerie Pryor, on the other hand, has done very well for herself, thank you very much. According to her credentials, she placed respectably in several local dance events, studied under some excellent teachers, and caught the nation's attention when she appeared on *Dance or Die*, spending most of the season as a legitimate front-runner for the grand prize.

I'd probably hate her if she wasn't my secret identity. As it is, I'm just plain jealous.

And if I ever prove I can make it in the world of competitive dance, I'm going to have to become her all the time. There's no way a Price can risk herself on the public stage. It would be an invitation to assassination. So for right now, I can use that as a justification for never bothering to remember the names of most of the dancers I deal with: they don't remember mine. The fact that they've never had the chance to learn it is academic.

"Now calling group seventeen to the main stage," boomed the intercom, sounding surprisingly free of static. The hall might be cold, but it was better-maintained than most of the places willing to host entry-level competitions. "First dance will commence in five minutes."

I straightened, reaching up to check my wig in a gesture designed to look like I was just checking my hair. All the pins were still in place. "Let's dance," I said quietly to myself, and started for the doors to the main stage.

Explaining the rules of professional ballroom dancing would take the better part of a week, and probably wouldn't help once I got to the difference between professional and amateur dancing, the way steps are ranked, and who pays what fees to enter a competition. Here's what you really need to know:

There are two major schools of competitive ballroom dance. International is the standard for most of the world, and focuses on crispness, precision, and the formality of the steps. There are International dancers from the United States, but they aren't regarded very highly by the rest of the world, largely due to the existence of American ballroom. American is looser, showier, and a lot more fun to watch on television. Most of what you'll see in movies and on reality-based dance shows is American ballroom. International is gorgeous if you know what's going into those tight, precise steps and twirls. American, on the other hand, doesn't require you to have any actual understanding of ballroom dance. It just wants you to stay awake.

Once you get past the whole International-vs.-American divide, you run into the second major division within the ballroom world: the smooth styles vs. the Latin dance forms. In International dance, the smooth styles are the slow waltz, the tango, the Viennese waltz, the slow foxtrot, and the quickstep, while the Latin styles are the cha-cha, the samba, the rumba, the Paso Doble, and the jive. In American dance, the smooth styles are the waltz, the tango, the foxtrot, and the Viennese waltz, while the Latin styles are the cha-cha, the rumba, the bolero, and East Coast Swing.

Confused yet? Now, just to up the ante a bit, please note that "Argentine tango" is nowhere on either of those lists. The Argentine tango is a horse of a different color, belonging to neither International nor American ballroom, and refusing to fit neatly into any specific style designation. The Argentine tango isn't here to play nicely with the other children. The Argentine tango is here to seduce your women, spill things on your rug, and sneak out your bedroom window in the middle of the night. It's the unabashed tomcat of dances, consisting primarily of swagger and sex, and it's a hell of a lot of fun. Which is why you'll find dancers from every side of the fence showing up for the competitions, wearing painted-on pants and lingerie disguised as dresses, all of them ready to get their freak on. Under carefully controlled and rigorously judged conditions, that is.

The Argentine tango. Because, sometimes, dirty dancing comes with rules.

Group seventeen consisted of ten couples. All twenty of us were dancing at the professional level; only four were paid partners, which is a remarkably low number for a group our size. According to the posted rosters, we'd all checked in by eight o'clock in the morning. I hadn't seen more than five of the people I'd be dancing with, and I'd only seen my partner once, across the crowded lobby. He'd been deep in conversation with his boyfriend at the time, and I'd decided not to bother them. If we weren't prepared by the time we paid our registration fees, we were already screwed.

(At least this was one of the more affordable competitions; buy-in had only been two hundred dollars for professionals, nonrefundable under any circumstances, including death. Only the top three couples would be getting cash prizes, but the top twenty would be going on to the regional division competition. That's all I was hoping for. A regional would give me something to justify taking more time to practice, even if more practice meant having less time to worry about what the hell might be making the city's cryptid population go bye-bye.)

The hall where we'd be going through our paces was a beautiful combination of "overly shadowed" and "overly bright." Desk lights lit the workspaces of the individual judges and floodlights lit the stage, while the tiers of frozen spectators weren't really lit at all. I used to find the silence from the audience creepy. The people who show up to watch competition ballroom dancing are sort of like the people who show up to watch really high-stakes tennis: completely silent, never gasping, applauding, or giving any sign that they're not all dead. I've never understood the appeal. There's a vast attraction to being the one on the floor, and watching televised dance competitions can be a lot of fun, if there's booze involved. But sitting around playing wax dummy for hours on end? What's the point?

I scanned the crowd of dancers for James as we made our way onto the floor. When I'd seen him earlier, he was wearing the standard-issue skintight pants, and a

deep green shirt chosen to match my dress and complement the apparent color of my hair. (Of the three professional partners I'd worked with before coming to
New York, James was the only one who'd ever realized I
wasn't a natural redhead. That wasn't a problem for either of us, since I was the only partner he'd worked with
who realized he wasn't a natural human. Chupacabra
may not be good for the livestock, but damn, those guys
can dance.)

"Positions, please," said one of the judges. His ampli-
fied voice boomed through the speakers, making it impossible to tell which of the shadowy figures was
speaking. Couples began pairing off all around me, and
there was still no sign of James. I was starting to worry.
Couples enter *as* couples, and there are no substitutions
allowed once the event program has been printed. There
definitely aren't any substitutions allowed after you're
on the floor.

The other nine couples had fallen into ready position,
leaving me all-too-visibly alone in the middle of the
floor. I barely managed to keep from wincing as the
speakers clicked on again.

"Number one hundred eighty-four, please join your
partner."

I scanned the floor again, looking for James. If I didn't
find him in the next few seconds, I'd be disqualified by
default. I couldn't afford to lose the entry fee. More importantly, I couldn't afford to lose the shot at the regional competition. I needed that title.

Still no James. I took a step backward, anticipating
the instruction to leave the floor, and stopped as my
shoulders bumped up against a man's chest. "James," I
sighed, utterly relieved. My arms automatically raised to
form the proper frame as I turned.

"If you like," Dominic replied, catching my right hand
and pulling me into a tango stance. I gaped at him, but
there was no time to argue. The music was already starting. Instinct was the only thing that saved me, relaxing

my shoulders as my back straightened, pulling me into the correct posture.

With no more fanfare than that, the dance began.

The Argentine tango isn't as devoted to creating a frame between dancers as most of the structured forms; it's hard to look like you're ironing the wrinkles out of the front of your dress with your partner's chest if you're going to be all fussy about keeping the appropriate distance. Dominic was doing a passable standard tango, and I let him be the one to hold the structure of the dance, sliding closer in what would hopefully look like a practiced dance step as I hissed in his ear, "What are you doing here?"

"Looking for you," he replied, and pushed me into a half-turn before yanking me back. He definitely wasn't going to win me any points in technical style if he kept flinging me around like that. At least he looked the part, in skintight black jeans that were probably reinforced with Kevlar linings, a button-up red silk shirt, and a black half-duster that had to be murder in the heat, but allowed him to cut a dramatic silhouette, as well as hiding a hell of a lot more weapons than my own frothy confection of a costume. It was a step up from his generic monster-hunter trench coat. "This seemed like the best way to catch up."

"You could have called," I snapped. A little too loudly—one of the neighboring couples glanced in our direction, forcing me to move in even closer as I stage-whispered, "You had my number. Now where the hell is my partner?"

"The 'gentleman' with whom you were prepared to perform this parody of dance is currently indisposed." The way he stressed the word "gentleman" made it clear he knew James wasn't human.

I jerked back and stared at him, barely stopping the motion from turning graceless. "Did you kill my partner?" My voice came out steady and calm. That was due to the fact that my mind was otherwise occupied with trying to figure out how quickly I could get to my concealed weapons.

"Kill? No. I assumed it would upset you, and endanger our working relationship." Dominic looked down his nose at me. No small task while we were spinning around the dance floor. "He'll wake up in an hour or so."

There was no possible way to salvage the competition. Even bribing the judges and claiming James had suffered some sort of unexpected medical emergency (one which happened to mysteriously clear up in time for us to join the final group) wouldn't do it after I'd shown up on the floor with another man. It was going to look like we'd tried to pull a bait and switch. Worst of all, it hadn't even resulted in my appearing with a better partner. Dominic was a decent tango dancer—that was clear from his posture and footwork—but he'd just as clearly never danced the Argentine tango in his life. He stepped mechanically through his paces while I flung myself around him, trying to pretend we were doing the same dance. It might have passed muster in a social situation, but here? It was suicide.

"You could have called," I hissed again. "What the hell is wrong with you?"

"That I should refuse the discussion of serious business matters over an unsecured phone line? I'm sure I don't know, but I hope it's never corrected."

"That's *it*," I snarled. I pulled back and mimicked the beginning of a partner-assisted spin before shouting in mock-pain and dropping down to clutch at my left ankle. Looks were cast in our direction by the other dancers, some sympathetic, some openly and maliciously pleased. One less couple in the competition meant one step closer to victory. Cold math, but as Sarah was so fond of telling me, numbers don't lie. Everything else does, but numbers? Never.

Dominic stared at me, actually looking concerned as

he stooped to kneel on the floor. "Have you twisted it? Those shoes you're wearing—"

"Are appropriate for the occasion," I hissed. "Now help me out of here."

Taking help, even fake help, from a member of the Covenant rankled, but it was necessary if I wanted my "injury" to seem realistic. Leaning heavily on the arm he offered for support, I limped out of the tango competition with my head held high and entirely real tears shining in my eyes.

So much for making it to Regionals.

The nature of my disguise meant I couldn't go from Valerie to Verity in the dance hall bathroom. I limped my way back to the coat check, where I reclaimed my duffel bag and coat. Dominic trailed behind me, looking puzzled. His look of puzzlement grew deeper when I stomped out of the dance hall, limp fading with every step I took away from the doors.

"You were faking?" he demanded.

"You couldn't pick up a damn phone?"

"How could you be faking?"

"You thought coldcocking my partner and stuffing him—where *did* you stuff him?"

Dominic glanced away. "A storage closet."

"Right. You thought coldcocking my partner and stuffing him into a storage closet before crashing my dance competition was less risky than picking up a damn phone and saying, 'hey, want to talk to you about all the dead stuff in the city'? You're crazy!" I started walking faster. "Certifiably crazy. And you owe me a refund on my entry fee, in addition to the five hundred for keeping my shirt on last night."

"My apologies if I thought the threat we may be facing was more important than your little diversions."

Something inside of me snapped. I'd put up with side-long looks and subtly disapproving comments from my family for years. Getting outright disdain from a member of the Covenant of St. George was the last straw. I wheeled on him, jabbing a finger straight at the center of his chest. "Look, asshole, dancing is not a 'little diversion.' It's my life, you got that? You had no right to track me down like this, and you *really* had no right to intrude. You don't approve of my life? Well, screw you. At least I have one."

He blinked at me, nonplussed. "I—"

"Save it and come with me."

"What?" His expression turned wary. Not a bad call on his part. I was just about angry enough to shove his body into the nearest dumpster and take my chances on some concerned citizen finding him before the local ghouls did.

"You've fucked up my day, you've fucked up my chance to qualify for the next big competition, and you may have fucked up my cover. You're not getting out of here without telling me what you came here to tell me. Now come on."

I was starting to realize that the last of the items on that list was the one that represented the real danger. He'd blown my cover. A member of the Covenant knew that Valerie Pryor was actually Verity Price in insufficiently concealing clothing. Depending on what happened next, he might not have disqualified me from a single competition; he might well have disqualified me from my entire career.

It was a horrific thing to even think about, but if Dominic De Luca wanted to, he could make certain I'd never dance professionally again. I didn't want to kill him. It was looking increasingly likely that I wasn't going to have a choice.

I'll give Dominic this, even if I didn't want to give him anything else: he followed me without complaint, despite the havoc the heat outside had to be wreaking on his overly heavy attire. I marched him down the street, around a corner, and through the back door of a greasy spoon that stank like a hundred years of deep-fried dinners. He hesitated when he saw the kitchen, and I grabbed his jacket sleeve, dragging him deeper in. The fry cook on duty was a hulking shape in dirty whites, his back to us as he chopped some unidentifiable cut of meat into smaller and smaller chunks.

"Hey, Nigel," I said.

He grunted, waving us on.

Dominic picked up the pace slightly, drawing close enough to hiss, "Is he—" in my ear.

"Wouldn't you like to know?" I shoved open a door at the back of the kitchen, revealing a rickety flight of stairs leading to the storage rooms overhead. I took the steps two at a time, focusing my anger on the difficult task of not punching my five-inch heels through the half-rotten wood. It helped, a little. If I was thinking about *not* puncturing things with my shoes, I wasn't thinking about how easy it would be to impale Dominic with them.

He managed to stay quiet until we reached the second floor. The hallway was choked off with boxes of old newspapers and stacks of dishes retired after they became too chipped for even the establishment downstairs. I wove between them, careful to keep from triggering an avalanche.

Dominic wasn't so lucky. There was a shattering crash, followed by the sound of him swearing in loud, enthusiastic Italian. "Keep walking," I said, in a singsong tone.

"What are we *doing* here?" he demanded.

"I need to change." I looked back over my shoulder, smiling sweetly. "If you'd called, you wouldn't be following me into the place where dishes go to die. Think about that the next time you decide to mess with my competition schedule."

"Because God forbid something gets in the way of your dancing," he sneered.

"Damn right," I said, and half-pushed, half-slammed the nearest door open, storming into the mostly-empty storage room on the other side. More crashes and clattering punctuated Dominic's progress as he followed after me.

More things that don't really survive their first encounter with the glamorous, exhausting world of professional ballroom dance, much less their first encounter with the glamorous, exhausting world of professional cryptozoology: modesty. Sure, I'd scream like any other girl if someone walked in on me in the changing room at Victoria's Secret—probably right before I kicked that someone in the head—but when it comes to changing into street clothes, I could do it in the middle of Fifth Avenue. I knew Dominic had entered the room when I heard his breath catch, and twisted to look over my shoulder at him, eyebrows raised in silent question.

"You . . . ah . . ." he stammered, eyes darting around like he wasn't sure where he should look. It wasn't like there was a shortage of targets. I was, after all, standing there in emerald green thong panties, thigh-high sheer stockings, stiletto heels, and an assortment of holsters, having already shucked my costume to the floor.

If I took my arm away from my chest, he'd probably die. Maybe not a standard way to kill a man, but hey, beggars can't always be choosers. "Yes?" I prompted.

Dominic swallowed. "You dance with a gun at your back?"

"Wouldn't you?" I crouched to start digging through my duffel bag, producing a plastic baggie full of Ace bandages before I straightened up. Wrapping is pretty standard after a competition—it helps to keep me from injuring myself when I inevitably go running across the rooftops to burn off all my extra adrenaline. Plus, a nice layer of Ace bandage counts as at least minimal armor, which is always nice.

I would normally have stayed low while I wrapped my ankles and knees, but I didn't feel like doing Dominic any favors. I stretched my left leg into a full extension instead, staying balanced on the right as I started winding bandages around my knee. "Worst thing about the Argentine tango: you can't fit more than a few weapons under your costume without it getting really obvious. The waltz is better. You can hide a regulation machete under a waltz costume."

"Er, yes. Of course." It sounded like he still didn't know where he was supposed to be looking. Tough. "I suppose you'd like to know why I felt the need to seek you out."

"Because you're a pompous asshole who didn't get a decent cell plan? I could be in your network. All calls would be free." I bent my leg back to make it easier to get to my ankle, and repeated the wrapping process. "Yes, Dominic. I would like to know why you decided to ruin my day and damage my career. Please, enlighten me."

"I believe I've discovered the reason for the local disappearances." He sounded a bit more sure of himself as he made the pronouncement, some of his usual arrogance coming back into his voice. He understood making dire pronouncements. Apparently better than he understood seminaked, highly flexible women. The poor guy must have led a *very* boring life.

"What would that be?" I asked. My left knee and left ankle were wrapped, and would be able to take a lot more pressure without getting damaged. I strapped my left ankle holster on over the Ace bandage and switched legs.

"I've been examining the Covenant's records on this area going back several hundred years—"

A needle of jealousy stabbed me in the chest. We're lucky when the family records extend back to my great-great-grandparents arriving in America. "There's a luxury some of us don't have," I muttered.

"What's that?"

"Nothing." I started wrapping my right ankle, trying

not to let irritation make the job turn sloppy. "What did you find in the records?"

Dominic paused portentously, and said, "I believe there is a dragon sleeping under this city."

I fell on my ass.

Ten

"A lady is never truly embarrassed. And if
she is, a lady is never gauche enough to
leave survivors."

—Evelyn Baker

The upstairs storage room of an unnamed and highly questionable diner

FIVE MINUTES, A HASTILY-COMPLETED WRAPPING JOB, and
a pair of jeans later, I was sitting atop an antique
stove and running my weapon checks, watching Dominic out of the corner of my eye. He was pacing back and
forth along the length of the room, his steps thudding in
an almost martial rhythm. It was a stable enough beat to
be soothing, and there was a decent chance that he'd hit
a rotten patch and fall through the floor into the diner
below us. That kept it interesting.

"There's one major problem with your 'solution,'" I
said. "Dragons are extinct. The Covenant wiped them
out centuries ago."

Dominic favored me with a look of withering disdain.
"Did we?"

"Hello, not the one who writes the propaganda, remember? But, yeah, according to everything I've ever
read and everyone I've ever talked to, human or cryptid." If the dragons were still alive, the dragon princesses
would know about it—they'd *have* to know, since all the

old bestiaries claimed that the two species lived in a sort of symbiosis. If there were still dragons, the dragon princesses probably wouldn't be working in strip clubs and living in neighborhoods just this side of demilitarized zones.

"Nonetheless, it seems that a few may have escaped extermination."

I looked up from securing my ankle holster, fixing him with a disgusted stare. "Here's a tip: wiping out a sentient species isn't 'extermination.' It's genocide. Get your terminology straight."

"Dragons fed on humans."

"When humans went into their caves to steal their stuff, you're damn right they did! If the dragons had been from Texas, they would've gotten awards from the homeowners' association, not a gang of medieval vigilantes looking to skin their asses."

Dominic looked at me blankly. "What does Texas have to do with anything?"

"Wow, they didn't give you any cultural acclimatization before they dropped you here, did they? Did the Covenant *want* you to get eaten?" I slid off the stove. "Okay, so fine, let's assume you're right, and everything we thought we knew is wrong, and there's a dragon sleeping somewhere under the city of New York." I paused. "Not the *entire* city, or even a borough, right? Just a few blocks or something? Because I don't think I'm equipped to deal with a dragon that's actually the size of New York." A dragon the size of Manhattan was too much to think about, especially if there was a chance it was hostile. The old family story about Grandma taking on an entire hive of Apraxis wasps with nothing but some concussion grenades aside, we're taught never to go up against impossible odds if there's any other choice.

"Not the entire city," said Dominic. He paused, a discomfited look crossing his face. It was an oddly attractive expression on him, softening his features from their usual perpetual arrogance and turning them into something a girl wouldn't mind seeing, say, on the other side of the table at breakfast. "At least, I don't believe so. The largest recorded dragon was no larger than a blue whale."

"I probably shouldn't find that as reassuring as I do." I picked up my bag. "So we're assuming there's a dragon. I don't want you calling reinforcements, since they'd just wipe out the cryptids I'm trying to protect, and I'll bet you don't want me calling reinforcements either."

"Not particularly," he said, his normal arrogance creeping across his face like frost across a window on a cold morning. "You already have me far too outnumbered to enjoy."

"Me and my army of cryptids that don't listen to a damn thing I say, we're scary," I agreed. "Why do you think there's a dragon?"

"I'd rather not say just as yet," Dominic replied, stiffly.

"Great." I sighed. "Let's say I believe you. So now what do we do?"

"I suppose we determine whether or not I'm correct, and decide what to do from there."

I gave him a thoughtful look. Something in the way that he was standing . . . "You don't *want* to be right, do you?"

"Not particularly."

"Why not? I mean, if it's a dragon, I can't really stop you from killing it. Not unless it speaks English and likes blonde girls well enough to listen to one and, even then, only if it feels like turning you into a charcoal briquette."

Dominic smiled briefly, eyebrows rising. "Good to know that your plans for me include immolation."

"I'm flexible. I can flex." I shrugged. "I'll happily dispose of your corpse in a nondraconic manner, once we know what's really going on."

"Fair enough. As for why I'm not terribly pleased about the idea of being right, well. This is my first time in the field. I'd rather not start my career with a failed dragon slaying." There was something else there—something he wasn't saying to me yet. I could see its shadow in his eyes.

Better not to push. "That's cool. I don't want to call my folks."

"Then we're in agreement. I suppose that once we've determined the true nature of the threat at hand, we'll . . ." He stopped, mouth continuing to move for a moment with no sound coming out.

It was hard not to feel bad for the guy. Sure, he was a stone killer, but he'd been raised that way, and you don't blame a snake for biting. He wasn't used to being lost like the rest of us. "You don't know either, do you?"

Clearly frustrated, Dominic shook his head. "No. I'm not accustomed to lacking a plan of action."

"That's okay." I smiled wryly. "I'm a Price. We're basically the reason the universe invented improv."

"Well, then, I suppose I had best stick with you."

"Don't think this means I'm not still pissed at you for fucking up my competition," I said. "Now come on. Let's go dragon hunting."

My usual means of information gathering involves hitting the homes and workplaces of the local sentient cryptids and asking what's been going on at (or sometimes under) the street level. That wasn't an option with Dominic along. Neither was my customary overland approach. While he wasn't uncomfortable on rooftops, exactly, he drew the line at throwing himself over the edges.

"Oh, come on," I cajoled, as we walked down a dark alley that stunk like human urine and recycled grease from the vents of the Chinese deli. There was also the sweet, slightly spicy scent of gingerbread undercutting it all; this was part of a Madhura's feeding ground. That was comforting. I hadn't been aware that we had any Madhura left in the city. Things couldn't be that bad if they hadn't all fled.

Dominic's eyes moved constantly as we walked, darting from side to side as he took in the alley walls around us. He wrinkled his nose when the stink first became apparent, but he hadn't said a word about the Madhura. Lack of practical experience was definitely not an asset for new Covenant field agents. "I said no. Gravity is not a toy."

"It's not like I'm asking you to let me cast some sort of flight spell on you." He gave me a sharp look. I raised my hands. "I didn't say I *could* cast a flight spell, you dork. I'm not a witch. I'm just saying this would go faster if we weren't restricted to the speed of our feet."

"Again, no. You may take pleasure in taunting the laws of physics, but I prefer to save my brushes with death for times when they're actually necessary."

"Now you sound like my father."

Dominic snorted. "God forbid."

I stopped where I was, giving him a narrow-eyed look. "Exactly what is that supposed to mean?"

Dominic turned to face me, crossing his arms over his chest. "Do you really want to have that conversation here and now, when I may be the only chance you have of finding this creature before it does real damage to your precious city?"

"Yeah, I think I do. What, exactly, is that supposed to mean?"

"Only that no respectable member of the Covenant wishes to be told he sounds like a traitor."

"Uh, first, mister, my father's not a traitor. He never belonged to your stupid Covenant. None of us did. If you want traitors, you'll have to go back at least two generations, and if you ask the mice, they weren't traitors even then."

Dominic blinked, looking nonplussed. "Ask the what?"

I was just getting warmed up. "Plus, what makes you

God's gift to cryptozoology? Why are you my only shot at finding something that may 'only' be the size of a blue whale? I'm a Price, but I'm not an idiot. I'm pretty sure I can find something that big without your help. All you're doing is keeping me off the rooftops, scaring the local cryptids, and slowing me down."

"And what is it that you think you can do for *my* search, exactly? Are you planning to tango gaily down the yellow brick road to victory? You're a traitor, from a family of traitors, and there's not a damn thing you can do that I can't do without you!"

"Oh, yeah?"

"Yes!"

I was having a heated argument, verging on a shouting match, in a deserted alley with a member of the Covenant of St. George who had seen me get dressed, and thus knew where all of my weapons were located. I'd been monitoring escape routes the whole time, and the prospects were pretty bleak; if he didn't have anything ranged, I might be able to make it to the dumpster and use that to boost myself to the exhaust vents from the deli. After that, I'd have to improvise.

Dominic stepped closer, sensing victory in my hesitation. His chin was slightly raised, giving me an excellent view of his arrogant, irritating features. My chest tightened as my already sped-up pulse kicked into overdrive. I was essentially cornered. I could flee, or I could fight . . . and if there's one thing I've spent my life learning, it's that there's always more than one way to wage a war.

"Try doing *this* without me," I said. Leaning onto my toes with the ease that comes from dancing a thousand rumbas with men half a foot taller than me, I put a hand on the back of his head and pressed my lips to his.

Kissing a man is a lot like dancing the tango: somebody leads and somebody follows, and the traditional form says it's the man who controls the dance. I've never been one to stick to tradition when it isn't essential. And that turned out to be a good thing, because the kiss was, well . . . I've had better. Maybe because I wasn't sure, from the way Dominic was kissing me back, that he'd ever had anything at all.

I've had a lot of practice at dancing with amateurs. I kissed him with more urgency, waiting for his instincts to kick in and remind him of the steps his hindbrain almost certainly knew. There was a moment of puzzled hesitation on Dominic's part, like he didn't quite understand what I was doing. Then his arms were around me, crushing me against his chest and surrounding me with the warm, masculine scents of leather and clean sweat. There's nothing sweeter than the smell of a man who likes to keep himself clean and has managed to run himself into a lather. It means somebody's been doing something physical, and it means something else physical might be on the table. I felt my body responding and pressed myself harder against him. The buckle of my holster bit into my belly hard enough to leave a bruise. He'd have a matching one, if the angle of our bodies was any indication. I had more important things on my mind.

He kissed with an urgency that was entirely out of keeping with his businesslike demeanor, possibly because he wasn't getting kissed nearly often enough. The muscles in his torso were as hard as I'd expected them to be. That wasn't all that was hard—if there'd been any question about how enthusiastic he was about returning my advances, it was answered by the feeling of him pushing up against my thigh.

The answer changed as he abruptly pushed me away, hard enough to send me staggering into the alley wall. "Hey—" I protested.

"What was the meaning of that?!" He glared at me, cheeks darkening as some of the blood began returning to his head. Pity. I'd liked it better when it was busy with certain other parts of his anatomy.

"You said there was nothing you could do with me that you couldn't do by yourself." I was cranky enough over being shoved away that I decided to twist the knife, and blew him a mocking kiss. "If you can do that by yourself, you should look into getting a place with the circus."

"You are an insolent, irresponsible, immature little bitch!"

"And you're an arrogant asshole, and there may be a dragon under this city. Now can we stop the dick waving and start figuring out how we're going to deal with this? Or do I have to kiss you again?"

Dominic hesitated, making me wonder, for a brief second, whether he wanted to be kissed as much as I wanted to kiss him. Then he glowered, shaking his head. "Fine," he said sullenly. "What do you suggest?"

"First off? I suggest we go and find the Madhura that lives in this area. She may know something."

"The what?" He looked at me blankly.

I almost had to laugh at that. "Oh, man. For a big, bad dragon hunter, you sure have a lot to learn. Come on."

We found our Madhura behind the counter of a tiny café called "Gingerbread Pudding." She was a petite, attractive woman of Indian descent, wearing a sapphire blue T-shirt and a bright red apron embroidered with "Come catch me! Be a Gingerbread Fan!" Her thick black hair was bound into two long braids that dangled over her shoulders as she served a slab of dark brown gingerbread and a cup of hot chocolate to a customer, smiling all the while. The Madhura are attracted to sweet things. They thrive on honey the way dragon princesses thrive on gold, or bogeymen thrive on information. Working in a place that specialized in desserts was probably close to her inborn idea of Heaven.

Dominic eyed the Madhura with evident bewilderment as we waited for our turn to approach the counter, nostrils flaring slightly as he detected the distinct spiciness of her pheromones. A happy Madhura is close to irresistible. It's part of what's kept them alive for so long. "What is she?" he asked, voice pitched low.

"Madhura. They're originally from the Indian subcontinent. They used to be worshiped as gods and goddesses of plenty, because they always knew where the honey was." We took another step forward as the line advanced. "They're harmless, they're friendly, and they usually know what's going on."

His expression darkened. "I don't believe we share the same definition of 'harmless.'"

I dug an elbow into his side. "Just shut up and let me talk."

He glared but fell silent as the last customer collected his purchases and went to take a seat, letting us step forward. The Madhura turned her smile in our direction, saying, "Welcome to Gingerbread Pudding. I'm Piyusha. What can I get for you today?"

"Whatever you think is good, and some information." I did my best to look harmless as I offered a return smile, and said, "My name's Verity Price. This is my . . . friend . . . Dominic. We wanted to talk to you, if we could."

Piyusha's smile froze in place as she glanced between us, finally saying, "Verity *Price*? As in . . . ?"

"Yes. I'm trying to figure out what's going on. Please?" Dominic was still glaring. I dug an elbow into his side. He grimaced. "I promise we won't take up too much of your time."

"All right." Piyusha nodded toward a door marked "Employees Only." "Head in the back. I'm going to get one of the other girls to take the counter, and I'll be right with you."

"Thanks a lot," I said, and took Dominic's hand, towing him along with me as I followed Piyusha's instructions. The people who had been in line behind us grumbled darkly as she slipped out from behind the counter, leaving them temporarily without a server. The door between us and the café swung shut, and we were left alone.

Piyusha was true to her word: she came into the small employee break room about eight minutes later, carrying a tray loaded with two slices of frosted gingerbread, two large mugs of chocolate milk, and a small plate of graham crackers and honey. She took a seat across from us at the card table that dominated the break room, putting down her tray so that the gingerbread was oriented toward me and Dominic, while the crackers and honey were closer to her.

"Now," she said, focusing her attention on me, "to what do I owe the honor of the attention of your family?"

"We want information about the dragon," said Dominic, his tone barely short of rude.

Piyusha froze in the act of reaching for one of her graham crackers, simply staring at Dominic. Finally, she allowed her hand to drop to her lap and looked to me once more, asking politely, "Is he a member of your family, or is he a member of the Covenant?"

"The latter." Seeing the burgeoning panic in her eyes, I added, "But he's promised not to hunt anyone who helps us in our investigation unless they become an active threat to the local human community." That was a transition that would mark them for a hunt by my family, as well as by the Covenant. No matter how much we may like a cryptid, once they start hunting people, they have to be put down. That's part of the service we provide to the local ecology of the places we live.

Dominic glanced at me, frowning. I kicked him under the table. We'd discuss the promises he hadn't actually made but was damn well going to adhere to later, after I'd calmed down our friendly neighborhood Madhura.

"I . . . see," said Piyusha, relaxing marginally. She picked up one of her graham crackers, dipping it into the honey. "I'm not the most connected in this city. I work in a dessert café, y'know? But I do hear things, sometimes. Things that aren't always all that nice." She looked between us, still spinning her graham cracker in the honey. "You swear he's not going to come back here and hunt me?"

"I swear. If he does, he's the one endangering the ecosystem, not you."

Piyusha relaxed further. "You should try your gingerbread. It's really good. Secret café recipe, people have the stuff shipped all over the place, because you can't get it anywhere else."

"Cool. Thanks." I picked up my fork, using it to slice off a sliver of gingerbread. Dominic grudgingly did the same.

That seemed to have been the last piece Piyusha needed to convince her that we weren't intending to set her on fire. "Like I said, I'm not the most connected person around, but what I've heard is that not everyone who's leaving is actually, y'know, *leaving*. Some of them just disappear. No notes, no forwarding addresses, nothing."

"Well, that happens," I said. "Especially with news of the Covenant being in town getting out—"

"Does it usually happen with the lamia?"

That stopped me. The lamia are sort of like centaurs, if you expand your definition of "centaur" to include "body of the world's biggest fucking snake." They're more clannish than the dragon princesses, with even better reason. They can't blend in human society, and their endothermic metabolisms mean that they're weak and disoriented whenever the weather gets too cold. "Safety in numbers" is the lamia creed . . . and no lamia I've ever known or read about would abandon their nest without a damn good reason.

Seeing my confusion, Piyusha pressed, "How about the hidebehinds? Four of them have disappeared."

"How can you tell?" I asked automatically. Then I shook my head. "Sorry. That was flippant and speciesist. I just . . . why hasn't anybody told me this?"

"Maybe because there's a member of the Covenant in town? I mean, you brought him here. To me. You *led* him to me." Piyusha worried her lower lip between her teeth before adding, "It sort of creeps me out."

"Madam, I assure you, I could have found you on my own," said Dominic, frostily.

Piyusha met his eyes straight-on, squaring her shoulders. "Would you like to bet on that?"

"This is fun, but it's not helpful," I said. "Do the ones who've disappeared have anything in common? Species, geographic location, anything?"

"They were all female, and they were all unmarried or unmated," said Piyusha. She worried her lip again, and then added, "Some went missing during the day, and some went missing at night. A few were regular customers. I've been thinking about getting out of town."

"That just might be a good idea." I pulled my wallet out of my bag and produced a business card, setting it on the tray next to her graham crackers and honey. "Call me if you need anything, or if you find anything else that might help us figure out what's going on. If it really *is* a dragon—"

"I'll call you," said Piyusha. Looking at her face, I could almost believe she meant it. She picked up the card, laughing nervously as she tucked it into her pocket. "My brothers aren't going to believe that I met a real Price. Sunil's convinced you people are just fairy tales."

"We don't get enough happily-ever-afters for that," I said.

Piyusha's expression sobered. "No, I guess you wouldn't." She glanced at Dominic. "That's all I know. I'm sorry I couldn't help more."

It wasn't hard to catch her drift. "Don't worry. You've helped more than enough. Hasn't she?"

"Yes," said Dominic. He managed to make the word sound like it pained him.

I stood. "We won't take up any more of your time. You'll call?"

"I'll call," Piyusha said firmly.

We exchanged polite farewells as Dominic rose, and she walked the two of us to the door, waving off my offer of payment with a laugh that only sounded slightly forced. I found myself liking her more by the moment. Through the glass, I saw her returning to her place behind the counter. Then we walked away, and I never saw her alive again.

Eleven

"If you offered me the chance to do it all
over, knowing what I know now, after the
things I've seen . . . I'd shoot you in the
head. That ain't the kind of thing you ask a
lady."

—Frances Brown

*The sidewalk outside Gingerbread Pudding, a dessert café
with good taste in servers*

DOMINIC'S RESTRAINT SURPRISED ME; he waited until
we couldn't be seen from the café's front window
before grabbing my elbow and jerking me into the nearest alley. The maneuver was sudden enough to throw me
temporarily off-balance, and I stumbled against him,
giving him the leverage he needed to get hold of my upper arms. His fingers dug in hard enough to pin my arms
to my sides, without quite holding hard enough to hurt
me. I appreciated that. I wasn't really in the mood to
break his jaw.

"You presume too much, woman," he hissed, eyes
narrowed. "How *dare* you? That inhuman *thing*—"

"Her name is Piyusha," I said. I made an effort to
keep my tone level and reasoned. "She's a Madhura. She
has a human life span. She has no physical advantages.
She's not a predator. Since she's an unmarried female,
she's probably living with her parents or siblings, and

working in the café because the day-olds contain sufficient sugar to keep them all in good health. She'll marry when she meets a male who smells right. Wherever they live, the whole neighborhood will benefit, because the milk won't spoil, the bread won't go stale . . . hell, living near a Madhura even retards tooth decay."

His fingers loosened, a confused expression crossing his face. The confusion passed quickly, replaced by pure fury as he clamped down again, harder than before. "Witch!" he spat. "You're trying to twist my mind with your propaganda."

It was the confusion that did it.

When my family left the Covenant, they told us we were wrong, that we had no idea what we were doing—that we were traitors not only to "the cause," but to the entire human race. There's one thing I've never encountered, either in the accounts I've read of the departure or in the reenactments of the Aeslin mice: confusion. The members of the Covenant were absolutely convinced of their truth, every step of the way. But Dominic . . . he might not agree with me, he might *never* agree with me, but the confusion I sometimes saw in his face told me there was a chance. And if there was a chance, I was going to take it.

"Propaganda? What, you mean I'm trying to make you listen to reasonable arguments about why you shouldn't go killing people in my city?" He was starting to cut off circulation to my arms. I squirmed. "Okay, how about this: let go of me, or I'll knee you in the balls."

Dominic let go.

I took a step back, smoothing imaginary wrinkles out of my shirt with the heels of my hands before crossing my arms and falling into a casual, hipshot position. Guys hate it when girls look at them like they don't matter. Dominic appeared to be no different; he scowled at me even harder. "Look, I get that we're on different teams most of the time, but we've agreed that having a dragon get loose in New York would be bad for everybody. You need to get it through your head that not every cryptid is actually evil. A lot of them serve important ecological functions."

"Bull—"

"My great-great-grandparents left the Covenant because Dr. John Snow discovered the mechanism by which cholera was able to spread through England."

The change of topics appeared to completely baffle him. That was reasonable; it was a bit of a non sequitur if you don't know the family history, and I was betting the Covenant had never put Great-Great-Grandpa Healy's actual reasons for leaving into the record. "What?"

"Cholera is a bacterial infection spread through polluted water." I took a step toward him, arms still crossed. "It didn't start getting bad until the 1800s, which a lot of people attribute to the increase in the population of the world's cities. The worst outbreak anyone had ever seen occurred in 1832, when it killed a truly ridiculous number of people in London and Paris." He was still looking baffled. I took mercy. "The last known unicorn in France was killed in 1831."

That put Dominic on more familiar ground. "Unicorns are feral beasts. They kill—"

"I know the stats on unicorn kills." One more step closed the distance between us. He didn't grab me. I didn't knee him. "Unicorns cleanse the water in the areas where they live. Cholera comes from tainted water. A unicorn in the wild will kill one, maybe two people a year. A cholera epidemic kills thousands. So, yeah, when John Snow's findings were published, my family had some questions, and when we were told 'it doesn't matter, we're doing God's work,' we left. Still think it's propaganda?"

"I . . ." Dominic stopped. "They're monsters."

"Some of them are, sure. But by any objective measure, so are lions, and tigers, and bears. What do you think the sapient cryptids, like Piyusha's family, think about you?"

There was a long pause before he said, "I don't know."

"That may be the first totally honest thing you've said to me." I unfolded my arms, sticking out my hand. "Hi. My name's Verity Price. I will forgive you for the rooftop snare and the dead ahools and the attitude problem if you'll forgive me for kicking your ass if you try to hunt anybody who isn't actively threatening my city. Deal?"

Looking faintly amused, Dominic took my hand and shook, twice. "Deal. Although I'm actually forgiving you for making the attempt. I'm not as certain of your success as you are."

"That's fair." I reclaimed my hand, stepping back out of his personal space. "So you're the guy with the record books. Is there anything in them about dragons having a thing for unmarried women?"

"Only in that a village in the process of trying to placate a dragon was likely to use virgins as the main course." Dominic shook his head. "I don't know whether that means they actually demanded them . . ."

". . . or whether the village elders just figured nobody would miss a few virgins. Got it. I'll ask my dad. He may know." And then I'd ask the dragon princesses. I was willing to introduce Dominic to a few members of the cryptid community while we were getting the ball rolling, but if I brought him near the princesses, they'd disappear in a heartbeat. If there was actually a dragon in the city that would be the last thing we wanted. "In the meantime, we need more information."

"I can contact my superiors and request that any information about the dragons not presently included in the primary records be sent for my review. It may take a few days."

I gave him a sidelong look. "Won't that make them suspicious?"

"Dragons are extinct, remember?"

"I swear, if you're trying to pull a fast one and call down an air strike—"

"Would I have bothered informing you of my suspicions?" Dominic tucked his hands into his pockets, studying the alley wall. "I don't want to trigger an assault unless I have to."

"Why not? I thought that's what you were trained for?"

"There are . . . complications."

"Complications like what?"

He cast a sidelong glance in my direction. "How quickly can you get yourself, and everything you claim to be protecting, out of this city?"

That stopped me. Until that moment, I hadn't really considered the fact that Dominic—annoying, overbearing Dominic, who'd spoiled my shot at Regionals— might actually be trying to help. I eyed him. "What's in it for you?"

"I don't get the Covenant spoiling my first solo mission." Dominic shrugged. "They're very big on initiative. They're also very big on claiming credit. If it's a dragon, I want to be the one who finds it, not the one who reports it and winds up with a footnote in the official records."

"What about that whole 'I don't want to start as a failed dragon slayer' thing?"

"I said I wanted to find it. I didn't necessarily say I wanted to prod it with a sharp stick."

I could have kissed him for that. "See, I'll just be happy if I don't get eaten." I paused, considering, before asking, "Are you going to be cool about the fact that not all cryptids are the bad guys here?"

"For the moment, I'll allow it."

"Okay. Then I've got someone we should talk to."

Dominic quirked an eyebrow. "Oh? And who's that?"

"My cousin."

The disapproving eyes of the concierge tracked us across the lobby of the Plaza Athenee, a five-star establishment whose suites cost more per night than I made in a month of waiting tables at Dave's. It was the sort of place where they'd film movies, if the management didn't consider Hollywood film crews too déclassé to trust near their marble floors. Even the air tasted like money, a delicate blend of expensive perfumes and unobtrusive all-natural cleaning products.

"What are we doing here?" hissed Dominic.

"I told you, we're visiting my cousin." I stopped in front of the elevators, smiling at the operator—yes, the real, live elevator operator—responsible for keeping the buttons from soiling our dainty fingertips. "Penthouse, please. Sarah's expecting me." It wasn't entirely a lie. I didn't call ahead, but once a cuckoo is telepathically attuned to someone, they can "hear" them coming a quarter of a mile away. I haven't been able to sneak up on Sarah since I was eleven.

Dominic gave the lobby another mistrustful glance as the elevator operator pressed the button for the penthouse. "Your cousin is staying *here*?" he asked.

"You don't have to sound so doubtful," I said. The elevator doors opened. Tossing a smile to the operator, I grabbed Dominic's arm and tugged him with me into the elevator, which was as lush and lavishly appointed as the lobby. The doors closed. I released his elbow. "She likes hotels."

Dominic looked at me, stone-faced, and said nothing.

Even if his discomfort amused me, I could at least understand it; I used to feel grubby when I visited Sarah "at home," no matter how nicely I dressed. Sample sale Prada and secondhand Alexander McQueen does not quite live up to the standards set by the sort of hotels she likes to take advantage of. Poor Dominic had to feel like he'd just been dropped into the middle of a Bond flick without having the time to get his tux out of storage.

Over time, I've learned that once Sarah has successfully "nested," the hotel staff doesn't really care how I look. I'm there to visit Sarah Zellaby, and that's good enough for them. Besides, it's not like Sarah makes any sort of effort with her appearance when I don't force her into it. Ninety percent of her wardrobe is essentially shapeless, the sort of bulky sweaters and knee-length skirts that people tend to gravitate toward when they're Velmas instead of Daphnes. No amount of telling Sarah to embrace her Daphne-ocity has managed to fix her fashion sense.

(Cuckoos are natural thieves. They want something, they take it. Sarah was raised to play nicely with the other children, so she doesn't go for the normal cuckoo targets—bank accounts, houses, husbands, other things that can destroy your life. She restricts her nest snatching to hotel chains and big corporations, where she figures it'll never be noticed and won't really be hurting anyone. She's basically right. She's also basically proof that some forms of credit card fraud will never be stopped. But she always tips the bellboys and maids really well, and the people who remember her once she's moved on are always sorry to see her go.)

The elevator slid upward with silent, well-oiled precision. I wouldn't even have known we were moving, if not for the numbers above the door. "About Sarah . . ." I said.

"Yes?"

"She's a cousin by adoption, but she's still a cousin. So hassling her is hassling family, and we don't tend to react very kindly."

His eyebrows rose. "Is there a particular reason I'll want to 'hassle' your cousin?"

"Just be cool."

The elevator stopped with a ding, and the doors slid open to reveal the penthouse. I stepped out. Dominic followed half a beat behind.

If there's ever been a race of cryptids that came close to justifying the Covenant's "shoot on sight" attitude, it's the Johrlac, colloquially known as "cuckoos." They're the perfect ambush predator, capable of blending into crowds anywhere in the world without leaving so much as a ripple to track them by. They look human on the outside, and their particular brand of telepathic camouflage means that even when you cut one open, if it's still breathing, you're still going to see what the cuckoo *wants* you to see, rather than whatever's really there. They have clear blood, no hearts, and a decentralized circulatory system that looks like somebody's drunken knitting project. There's no way you should be able to mistake that for human . . . but people have been doing it for centuries, because the only ways to see a cuckoo clearly are for the cuckoo to decide you're allowed, or for the cuckoo to die.

If cuckoos were just mimics, they wouldn't be a problem. There are lots of cryptids that specialize in pretending to be human, and for the most part, they make pretty decent neighbors. But cuckoos are telepaths, cuckoos are predatory . . . and cuckoos are mean. The average cuckoo has no qualms about destroying a person's life just because they want to, and given their natural *Invasion of the Body Snatchers* talents, they're damn good at what they do.

The Covenant of St. George never confirmed the existence of the cuckoos. They suspected, sure, but how do you find something that's wearing the perfect disguise?

You look for the holes.

Great-Great-Grandpa Healy started hunting for the cuckoos shortly after the family moved to North America. It was the Salem witch trials that set him off; there was something about how the behavior of certain key parties kept changing that just didn't ring true. He dug. When he hit rock bottom, he reached for the jackhammer, and he kept digging. What he found was a pattern of replacements, sudden personality changes, and horrible atrocities that went back as far as he cared to go. That, and a marked lack of Apraxis wasps.

Nothing scares the Apraxis. They're thirteen-inch-long parasitic wasps that band together to form a tele-pathic hive mind, and they were designed to be scary, not to be scared. Normally, when a hive gets settled, they stay and slaughter the locals until they get burned out or run out of locals, whichever comes first. Only sometimes, they run for the hills, usually just before one of the peo-ple the Apraxis were preying on goes apeshit and starts *really* messing things up. Great-Great-Grandpa started tracking Apraxis wasps, and—when he found a hive es-tablished in Colorado—he sent my great-grandfather to get the lay of the land. Great-Grandpa Healy came home with a fiancée, a police record, and proof that the cuckoos existed. So it was a good vacation.

I won't be all dramatic and say the cuckoos are our family's arch-nemesis or anything—for one thing, we're related to at least two of them—but they're definitely something we keep an eye on. Invisible telepaths who like to kill people for fun? Not helping the cryptid cause. Not helping one little bit.

The penthouse at the Plaza Athenee was palatial verg-ing on outright ostentatious. The carpet was plush enough to complicate walking, and the wallpaper was gilded with genuine gold leaf. The upholstery on the couch and settee was a stark ivory white, the sort of thing that only stays clean if you have an army of maids steam cleaning it on an almost daily basis. There was even a crystal chandelier hanging in the foyer—because every hotel room needs a foyer.

It was also trashed.

Room service dishes covered the dining area table, and fast food bags littered the area around the couch, which was almost entirely hidden under textbooks and sheets of notebook paper. The coffee table had been repurposed into a mini-computer lab, with three laptops all doing their weird computer things. A trail of discarded clothing marked the way to the bedroom, like Hansel's bread crumbs if he'd been working with ladies' undergarments instead of bread.

"What happened here?" asked Dominic, sounding faintly awed by the sheer scope of the mess.

"Sarah did." It's not that Sarah is a destructive person. She's not, especially when measured against the standards of her species. She's just distracted most of the time, and the sheer effort of staying focused tends to interfere with silly things like "laundry" and "cleaning up after herself." Grandma Baker is the same way. Telepaths living in a non-telepathic society deal with a lot of white noise from the people around them, almost none of whom know how to construct a proper shield against mental invasion. The telepaths wind up easily distracted almost as a form of self-defense.

Dominic's eyes narrowed. "This is the Sarah I'm not allowed to 'hassle,' correct?"

"Yup."

"You still haven't told me why I'd want to."

"Because as a member of the Covenant of St. George, you consider yourself morally and ethically compelled to exterminate me for the sin of not having been present on the Ark. Although I think I could make a case for it being impossible to tell whether or not my species was there." Sarah walked out of the bedroom as she spoke, offering a vague smile in our direction. "Hey, Very. Hey, Very's friend from the Covenant. Should I be running for cover about now?"

"No, he's promised to play nice." I gestured to Sarah. "Dominic De Luca, meet my cousin, Sarah Zellaby. Sarah, meet Dominic. We're looking for information, and I was hoping you could help."

"Just what every cryptid girl wants. A Covenant member in her hotel room." Sarah shrugged, heading for the kitchen. "I'll do what I can. Come on. I think there are some chairs in here."

I shrugged and followed. Dominic trailed after me, half-scowling as he studied Sarah, looking for a clue to her species. He wasn't going to find one. I elbowed him lightly, saying, "Remember, no harassing my cousin or hunting the cryptids who help us with this thing."

"You're certainly putting a lot of faith in my good behavior," he muttered.

"No, I'm putting a lot of faith in the fact that I have a lot of knives and you're outnumbered," I said. "Besides, you didn't kill Piyusha. There's no point in starting with Sarah. She's a math geek."

Sarah stuck her tongue out at me.

"But what *is* she?" he demanded.

"The technical name for my species is 'Johrlac,' but more colloquially speaking, I'm a cuckoo." Sarah swept the papers off the loveseat in the breakfast nook—my *apartment* doesn't have a damn breakfast nook—before doing the same with the matching easy chair and dropping herself unceremoniously into it. "As Verity so kindly told you, I usually identify myself as a mathematician. Neither this nor my species gets me many dates."

Dominic had the good grace to look faintly embarrassed as he sat beside me on the loveseat, careful to keep his knee from touching mine. "I'm sorry, miss. I don't believe I've encountered your species before."

"Oh, you probably have," said Sarah, with the small grimace that always accompanies her talking about the rest of the cuckoos. "You're just lucky: you didn't notice."

Dominic gave her another appraising look. I'll admit she wasn't at her most threatening: she was wearing jeans with the knees worn through, a green T-shirt two sizes too big, and white ankle socks. Her thick black hair was gathered into a sloppy ponytail, and didn't look like it had been brushed since the last time I'd seen her. As "big scary cryptids" go, she wasn't even making the junior leagues. I could almost see him dismissing her as harmless. That was a mistake, although I wasn't going to call him on it.

"I suppose I'll take your word for it," he said finally.

"Thanks," said Sarah, and focused her attention on me. "What are you looking for, and why am I your girl?"

"Dominic thinks there's a dragon somewhere under the city."

Sarah stared at me.

"If he's right, it's probably asleep, since I haven't heard any reports of Godzilla's scary older brother rampaging through Central Park."

Sarah continued to stare at me.

"We met a Madhura who said there have been disappearances in the local cryptid community. Like, actual 'has anybody seen Mary' disappearances, not just people moving out of town to avoid Happy Boy here." I jerked a thumb toward Dominic, who scowled. "She said it's all females, all unattached."

"Implying all virgins, if you're an archaic prick," said Sarah, beginning to nod slowly. "Have you called Uncle Kevin?"

"Not yet—that's my next stop. I wanted to see if you could do a scan for subterranean hostiles. See if we're about to have the world's biggest iguana come out and start eating people."

"Scan?" said Dominic.

"I'm a telepath," said Sarah, in a distracted, matter-of-fact tone. Ignoring the fact that it was now Dominic's turn to stare, she continued, "You realize that in a city this size, you're basically asking me to buy two first-class tickets on the Migraine Express, right?"

"I know. But if we're going to go down there and check things out—"

"You'd like to know you won't be eaten. Fine." Sarah sighed, digging a cell phone out of the pocket of her jeans. Dominic continued to stare as she dialed a number, waited a few seconds, and said, "Hi, Professor Hines, this is Sarah. I just wanted to call and let you know that I ate some bad sushi, and I won't be able to make it to tonight's review session. I'm really sorry, and I'll make sure to get Tanya's notes before next week's class." She hung up. "There. I can now incapacitate myself for your pleasure."

"She's a *telepath*?" demanded Dominic.

"And he catches up with the conversation." I patted his knee. "Yes, she's a telepath. Sarah reads minds. Don't worry, she's not reading yours."

"It would be rude," said Sarah. Putting her phone down, she began arranging herself carefully in the chair. "Telepathic ethics say you should never read a sentient creature's mind without permission, provocation, or legitimate reason to fear for your life."

"Telepaths have ethics?" Dominic's eyes narrowed, tone and posture united to convey his disbelief.

"My mother and I do," said Sarah, letting her head settle against the back of the chair. "We mostly got them from *Babylon 5*, but they still work."

"It's a long story," I said, cutting Dominic off before he could get started. "Anything you can find will be a big help, Sarah, really."

"Got it," she said, and went limp, eyes staring sightlessly at the ceiling.

Little exercises of telepathy—like scanning a crowded club for a known killer—can be difficult, but Sarah can still manage to carry on a conversation while she does them. It's the big things that are dangerous. They take too much effort, and too much focus, to let her do anything else. A cuckoo in the middle of something big is essentially defenseless. That's why I left my hand on Dominic's knee, keeping him from getting up. He'd only promised to leave her alone under duress, and I didn't want to risk it. I just wanted him to see a cryptid doing something to help us, rather than being something he needed to be afraid of.

Besides, it wasn't like he'd ever find her again if she didn't want him to.

Sarah's breathing got shallower and shallower as she continued to stare at the ceiling, eyes wide and startled-seeming. She didn't blink. After about thirty seconds, her irises began to glaze over, going from icy blue to a milky, cracked-ice white. Dominic stiffened.

"This is unnatural," he hissed.

"For us, yes. For her, no." I squeezed his knee, keeping my eyes on Sarah. "This is perfectly natural. It's what she evolved to do." It's the reason she stays near one of the cousins at all times. So that if she ever goes back to her killer-cuckoo roots, there's someone around who knows how to stop her.

"Still—"

"There's something there," said Sarah, in a remote, utterly disconnected tone. Dominic stopped. "It's big. It's old. And it's hungry."

"Where is it, Sarah?" I asked, keeping my voice level. Most telepaths respond better when people don't sound concerned by the fact that they've fallen into a fugue state. I don't understand the psychology behind it, but I'm not the telepath.

"I don't know. Close. There's too much earth between here and there, and the subway system is in the way—I can't see it clearly. But it's big." She hesitated. "Did I say it was big?"

"You did," I said soothingly. "How big is big? Is it bigger than a bulldozer?"

"It thinks big thoughts. It dreams big dreams." Sarah twitched. "It's asleep. It's been asleep for a long time. I think . . . I think it's hibernating. Waiting for something to change before it wakes up again."

"Is it a dragon?" demanded Dominic. I shot him a warning look. His attention was focused fully on Sarah, posture tight with a degree of tension that I recognized from my own mirror. He was itching for a fight.

"I don't know," said Sarah, a note of peevish irritation creeping into her voice. "What does a dragon think like? You tell me, and I'll ask it."

"She can't really do that," I said, before he could ask her. "Sarah, is there anything you can give us as a pointer? What direction do we need to go?"

"Down." She blinked, the blue returning to her eyes as she sat up in the chair and looked at us gravely. "You need to go way, way down, Very. And you need to go now, because I think somebody's trying to wake it up."

Twelve

"The problem with people who say monsters don't really exist is that they're almost never saying it to the monsters."

–Alice Healy

Central Park, a block and a half away from the Plaza Athenee, preparing to do something stupid

THE FIRST OUT-OF-THE-WAY MANHOLE COVER we could find was located on the edge of Central Park, about a block and a half away from the hotel. It was mostly hidden in the middle of one of those little seating areas that spring up around the city like mushrooms after a hard rain. The few people who did walk by pretty much ignored us. "I love big city life," I said quietly.

"What was that?"

"Nothing." Dominic had removed his duster and shirt before taking the crowbar Sarah somehow managed to wheedle out of the hotel manager—when a cuckoo gets involved, it's better not to ask exactly how they accomplish things—and setting to work. Sarah was back at the hotel, gulping Tylenol and keeping a telepathic "eye" on the area. She'd let us know if she saw trouble coming.

In the meanwhile, I was absorbed with the all-important task of checking my weapons, including the emergency throwing knives and smoke grenades I'd retrieved from Sarah's closet. Well, that, and watching the way the muscles of Dominic's back moved every time he strained to get a better degree of leverage on the manhole cover. Sure, he was Covenant, and I might have to kill him before everything was said and done, but the man had the sort of physique professional athletes would kill for. In his case, he probably had. All the training in the world won't take the place of knowing that your performance on the field literally means the difference between life and death. So what if he was a dead man walking? He wasn't dead yet, and the way he was carbonizing my hormones reminded me, graphically, that neither was I.

Dominic glanced up, as if he could feel my eyes on him, and scowled. "You could help, you know," he said sourly.

"There's only one crowbar, and I'm busy making sure we get back from the lizard hunt in one piece." I slotted another throwing knife into its holster. "Don't worry. It'll be my turn to sweat soon enough."

Muttering something in a language that sounded suspiciously like Latin, Dominic shook his head and went back to work.

You do *realize you're broadcasting, right?* asked Sarah, implied laughter coloring her mental "voice."

I nearly stabbed myself in the leg. The first time she pulled that trick, I actually did—cuckoos mature into projective telepaths in their teens, riding what Antimony and Sarah call "the X-Men effect." (My sister and my cousin: both enormous nerds.) Before that, she'd been strictly limited to feelings and vague impressions that were to actual sentences as interpretive dance is to the Viennese waltz.

Shut up and get out of my head, I shot back. I'm not a telepath, but that hasn't stopped me from learning how to communicate with them, if only out of self-defense.

So are you going to jump his bones? I ask purely out of academic interest, and because if you're taking brood-

ing, dark, and inappropriate home with you, I'm not auditing any classes near your apartment for a week.

"God, Sarah," I muttered. Dominic glanced sharply in my direction, and I offered him a quick, reality-show-perfect smile. He shook his head again, looking baffled as well as disgusted, and bent back to his work. *Don't you have anything better to do?*

Not until you get back. Safely, please.

I'll do my best, I replied, approvingly. Dominic was shoving the manhole cover off to one side, releasing an unpleasant gust of sewer smell. I wrinkled my nose. *Looks like we're ready to head down the rabbit hole. Thanks for all your help.*

Call me when you get back above ground. The soft background static of an active telepathic connection cut off as Sarah turned her attention elsewhere, leaving me alone with a half-naked member of the Covenant of St. George, an open manhole cover, and a plan consisting mostly of "look for something to hit."

"One subterranean tour of the island of Manhattan, coming right up," I said, sheathing my last knife before sliding off the dumpster I'd been perching on. I trotted over to help Dominic get ready to descend into the darkness. The things I do to keep potentially extinct monsters from eating the human race, I swear.

The New York City subway system is a large part of the reason for the city's massive cryptid population. Many species of cryptid prefer to live in darkness—hence the popularity of creepy old houses, supposedly haunted forests, and complex cave systems. When those aren't available, a sufficiently large and complicated subway system will suit most cryptids just fine. As an added bonus, city subways tend to come with water and power systems that can be tapped with relative ease, allowing city cryptids to live in comfort, yet not miss out on their modern conveniences. A surprisingly large number of bugbears really enjoy their daytime talk shows.

Because of the city cryptids' tendency to retreat underground when given the opportunity, I never go anywhere without a light, bug spray, and a water bottle in whatever bag I happen to be carrying. Just in case.

The manhole opened to reveal a rusty metal ladder bolted into the concrete and pointing straight down into the sewer system. Dominic insisted on taking the lead, presumably so he'd have the first opportunity to fight off anything that felt like attacking us. I didn't object. If he wanted to feed himself to the monsters, it would both keep them from eating me and solve that nagging question of whether or not to kill him. Two birds, one stone.

By bracing my feet against one side of the narrow tunnel and my shoulders against the other, I was able— barely—to get sufficient leverage to let me pull the manhole cover back into place. Most of the light died once the opening was sealed, leaving only a few narrow beams to illuminate our descent.

"In a sewer, in the dark, with a Covenant member," I muttered. "Can this day *get* any better?"

The ladder ended after about fifteen feet, when my questing foot hit a chilly layer of half-congealed water. Grimacing, I dropped off the ladder, letting water soak through my socks, and pulled the cave light out of my bag, clipping it to my belt before saying, "Close your eyes. I'm going to turn the light on."

"What?" asked Dominic.

I flipped on the cave light—a miniature halogen designed for deep spelunking and hunting basilisks in the woods on moonless nights. Dominic's pained yelp told me he hadn't listened. "I warned you," I said, and turned to survey our surroundings.

I wouldn't have been surprised to learn that the tunnel we were in was labeled as "generic New York sewer tunnel, model 16-C" on the official maps. The walls were just the right shade of grimy, slightly-mossy concrete gray; the slime covering the floor was just the right depth, with just the right questionable texture. I glanced up and nodded, satisfied. "Thought so."

"What *are* you talking about, you insufferable woman?" demanded Dominic, still scrubbing at his eyes in an effort to recover from looking directly into my halogen light. The gesture was made amusingly awkward by the short sword he was holding in one hand, which begged the question of where, exactly, he'd been hiding the sword before he got into the sewer.

"Look up." I jerked a thumb toward the ceiling to better illustrate my point.

He looked, scowl turning slowly into a bewildered frown. "What am I looking *at*?"

I decided to take pity. If I didn't, we'd be standing in the faux sewer all afternoon, and that was so not the way I wanted to spend the hours before my shift. "Look at the light fixtures."

"I don't see what you're talking a—oh."

"Yeah." The light fixtures dangling from the concrete ceiling were ostensibly for use by city maintenance personnel. That would have worked fine, if they'd actually been *functional*. With my cave light directed at the bulbs, it was clear that they might look like lights from a distance, but were really nothing but blown glass covered in Halloween store cobwebs. They even had lengths of yarn where the filaments should have been, guaranteeing that no amount of tinkering would get them to turn on.

"Monstrous deceits," snarled Dominic.

I turned to face him, careful to keep my light aimed downward as I gave him a dubious look. "What, swapping a light bulb for a decoy is a monstrous deceit in your world? Remind me never to eat the last of the Thin Mints."

"What's a Thin Mint?"

"That's it: after we save the world, we're finding some

Girl Scouts to mug for cookies." I did a slow turn, checking the tunnel branches around us. There were three. Two of them looked naturally broken-down and unpleasant, while the third wouldn't have looked out of place in a midnight monster movie. "That way."

"How do you know?"

"Because that's the one that looks like it should have a sign warning us not to go near the castle. Come on." I started picking my way carefully through the sludge. It might be there for effect, but that didn't mean I wanted to get any more of it into my shoes than I had to.

"I don't understand," said Dominic. This didn't stop him from muscling his way forward until he was pacing next to me, his shoulders making the tunnel a substantially tighter squeeze than it would have been if we'd been walking in sensible single file.

"Look: we're not actually going to walk into anybody's living room," I hoped; the city cryptids would *never* forgive me for that, "but we're definitely walking into somebody else's territory. Most of the sewers and subway systems are inhabited, and I don't mean by the human homeless. Although the humans may make up a serious chunk of the total population. I don't know, I don't keep track. What I do keep track of is our local cryptids, and this 'don't look here, ooh, spooky' sort of setup is classic bugbear."

"Doubtless you're overlooking the human homeless because they're supplementing the diets of your precious bugbears."

I rolled my eyes. Thanks to the dark, he never saw it. "Bugbears don't eat people. What are they teaching you Covenant kids, anyway?"

"So what *do* bugbears eat?"

"Usually? Trash, half-rotten meat, whatever they find that looks interesting and isn't actually alive. They're not big on eating living things. Or hunting. Or cooking." Your average bugbear can set an apartment building on fire trying to make a bag of microwave popcorn. It's either a supernatural power, or they're really, really dumb about technology. Possibly a little of both. "They're not harmless, but they're not big contenders in the 'fucking with you' department."

The sludge on the floor dried up as we walked, giving way to smooth-worn concrete. The tunnel slanted down shortly after that, easing us deeper into the bowels of Manhattan. I glanced at Dominic, trying to assess whether he'd caught the descent. Judging by the way his lips were narrowed, he had.

The walls were beginning to look less horror movie "all hope abandon," and more legitimately weathered. The lower we got, the less effort the locals would have needed to put into making the transit authorities look elsewhere. "The top layers are likely to be bugbear and maybe—*maybe*—Jersey devil territory. Under that, we'll have the hidebehinds, and under them, the subterranean bogeymen." There were various other underground races we might encounter, but those were the big guys: the ones with sufficient numbers to have a say in what passed for local "government," and sufficient intelligence not to mess with us unless we threatened them.

"Beyond that?" asked Dominic.

"Beyond that, according to Sarah, we'll find our dragon." A rat squealed ahead, alerting its relatives to our presence before darting back into the shadows. Its presence was a good sign. If there'd been cave basilisks around, there wouldn't have been rats. I'd rather risk a little bubonic plague than a lot of turning to granite, thanks.

"I'm not equipped to kill a dragon," said Dominic, sounding uncertain and faintly peeved. "I'm not even sure how you're supposed to *start*."

"Neither am I, but we're not killing it, remember? We're just finding out what the situation is, and if somebody's stupid enough to be trying to wake the damn thing, we stop them." The tunnel in front of us divided at a Y-bend, both branches proceeding identically into the dark. I stopped, frowning. "Cute."

"I don't suppose you have some great wisdom in the arena of sewer exploration?" Dominic asked. I shot him a look, and he met it with an amused quirk of his lips. "You seem to know everything *else*. I thought perhaps you'd been concealing a background in spelunking until the right dramatic moment to reveal it."

"No, that's my grandmother's hobby, not mine." I dug through my bag until I found a pair of high-bounce balls I'd purchased earlier from supermarket vending machines. I held them up for Dominic to see. "We can, however, consult the oracle."

His expression turned dubious. "Your oracle is a pair of rubber balls?"

"*Round* rubber balls," I said, and stepped forward, bending to place the balls carefully at the mouths of the two tunnels. "Okay. Watch the balls, not my ass."

"I assure you, madam, your, ah, ass is of no pressing interest to me whatsoever."

I smiled into the darkness. "Of course it's not," I said, and let the balls go.

Any kid can tell you that a high-bounce ball, when released, will immediately start making a break for freedom—even if you put it down on a completely level surface. The sewer tunnels were far from level. The two balls began rolling forward at the same pace, but the ball on the left started gaining speed almost immediately, accelerating until its brother was left in the proverbial dust. I straightened.

"We go that way," I said, pointing down the leftward fork.

I was expecting at least a token argument, but to my surprise, Dominic nodded. "We're trying to go down, so that makes sense. I do have to wonder—how long were you intending to wander around blind?"

"You didn't have a problem with it when we were deciding to come down here," I said, starting down the left fork. The light went with me. Dominic, not wanting to be abandoned in the dark a considerable distance beneath the streets of New York, followed.

"Since I don't think maps exist for this sort of thing, I still think this is the best idea. But is there any way to start narrowing down where we ought to be looking?"

"There *are* maps of the New York sewer system, but they probably won't extend to cover the areas we're heading for." I sighed. "I wasn't expecting to come down here without having time to prepare. This day has so not even been in the neighborhood of what I was expecting."

"I suppose I should apologize for that," said Dominic. Tone gone wry, he continued, "I'm not sure what I was trying to prove. Maybe that you weren't as well hidden as you seemed to think. I still don't really understand why it's so important to you. The dancing, I mean. But I'm sorry to have been as much of a disruption as I apparently was."

"Thanks for that. It won't get me into Regionals, but . . . thanks." The decline was more pronounced in this tunnel. We were moving downward at a faster clip now, probably skirting at least one major transit line in the process. "To take your first question first, we're going to go as deep as we can, and then I'm going to find the locals. If there's a dragon down here—and there's not really much 'if' about it, not if Sarah can spot the thing—then anybody who lives close enough to it should be feeling the effects. Whatever those are. So we're just going to find the bottom, and then we're going to ask for directions."

"How civilized."

"I try."

"You said that was my first question. What was my second?"

"The dancing." I smiled wistfully into the darkness. "Why it's so important to me."

"It is . . . odd, you must admit," he said, sounding a little embarrassed. "Here you already have a purpose in your life, and yet you're choosing to spend your time—doing something else."

I could hear all the slurs and accusations of goofing off that my dance career has received in his hastily-swallowed words, and I appreciated them. Not the insults; the fact that he managed to stop himself from saying them out loud. "You remember that whole 'traitors' thing?"

"I doubt I could forget."

"Well, after Dad and Grandma managed to convince the Covenant that we were all dead, we pretty much went into hiding. I don't know what's going to happen now that you know we're still around. Since we can't exactly quit the family business—there are too many people out there with serious grudges against us, and I'm not talking just cryptids—we have to keep learning how to fight. But we can't go through standard channels. Not if we want to get as good as we need to be."

"Why not?" he asked. He sounded honestly puzzled. Maybe we needed to spend more time in the sewers. I was definitely coming to like him better down here.

"Because most martial arts and organized sports publish their rankings once you get to a certain level of competition," I replied. "My . . . one of us couldn't even take fencing in college, because the entire Fencing Club got called out in the local paper." Alex was *livid* when Dad found that out and told him he couldn't fence. He wound up joining a historical reenactment group to learn how to handle a saber, since basically no one looks at those membership lists with an eye toward "spot the enemy presence." We've been giving him shit about Renaissance Faires ever since.

"Oh," said Dominic. I glanced toward him again,

and saw the horror in his face. He'd clearly never stopped to consider what it meant to be hiding from a global organization that monitors the news for signs of cryptid activity. "So you went into ballroom dance because . . . ?"

"It's a viable way of building some of the same muscle groups as martial arts and gymnastics, but it isn't monitored the same way. Plus, since it's not 'dangerous,' it's easier to do under an assumed name."

"And you liked it?"

"I loved it. I still do." I couldn't keep my voice from turning wistful. "When you're on the stage, nothing else really matters. Nobody's trying to kill you; nobody wants to see your credentials or needs you to get them the gorgon antivenin. It's just you, and the music, and knowing how you're supposed to move. Dancing is all I've ever really wanted to do. I'm here partially so I can prove that I can make a career of it, before I get sucked into cryptozoology for keeps. That way, whichever way I go, it'll be a choice."

"Assuming you survive the dragon long enough to make choices."

"There is that." We kept walking. At our rate of descent, we were going to pass out of bugbear territory before we saw any of the locals. That was fine by me. Bugbears aren't very helpful when interrupted, and we'd have better results with the hidebehinds or the bogeymen.

"Also assuming I don't turn you in to the Covenant when I get home." Dominic shook his head, causing his shadow on the wall to flicker and shift. I gave him a startled look. He smiled. "*If* I get home, that is. I know you're thinking it. I may be an arrogant bastard by your standards, but I'm not foolish."

"The thought had crossed my mind," I admitted slowly.

"Given the natural conclusions of that thought, I'd

like to propose a truce. I won't tell anyone you exist, and you won't attempt to kill me, until after we've dealt with the current situation."

Did I trust him? Well, I was deep beneath the city streets, alone, in a narrow tunnel that left very few avenues of escape, and made gunfire a questionable option at best. I'd already trusted him further than I would have expected. At this point, did trusting him a little further really make that much of a difference?

Probably not. "Deal," I said, shoulders slumping slightly with relief. I hadn't been looking forward to trying to kill the man. For one thing, it would leave me with no one to move manhole covers for me. For another, annoying and impossible as he was, it was actually sort of nice to have someone male and human who wasn't related to me and didn't look at me like I was crazy when I slipped and used the word "Sasquatch" in casual conversation. Not that we'd had much opportunity for casual conversation—all our conversations so far had been focused on killing each other, killing something else, or trying not to get ourselves or anybody else killed. He just didn't seem like the kind of guy who'd think Bigfoot was a synonym for "bonkers."

"Excellent," he said. Behind us, in the darkness, I heard the distinctive scrape of metal against metal. Tone deeply apologetic, Dominic continued, "Now, about dealing with the current situation . . ."

"Fan-fucking-tastic," I snarled.

We turned to press our backs together, Dominic's short sword held out in front of him, my halogen light bathing the tunnel walls. I pulled the telescoping baton from my belt, snapping it open and locking it in that position. There was no sign of whomever—or whatever—had drawn the knife, but I could hear the scuffle of claws on concrete, too large and too heavy to belong to the rats.

"What are our escape routes?" Dominic asked tightly.

"Forward and back," I muttered. More loudly, I said, "Okay, people. If you want to talk, we're prepared to talk. And if you want to dance . . ." Again the sound of metal on metal, from a different direction this time. Well. That answered that. "Okay. Let's dance."

Thirteen

"Nothing lasts forever. That's the tragedy
and the miracle of existence—that everything is impermanent. Everything changes.
All we can do is make the best of the time
we have. And go down shooting, naturally."

–Enid Healy

Deep beneath the streets of Manhattan, about to be attacked

THERE WAS A PAUSE AFTER MY LAST bravado-fueled
comment, long enough that I was starting to feel a
little silly standing in a sewer in a defensive posture, my
back pressed up against a member of the Covenant of
St. George, waiting to be attacked like a coed in a horror
movie. I was about to suggest we start moving again
when the walls around us bulged, transmuting from flat
stone into lumpy, uneven crags. The crags split away
from the walls, becoming a group of roughly-humanoid
figures in tattered, mismatched clothing.

I gasped. It was a stupid, girly thing to do, but I
couldn't help myself. I've been studying cryptids since
before I knew my ABCs. I've been specializing in the
humanoid cryptids since second grade. But these . . .
whatever they were, it was nothing I'd ever seen before.
That realization was almost as chilling as the one that
accompanied it.

We were trapped.

The figures continued to separate from the walls around us; I counted at least ten, maybe more, since the way their outlines shifted and blended together made it difficult to say for sure. They were hairless, about six feet tall, and covered head to toe in tiny green-and-brown scales. None of them was carrying a gun, thank God, but they all had at least one weapon in their hands, and in close quarters, knives and lead pipes will get you just as dead as bullets. Holes torn in the seats of their pants allowed their long whipcord-thin tails to wave free. Several of them were clutching additional weapons with those tails, waving them with prehensile menace.

"Oh, fuck, killer Sleestaks." I pressed further back against Dominic. They had us outnumbered, and while they might have fought against humans before, I'd never fought against *them*. I wanted to watch them move for as long as I could.

"You know what these are?" he demanded, sotto voce. "How do we defeat them?"

"I so don't have time to explain *The Land of the Lost* right now." I shifted my weight onto the balls of my feet, assuming the position I'd use to start a samba. Samba, street fight, it's all the same once you find the rhythm. Pitching my voice toward the lizard-men, I said, "My name is Verity Price. My companion and I mean you no harm. We're just passing through, on important business."

Three more of the lizard-men produced knives from inside their grimy shirts. So much for that tactic.

Time to try another approach. "I work for Dave Smith," I said. "The local bogeyman community will vouch for me." They definitely understood that, since their reaction was different this time: two of them hissed balefully, and one produced a nasty-looking hacksaw from inside his vest.

I said "different," not "better."

"I don't think you're talking us out of this," said Dominic. Despite the precariousness of our position, he couldn't quite keep the amusement from his tone.

Great. The man finally gets a sense of humor thirty seconds before we die. "I guess we're just going to have to go the old-fashioned route."

The lizard-man with the hacksaw hissed. That must have been a signal. The rest immediately stopped their baleful glaring and began to advance, clawed feet clacking on the sewer floor.

"What's that?"

"Let's kick some lizard ass."

With a wild, ululating cry that was half reptile, half human, and all nightmare-inducing, the creatures charged. I took advantage of the fact that I was still braced against Dominic, leaning into him just long enough to kick the first of the attackers in the chin. Its jaws snapped shut on its serpentine tongue, and it made a wordless sound I assumed was lizard-man for "Ow." My heel caught him in the forehead as I brought my foot back down. Then Dominic was lunging for a target of his own, momentum carrying him away from me and leaving me to dance my side of the battle solo.

Ten lizard-men, a Covenant trainee, and a Price girl: there's no way to turn that into even odds. The lizard-man I'd kicked in the head was on his knees, blood running from the sides of his mouth. I kicked him a third time, sending him over backward before jumping up and using his chest as a source of higher ground. Without that extra bit of height, the lizard-men had more than six inches on me.

Six of the lizard-men were engaged in combat with Dominic, their tails whipping around to strike his back and shoulders as he hacked his way grimly forward. My count had been off by two, because even with my new stepstool groaning and motionless beneath me, there were six more closing in on my position. The odds were more than reasonably good that we were screwed.

"I've always loved a challenge," I said—more for effect than because I meant a word of it—and leaped, baton raised, toward the next of the lizard-men.

In the movies, when the hero is surrounded by a gang of ne'er-do-wells who mean to do him (or her) harm, they always offer the courtesy of approaching one at a time, thus letting themselves be mowed down by the hero's superior fighting skills and devastating repartee. Our lizard-men clearly hadn't seen that many movies, since they belonged more to the school of "run at the enemy until the enemy stops fighting back." I could appreciate the tactic—even respect it—but that didn't mean I appreciated being on the receiving end.

My first lizard-man didn't move even after I launched myself from his chest. I slammed my baton into the throat of the next one in the line, hearing the distinct breaking-plywood sound of his larynx giving way. He went down immediately, clutching at his throat. With two lizard-men down and five remaining, I was no longer devastatingly outnumbered, just horrifyingly outnumbered, and those were odds I was better-equipped to deal with.

I swung my baton at the next lizard-man, aiming for his kidneys at the last moment. Unfortunately, that was the moment when another of the lizard-men caught me in the back of the thighs with a length of what felt like rebar, sending me staggering for balance. The lizard-man I'd been swinging at whipped his tail around and yanked the baton from my hands, flinging it away into the darkness.

"Hey!" I yelped, from anger as much as from surprise. That baton was a gift from my brother. I didn't appreciate having it taken away by a crazy cryptid with territory issues.

Since I was already staggering, I let myself hit the

ground in a runner's crouch, pulling the throwing knives from the holster strapped around my left ankle. It was difficult to tell exactly where the lizard-men were—the distortion from the cave walls made it almost impossible to know what was the original noise, and what was just a decoy—but Dominic's breathing was distinct enough from theirs that I could tell where it *wasn't* safe to aim. Whipping myself around to face the attackers coming up behind me, I half rose and snapped my wrists forward in the throwing motion Antimony and I spent three summers studying with the local circus.

We may have driven the Incredible Christopher crazy with how long it took us to learn the fine art of knife throwing, but he would have been proud of me in that moment, assuming he could get past the part where I was applying his lessons to an underground battle with an unidentified race of lizard-men. The knives flew straight and true toward their targets, one burying itself in the throat of a third lizard-man, while the other caught the fourth in the shoulder. The one I'd hit in the throat went down like a sack of potatoes. The other remained standing, but squealed, losing his hold on the larger of his two knives.

A severed head went flying overhead from Dominic's direction, signaling that at least one of his opponents was no longer an issue. I was liking the odds better all the time.

My allotment of lizard-men was starting to advance again, faster this time, their tails waving wildly. Their hissing had acquired a distinctly pissed-off note, distinguishable from their earlier hissing only because it came with a healthy dose of snarling and exposed teeth.

"Dominic?" I shouted, barely ducking a blow from a lead pipe clutched in a scaly tail. "What's the situation on your end?"

He answered with a grunt of exertion before calling, "Somewhat busy!"

"I know!" I dodged another blow, pulling a stiletto

from my sleeve and stabbing the lizard-man's tail before he could pull it away. He shrieked as he yanked his tail back, taking my stiletto with it. Fighting in quarters this cramped was resulting in a surprisingly large number of lost weapons. "How many do you have left?"

"Three! You?"

"Two and a half!" One of the downed lizard-men staggered to his feet, and I amended, "Three and a half!" The nearest lizard-man lunged for me. I jumped clear, barely, jamming a hand into the waistband of my jeans as my left shoulder slammed into the wall. I hit stone, not concealed lizard-man; that was one possible complication down the drain.

"We need to retreat!"

"I know!" Yanking the .32 from my hip holster, I released the safety and opened fire.

Here's the thing about friendly fire: it isn't. Once Mr. Bullet has left Mr. Gun, he is no longer your friend. Shooting a firearm in an enclosed space is a dangerous proposition at best, because the closer the walls are, the more likely you are to set off a ricochet. Even if your bullets don't come bouncing back at you, there's a good chance that pieces of the wall will. Stone chips *hurt* when they're traveling at that sort of speed.

I fired first at my two most intact lizard-men, catching one in the forehead and the other in the throat. They went down hard. I put two more bullets into a third lizard-man, the reports leaving my ears ringing until I could barely hear the shrieks echoing through the sewers.

The lizard-men must have been even more sensitive to sound than humans. They stopped attacking, all of them turning to me as they hissed and bared their teeth.

Mouseguns are intended for self-defense and designed to be easily concealed in street clothes, not to hold enormous numbers of bullets. I kept my .32 raised, trying to look cool and unruffled, despite the blood I could feel trickling down my cheek from a cut near my hairline. I was going to be sore in the morning, assuming we lived through the night.

"I know you understand English," I said, focusing on the lizard-man with the hacksaw. He was still standing, and he was my best guess for the leader. "Let's see if you can understand this: back off and let us leave, or I start shooting again." If they knew firearms, they'd know I was bluffing. If they knew firearms, they'd probably have brought some.

Slowly, the lizard-men began to back up. They weren't backing away, exactly—the tunnel was too narrow for that—but they were clearing the necessary space for Dominic to move to my side, his short sword still at the ready, and a long, curving dagger in his off hand. That explained how he'd managed to keep the lizard-men from gutting him while he was chopping off their limbs; he had something to stab with, even when he was blocking.

"Now what?" he muttered.

"Now you're going to lead me out of here, so I don't have to take my eyes off our new buddies," I said, keeping the gun aimed, unwavering, at the lizard-leader's forehead.

"Right," said Dominic. He stepped out of my field of vision. I felt his hand on my shoulder a moment later, tugging me back the way we'd come.

Even with Dominic making sure I didn't collide with anything solid, walking was a chore. The previously-dry floor was slippery with blood, and chunks of lizard-man kept getting underfoot, threatening to knock me on my ass. I was glad to be wearing sensible shoes for a change, and doubly glad that I'd wrapped my ankles before we started pounding the pavement.

The lizard-men stayed where they were as we moved away, their tongues flicking, snakelike, to sample the air.

Once we reached the first turn in the tunnel, I stepped back, lowered my gun, and looked to Dominic.

"This is where we run," I said.

He nodded firm assent, grabbed my free hand, and booked it back up the incline toward the place where we'd entered.

The sound of clawed feet striking stone followed us all the way back to the ladder leading to the surface. The lizard-men started out at least twenty feet behind, and only gained slightly. Panic is a great motivator when it comes to sprinting. At the bottom of the ladder, I stopped and shoved Dominic forward, shouting, "Go! I'll be right behind you!"

"Verity—"

"Don't be a chivalrous idiot! I'm the one with the gun!"

He went.

Light flooded the tunnel as he shoved the manhole cover off to one side. I heard squeals of reptilian anguish coming from the direction of our pursuers. Looked like our subterranean Sleestak knockoffs couldn't stand the sunlight. I drew my gun and fired once into the darkness, just to keep them from getting any funny ideas, and followed Dominic up, into the light.

The familiar mental static of Sarah's proximity snapped on as soon as I got to ground level. Dominic grabbed my hands and pulled me off the top rung of the ladder, setting me on my feet before he returned to what he'd been doing: shoving the manhole cover back into place. A momentary chill washed over me as I realized that I'd been practically screaming "here I am, entomb me" to a member of the Covenant.

But he hadn't. And judging by the quick, worried glance he cast my way before throwing all his weight onto the crowbar and forcing the manhole cover to move, he hadn't been intending to. The screech of metal moving over blacktop would have been painful under normal circumstances. At the moment, it was music to my ears.

Telepathy gets harder the farther people are from each other. I was too tired to perform the internal gymnastics of trying to shout without using my mouth, and Sarah had to be as aware of my presence as I was of hers. Being a telepath means never needing to say "I'm lonely." Digging my phone out of my purse, I leaned hard against the nearest lamppost and dialed her number.

She picked up before the first ring had time to finish. "How badly injured are you?" she demanded.

"I'll probably never play the piano again, but my wounds are mostly superficial. I'm going to have some awesome bruises." I could feel them forming across the back of my thighs where the lizard-man caught me with the rebar. "Not sure what Dominic's status is. We were fighting pretty much blind."

"Come back to the hotel. I'll meet you in the lobby and walk you up to my room. Don't argue!" The fierceness of her tone would have been comic under almost any other circumstances. "Aunt Evelyn would have my ears if I let you leave here without checking you over."

"Technically, she's your sister." As attempts to tease go, reminding Sarah that her adoptive parents—my grandparents—are also Mom's adopted parents was a pretty lame one.

It still seemed to reassure her that I wasn't intending to bleed to death. "Get moving," she said, much less fiercely, and hung up the phone.

I snapped my phone shut, shoving it into my bag and straightening up. Dominic had managed to get the manhole cover back into position. He was standing half-bent, hands braced against his knees and his feet apart. He looked exhausted. I shared the sentiment.

"You okay?" I asked, walking over and putting a hand on his shoulder.

His head jerked up, expression reflecting a startlement that changed quickly to concern. "You're bleeding," he said, eyes going to the cut in my forehead.

"Superficial," I repeated. Comforting a cryptid and a member of the Covenant in the same five minutes. Who says the age of miracles is over? "What about you?"

"Some minor bruises and abrasions, and a possible sprain to my left shoulder." Dominic's expression darkened. "We could have been killed down there. Do you still want to insist that we befriend the monsters?"

"Not all of them. Just the ones smart enough to be on Facebook." There was a shininess I didn't like to the fabric on the right sleeve of his duster. I reached out, brushing my fingers against it. They came away slick and slightly sticky. "Your blood, or someone else's?"

"Both." Dominic glanced at the manhole cover. "I gave as well as I got."

"So much for minor abrasions." I stepped back. "Sarah's going to meet us at the hotel. She can give us a once-over before we head out of here."

He raised an eyebrow. "What makes you think I would ever allow a *cryptid* to examine my injuries?"

"Your total inability to take them to a New York emergency room without getting the third degree." That wasn't true—he could probably just claim to have been mugged, and since he didn't have any bullet wounds, it wasn't likely they'd report it to the police without his consent—but he didn't need to know that.

Dominic sighed. "I cede the point. Any hostile actions, however . . ."

"Hey, after the Sleestaks, I'm jumpy too. Don't worry. She'll be careful."

"That reminds me."

"Of what?"

"What, exactly, is a 'Sleestak'?"

I made it halfway through my explanation of *Land of the Lost* before we reached the Plaza Athénée. Sarah was waiting for us on the sidewalk outside, eyes wide and bleached from their normal glacial blue to an icy blue-white. Her telepathic shields were down, leaving her an open receptor for anything in range. It was dangerous as hell, and not something she did very often, but I had to admire the sense behind her actions. If any of the lizard-men had managed to follow us out of the sewers, she'd "hear" them before they could attack us.

"Hey, Sarah," I said, offering her a wave with one grimy, blood-mottled hand.

Her relief was visible. A small measure of the color bled back into her eyes, like ink spreading through blotter paper. "I can't leave you alone for five minutes without you finding something horrible to get into, can I? Come on, both of you. I've got everyone in the lobby primed to ignore us, but I can't keep it up for long."

"You're the one that sent us off to find a dragon," I pointed out, and followed her, waving for Dominic to do the same. Moving stiffly, he came.

Sarah was true to her word: although the lobby was full of people, none of them even glanced our way as we walked past them to the elevators. We were unkempt enough to have been a spectacle in a place as ritzy as the Plaza Athénée, even if we hadn't been covered head to toe in a delightful blend of sewage, blood, and slime. Somebody should have called the cops as soon as we crossed the threshold.

Dominic observed the oblivious hotel occupants with a dark scowl, shoulders going stiff beneath his duster. I realized, sickly, that Sarah's little Jedi mind trick probably wasn't doing anything to convince him that she wasn't a danger to the human race. It wasn't like he'd be able to find her after we left—not without me guiding him—but still. I made a note to remind her to change hotels again sooner rather than later.

The elevator came and we boarded without incident.

From penthouse to sewer and back again in a single afternoon . . . and the day was nowhere even close to over yet.

Sarah's eyes returned to their normal shade of slightly-alien blue as soon as the elevator doors closed behind us. When we reached the penthouse, she went straight for the kitchen, saying, "I'll get the first aid kit. You two figure out which of you is hurt worse, and just let me know where I'm starting."

Dominic glared after her, waiting until she was out of sight before turning to me and saying, darkly, "She controlled the minds of all those people. How can you—?"

"She couldn't have held them if she was an actual threat. Cuckoos are ambush hunters. That kind of open assault isn't their style." That wasn't entirely true—there were things she could have done, if she could keep concentrating while she was poisoning drinks—but it was true enough for him. I knelt, wincing, to start untying my shoes. "Get your jacket off. Sarah's going to need to see that arm."

Wow, you sure did find a sweetheart. Sarah's mental voice was sour. *You should keep this one, Very, he's a real gem.*

Stop eavesdropping if you don't want to hear it, I chided.

"I'm still not comfortable with this," said Dominic. Still, he shrugged out of his duster, revealing the thoroughly-shredded sleeve over his right arm. He made a sharp hissing sound as he studied the damage. I was too far away to get much more than an impression of equally-shredded flesh, and I was happy with that. "I take that back. I'm less comfortable with dying of septic shock."

"It's always good to know where I rate," said Sarah,

walking back into the room with a standard drugstore first aid kit in one hand and a paring knife in the other. She put both down on the coffee table, extracting a cup from the first aid kit before looking the two of us studiously up and down.

"Worse injuries?" she asked me.

I pointed to Dominic.

"I figured as much. Dominic, could you take off your shirt and come over here?" Sarah picked up the paring knife, shooting me a sour look. I knew what was coming next, and mouthed the word "Sorry" at her. She sighed. "Ah, the joys of alternative biology," she said, and slashed the knife quickly along the curve of her left bicep. A thick, clear substance started leaking out of the cut. Still wincing, Sarah traded the knife for the cup and began collecting it.

Dominic froze midway through removing his shirt, staring at her. I straightened and planted a hand against his upper back, pushing him forward.

"Trust me," I said.

Maybe it was the fact that we'd just survived an attack by subterranean lizard-men; maybe he was just too tired to keep fighting with me. Either way, Dominic's shoulders slumped slightly, signaling his submission even before he finished removing his shirt, crossed to Sarah, and sat down on the couch. I decided to ignore the fact that he was swearing under his breath in Latin. He wasn't stabbing anybody. That was all I could ask for.

Sarah studied the viscous fluid coating the sides of her cup, nodded, and put it aside, reaching for a gauze pad. "I'll start on your arm in a second," she said, unwrapping the gauze. "I'd rather not faint from blood loss while I'm trying to clean out your wounds."

"That *is* blood?" asked Dominic, sounding horrified.

"It comes out when you cut me, and it keeps me oxygenated, so yes, it is." Sarah slapped the gauze over her bicep, taping it down. "Cuckoo biology. Putting a healthy dose of 'what the fuck' into your daily life."

"You took the words right out of my mouth."

She flashed me a tightly amused smile. "I know."

Telepaths suck. "Cuckoos bleed sort of a biological antifreeze," I supplied, moving to sit next to Sarah on the couch. I dug through the first aid kit as I continued, "It's the best topical antibiotic we've ever found, and it doesn't really have any nasty side effects."

"If you don't count me having to bleed, which Very clearly doesn't," said Sarah dryly.

"Wait!" Dominic pulled away from her, staring at me. At least he knew who he was supposed to blame. "You expect me to sit here and passively allow her to *bleed* on me?"

"It'll prevent infection, it'll reduce scarring, and it's that or the hospital, so yes, I sort of do." I shook my head. "Suck it up and trust me, okay?"

Dominic scowled at me for a moment, and then subsided, sagging into the couch.

"Thank you."

He muttered something in Italian. It didn't sound like a compliment.

"Same to you," I said, and passed Sarah a hand towel from the first aid kit. She folded it over twice, beginning to wipe the worst of the blood from his arm. He hissed in pain. I hissed in surprise.

Four parallel slashes cut across his arm, not quite deep enough to hit the bone, but definitely deep enough to hurt like a bitch. I upgraded my assessment of his pain tolerance. Dominic looked stoically at the wound, and said in a clipped tone, "I've had worse."

"How macho," said Sarah. Putting the towel aside, she picked up the cup and began carefully dribbling its contents over the wound. "How's that feel?"

". . . soothing," said Dominic, sounding bemused. "Why?"

"Natural painkiller. Trust me, you'll be glad," said

Sarah. She put the cup down, looking to me. "Ready, Verity?"

"Ready." I picked up the suture kit, and smiled apologetically. "Time for your stitches. This may sting a little."

Dominic blanched.

Fourteen

"First, check your ammunition. Then,
check your escape routes. Finally, check
your hair."

–Frances Brown

*A semilegal sublet in Greenwich Village, about two hours
later*

DOMINIC HAD DEFINITELY COME OFF THE WORSE in our
fight against the lizard-men. I had some minor cuts,
a lot of bruises, and a certain stiffness in my left knee
that would work itself out after a couple of days. Dominic had those lacerations down his right arm, another set
across his ribs that wasn't as deep but looked just as bad,
and a full complement of minor cuts and bruises. It took
Sarah two full cups of blood to clean our wounds, and by
the time I finished stitching up his ribs, Dominic looked
ready to vomit. He seemed almost grateful when I said
we needed to go back to our respective homes, collect
our research materials, and regroup. Anything to get
away from the crazy girls who kept smearing him with
blood that looked more like corn syrup and stabbing
him with needles.

The concierge summoned two taxis at Sarah's request. I got into mine gratefully, letting myself sag into
the seat. Pride might have made me insist I was perfectly okay to take my usual overland route home, but

if Sarah was offering, well, I couldn't be *rude*, now could I? Also, I didn't particularly want to walk home barefoot, and there was no way I was ever wearing my sewer-soaked running shoes again. Sarah had promised to dispose of them for me. I didn't want to know any more than that.

I saw Dominic get into his cab. I didn't see where it went. I was too busy giving directions to my own driver, and planning out just what I'd tell my father. Hopefully, "Daddy, I found you a dragon" would be a bigger deal than "Daddy, I went into the sewers with a member of the Covenant and got attacked by killer lizard-men." Hopefully. Personally, I wasn't placing any bets.

My taxi pulled into midafternoon Manhattan traffic. I relaxed as best I could as we rattled over potholes and swerved to avoid tourists. If the past six hours had been anything to go by, this was the last break I was going to get for a while. And I still had to go to work.

Cries of exultation greeted my key turning in the lock. I opened the front door to find the entire Aeslin congregation gathered on and around the tiny table where I kept the mail. Several of them were waving tiny banners made of tissue paper that had been meticulously painted with drops of blue, black, and red ink.

"Hail!" shouted the head priest, waving his banner with extra enthusiasm.

"HAIL!" agreed the congregation.

"Hail," I said tiredly, and shut the door. "What's the occasion?"

"Today is the Holy Feast of I Swear, Daddy, I'll Kiss the Next Man That Walks Through That Door," said the priest, sparking a second, more solemn declaration of "Hail" from the rest of the mice.

"Cool." I started for the living room. The mice scampered after me, still waving their banners wildly in all directions. Aeslin religious rituals are nothing if not enthusiastic. "Do I need to do anything?"

One of the novice priests looked at me like she wasn't sure whether or not I was joking. "Priestess . . ."

"Right, right. I have to kiss the next man who walks through the door, right?" Cheers from the mice, interspersed with more cries of "Hail." "Got it. At least I'm not expecting company." I dropped my dance bag on the couch, looking toward the bedroom, where my computer was. Check email, or call home? Which was more pressing?

The odds that Dad was going to insist on coming when I called were high. The odds that he'd bring Alex and Antimony were lower, but still good enough to make me less than happy. There might, however, be something in my email that I could use to mollify him, like reports from a reliable source indicating a giant Gila monster or something living under the city. Anything but a dragon.

The mice had returned to their vigil at the door, having deduced that I wasn't going to kiss anyone immediately. Occasional cries of "Hail" broke the silence, muted enough to be reduced to the level of background noise. Things like this were a perfect illustration of why Alex was my date to my Junior Prom, and why I never brought any of the boys from my dance classes home.

Not any of the human boys, at any rate.

I swung by the fridge on my way to the computer, nabbing a can of generic diet ginger ale and the Styrofoam box containing all the leftovers from my previous shift. The kitchen at Dave's Fish and Strips isn't particularly interested in saving the planet from the scourge of nonbiodegradable plastics, but boy, are they happy to clog your arteries.

I sat down at the computer, munching a deep-fried zucchini stick as I waited for my email to load. I maintain three different addresses—private, personal, and cryptozoological—and thanks to Artie, they all feed into the same mail reader. (He said he was doing me a favor. I think he was actually tired of Sarah bitching when I didn't answer her mail.) When the download finished, the display at the top informed me that I had five hundred and thirty-seven new messages. I groaned. So much for making this fast.

More than half the messages were Facebook updates for Valerie, who has a lot more friends than I do—something about having been on national television upped her stock with the public. The remainder consisted primarily of spam and messages from my mailing lists. I flagged a few threads to come back to later—the reports of werewolves in Florida were starting up again, and there'd been another Bat-Boy sighting, this time at a strip mall in Boise—but shoved most of it into folders to get it out of my inbox.

Only seven messages remained by the time I was done. One was from Alex, telling me I'd better not do anything to get him sent to New York while his basilisk breeding program was still in such a delicate stage. Two were from Aunt Jane, updating me on the total lack of clues on the "what's going on in New York" front. Her second message, sent while I was waiting to go on at the tango competition, included the information about the disappearing cryptid girls. If the gossips outside the city were picking up on it, it was definitely spreading.

As expected, the message immediately *after* Aunt Jane's second email was from her son, my cousin Artie, demanding to know whether Sarah was okay. He'd clearly been worried when he sat down at his computer; two of the words were misspelled, something an enormous nerd like Artie would normally see as a crime worthy of hard time, or at least community service. He and Sarah have been sweet on each other since we were all kids. Not that she knows it's mutual, and not that he'll tell her. Eventually, I'm going to bang their heads together and lock them in a closet to work things out, before I'm forced to drown them both.

I fired off a response to Artie, assuring him that Sarah was fine. (I left out the part where she'd spent a chunk of the afternoon providing medical care for a member of the Covenant of St. George. There were things he didn't need to know.) I emailed Aunt Jane next, relaying the information we got from Piyusha. I didn't tell her about the dragon. She'd find out eventually, but I wanted to talk to Dad before I went spreading that information around.

The remaining three emails were from Dad, containing everything he'd been able to find about the history of cryptids in New York. The file attachments were large enough to make it seem like he'd emailed me an encyclopedia. I downloaded them all and started a search, looking for the word "dragon." Maybe I'd get lucky. Maybe the search wouldn't—

The search box blinked, indicating a hit. Heart sinking, I clicked over to the indicated file. The highlighted word was in the title of an article. "The Last Dragon?" Opening the article, I read:

> *Early settlers to the Island of Manhattan laughed at the local stories detailing how "the sun himself" had come to sleep beneath the island's stone. The sun, according to the legends, was vast enough to blacken the sky, and when he walked, the very stones shook and trembled in their fear. He came cloaked in darkness, sending golden handmaids to convey his requests. He troubled not the people of the land, but still requested tribute, in exchange for all that he provided in his warmth and in his light.*
>
> *The golden handmaids of the sun collected the tribute and carried it to him deep beneath the world, while every day he sent his magic into the sky, bringing heat and life. The handmaids were human in appearance, but the heat of the sun did not burn them, and the sharpness of stones beneath their feet did not cut them. Some among the settlers found the*

lure of the sun's handmaids irresistible, and went to the cave indicated by the legends as the place of tribute. The sun's seven golden handmaids came, and the men, dazzled by their beauty, took them as their wives. When locals protested this disruption of the tribute, they were chastised, and told that the sun did not sleep beneath the island, but that the golden women had tricked them.

No pictures survive of the "golden handmaids," but their description and purpose matches that most often ascribed to the so-called "dragon princesses," a symbiotic cryptid race which evolved to live in parallel with the dragons. It is possible that the last of the great dragons, fleeing the Covenant of St. George, may have taken refuge in the caves beneath Manhattan, bringing as many of the symbiotic race as possible into exile. Once the dragon died, possibly of wounds sustained before coming to Manhattan, it would be an easy matter to remove the dragon princesses from their home. There can be no question that the dragon died, if it was there at all; no living dragon would allow the dragon princesses to be removed.

The article went on to describe the various physical and psychological characteristics of dragons from around the world. There were—or had been, before people got tired of being on the buffet menu—six known species of "Great Wyrm," which is cryptozoologist for "enormous fucking lizard with wings." They all liked caves and precious metals, they all traveled with dragon princesses, and they were all, supposedly, extinct.

"And that, kids, is why we still have to depend on fieldwork," I muttered. I instructed the computer to print the file, and rose, picking up my phone as I walked toward the kitchen. After I got some ice packs for my leg, it was time to call home and let the parents know what I was dealing with.

"Can I help you?" inquired a flat, utterly nonhelpful female voice. The speaker's air of disdain was enhanced by a broad Ohio accent, making her sound like the stereotypical bored secretary from a bad sitcom.

I fell backward onto the bed, relief wiping the tension from my neck and shoulders. "Hi, Mom. It's Very. How was the Underworld?"

"Verity!" The disdain vanished in an instant, replaced by Mom's more customary brand of good cheer. My mother: one of nature's pep squad team captains. "How are you, honey? Your father said you were having some boy troubles."

The image of Dominic De Luca's face if he heard his presence referred to as "boy troubles" was enough to make me snort briefly with laughter. "Well, he's Covenant, and he's male, but I'm not sure that's the way I'd phrase it," I said. "When did you get home?"

"Just this morning. I've barely had time to rinse the brimstone out of my hair."

"There was actually brimstone this time?"

"Not literally, but close enough. There was this acidic slimy stuff that ate through the straps on our packs like they were sugar candy. Didn't melt skin or hair, though, so I can't complain overmuch."

I heard the faint resignation in her tone, and placed a guess: "No luck this time, either, huh?"

"None," she said. "I know she says she's sure he's still out there somewhere, but Very, I'm just not convinced. She was so certain that this was going to be the time we brought him home . . . maybe it's time she moved on."

"I'm not sure that she can."

Mom sighed. "To tell the truth, honey, neither am I."

Every family has their tragedies. My family has about a baker's dozen, starting with the death of my great-grandmother and increasing in unpleasantness from there. Grandpa Thomas is probably the worst of the lot. Somehow, he managed to get himself linked to one of the planes in the Underworld, probably by trying to pull off some sort of spell from the "no, really, don't do this" section of the family library. He spent years trying to sever the connection, sometimes on his own, sometimes with help. They never succeeded, and Grandma Alice was pregnant with my Aunt Jane when that link finally yanked him out of this dimension and into that one . . . wherever that one is. Grandma's been looking for him ever since. After forty years of chasing rumors and half-coherent clues across the dimensions, I don't know if she remembers how to do anything else.

Mom cleared her throat, breaking the melancholy silence that had grown up between us. "You didn't call to talk about this, though, did you? What's going on, Very?"

"Can you get Dad on the other line? I'd rather not go over this more than once if I can help it."

"Sure thing, sweetie; just hang on a second." There was a soft scraping sound as she set the receiver against her shoulder, and she shouted, sounding somewhat muffled, "Kevin! Pick up the phone! It's Verity!"

The line clicked as Dad picked up the extension in his office, saying, "Verity! How was your dance contest this morning?"

"It was a tango competition, and it was fine, until it got interrupted by an act of Covenant." I put an arm across my face, blocking out the light, if not the distant chatter of the mice. "Dominic decided the best way to get hold of me was to infiltrate the hall, stuff my partner in a coat closet, and get me disqualified for bringing an unregistered dancer onto the floor. Good times all around."

A long silence greeted this announcement. Finally, carefully, Dad asked, "Verity, has the Covenant blown your cover?"

"You mean 'does the Covenant know that Valerie Pryor is actually me'? Yeah. They do. But that's sort of secondary to the real problem at hand."

"If the Covenant knows—"

"So far, only Dominic knows, and he isn't telling anyone, because if he calls home, he's going to wind up losing control of this operation pretty much immediately."

There was a long pause before Mom asked the question that had to be preying on both of their minds—after all, losing my Valerie identity could mean the final end of my attempts at a dance career and, while they wanted me following in the family business, not dancing, this wasn't the way they wanted to win the argument. Her voice was almost hesitant, like she was afraid of what my answer would be. "Verity, if the Covenant knowing who you are is the secondary problem . . . what's the primary one?"

"Oh, yeah, that." I closed my eyes, bracing for the shouting I knew was about to start. "See, it turns out there's a dragon sleeping somewhere under Manhattan . . ."

My parents didn't disappoint. They both began talking at once, and quickly escalated to both shouting at once, less out of anger than out of sheer and utter bewilderment. I relaxed and waited, letting them get it out of their systems. As expected, they started winding down after a few minutes. Finally, cautiously, Mom said, "Verity? Are you still there?"

"I'm here. Just waiting for you two to calm down enough to listen. Are you calm?"

"That depends," said Dad.

"On what?"

"On whether you're getting ready to buy a plane ticket home."

I rolled onto my stomach, propping myself up on my

elbows as I replied, "Nope. I'm getting ready to go find myself a dragon."

"Verity—"

"Don't 'Verity' me. This is a *dragon*. A real, honest-to-God *dragon*. I'm not going to walk away from that. Could you?" Silence greeted my question. "I thought not. Anyway, I can't leave. The Covenant's in town, and their local representative is actually willing to work with me, at least until the dragon gets found."

"What happens then?" Mom asked quietly. "When you're alone with the dragon and a member of the Covenant, what happens then?"

"Well, then I guess we see whose point of view is faster on the trigger." I rolled onto my back again, staring at the ceiling. "I hate to admit it, but I need his help. I can't do this alone, and I'm not willing to have any of the rest of you fly out here—not when there's a chance that Covenant surveillance could ID you. I'm compromised, you're on the other side of the country, and that seems like the right place for you to be. Besides, I have Sarah here."

"Does she know about all this?" asked Dad.

"Know? How do you think *I* know there's actually a dragon? Dominic found the rumor, but it was Sarah who found the giant sleeping lizard." I hesitated, unsure as to whether I should tell them the rest. Common sense won out; if I was going to go off and get myself eaten, they'd need to know everything before they came charging in to recover my remains. "Oh, and there's one more thing. We think someone's trying to wake the dragon up."

It took a lot longer for the shouting to stop this time, at least in part because Antimony finally realized we were having a conference call and hopped onto the downstairs extension. Adding a third voice to the chaos—

especially a third voice that had to be brought up to speed on the situation—did nothing to make it quieter. I wound up holding the phone a foot away from me, listening to them yell at one another, and waiting for things to settle down.

Eventually, Dad realized I'd dropped out of the conversation. After vigorously hushing my mother and sister, he asked, "Verity? Are you still there?"

"Just waiting for the panicking part of our program to be over," I said, and brought the phone back to my ear. "Are you ready to listen calmly and without commentary to the rest of what I have to tell you, or should I send an email and turn off my phone?"

"We'll listen," said Mom firmly, before Dad or Antimony could say anything. "Go ahead, honey."

"Thanks, Mom," I said. "Okay, first, Dominic isn't responsible for the disappearances—not among the sentient cryptids, anyway. He killed a few of the nastier dumb ones. I was planning to kill a few of them myself, so it's hard to be too pissed. Anyway, *he* thought *I* was helping the local cryptids get the heck out of Dodge after I knew that he was in town. According to a local Madhura, most of the folks who've vanished have been young, female, and either unmarried or unmated, depending on the standards of their species."

"Someone's hunting virgins?" asked Antimony. "Gross much?"

"Pretty standard for the snake cults," said Mom. "I've never known a snake god who cared about virginity, but somehow, the idea that they do has managed to really take root with those people."

"So maybe somebody's applying snake cult standards to the dragon. Whatever the reason, Sarah says someone's trying to wake it up, and I believe her. When Dominic and I went down into the sewers—"

"Wait," Mom interrupted. "Are you saying you took this Covenant boy to meet your cousin?"

I bit back a groan. "Mom, she's a *cuckoo*. Like he's going to find her again if she doesn't want to be found? Give me a little credit, here."

"If he'd attacked at the time—"

"First, he didn't, and second, if he had, I would have been right there. Sarah and I together are more than a match for anything the Covenant can throw at us, and I know for a fact that I'm more heavily armed than he is. Can I get back to the sewers?"

"Please," said Dad.

I outlined the Sleestak encounter in the sewers as quickly as I could, paring the information down to the bare minimum. We went down; we found signs of cryptid habitation; we got jumped by rejects from another remake of *Land of the Lost*. We kicked ass, we ran away. End of story.

When I was done, I paused, waiting for someone to say something. No one did. Finally, I asked, "Well?"

"I have no idea what those are," said Mom.

"I'll check my books," said Dad.

"You got to have a subterranean grudge match with lizard-people, and I had to spend the day cleaning the library," said Antimony. "Some people get all the luck."

"Yeah, well," I said. "So that's the status. Are we agreed that I don't currently need backup?"

"No," said Dad. "You absolutely need backup. But . . ." He hesitated before saying, reluctantly, "We're agreed that we can't send any. Not right now. I want you to check in every day. The same goes for Sarah. If either of you fails to do so—"

"Cry havoc and let slip the dogs of war," I finished grimly. "I get the picture. I just know that if that dragon wakes up, we're going to have a serious problem on our hands, and it's best if we keep the number of us available for damage control as high as possible."

"I wish I didn't agree with you," said Mom.

"Oh, trust me, Mom," I said, sitting up and looking

out the bedroom window to the city beyond. The city that I was responsible for protecting, and that was dangerously close to becoming the setting for the first real-world *Godzilla* flick in the past several hundred years. I sighed. "So do I."

Fifteen

"There's nothing wrong with making a last
stand. Just make sure you bring enough
grenades to share with the entire class."

–Alice Healy

Still in that semilegal sublet in Greenwich Village

GETTING MY FAMILY OFF THE PHONE was simplified
when Dad got an email from Uncle Ted. Uncle Ted
was following reports of a basilisk sighting off I-5, and
really wanted some backup. (Basilisks are no laughing
matter. Not unless your idea of "funny story" involves
the phrase "and then the lizard turned my wife to
stone.") After delivering a few more hurried admonish-
ments about checking in and not letting myself end up
alone in a room with Dominic, Dad hung up. Mom and
Antimony were right behind him—the last thing I heard
was Antimony shouting, "Just let me get my crossbow!"
before blessed silence descended.

Well, blessed silence aside from the horns honking in
the street outside, the pigeons on my windowsill, and the
distant, ecstatic cheering of the mice. I wasn't feeling
picky. My family was staying in Oregon, and I had the
possible dragon all to myself.

I paused in the act of plugging my phone into the
charger. I had the possible dragon all to myself. Per-
versely appealing as that thought was, it also wasn't fair.

If there was even the slightest chance that the dragons weren't extinct, there were some people who needed to know about it.

The dragon princesses.

I wasn't actually scheduled to work until the next day. My job at Dave's Fish and Strips may be about as intellectually taxing as watching paint dry, but it's still exhausting, and I always try to take the days on either side of a major dance competition off. It's safer that way, and reduces the odds of my becoming so tired that I lose my ability to deal with idiots. Knocking someone's teeth out because they didn't tip well is not a swift route to job security.

After a quick shower and an unhealthy meal of leftover pizza, spray cheese, and corn chips, I changed into clean clothes, put on a new pair of running shoes, packed a few replacement throwing knives, and jumped out the kitchen window. The pigeons were getting used to me. There were a few ruffled feathers, and I got my share of irritated looks, but none of them actually took flight as I plummeted past them, grabbed the fire escape rail, and slung myself across the courtyard. It's amazing how quickly and completely the natural world can adjust. People forget that pigeons aren't hatched from cracks on the sidewalk; they're wild birds that have simply learned to exist in symbiosis with the human race. Their adaptation is proof that it can be done. We should applaud the pigeon as a survivalist totem, not call them "rats with wings" and shoo them off our windowsills.

The muscles in my thighs and shoulders loosened up as I ran, finding a rhythm that allowed me to compensate for the lingering stiffness in my left knee. My injuries hadn't been as bad as they could have been. The bruises didn't even slow me down much, although I felt them every time my heels made impact. I really hit my stride about halfway to Dave's, and finished the journey at full-speed, almost laughing from the sheer joy of feeling the wind against my face and the city beneath my feet. I felt like one of those spandex-wearing superheroes in the comic books that Sarah and Antimony swap back and forth when they think the rest of us aren't looking. I felt like I could fly.

Even Superman has to land eventually, even if it's just to talk to somebody who doesn't have super powers. I started slowing down as I got closer to Dave's, dumping speed by throwing needless tricks into my progress, so it would be less jarring when I finally touched down. I finished with a half-cartwheel that left me in a crouch, the remains of my inertia bleeding out through the sole of my right foot. I glanced at my watch. Decent speed, especially considering my injuries.

"Guess I'm going to live after all," I said, and straightened. Dust from the rooftops clung to my jeans and the palms of my hands. I took a moment to dust myself off before walking over to the rooftop door, testing the knob, and—upon finding it unlocked—letting myself inside.

The dressing room was deserted except for Carol, who was engaged in her usual mortal combat against her own hair. The tiny snakes covering her head writhed and snapped at her fingers, dodging frantically in their efforts to avoid the wig she was trying to clamp down over them. I couldn't entirely blame them. My hair was always sticky with sweat and matted in weird patterns when I had to wear my Valerie wig for any length of time, and my hair isn't independently alive. I knocked on the doorframe. She looked up, turning her head fast enough to give her bangs the opportunity to sink their fangs into her thumb. They did so, with gusto.

"Ow!" yelped Carol, dropping her wig and shoving

her injured thumb into her mouth, going cross-eyed with the effort of glaring at her own hair. The snakes, sensing danger, promptly withdrew into hissing clusters. "'toopid 'air," Carol mumbled around her thumb.

I winced. "Sorry about that. Are you going to be okay?" A lesser gorgon like Carol can't actually turn people to stone—their gaze doesn't work on anything much larger than a guinea pig—but that doesn't make them harmless. The bite of their serpentine hair (and yes, I realize exactly how that sounds) can kill.

Carol shook her head, pulling her thumb out of her mouth. She squinted at the rows of tiny puncture wounds. "We're immune to our own venom," she said, matter-of-factly. "Hi, Verity. I thought you weren't on duty tonight."

"I'm not. I'm here to see Candy—is she here?"

That got Carol's attention. She turned to blink at me, even her hair standing at attention and directing all of its several hundred eyes in my direction. "Seriously? Is this one of those 'if I tell you where to find her, you'll walk out of here with her head in a bag' situations? Because I don't like Candy very much, but I'm still pretty sure I'm not allowed to sell her up the river."

I rolled my eyes. "Gee, Carol, way to tell me what you really think of my loyalties. I don't want to hurt her. I don't even particularly want to call her nasty names. I just want to talk to her. So is she on duty or not?"

"Sorry. It's just, well . . . if anyone around here could inspire you to homicide, it would be Candy, right?" Carol shrugged, looking sheepish. "Yes, she's on duty. She should be taking her break soon, if you just wanted to wait here. You're not exactly, um, what Dave would call 'projecting a professional image' right now."

"You mean I don't look like a Playboy Bunny? My poor heart breaks." I walked over to perch on the edge of the dressing table, turning to peer at myself in the mirror. I was developing a pretty nice shiner around my right eye—I didn't even remember getting hit there—

and one of the only really visible scrapes ran down the same cheek. I looked like I'd been letting my boyfriend beat me up for fun. "You should've seen the other guy," I muttered.

"What?"

"Never mind." I hoisted myself up to perch on the makeup counter, careful to stay out of range of Carol's hair. "So what's been going on around here for the last couple of days? I am experiencing a drought of gossip, and demand the sweet rain of information."

"Well," said Carol, as she picked up her wig and resumed her efforts to stuff her hissing hair beneath it, "Kitty called from the road, and it turns out her boyfriend's band isn't doing quite as well as she expected, which *I* don't think is surprising in the least, but she, of course, thought they'd be the next big thing. Anyway—"

I leaned back against the mirror, listening to Carol talk, careful to nod at the right places and make the correct exclamations of surprise when prompted. Bit by bit, she coaxed her snakes under the wig, settling them one row at a time, like a general trying to control the world's most disobedient army. "You should get a beehive wig," I said, without really thinking about it. "One of those huge bouffant hairstyles. Then you could just hollow out the center, so you wouldn't have to squash your snakes when you put it on."

Carol's hands froze, eyes going wide and startled. "I never even thought of that!" she said. "Big hair is in again, isn't it?"

"Not quite *that* big—" I protested, but it was too late; the seed was planted. Carol resumed stuffing snakes beneath her wig, smiling bright as sunshine.

"I'll go to the wig shop after my shift. Thanks, Verity. You're the best."

"You're, uh, welcome," I said, unable to keep myself from thinking of those old urban legends about girls whose beehive hairdos turned out to be full of spiders, or earwigs, or other horrible things. How long before "and her hair was full of *venomous snakes*" joined the roster?

Oh, well. If you can't actually be an urban legend in your own right, I guess inspiring one is just about as good.

"Slumming in the bestiary again, Price?" asked a snide voice from the doorway. I glanced over. Candice was standing just inside the room, arms crossed defensively across her chest, model-pretty features drawn into a scowl. Her shoulders were set like she expected a fight. Maybe she did. I *had* told her the Covenant was in town not all that long before, and now here I was with another bombshell.

I slid off the counter, keeping my body language as open and nonthreatening as I could manage. "Hey, Candy," I said. "I actually came to talk to you, if you could give me a few minutes? It's sort of important."

Her eyes narrowed. "What could *you* possibly want to discuss with *me*?"

I glanced unobtrusively toward Carol, who was trying to look like she wasn't watching this little drama in the mirror. "It's sort of private. Would you mind coming up to the roof with me?"

"Why, so you can throw me off?" Candy demanded.

I bit the inside of my cheek and counted to ten before saying, very carefully, "I have no intention of throwing you off the roof, and if you'd rather we talk here, I'm perfectly willing. I just thought you might like to have the chance to decide whether or not to tell the Nest, rather than risking this getting into the rumor mill and reaching them some other way."

Carol rolled her eyes. "Thanks for putting such trust in my discretion."

"It's not you I'm worried about." I jerked a thumb toward the air vent. "You really think Dave doesn't have this place bugged?"

"Good point." Carol turned in her chair, half her

snakes still exposed and snapping fiercely at the wig. "Candy, go up to the roof with her. If you're not back down here in ten minutes, I'll get Ryan and come looking for you. Promise."

Candy still looked unsure. I sighed. "If you don't think my information was worth your time, I'll give you fifty dollars," I said, picturing my groceries for the week growing wings and flying away. I could always make do with leftovers stolen from the kitchen at Dave's. That was mostly what I'd been doing anyway.

"One hundred," countered Candy.

"A hundred—Candy, I make the same amount of money you do! Less, even, since you get better tips." She had an ice princess demeanor with a Playboy Bunny's looks. I'm no slouch in the looks department, but my tendency to break fingers that "accidentally" touch my ass means I don't tend to get the tables with the repeat customers.

"One hundred, or I don't go with you," said Candy, lifting her chin in an imperious gesture that telegraphed exactly how serious she was. Only the promise of money—all but irresistible to a dragon princess—was getting her to the rooftop, and fifty wasn't going to cut it.

I sighed. "One hundred, *if* you think my information isn't any good."

"Deal," said Candy, and unfolded her arms. Moving with quick efficiency, she untied her apron, placed it in her locker, and padlocked the whole thing, protecting her tips. She went through that ritual every time she took a break, and it had long since stopped being insulting; it was just another part of being who she was, a dragon princess surrounded by creatures that looked like her, but really belonged to another species altogether.

Sometimes I think evolution *really* didn't do the totally human-form cryptids any favors. It's so easy to forget that they aren't like the rest of us—geeky, like Sarah or Artie, or maybe a little spaced-out, like Uncle Ted, but still essentially just folks—and start judging them by human standards. You can't do that. It isn't fair.

"Ten minutes," said Candy sternly to Carol, and left the room, heading for the stairway to the roof.

Carol turned back to the mirror, her reflected lips mouthing the words "good luck" as she went back to stuffing snakes beneath her wig. I rolled my eyes beseechingly toward Heaven, and followed Candy out of the room.

Candy beat me to the roof by almost a minute—a minute I was sure she'd carefully deducted from my promised ten. She was more than ten feet from the door when I reached the top of the stairs. She raised her hand, saying sharply, "Stay there."

I raised an eyebrow, letting the door swing shut behind me. "You mean, stay here by the door?" Candy nodded. "You know, it's harder to keep secrets really secret when I have to shout them at you. Can you at least come a little bit closer?"

Candy narrowed her eyes. "How do I know you're not planning to throw me off this roof?"

I bit back the urge to groan. "Because if I was going to kill you, I'd just shoot you, okay? Gravity is *not* my weapon of choice. Look, the deal's off if you don't come close enough for me to tell you what I came here to tell you. So you'll have come up here for nothing."

That, at least, got through to her. Candy took several grudging steps forward, until she was still out of arm's reach, but at least close enough for me to talk to without shouting.

"Thank you," I said. Forcing my body language to remain as nonthreatening as possible, I asked, "Candice, have you *ever* heard anything—anything at all—to indicate that the dragons aren't really extinct?"

She reeled back as if I'd just hauled off and punched her in the face. When she focused again, it was to give me a look of such fury that *I* felt a little bit punched. "Is that why you brought me up here?" she demanded. "To make fun of me? What, cable isn't enough for you people, you have to find other ways to entertain yourselves? That's swell of you. That's just plain swell."

"Candy, we think we may have found a dragon."

She froze. Literally froze, dewy blue eyes gone so wide that I could see the whites all the way around her irises. I didn't think she was breathing.

"We weren't looking for it, exactly, but I have access to a telepath, and she says—"

"Where?" asked Candy. Her voice was barely a whisper, and mostly ripped away by the wind, but I recognized the shape of it on her lips. She took three long, runway-perfect steps forward and grabbed me by the shoulders, succeeding in shaking me twice before the surprise wore off and I pulled myself away. "Where? Don't you keep this from me, don't you *dare*, and if you're lying, I swear, if you're lying—"

"Candy, calm down!" I shook my head, holding up my hands defensively. "I only just found out, okay? I haven't been keeping anything from you. Anyway, we think there may be a dragon sleeping somewhere under the island, and we think it's connected to the recent disappearances."

Her eyes widened again—with anger, this time. "What, so you're blaming the dragon? Is that why you wanted to talk to me? You're looking for bait?"

"What? No! I'm blaming the disappearances on humans, some sort of snake cult, probably, trying to wake the dragon up the way they'd summon a snake god." I let my hands drop back down to my sides. "If there *is* a dragon, I want to protect it. I want to prove that it's not the source of the trouble we've been having recently. And I wanted the Nest to know as soon as possible, because this affects you."

"More than you know," she said bitterly. Shaking her head, she asked, "So what do you want from me?"

"I want you to go to the Nest. I want you to tell them what we've found, and that I'm trying to find a way for you to get to the dragon. If there's anything that might tell me where to start looking, anything at all, I need to know."

Candy studied my face, tilting her head slightly to the side as she asked, "Why should we tell you? Why shouldn't we just go looking on our own?"

"Two reasons. First off, if there's some sort of snake cult in town making virgin sacrifices, they probably already know how to get to the dragon. I'm sure they'd look at you and the Nest as a perfect virgin buffet."

Candy blanched. "And the second reason?"

"I went down into the sewers earlier today, looking for clues." I decided not to mention the fact that Dominic had gone down with me. That seemed like a little bit too much for Candy's nerves. "I got jumped by a bunch of lizard-dudes I'd never seen before. It was like *The Land of the Lost* down there. Unless you're sure they'd be happy to see you, you probably need some sort of—" I stopped midsentence. Candy had gone pale and started to shake, suddenly looking like she was on the verge of tears. "Candy? What's wrong?"

"There's a dragon," she whispered. "There's definitely a dragon, and somebody's hurting him. They have to be hurting him if they're making servitors. Oh, Verity!" My name came out as a wail, and she was suddenly doing something I would never have expected in my wildest dreams: she threw her arms around my shoulders, burying her face against my chest. "We have to find him!"

I patted her awkwardly on the back. "Don't worry," I said, as confidently as I could. "We will."

Apparently, "I may have found you a dragon" counted as big enough news that Candy didn't make me pay her for going up to the roof with me. Good thing, too—at a hundred dollars for ten minutes, I would have been borrowing money from Ryan just to pay off my debt to Candy. Never owe money to a dragon princess. Their interest rates are murder.

As for the pressing question of the night, namely— "What's a servitor?"—Candy was willing to answer it in detail. Too much detail. After providing a vivid installment of *Things I Never Wanted To Know Theater*, Candy promised to speak with the rest of the Nest about the dragon and call me with anything they knew, and went back inside to finish her shift. I watched her go, then went racing back across the rooftops to my apartment. Her surprise had been genuine—I was certain of that— and with what I'd just learned, I needed to check in sooner rather than later.

No one was picking up at the house. That wasn't a surprise, considering they'd left for the basilisk hunt not that long before, but I still said several words we're supposed to be careful about using in front of the mice as I hung up. General cheering greeted my profanity, along with a few ecstatic mentions of the Feast of Washing Out Mouths With Soap. I didn't have the energy to tell them to keep it down. If the mice wanted to have a party, let 'em. I had bigger—much, much bigger, as in "dragon-sized"—fish to fry.

I was sitting down at my computer, composing an email with everything I'd managed to learn so far (not nearly enough) when there was a knock at the apartment door. My head snapped up like a jackalope scenting a pack of coyotes. My presence in the apartment was, after all, technically illegal, since the original lease forbade subletting and the apartment's actual tenant was on extended vacation somewhere in Canada. I didn't exactly encourage things like "visitors," especially since a lot of the people who'd be coming to visit couldn't pass for human in a dark alley on a moonless night.

The knock came again. The mice gave a subdued cheer. "Hush!" I hissed, standing. "You get out of sight while I answer the door."

"But, Priestess, the Holy Feast—"

"Will be honored, *if* it's a man, and *if* I let him through the door," I said. "Now *hide*." The mice scattered, vanishing under furniture and into hidey-holes. Only a few pennants and some pigeon-bone accessories were left to show that they'd ever existed, and those could be excused as my having morbid taste in dolls. (Antimony did that once, taking a bunch of mouse-designed ceremonial gear to school as part of an art project she billed as "Barbie Meets Modern Primitive." She got an "A," and an appointment with the school counselor.)

The knocking came a third time. It was starting to sound impatient. "Shit," I hissed, giving the room a quick once-over for obvious weapons before shouting, "I'll be right there!" I triggered my screensaver—no point in giving some nosy neighbor an eyeful—and half-ran across the room, yanking open the door.

Dominic De Luca gave me a look that was half-exasperated, half-amused, and held up a large paper sack which smelled enticingly of fried chicken and the usual assortment of sides. "Before you begin shouting at me for having your address, I wish to note that I come bearing peace offerings, and am prepared to apologize for further intruding on your privacy. I simply thought we should speak, and I no longer trust you in coffee shops."

"Fair," I said, and grabbed his arm, hauling him into the apartment before shutting the door firmly behind him. "Sorry, I'm trying to avoid attracting the attention of the neighbors. Technically, I can't legally be here, so—"

The room erupted into cheers. Quite literally: with mice crammed into every cushion and hidden under every piece of furniture, it sounded like the apartment had suddenly been possessed by the spirit of Super Bowl Sunday. Dominic's head whipped around, eyes going wide. "What in God's name—?!"

"Oh, *crap*," I groaned, putting a hand over my face. "I should have expected this. I should have *known*, and spent the night at Sarah's or something. This is all my fault."

"Why is the apartment shouting at us?" Dominic groped for his belt, presumably to produce something he could use to attack the cheering, hostile . . . apartment. If he had a knife intended entirely for stabbing haunted sublets, I didn't want to know about it. I uncovered my face and clamped my hand down over his, holding him in place. He gave me a startled look.

"I'm really, really sorry about this, but it's the Holy Feast, and it's just not going to stop until I do this, so please don't take things the wrong way, okay?" He was still looking completely baffled. "Oh, to hell with explaining." Stepping into his personal space, I leaned up, and kissed him for the second time.

The cheers got even louder. But after a few seconds, I don't think either of us was listening to the mice.

Dominic tensed for an instant before he was kissing me back, all the urgency I'd sensed in him earlier returning, and joined by a strange sort of relaxation, like he'd come to terms with the reality that I was kissing him. Things got good faster this time; he wasn't holding back. With one hand pinned under mine, and the other filled with fried chicken, it wasn't like he could exactly put his arms around me, so he turned us around instead, pinning me up against the wall beside the door. It didn't feel like being trapped. It felt like an embrace, one that couldn't use the standard materials, and so had to find a way to improvise. I like a man who knows how to think on his feet.

Our first kiss ended when he pushed me away. This time, there was no pushing. He leaned into me, and I strained to press myself more solidly against him. Dominic made a small growling noise in the back of his throat, clearly frustrated by the unavailability of his hands. The cheers were tapering off, and my hormones were starting to go insane. Right. If I was going to get the situation—and myself—back under control, this was the time to do it. Right now. Not in five minutes, despite the fascinating thing Dominic was doing with his tongue. Right *now*.

Pulling back with a gasp, I looked into Dominic's eyes, seeing my own thin control reflected there, and gasped, "You just walked in on the Holy Feast of I Swear, Daddy, I'll Kiss the Next Man That Walks Through That Door. It was the only way to make them stop."

He blinked.

"Seriously."

Dominic blinked again. Seeming to realize that the cheering had faded, he stepped back, letting me move away from the wall. "They . . . who?" he asked blankly.

"My resident colony of Aeslin mice." Sensing that the mood was irreparably broken, I took the bag of chicken from Dominic's hand and called, "You can come out now!"

"HAIL!" replied the mice, popping into view from places all over the room. It looked like a bad special effect on a Jim Henson TV show, and I'm used to them. It's really no surprise that Dominic jumped, eyes going enormously wide in his suddenly-pale face.

"Your apartment is full of talking rodents," he said, like this was somehow going to be a surprise to me.

"Yes," I said.

"Your apartment is full of talking rodents, and you just kissed me again."

It seemed safest to keep agreeing with him. "Yes."

Dominic nodded slowly. "All right. You mentioned a . . . Holy Feast of some sort? Was that the motivation behind . . . ?"

"Yes. I mean, no. I mean . . . chicken?" I held up the bag, forcing a smile that probably looked more like the painted grin of a crazy clown. "Come on. Kitchen's this way."

Of course, my kitchen was so small that there was no chance we could sit down. Even eating standing up at the counters wouldn't work, unless we wanted to eat with our backs to one another. Somehow, I didn't think that was going to reduce the tension between us.

The living room was out, unless I wanted to risk getting chicken grease all over my costume rack. The bathroom might work, if one of us sat on the edge of the shower stall, and the other sat on—no, the bathroom was out. That really left only one option, and given the Holy Feast we'd just been celebrating—given how much I'd really *enjoyed* the celebration—I wasn't sure it was a good idea.

Dominic stopped in the kitchen doorway, looking first at the tiny room, and then at me. He didn't say anything. He didn't have to. I opened a cabinet, producing a pair of plates, and offered him another overly-strained smile. "This may sound a little weird, but I think we're going to have to eat in the bedroom. That's the only place in this apartment with enough space for us both to actually sit down and eat."

"Is that so?" Dominic raised an eyebrow, looking very marginally amused. "Are you sure this is not the second stage of your rodent-inspired 'Holy Feast'?"

"Yes." I nodded so vigorously it felt like my head was at risk of coming off. "That's a different celebration."

Dominic blinked. "You are very, very strange," he said, after a long pause. He reached out to take the plates from me and then stepped back out of the kitchen doorway, allowing me to lead the way to the bedroom. I scanned constantly as we walked, looking for anything that would cause me to die of embarrassment. So far, I wasn't seeing anything. There was a quiver of arrows leaning against the hallway wall—no big deal—and I'd left a hand ax out on my dresser. Sloppy, but still not a problem. I was more worried about the important things, like dirty underpants left out on the floor.

The fates were with me; all my delicates were safely out of view in the laundry hamper. I breathed a sigh of relief, setting the sack of greasy goodness on the edge of the bed. Having the blankets dry cleaned would cost a lot less than doing the same for my costume rack. I sat down on one side of the sack of chicken, motioning for Dominic to sit down on the other side. Safely distanced by calories and cholesterol, Dominic sat, passing me a plate as he did. I smiled wanly.

"So, dinner," I said, leaning over to open the sack. "That was very sweet of you."

"It seemed like the least I could do, given the circumstances." Dominic reached into the fried chicken bag, pulling out a container of mashed potatoes and setting it delicately on the bed. "I wasn't sure what the appropriate 'I'm sorry I took you into the sewers without proper preparation and got you beaten up by lizard-men' gift was."

"Brass ammunition or an anti-incubus charm," I said automatically. Then I paused. "Er . . ."

"You really are the *strangest* woman I have ever met." Dominic sounded almost admiring. "Now, will you please explain the talking rodents, and how their religious observations led to you accosting me in your front hallway? I'm still trying to decide whether or not to feel taken advantage of."

"They're Aeslin mice." I pulled the chicken bucket out of the bag, selecting a breast and a thigh before offering it to him. "Religious observations are sort of what they do."

"I've heard of them, but I've never actually encountered them before." Dominic glanced speculatively toward the door back to the hall. "They're cryptids, aren't they? Of a somewhat more diminutive variety than those we generally find ourselves opposing?"

"I try to avoid opposing cryptids of any size, but yes, they're a type of cryptid. A very religious-minded type of cryptid. They've been living with my family for generations—since before we left the Covenant." I started peeling the skin delicately off my chicken. "One of my multiple-great-grandmothers found them, and she just couldn't bring herself to kill them, so she brought them home."

"Maybe that was part of what made it so easy for your family to leave," said Dominic. I shot him a speculative look. He shrugged. "They had already deviated from the laws."

"Maybe so, but . . . it still wasn't easy." I looked down at my chicken. It was easier than looking at him. "I've read the diaries. We all have. It was a big decision, both times that it happened. For my great-great-grandparents, and then again for my grandfather. I mean, it was *hard* on them. They were turning their backs on everything they'd ever known, because they'd decided there was something that mattered more than doing what they'd been taught to do. Hell, what they'd been *raised* to do. This wasn't a choice they made on a whim. This was everything to them."

Dominic's hand touched my knee almost tentatively. I raised my head, looking at him warily. He met my eyes, expression grave, and said, "I understand loyalties being called into question. I may not fully understand the choices they've made, but . . . I understand what could have inspired those choices."

"Hey. Baby steps." I smiled a little, and took a bite of chicken. It tasted amazing, possibly because I hadn't eaten a decent meal in days, and combat burns a *lot* of calories. Lucky for me, Dominic was in a similar state, or the speed with which I inhaled both pieces on my plate might have convinced him that I was some sort of cryptid. Never a good conviction to inspire in a Covenant member, unless you feel like having an ash-wood stake driven through your chest.

"I always wondered what had caused your ancestors to throw their lives away like that," said Dominic, attention apparently going to his chicken. He didn't look at me as he continued, "It seemed a particularly arrogant means of committing suicide."

I didn't say anything. I just waited.

"The teachings of the Covenant are what allowed mankind to survive, once, when competition for resources was stiffer—when sometimes we *were* the resources in question. Without the willingness to kill, we could never have lived long enough to develop the capacity for mercy."

"That's probably true," I allowed. "I think we have that capacity now, though."

"Do we?" Dominic looked at me. "Sometimes I wonder."

"Maybe wondering is enough."

"Maybe so."

We ate in silence for a few minutes after that, broken only when I asked him to pass a biscuit. Finally, Dominic set his plate (with its associated chicken-bone graveyard) aside, touching my knee with the fingers of one hand. He was less tentative this time.

"You kissed me once to prove a point," he said. "Then you kissed me again to honor a rodent religious ritual."

"It was the only way to make them stop celebrating," I protested.

"Indeed." Looking at me thoughtfully, he asked, "What would it take to get you to kiss me a third time, do you think?"

My heart didn't literally stop, but for a moment, it sure as hell felt like it had. I coughed a little, getting my cardiac rhythm back on track, and managed to say, "Well, I guess you kissing me once might be a decent way to start."

"And after that?"

"Well, after that, I'd say the odds of my kissing you again would go way, way up." Suddenly, the brown paper sack didn't seem like nearly enough of a barrier between us. In medieval times, unmarried couples had to sleep with a sword between them to make sure they wouldn't get up to any funny business. About half of me wished I'd followed their example. The other half was joining the mice in cheering wildly. I gasped. "Oh, God, the mice!"

"What—?" Dominic stared after me, bewildered, as I grabbed the sack, jumped to my feet, and ran to the bedroom door.

"Bedroom privileges have been revoked for the remainder of the evening!" I shouted, chucking the chicken bag into the middle of the hallway, where it was immediately besieged on all sides by tiny, furry bodies. "I invoke the Sacred Law of Food for Privacy! Feast, and leave me alone!"

I slammed the door just in time to mute the cheering. Turning back to Dominic, I asked, "So, what were we talking about again?"

"I believe we had just reached the point of deciding that it was my move," he said, and stood, taking two long steps forward to my position. Cupping his hands around the sides of my face, he tilted my head up toward him, bent forward, and kissed me soundly.

Sixteen

"Something about those Covenant boys—
mmm. Maybe it's the trousers. Takes a certain class of man to carry off trousers cut
to hide that many weapons, and I always
find myself lost in thoughts of getting
those trousers off them."

–Enid Healy

*The mouse-free bedroom of a semilegal sublet in Greenwich
Village*

IF I'D THOUGHT DOMINIC'S KISSES in the alley were urgent, they were nothing compared to the five-alarm
fire motivating him now. He kissed me like all the oxygen was running out of the room, and the only way for
either of us to survive was to learn how to manage on a
single person's breath. I wasn't worried about him hurting me—with my training, that sort of concern is generally oriented in the other direction—but the knowledge
that he was one of the few men I'd ever met who *could*
take me in a fight was enough to make my knees go
weak. I matched his five-alarm fire with one of my own,
feeling the answering tension in his wrists as he tugged
me closer to him.

When he dropped his hands from my face and pulled
his own face away, it was like he'd just announced that
they were canceling Christmas. My eyes, which I didn't

remember closing, flew open, and I gave him a disappointed look, asking, "Did I do something wrong?"

"Did you—God, woman." He laughed, mumbling something in Italian. It sounded like it was directed at himself, so I decided not to take offense; I just kept making puppy-dog eyes at him, waiting for him to tell me what was wrong. "You are the most insane, insufferable, infuriating excuse for a female that I have ever met."

"Well, yeah," I said, blinking. "You knew that before you brought me chicken. Are you mad that I gave your chicken to the mice? Do I need to get more chicken before you'll start kissing me again? Because I can go and buy more chicken if you'll just promise to wait he—" He cut my protests off with another kiss. I've never much cared for being interrupted, but if all the interruptions were going to be of this caliber, I could probably learn to live with it.

Since Dominic's hands weren't setting the terms of our dance anymore, I stepped closer, leaving no space for air between us as I pressed myself against his chest. His arms went around my waist, reeling me in, and I gladly let my heels leave the floor. This kiss wasn't as urgent. It didn't need to be. It went on and on, until I began to wonder if it was possible to spontaneously combust just from kissing.

Dominic turned his head abruptly to the side, but didn't let me go. "This is . . . I shouldn't be . . ."

"Oh, you should." I nodded vigorously, sliding my hands down the planes of his shoulders, feeling the interplay of the muscles there. He was muscled almost like a dancer, all long, hard sinew and corded strength. A lifetime of training to fight for your life will do wonders for the physique. "You really, really should. It's actually recommended for solo Covenant agents on their first trip to North America. See the sights, stalk the locals, sleep with a Price girl."

"You infuriating creature," he breathed, somehow turning the words into something verging on an endearment. He turned back to face me, letting me see the barely-restrained hunger in his dark brown eyes. He was looking at me the way the mice look at cake on a feasting day; like devouring me wouldn't just be a pleasure, it would be a holy ritual. "Do you have any idea what you're doing?"

"I do," I said, and leaned forward to place a kiss on his chin before he had the chance to pull away. "I am an adult, and you are an adult, and I am doing my damnedest to seduce you right now, or to convince you that it's worth the trouble of seducing me. Dealer's choice. Just don't tease me."

He barked a short, sharp laugh. "Tease *you*? Me, tease *you*? I'm not the one who runs across this city's rooftops wearing a skirt barely deserving of the name, or fights like it was some sort of ballet routine."

"My grand jeté kills 'em back on the farm," I said solemnly. Then he was kissing me again, arms pulling me into his chest until there really wasn't any room between us, not for hesitation, not for *anything*. The pressure of my thigh holster digging into my skin was just a delicious reminder of how close we really were, how close I was to feeling his body moving naked against mine, and, oh, God, if the Covenant taught all their field agents to kiss like this, it was a wonder they ever made it from the bedroom to the battlefield in the first place.

Dominic gave a small growl of frustration as he realized that he couldn't possibly get me any closer to him. Not changing his grip on my waist at all, he lifted me off the ground, turning toward the bed. A lifetime spent learning how to negotiate difficult lifts with a partner made my next motion automatic, as I brought my legs up and wrapped them around his waist, eking out another half inch of closeness even as he was turning us toward the bed. Through the haze of rising hormones and distractingly searing kisses, the small part of my brain that was still on duty managed to identify two throwing knives and a strapped-on vial of what was probably more holy water. That just made me kiss him with more fervency. There's nothing in this world sexier than a man who comes prepared.

Rather than attempt to loosen my limpet-like hold, Dominic sat down on the bed's edge, hands starting to explore the unfamiliar territory of my body. It only took him a moment to get my shirt worked loose from the waistband of my jeans, and then his fingers were underneath it, running up my sides and sending shivers through my entire body. I broke off our kiss and unclasped my arms from his shoulders long enough for him to pull my shirt off over my head. Then I leaned back and watched him, waiting. He'd already seen me mostly naked, after the tango competition he so rudely disrupted. But this, here, with me wrapped tight around him and his breath coming in short, hard gasps . . . this was different. I knew his body wanted this as badly as mine did; even if he'd wanted to *lie*, my position, settled firmly in his lap, would have made that impossible. I just wanted him to have one last chance to change his mind.

Eyes solemn, Dominic touched my collarbone with the tips of his fingers, watching as my back arched involuntarily. His eyes remained on my face as his fingers glided down, over the top of my left breast, along the shallow divide of my breastbone to my stomach. They brushed across my navel, finally coming to rest at the waistband of my jeans.

"I am assuming," he said, words tight, like he was almost out of breath, "that this is you giving me one last opportunity to come to my senses?"

I didn't trust myself to speak. I just nodded, my hands still lowered, trying not to move too much. In his position—in my position—that wouldn't have been fair.

Dominic smiled, the expression lighting up his entire face. "You foolish creature," he breathed. "I have gone well past the point of such an easy escape." And then his arms were around me again, and my arms around him, and we were falling, but that didn't matter: the bed was there to catch us as our hands began the fevered, frantic removal of clothing, weaponry, and barriers. We were on different sides of this war. One of us might have to die before this ended. But in that moment, with him whispering in Italian in my ear and my every nerve on fire, there were no more boundaries between us.

The intoxicatingly mingled scents of sex and sweat perfumed the bedroom air, making me want to fight an army, dance a tango, and take a long nap, not necessarily in that order. Clothing and weapons littered the floor around the bed, making it look like we'd already fought an army. If we had, I wasn't entirely sure which one of us had won.

Dominic lay on his back, breath still a little uneven. I was stretched out at a slight diagonal, so that I could pillow my head against his chest while still dangling my feet off the edge of the bed. Rotating my ankles while I reclined helped to keep them from stiffening up, especially after the day I'd had. I'd have to rewrap them before I left the apartment again.

Lizard-men, rooftop marathons, overemotional dragon princesses, and to cap it all off, sheet-scorching sex with a member of the Covenant of St. George. This was going to be a fun one to try writing up for the family record. Maybe I could file it under "diplomatic relations" or something . . .

"So," I said finally. "Did you come over for a reason? Beyond the delivery of dinner and ravishment?"

"Insufferable," said Dominic. This sounded even more like an endearment than "infuriating" had. "I was coming to let you know that I checked what records I can access without drawing too much attention, and there was nothing definitive on the nature of the creatures that attacked us. Rumors and legends of manlike reptiles, but nothing coherent."

"Oh, Hells!" I sat bolt upright, heedless of the fact that I was clothed in nothing but the sheet—and, by the time I finished sitting up, not even that. "I got so wrapped up in the Holy Feast and the chicken dinner and the . . . well, and everything, I didn't get around to telling you. I know what they were. Are. I know what the things that attacked us in the sewer are, and there are going to be more of them if we don't find out who's messing with the dragon."

Dominic pushed himself onto his elbows, eyeing me with a mixture of surprise and irritation. "You didn't think to say this before? What are they? Why are there going to be more? Are they breeding down there?"

"I was distracted! You're *extremely* distracting." The sight of him shirtless in my borrowed bed was enough to start distracting me all over again. The desire to throw myself at him and beg him to have his way with me a few more times before we had to worry about the dragon wasn't really a surprise, but it was definitely inconvenient. "Anyway, I spoke to a representative from the local Nest of dragon princesses." Catching the shift in his expression, I hastened to add, "She wasn't aware that there was even a chance that there might be a living dragon around here. She was honestly surprised when I brought it up, and I don't think she's a good enough actress to fake something like that. I'm a performer. We know how to judge our own kind."

The brief darkness cleared from Dominic's eyes, and he nodded, saying crisply, "Proceed."

"So you know, the military precision thing, really not nearly as effective when you're starkers. Anyway, I told her about the lizard-men in the sewer and she flipped out, big-time. She says they're called 'servitors.' They exist to serve the dragon—or, if the dragon isn't in a position to be giving orders, say, because it's still in the middle of nap hour, to serve whoever's giving them the clearest instructions. They're not very smart, but they take directions real well."

Dominic frowned, a line appearing in the center of his forehead. I had to fight off the urge to lean over and kiss it away. Bad Verity. No Covenant hottie for you. "Why don't we have any clear records on these 'servitors'? You'd think *we'd* at least have something on them." The unspoken "even if you don't" hung between us for a moment before he turned his face away, looking faintly ashamed.

I cleared my throat to break the sudden tension, and asked, "What do your records say about the dragon princesses?"

"They're inconsequential; as harmless as any cryptid can be. They look human, from the outside, although their anatomy reveals certain . . . inconsistencies . . . if examined in detail." He didn't look back at me as he spoke. He probably had a good idea of my reaction to the idea of cutting up something he'd just admitted was harmless to see how it worked. "They may have served as bait for the dragons, once. It was never conclusively proven, one way or the other."

"And then there were no more dragons, and they just sort of vanished into the human population. You can't hunt what you can't find. They fell off the radar and stopped being a going concern," I said, concluding his little history lesson.

Dominic nodded mutely.

"Okay, so here's one of the pieces we've been missing all this time. The reason alchemists were always so damn hot to get their hands on dragon blood? It's a natural mutagen. I mean, we're talking some *Teenage Mutant Ninja Turtles*-level crap here." Dominic turned, giving me a blank look. I sighed. "Dragon blood alters human DNA if it's ingested. That's why people disappeared when they got too close to a dragon's lair. If the dragon caught them, and if they were too much of a danger to release, it . . . changed them. That way it didn't have to kill them, but they couldn't go running off to tell the local villagers where the lair was."

A look of slow horror swept over Dominic's face, washing away all the regret and understanding—and yes, the affection—as it passed. "You're saying that those creatures we fought . . . those creatures used to be *men*?"

"Yes, but the dragon's still sleeping. I mean, the dragon's not the one that's doing this. Whatever fucked-up snake cult is trying to wake the dragon up—almost certainly a *human* snake cult, snake cults are pretty much always human, the assholes—they're the ones feeding dragon blood to humans. They're the ones creating servitors, and telling them where to go, what to do. The dragon's just sleeping. It isn't doing anything wrong."

"Its existence is wrong," Dominic spat, sliding out of the bed. I'd been too busy before to really appreciate the symmetry of his naked body, scars and all. He was gorgeous, possibly the most gorgeous man I'd ever had the pleasure of having my way with.

Pity he was turning out to be a total asshole.

I straightened, locking my shoulders like I was preparing to tango for my life, and glared at him. The power of my glare was somewhat diminished by the fact that I wasn't wearing a stitch of clothing. Fortunately, I've had a lot of practice looking fierce while practically nude; this was just taking it to the championship level. "Its *existence* is the result of evolutionary pressures, the same as yours. Or do you want to start the argument against humanity? Because right now, you're offering one hell of an example in the 'negatives' column."

"You don't understand what you're talking about!"

If he'd wanted to make me mad, that was the way to do it. "Why? Because I didn't have the benefit of all your precious Covenant training? Your resources? Your centuries of doing it all exactly the same way every time?"

"Yes!"

"Even when the way you've been doing it is *wrong*?" My voice peaked on the last word, nearly breaking.

Dominic looked at me impassively, somehow managing to look dignified, even though he was just as naked as I was. In that moment, I realized how different we really were. We could fight together, we could bleed together, but in the end, he would always be Covenant, raised to view anything that wasn't human as a danger to be exterminated, while I . . .

I would always be a Price. Nothing I could ever do in my life, from ballroom dancing to poorly-considered trysts with cute Covenant men, was going to change that. His monsters were my family, and that was a chasm I didn't think either of us was capable of bridging.

He must have seen the same reality reflected in my expression. Something that looked like regret flickered in his eyes before he turned his back on me, bending to begin gathering his discarded weaponry. "This was a mistake," he said quietly. "This should not have happened."

I was glad he was facing away from me. It kept him from seeing the way I flinched when his words struck home. "As long as we're in agreement about that," I said, keeping my shoulders locked and my chin lifted. All I had to do was pretend that it was another competition, another stupid cattle call where I had to keep that brave face turned toward the audience until the winners were announced. "Sometimes things can get a little confused after a big fight. You make decisions you didn't actually intend to make, and then you can't take them back."

"Yes, I suppose that's true," said Dominic, grabbing his trousers and pulling them roughly on before he turned to face me again. "I appreciate your assistance in obtaining more information regarding this threat, and apologize if I have misled you in any way."

"Oh, is *that* what the boys are calling it these days?" I regretted the jeering tone of my words as soon as they were out of my mouth, but there was no way to call them back. Maybe it was better that way. It's not like the women of my family can exactly be said to respond reasonably when men from the Covenant get involved, and it was becoming increasingly clear what the math of this situation really was: Dominic, or the dragon. My survival wasn't really part of the primary equation, as Sarah would have said.

There was just no way all three of us were walking out of this alive.

Dominic yanked his shirt on, barely covering the holster buckled around his waist. "I believe we're done here."

"I believe you're right." I grabbed the sheet, wrapping it around myself with as much dignity as I could muster before marching to the bedroom door and wrenching it open. Dominic gave me a withering look and stalked out into the hall, only to be confronted with a sea of silent Aeslin mice watching him with black, unblinking oil-drop eyes. He stopped dead, staring back.

I stepped out of the bedroom behind him, and sighed. "Tell the mice you're leaving now, Dominic. It's the only way to make them go away."

"How do I . . . ?" He waved his hands helplessly.

The icy core of anger in my chest thawed a little. It was impossible to give serious thought to pitching him out the kitchen window when he was so clearly baffled by the mice. Still tempting, just less so. "They speak English. Tell them you're leaving."

"Ah." He cleared his throat before addressing the rodent throng: "I will be going now. Thank you for your hospitality."

"At least the man can be polite to my mice," I muttered, pushing past him to the front door as the mice scampered back to their business, only the occasional cry of "Hail!" marking their retreat. I paused with my hand on the doorknob, a thought striking me. "By the way, I realize that Aeslin mice may not fit your high standards for what does or does not 'deserve' to live, but I swear, if you come back here, if you hurt them—"

"Insufferable woman," said Dominic, tiredly. "I won't hurt your damned demon mice." He put his hand over mine. For a brief instant, the contact made me forget how furious I was with him as sense memories of his body moving against mine threatened to overwhelm me. Then he clamped his fingers down, turning my hand and the knob at the same time, yanked the door open, and was gone, storming down the hallway while I stared after him.

After a moment, I realized I was standing in the apartment doorway wearing nothing but a sheet. Not exactly the sort of display I wanted to present to the neighbors I wasn't supposed to have. I slammed the door, locking the deadbolt before spinning to press my back against the wood, like that was somehow going to be the final barricade to keep him out if he wanted to come storming back. He knew where I lived. A member of the Covenant knew where I *lived*. Worse, I'd just had *sex* with him, and now I was probably going to have to defend the last dragon in the world from him. I sank slowly into a sitting position, my knees pressing up against my chest.

"Look on the bright side, Verity," I said sternly. "There is no possible way this night can get any worse."

"*LET THE CELEBRATION OF THE HOLY FEAST OF KISSING THE NEXT MAN WHO WALKS THROUGH THAT DOOR COMMENCE!*" shouted the mice, with the utter glee that normally signaled the beginning of a multi-hour religious ritual.

I groaned, dropping my head forward so that my forehead rested against my knees. "My mistake," I muttered. "It can *always* get worse."

All around me, the mice exulted.

Seventeen

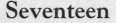

"We all make mistakes. Luckily for us,
there are very few mistakes that can't be
solved with a suitable application of either
lipstick or hand grenades."

–Frances Brown

The penthouse of the Plaza Athenee, sometime around midnight

"THANKS AGAIN FOR LETTING ME STAY." I sank a little deeper into the overstuffed couch, pulling my knees toward my chest. A chenille bedspread was wrapped around my shoulders, and Sarah had even managed to produce a pair of pajamas in my size. They were cute, if you liked blue silk with sushi prints. Given that Sarah is six inches taller than I am and rarely wears anything with a pattern, I wasn't sure where they'd come from, and I didn't want to ask. There was too good a chance that her reply would involve the room's previous occupants, who might not have had the opportunity to pack their things before they were evicted.

Sometimes having a cuckoo for a cousin can be morally troubling. (To say nothing of having a cuckoo for a grandmother. Although Grandma Baker's ability to get into anyplace she wanted just by walking through the front gates was pretty awesome when I was a kid and she took us all to Disney World. Mom says we don't need to feel guilty about that, since the park still owes the family for handling that whole bug-a-boo problem they had back in the eighties.) At the moment, I was just glad to have someplace to go that didn't involve a full-scale rodent bacchanal going on in the living room.

"It's no problem," said Sarah, walking back out of the penthouse kitchen with a pair of steaming mugs. "Here. Hot chocolate laced with brandy, just the way you like it."

"And getting me drunk guarantees I won't go running out and do something stupid, huh?" I wrapped my hands around the mug she handed me, breathing in the steam before taking a careful sip. She'd added the brandy with a generous hand. That, more than the temperature of the liquid, made it burn all the way down. "Oh, perfect."

"I figured you needed it, after the day you've had." Sarah settled into an armchair, curling her legs up under her body like a cat as she sipped from her own mug. I could smell its contents from where I sat, and hastened to take a larger gulp of my cocoa in order to cover up the scent. I like ketchup. I just don't think of it as a beverage, especially not heated and mixed with orange juice. Cuckoo biology is not for the faint of heart. "Did he really show up at your *apartment*? How did he find out where you live?"

"I don't know," I said glumly, staring into the muddy depths of my hot chocolate. If it contained the secrets of the future, it wasn't sharing them with me. "He's Covenant. Maybe they have some sort of magical tracking device."

"Or maybe he swiped your registration papers while he was invading the tango competition." Sarah took another sip of her ketchup, wiping her mouth delicately with the back of her hand. "Either way, it's not safe for you to go back there."

"So where am I supposed to go? I can't go back to Oregon until this whole dragon mess is sorted out."

Sarah shrugged. "So come stay with me. It's not like I don't have the room."

"That's a sweet offer, but what about the mice? I couldn't bring them here. I mean, even if you could convince the staff to ignore me, all it would take is one novice getting too enthusiastic and going on pilgrimage to the kitchen for cake, and then blammo. The hotel would call the Health Department so fast even you wouldn't be able to stop them."

"I know, but—"

"Plus, if I vanish, he could just come looking for me."

"See, that could be amusing." Sarah grinned a little. "He'll never find you here. We could watch him and take bets on his progress."

"You mean we could watch as he tracked down every cryptid he's encountered since he got here, looking for someone who could tell him where I was. Plus, if he hasn't told the Covenant about me yet, disappearing completely would be a surefire way to make him do it. He'd be sure I was going for reinforcements."

"What makes you think he hasn't told the Covenant about you?" asked Sarah, eyebrows rising. I glanced guiltily down into the recesses of my mug, and she gasped. "You *didn't*. Oh, no, you *did*. You so totally did!"

I looked back up to find her staring fixedly in my direction, eyes bleached a shade or two lighter than their normal arctic blue. I glared. "Hey! What happened to telepathic ethics?"

"Please, like those apply when you did *that* with a boy from the Covenant? Verity, that's disgusting!"

"Mmm . . . no, it wasn't." I couldn't quite prevent myself from smiling at the memory. "God, with a body like that? There was no possible way for it to be disgusting. A terrible idea, sure, but disgusting, no way. You should have seen him, Sarah. I mean, the guy is gorgeous."

"I did see him, remember? And our standards are a little bit different. You like the dark, brooding, on-the-wrong-side type, and I—"

"Like the geeky, frustrating, you-should-tell-him-already type. Yeah, I know."

Sarah didn't blush—her biology doesn't allow for it—but she did shoot me a mortified look before clearing her throat and saying, "So what are you going to do?"

"I'm not going to sleep with him again, for starters." No matter how much I wanted to. "First step is going to be swinging by Gingerbread Pudding to let Piyusha know that Dominic's decided to go off on his own. I'd rather she wasn't standing in the line of fire if he decides to start small with the cleanup. After that, I should go to the Nest, warn the dragon princesses that there's somebody—somebody *else*, I mean, beyond the snake cult that's making its own little army of happy homicidal lizard-men—somebody else out to hurt the dragon. And then I should go to work." I heaved a sigh, topping it with another mouthful of cocoa. "Dave isn't going to give me the night off just because I'm having boy troubles."

"Poor Verity," said Sarah, not without sympathy. "No wonder you're all stressed out. Why don't you go ahead and take the bedroom? You need to get some rest."

"What about you?"

"I have homework," she said, glancing into her mug of ketchup. I glanced at the clock. It was twenty minutes past midnight, which made it twenty past nine on the West Coast. Prime Internet chat time, if you happened to be a comic geek like Cousin Artie, or, say, a lonely mathematician like Sarah.

I smothered a smile as I stood, leaving the chenille bedspread and taking the hot cocoa. "Okay. You enjoy your homework, and I'll get out of your hair. Thanks again for letting me stay. I really couldn't handle another night of listening to the mice party down."

"Hey, what else is family for?"

"So true." I waited until I was halfway to the bedroom before calling back, casually, "Say 'hi' to Artie for me."

"I will," she replied thoughtlessly. I glanced over my shoulder just in time to see her wince. "Verity!"

"Good night!" I chirped, and giggled all the way to bed.

Sarah was gone when I woke up in the morning. She'd left a note on the coffee table, written in her usual semi-comprehensible scrawl:

> *V—*
> *Had to head for school or miss the start of the lecture session. Don't like eavesdropping on the thoughts of the other students just because I was too lazy to get to class in time to take my own notes. Order anything you want from room service, it all goes on my bill anyway. Love you lots, and please try not to get yourself killed today. Your parents would never forgive me.*
> *—S.*

I rolled up one silk sleeve, scratching at my elbow as I considered her note. Room service sounded good. A hot shower, a chance to fix my hair, and breakfast at Gingerbread Pudding sounded even better. I could talk to Piyusha, give her a little heads-up on the situation, and score some gingerbread to bring home to the mice as a peace offering. They didn't like it when I stayed out all night. Fortunately, their love was easily bought, and always for sale. And according to the clock, I had a little more than seven hours before I was expected at Dave's Fish and Strips—enough time to eat a leisurely breakfast, talk to Piyusha, check in with Dad, and change into a clean uniform before I had to go to work.

"No rest for the wicked," I said, and scribbled a quick "Gone out, thanks again, call you tonight" on the bottom of Sarah's note before heading for the penthouse bathroom. I might not be willing to take advantage of her room service, but the chance to shower in a full-sized tub? Oh, *Hell*, yes.

According to the hours in the window, Gingerbread Pudding was open from seven AM to nine PM every day. According to my watch, it was almost ten. So why were the doors still locked?

Usually, if I encountered a business that was closed during normal operating hours, I would assume they were having a private party or doing inventory or something. That might have been the case at Gingerbread Pudding. I just needed to talk to Piyusha too badly to take that chance. I'd already lost too much time by having a good night's sleep—even if I was pretty sure sleep was going to be in short supply from here on out. I rapped my knuckles briskly against the café door. No one came to let me in. I waited a few minutes before rapping again, harder this time.

The door creaked slowly open, revealing the narrow, anxious face of a man with a pronounced family resemblance to Piyusha. They had the same dark hair, and his features were practically a masculine version of hers. "Yes?" he asked suspiciously. The door creaked a bit farther open, letting me catch the sweet smell of honey and fresh ginger wafting from his skin. He gave me a quick up-and-down glance, assessing my jeans (designer) and burgundy halter top (silk, shamelessly "borrowed" from Sarah's closet) before reaching a decision, and saying, "I'm sorry. We're closed."

"Hi," I said, offering him the sweetest smile I could muster. "You must be one of Piyusha's brothers. I'm Verity. I realize you're probably busy, but this will only take a few minutes, and I really need to talk to her. Is there any way you could get her for me?"

The man's expression froze. "Verity Price?" he asked.

"Yeah," I said. "Piyusha may have mentioned that I dropped by—?"

"Yes, she did," he said, expression still not wavering. Opening the door fully, he stepped to one side and asked, "Won't you come inside?"

"Thanks." I stepped into the darkened café, flashing him another smile as I went. He didn't return it.

As soon as I was past the threshold an arm reached out from the space behind the door, locking itself around my neck and hauling me backward. It was surprising enough that I didn't fight immediately. I felt myself pressed against the chest of a second, shorter man. He smelled less like honey, and more like a mixture of cinnamon and ginger. That was something. At least if this turned into a serious fight, I'd know where to aim my kicks—even if I couldn't see to tell them apart, I'd be able to smell the difference.

The door swung shut. "Now," said the man who'd let me inside in the first place. "You're going to tell us what you've done with our sister."

Intelligent cryptids come in two major types: loners, like the cuckoos and the gorgons—most of whom would be perfectly happy if the rest of their species disappeared off the face of the planet—and the more social sorts, like the dragon princesses and Madhura. Social cryptids live and die by the concept of family. For many of them, that dependence on the company of their own kind is what has allowed them to survive into the modern era. That gives them a sense of family that would put my own to shame.

The Madhura with his arm hooked around my neck tightened it slightly, not quite choking me, but definitely making it a bit harder to breathe. I wasn't that worried. He was strong enough to be an inconvenience. That didn't mean he had the training necessary to hold onto me once I decided I was done being held. Strength is cheap. Technique is what really counts.

Keeping my chin up and my voice calm, I said, "I haven't done anything with Piyusha. Is there a reason you're assuming I did?"

"Hold her, Sunil," commanded the first man. Turning, he locked the door before walking toward me and my captor, the newly-identified Sunil. "You're Covenant. Why should we assume anyone else was responsible?"

"I'm terribly sorry to disappoint you but, not only am I not responsible for Piyusha going wherever it is she's gone, I'm not Covenant. I'm a Price."

"There's no such thing," said Sunil, breath hot against my ear. "They're a lie you Covenant bastards spread to make us think that some of you can be trusted. You fooled our sister. You won't fool us. We're nowhere so gullible."

I was starting to get annoyed. I focused on the man in front of me. Much as I wanted to start yelling at both of them—no one calls me Covenant and gets away with it—I needed to be reasonable as long as I could. "If you want to take my wallet out and check my driver's license, I promise you, it'll tell you that my name is Verity Price. And no woman has *ever* voluntarily carried fake ID with a picture that ugly. What happened to Piyusha?"

"That's what you're going to tell us," snapped the man in front of me, jabbing a finger at my chest. He didn't quite make contact.

Raising my eyebrows, I asked, "Is that the best you can do? Threaten to poke me? Wow, do you not have any talent for interrogation." I reached up with both hands—which neither of them seemed to have thought might need to be pinned—and grabbed Sunil's arm, twisting hard. He yelled. I yanked down. In a matter of seconds, I was free, and both Madhura were staring at me like I'd suddenly demonstrated the ability to walk through walls.

"I'm really not in the mood for games, and I have way bigger problems than the two of you," I said sternly, producing a throwing knife from inside my shirt and holding it at a defensive angle in front of me. It's normally a bad idea to be the first one to draw a weapon, but they had me outnumbered, and I needed to even the playing field a bit. "Does one of you want to tell me what you think I did, so we can clear this up, or do you just want to piss me off?"

"Our sister came home telling fairy tales about a Price woman and her friend from the Covenant," spat the taller of the two men, glaring. "Twelve hours later, she was gone. Do you really think we wouldn't put the pieces together?"

"Rochak, I think she's serious," said Sunil, frowning as he studied my expression. He shared the family resemblance, although his hair was a deep burnt-toast brown, rather than the black shared by his siblings, and his eyes were slightly lighter. He looked like the human incarnation of the Gingerbread Man. Assuming that you'd always pictured runaway pastry as a smoking-hot Indian dude in his mid-twenties. "No one looks that clueless when they're lying."

"Hey!" I yelped. "I'm blonde, but that doesn't make me a dumb blonde." I paused. "But I really am that clueless, at least right now. You're telling me that Piyusha is actually gone? As in, missing, disappeared like the others, didn't just cut out to see her boyfriend *gone*?"

"Yes," said Sunil, gravely. "She went out for groceries and she didn't come back. We tried calling her phone after an hour had passed. She didn't answer. We were concerned, and started looking for her. She . . . there were signs of a struggle."

"Blood?" I guessed. He nodded. "Are you sure it was hers? I mean, how could you tell?"

Sunil turned to Rochak, looking vindicated. "See? She's serious. This is not the one who hurt our sister."

"Why does this please you? It means we still have no

idea who *did*." Rochak scowled at his brother before looking at me and saying, flatly, "My apologies for the accusation. You must see why you would be a reasonable suspect."

"I do, but does someone want to tell me why you're suddenly willing to believe me?" I lowered my throwing knife. I didn't put it away. "Blood is blood, usually. Unless it's not."

"Our blood is not precisely like yours."

"Really?" I asked, with what must have seemed like a bit too much enthusiasm. They both gave me uneasy looks. I sighed. "I'm not going to cut you open to see what *your* interesting inside bits look like. I'm just curious."

Rochak said, uncomfortably, "Still, it is something we'd rather not discuss."

"Have it your way." I'd just have to let Dad know that the database entries on the Madhura needed to be updated to reflect undocumented physiological oddities. That's the trouble with not dissecting everything you meet: so much remains a mystery. "What time did she disappear?"

"She left for the store a little before ten o'clock last night," said Sunil. "We became concerned when she didn't come home or call by eleven."

I breathed out a silent sigh of relief. Dominic hadn't been responsible. He'd been at my house well before that, and he hadn't left until sometime after eleven-thirty. Piyusha probably wouldn't have shared my relief—whether she'd been taken by the Covenant or taken by crazy people who wanted to sacrifice her to a sleeping dragon, she'd still been taken—but at least I knew I hadn't led death to her front door. Not directly.

If I warned her brothers about Dominic, they might decide that I really had been responsible for Piyusha's disappearance. If I didn't, and he came back here on his own, they'd be completely unprepared. Either way, I was taking a risk.

Only one of those risks stood a chance of leading me to the dragon. If I didn't find the dragon before Dominic did, an entire species might go extinct. Mustering the most sincere "I'm here to help" expression I could, I asked, "Can you show me where you found the blood?"

Sunil and Rochak led me out the back door of the café and down the street to a tiny hole-in-the-wall bodega. There was a faded sign propped in the window, advertising a two-for-one sale on canned tomatoes, and a milk crate of sad-looking apples was doing double duty as a doorstop. "Here," said Sunil, indicating a reddish smear on the wall next to the bodega's window. It looked more like thickened sap than blood. I leaned closer, and the overpowering sweetness of it hit me. It was like pine resin mixed with molasses, with only the slightest hint of copper to confirm the mammalian origins of the one who'd lost it.

"We knew it was dangerous to let her go out alone, but she said she felt perfectly safe; she said nothing would touch her with a Price this close." The accusation in Rochak's eyes was impossible to bear. I focused my attention on the bloodstain instead, trying to pretend I knew anything about blood splatter analysis that hadn't been learned from watching reruns of *Dexter*. "I suppose she was incorrect."

"Guess so," I mumbled. Glancing to Sunil, I asked, "Did she make it into the bodega?"

He nodded. "The clerk said that she had been in and out right around ten. That she was in good spirits."

Neither one of us was going to mention the fact that the clerk might have been the last one to speak to Piyusha before she was grabbed, hauled underground, and sacrificed to a giant sleeping lizard that really couldn't have cared less. "So we have a window on when she went missing. That's something at least." I straightened, moving back until I could no longer smell the cloyingly sugary scent of Piyusha's blood. "Thank you for showing me this. I'll look for her, and if I find anything—"

"You won't," said Rochak, quietly.

"Maybe not, but you'll still be the first to know." I shrugged. "It's all I can offer. Stay together. If you have any other sisters, don't let them go to the store by themselves."

"You'll really look for her?" asked Sunil.

I nodded. "I really will."

"How do we know that we can trust you?" asked Rochak.

"You don't. But right now, I think I'm about the best chance your sister's got." All three of us looked at the smear on the wall. None of us said anything after that. No one really needed to.

Things that I am: impulsive, foolhardy, occasionally too convinced of my own invulnerability. Things that I am not: completely stupid. After I bid Piyusha's brothers good-bye, I scaled the nearest fire escape, got myself back up to rooftop level, and pulled out my cell phone. Leaning against the side of an ornately-carved gargoyle (after first checking to make sure it wasn't a real gargoyle taking a nap), I called home. The answering machine picked up: fifteen seconds of silence followed by an ear-shattering "beep." Another safety precaution.

"Hey, guys, it's me. Pick up." I waited a few seconds. No one picked up. "Come on, if you're there, pick up." No one picked up. I sighed deeply. "You'd better not all be dead right now. I'll try your cells. If you don't hear from me again, send reinforcements. With tanks, if at all possible." I hung up.

Calling Mom, Dad, and Antimony's phones got the same result: a quick ring to a blank voicemail prompt. I left basically the same message with all three of them, and considered calling Uncle Ted. They'd been going on a basilisk hunt . . .

And those can take days, I reminded myself firmly, and *someone* would have called me if things had gone wrong. Maybe just Aunt Jane, but still. *Someone.* I sighed, pushing my concern as far into the back of my mind as I could, and dialed the person I'd been trying to avoid calling. My brother.

Unlike the rest of the family, Alex has always stayed in the habit of answering his phone. That's because he's the only one—apart from me—at least pretending to have a life outside the family business, and since *his* job comes with nine-to-five hours and an actual paycheck, when the phone rings, he's there to answer it. True to form, the phone only had time to ring three times before it was picked up on the other end. I smothered a small sigh of relief.

"Alexander Preston's phone, Alexander Preston speaking." My brother, as always, sounded distracted. He probably had a book in one hand, some kind of lizard in the other, and the phone on speaker.

"Hi, Alex," I said. "It's your best-beloved baby sister. You got a moment to chat?"

"Verity?" His tone turned wary. I could practically feel the full force of his attention being turned in my direction. "Where are you?"

"Still in Manhattan. Dad keeping you posted on the local news, or do I need to bring you up to speed before I start asking for your help?"

"You mean the part where you're claiming you may have an actual dragon on your hands? Yeah, I've heard."

"Oh, see, you haven't heard the *best* part. My dragon's been upgraded from 'may have' to 'absolutely have.' It's here. It's sleeping, which is the good part, but, well. There are a few bad parts."

"Why don't I like the sound of that?"

"If I have to take a guess? Because Mom wasn't in the practice of bouncing you off the pavement when you were a baby. Bad part number one, I think we've got a snake cult. Or, well, whatever you call it when you have a bunch of idiots worshiping a reptile that isn't actually a snake. Dragons have legs, right?"

"Yes, dragons have legs," said Alex, slowly. "They're like very large lizards. What makes you think you have a snake cult?"

"Didn't Dad tell you about the virgin sacrifices?"

There was a long pause before Alex spoke again—long enough for him to count silently to ten. I know that pause very well. He's been incorporating that pause into basically every conversation we've had since I turned twelve. "No, he didn't tell me about the virgin sacrifices. Verity, why are you *calling*?"

"Because I'm about to do something really stupid." Silence greeted my proclamation. I sighed. "The snake cult—dragon cult—whatever—it's been snagging cryptids all over the city. Maybe humans too, for all I know. They've taken a Madhura I know, a girl named Piyusha. I have to at least try to get her back."

"What do you mean, 'get her back'?"

"I mean I'm going to go down into the sewers where I got attacked by Sleestaks—it's a long story, turns out dragon biology is even wackier than we thought it might be, and now there are Sleestaks under New York—to find Piyusha. I had backup last time I was down there, and it was still pretty close. So I want to make sure someone knows what the situation is, and can sound the alarm if I don't call back in an hour. I'd have called Mom, but they're all out chasing basilisks around Oregon."

"Verity . . ."

"There's no one close enough to get here while she still has a chance in hell of being alive, and if I can't at least try to save her, what's the point of my even being here?" Silence. "You know I'm right."

"What about Sarah?"

"I'm not taking her down there with me, if that's what you mean. She'll be fine on her own until the cavalry can get to town. Piyusha doesn't have that long."

There was a long pause before Alex said, voice stiff with resignation, "If you haven't called in two hours, I'm catching the next plane to New York. And if I find you hanging out in some dance club because you didn't think I needed an update, I'm going to beat your ass. We clear?"

"As crystal. I left messages with Mom, Dad, and Annie, so if any of them call you—"

"I'll tell them you're insane but being responsible about it."

"Thanks, Alex."

"You better remember this the next time I ask you for a favor." He hung up without saying good-bye. I was sort of expecting that. What I wasn't expecting was the pang that went through my chest as the silence fell and I realized that I was truly getting ready to do this. I closed my phone and gazed across the rooftops around me. This was where I belonged, out in the open, with a thousand directions to escape in. Not down there, in the dark, alone.

Piyusha was an innocent. She'd answered all the questions Dominic and I asked her, and she'd trusted in my presence to keep her safe. There's a sort of responsibility that has to come with having that sort of a reputation. I had to try. No matter how much I didn't want to.

I slid my phone into my pocket and stood, stretching out my hamstrings before stepping delicately off the edge of the roof. Time to get to work.

Eighteen

"This isn't the sort of business that comes with a lifetime guarantee. You start because it's the right thing to do, and by the time you realize that the only way to quit is a closed casket funeral, it's too late to get out. That's just the way it is."

–Alice Healy

In the sewers under Manhattan, doing something stupid

THE SEWERS WERE DARK, OPPRESSIVE, and a little nerve-racking when I went into them with Dominic to watch my back and no reason to expect any trouble. Going into them on my own was a dozen times worse, especially now that I knew what was down there. I'm not a fan of close-quarters combat, and blind fighting is Antimony's thing, not mine. But Piyusha needed me, and there was no one else to call.

Stepping off the bottom rung of the ladder, I snapped my cave light on and clipped it to my belt. The light illuminated what looked like a perfectly normal stretch of sewer, from the water-stained brick of the walls to the unrecognizable sludge thinly coating the concrete floor. I drew my .45 and started forward, holding it in front of me in the classic television cop position. I was trying to keep my nerves in check. I knew what direction I was going, thanks to Sarah (and my compass). All I needed to do was get there without freaking out. And hopefully without encountering any more unwanted lizard-men. I'm not normally one to run from a fight, but if I could avoid this one, let's just say I wouldn't be sorry.

Fifteen minutes later, I'd walked probably half a mile into the dark beneath the city, descending gently all the while, and I hadn't seen anything bigger than a rat. (Not that the rats weren't plenty big. New York seems to take pride in trying to produce the largest rodents the world has ever seen. Fortunately, with size comes intelligence, and most of them took one look at my expression and scattered.) I was starting to think I was on a wild-goose chase when an air current wafted up from the depths and addressed my nose with an aroma that had absolutely no business being in the sewer:

The sweet scent of pine resin mixed with molasses.

Piyusha was somewhere ahead of me. Somewhere in the dark. Gritting my teeth, I adjusted my grip on the gunstock and kept walking.

The sticky-sweet smell of Piyusha's blood got stronger as I descended, becoming harder to ignore with every step. Part of me took careful note of the strength of the smell, analytically trying to figure out whether Madhura blood contained some chemical compound that made it smell stronger as it dried. Maybe it worked as a deterrent to predators, or as an attractant for some natural prey? (Not that Madhura have much I'd call "prey" outside of donuts, Snickers bars, and cotton candy.) Lots of cryptids have blood with interesting qualities, at least from a human standpoint. Cuckoos bleed antibiotics; giant swamp bloodworms bleed a gummy slime that attracts damn near any predator you'd care to name; incubi and succubi bleed something that's basically an open call to fornication. It's all part of the barely-comprehensible circle of cryptid life. Disney it's not, but it definitely keeps things interesting, especially when Mom forgets to label the plasma in her medical emergency kit.

It was easy to regard the smell of Madhura blood as a relief, given the sewer-stink alternatives . . . as long as I didn't think too much about what the strength of the smell meant. If Piyusha had been human, losing this much blood would have killed her for sure. Not knowing much about Madhura physiology, I just had to hope she had more reserves than a human girl her size.

Hope died when my foot hit something soft. I looked down and met Piyusha's staring, sightless eyes with something from the strange, empty country that sits between sorrow and disappointment. She was naked, with black runes sketched down the length of her body in what looked like it was probably Sharpie. It hurt my eyes if I tried too hard to focus on them. I holstered my gun before pulling my phone from my pocket, and whispered soft apologies as I took blurry digital photos of her corpse. I didn't know enough about her culture to know if this was considered desecration, but I needed to document those runes. Maybe Dad could tell me what they meant. Whatever it was, it wasn't anything good. Nothing written in Sharpie on a corpse ever is.

Once I was done with the unpleasant task of photographing Piyusha's body, I tucked the phone away and knelt, beginning the even more gruesome task of examining her wounds. Whoever took her had slit her throat just below her jaw, covering the runes on her chest and collarbones with a gummy-looking veil of watery red blood. There wasn't enough blood for that to have been the wound that killed her; she'd already been bled almost dry by that point, probably via the slashes running down the length of her forearms and calves. I just hoped she'd been numb before they cut out her heart. It was a small thing to hope for, given the obvious and undeniable violence of her death. It was the only thing I had left to hope.

Her expression was a mixture of terror and raw confusion, like she hadn't been able to believe what was happening to her. I blinked back tears as I reached down and brushed her eyelids closed. There was still a faint, lingering warmth to her skin, but not much; she'd been dead for a while.

"I'm so sorry, Piyusha," I whispered. "If I'd known this was going to happen, I wouldn't have left you alone. I'm so, so sorry."

She didn't answer me. There are ghosts in the world—my Aunt Mary is one of them, and she's a lot of fun at parties—but they almost never result from ritual sacrifices. That kind of death commits the soul to something else altogether, and doesn't leave anything behind. I just had to hope that stopping the bastards who'd done this would free Piyusha to move on to whatever afterlife waits for the Madhura.

I straightened, wiping tears from my eyes with the back of one hand. I couldn't move her alone, and I wasn't going to make her brothers come down into the dark. Maybe Ryan could help. Tanuki are stronger than they look, even when they're in their human forms; he'd probably be able to shift her without any real—

Something hissed ahead of me. My head snapped up, shoulders locking as I took in the vulnerability of my position. Retreat was probably the best approach in this situation. I could return to collect Piyusha's body, with Ryan to back me up and, more importantly, I wouldn't wind up dead in a sewer.

The hissing started up behind me, even louder than the hissing from the front, just before the hissing started from the sides. Okay. Maybe I wasn't going to be retreating after all.

I didn't want to open with gunfire in an enclosed space until I knew exactly how many opponents I was deal-

ing with. Since I lost my telescoping baton the last
time I tangled with the Sleestaks, I'd been reduced to
sharp things. That's okay. I like sharp things. I reached
back and drew the machete from behind my backpack
with one hand, drawing the flensing knife from my belt
with the other. Nice, sharp, and capable of hitting bone
in a single thrust if I was using it correctly. If I ever
wanted to see daylight again, I'd damn well better use
it right.

"Well?" I asked the hissing darkness. I couldn't see
anything in the area illuminated by my halogen light,
but there was a lot of sewer I couldn't see at all. They
had the advantage. "Are we going to do this thing, or
what?"

The darkness boiled, and out of it came the servitors.
There was no posturing this time; they moved with the
speed of striking cobras, coming too fast for me to count.
This gang was at least as large as the one Dominic and I
fought off together, and that had been a close victory. If
I couldn't find an escape route, the best I could hope for
would be a swift and reasonably painless death. Piyusha's body provided a mute, horrifying example of what
the worst would be.

I launched myself into a high kick, my toe catching
the lead servitor in the chin as I slashed out to either
side with my respective weapons. I felt, rather than saw,
the machete find a target, hacking deep into scaled
flesh. The flensing knife hit nothing but air, but at least
it drove back the attacker on that side, giving me a little
more space in which to maneuver. None of the servitors went down. That would have been too much to
hope for.

My lead foot finished its arc, hitting the floor just in
front of the servitor I'd kicked. He looked dazed. I took
advantage of the hole in his guard, bringing my other leg
up and kneeing him firmly in the groin. Whatever mutagenic process created the servitors, some attributes of

their mammalian origins remained intact; as soon as my knee hit his nuts, he doubled over, allowing me to bring my machete down across the back of his neck. He toppled.

I was still wrenching my machete free when a tail snaked out of the darkness behind me and wrapped noose-tight around my neck, jerking me backward. My hand lost its grip on the machete handle, leaving me with nothing but the flensing knife, which I didn't dare start waving around my own throat. I dropped it instead, frantically clawing at the tail that was in the process of choking me. Air had suddenly become a much more valuable commodity than weaponry.

My fingernails couldn't find traction on the scales covering the servitor's flesh. One of my nails caught and tore, the sharp flare of pain barely distracting from the all-encompassing pain in my neck. My vision was starting to blur around the edges as oxygen deprivation set in. I kicked and thrashed, but my feet didn't make contact with anything. Suffocation is one of those things you just don't learn how to fight through. Big problem, that.

A female voice spoke suddenly from up ahead in a language that I'd never heard before. It managed to be sibilant and fluid at the same time, like choral music written for snakes. The hissing around me stopped, replaced by confused clicking. The tail around my throat didn't loosen. I continued to struggle, but I was losing strength, and without the leverage to break the hold, I wasn't going to have much time to be curious about what was happening around me.

The woman spoke again, still in that strange snakesong language—but this time I recognized my name in amidst the trilling hisses. There was a distinct note of command to whatever she was saying. The clicking grew stronger, and the tail around my throat let go, sending me toppling to the ground. I managed to hit my knees and catch myself, preventing gravity from dropping me face-first onto Piyusha's body. My right hand hit her shoulder, fingers sinking into her flesh. I shuddered and scrambled to my feet, grabbing my machete and wrenching it free before I turned to look toward the woman who'd ordered my release.

Candy was standing in the opening of a connecting tunnel, the fingers of her left hand pressed up against her cheek. She was staring at the servitors around me with enormous eyes glistening with tears. I'd never seen a dragon princess cry before.

"Candice?" I rasped, and looked quickly around me. There were at least a dozen servitors, all of them watching her with the focused intensity of a snake wondering whether or not to strike.

"Don't make any sudden moves," she said, following it with another sentence in that strange sibilant tongue. "I don't know how much they actually understand me, and I can't hold them forever. Just . . . start walking toward me, and try to look like you're not worried."

"Right." Talking hurt my throat, so I stopped there. My flensing knife was on the ground near a servitor's foot. I stooped to grab it, and the servitor hissed at me, causing me to flinch back. He didn't make any hostile moves, so I kept moving, making my slow way toward Candy.

"Can you run?" she asked. One of the servitors took a step forward, and she snapped something harsh and hissing at him. He stopped before stepping back to his original position, looking oddly chagrined. I didn't know reptiles *could* look chagrined.

"I think so," I answered. "What are you saying to them?"

"I'm telling them they have to listen to me, because I speak the language of dragons," she said, not taking her eyes off the servitors. "It's an instinctive language. They weren't born dragons, but they should get some of the language through the blood when they're changed."

"Should?"

"It's not like anyone's been able to test this for a long time, you know." She cast a brief glance my way, an oddly bitter look in her eyes. "Dragons are extinct, remember?"

"I remember." I slid the flensing knife into my belt, keeping hold of the machete. "Now what?"

"Now we run." She grabbed my wrist, hissing a final command at the servitors before she turned and hauled me down the tunnel she'd emerged from. My lungs still hurt from my near-suffocation. I ran anyway.

Candy hauled me along for the length of the tunnel, until we emerged through a door in the wall into what was clearly a working subway tunnel. Rumbling in the distance made it sound like there was more than one dragon sleeping underneath the subway. Letting go of me, she pulled a smart phone from her pocket and glanced at the screen before motioning for me to follow her down the tracks.

"The next PATH train comes through in ten minutes," she said, not looking back. "Hurry up if you don't want to catch it."

"Wait—what? I thought we were in the subway."

"The PATH and the subway are different systems. Sometimes they connect. Both of them have trains." Candy did look back this time, since that made it easier to look at me like I was an idiot. "Nine minutes."

I hurried.

The Port Authority Trans-Hudson service runs trains between New York and New Jersey, under the Hudson River. They have a much more limited network than the main subway system, but they still get people where they're going and, more importantly, their trains will still squash you flat as a bug on a windshield. On the plus side, because their service is more limited, we were less likely to wind up flattened by a train that wasn't keeping to the schedule Candy had in her phone. That was something, anyway.

I stuck my machete back into my backpack, where I wouldn't frighten any late morning commuters. I didn't need to worry. The platform at the Christopher Street PATH station was deserted when Candy and I scrambled up onto it. She looked around, satisfying herself that we were alone, and dug into her pocket again, this time producing a MetroCard. "Here."

"What—?"

"Everyone knows you think you're too good to ride the subway, so I know you don't have one, and you're going to need it." She started walking toward the exit gate, giving me a chance to really look at what she was wearing: designer yoga pants, black, a silk tank top, also black, running shoes, and a sleek ponytail. In New York, that's the sort of thing you wear when you don't want to be noticed.

"Hang on." I hurried to catch up. "Were you *following* me?"

"Did you think I just stumbled over you down there? I'm not that into sewers." Candy turned to glare at me. "Of course I was following you. You don't get to tease us with the idea that there's a dragon somewhere in New York and then go running off after it. We don't trust you. You need to be watched."

"Who's 'we'?" I asked.

"The Nest." Candy shook her head. "You're coming home with me. My sisters want to talk to you. They don't believe me when I say that you're not going to hurt the dragon."

A bored-looking transit cop leaned against the fare gates, presumably to make sure we weren't carrying any dead bodies or trying to break anything. The bruises forming around my throat didn't even rate a change in his expression as he watched us exit the platform. I waited until we were up the first flight of stairs before asking, "So you saved me because you don't trust me?"

"I saved you because you're the best chance we have of actually finding the dragon. Whether I trust you or not is immaterial. He needs us."

"For what?" I asked. The look she shot me made me immediately regret the question. Her expression was a complicated mixture of longing and anger and resentment, and I couldn't even begin to unravel it.

"You're coming to the Nest," she said firmly, as we stepped off the last flight of stairs and into the tunnel connecting the PATH and subway systems. Grabbing my wrist again, she began hauling me along. "After that, you can ask me all the questions you want."

I needed to tell Piyusha's brothers that she was dead. I needed to tell my family that I was alive. I needed to go home and take care of my injuries before I went looking for more injuries to go with them. I needed to do a lot of things.

A dragon princess had saved me from the Sleestaks underneath Manhattan, and she'd done it by speaking to them in a language I didn't even know existed. If I was going to find the dragon before Dominic did—and before the snake cult had time to do to more cryptid girls what they'd done to Piyusha and the others—I needed to understand why she'd been willing to do that. What were the dragon princesses to the dragons, really? We'd been asking that question for years, but it was always very academic, something to ponder when you didn't really have anything else to do with your time. Suddenly that "very academic" question might be the answer to everything.

"I hate the subway," I muttered.

Candy cast a smugly vicious look in my direction. "I know," she said.

For the second time in a single day, I started down into the darkness beneath New York City. At least this time, all I'd have to deal with were the people who rode the subway.

Nineteen

"Learning something new about the world
in which we live is always a wonderful
thing. Unless you're learning what a wendigo looks like from the inside."

–Evelyn Baker

The Meatpacking District, which is nicer than it sounds

WE POPPED OUT OF THE SUBWAY in the Meatpacking
District, a rapidly-gentrifying neighborhood that
used to be devoted almost entirely to, you guessed it,
meat. (There are still working slaughterhouses there
which is both a real blessing to the city's cryptid community and something for the tourist bureau to work as
industriously as possible on hiding. Somehow, "come to
New York for all your goat-slaughtering needs" just
doesn't have the right ring to it.) The lunch crowd was
out in force, clogging the sidewalks with tourists and
well-dressed business people out to grab a quick bite before diving back into the fast-paced world of whatever
kind of job you need to pay for real Manolo Blahnik
patent leather heels. I swallowed my drool, resisting the
urge to clock a yuppie and make off with her shoes.
There wasn't time to mug passersby for their clothes, no
matter how much they were abusing them by grinding
the heels against the pavement.

Not that I was one to talk. Candy was impeccable, as

always, but my clothing was covered with an exciting mix of sewer slime and three kinds of blood—Neapolitan gore. I could probably pass Piyusha's blood off as maple syrup, and the blood from the lizard-men as some sort of tar. My own blood couldn't be mistaken for anything other than what it was, especially since several of my smaller wounds were still leaking. People recoiled as I passed, expressions reflecting everything from confusion to horror. I didn't stop to reassure them. As long as I kept following Candy, who clearly knew where she was going, it wasn't likely that anyone would ask if I needed help, and that was good; the last thing I needed at the moment was a Good Samaritan. For one thing, I was too damn tired. The events of the last few days were starting to catch up with me and, no matter what happened with the dragon princesses, I was still going to need to tell Piyusha's brothers that she was dead.

"All this, and I have to work tonight," I muttered darkly, dodging around a touristy-looking woman with eighties bangs and a pair of grubby toddlers that seemed to be occupying the majority of her attention.

"What was that?" asked Candy.

"Nothing."

"Good. We're here." She opened the door of a small, spotless bodega crammed between a wine bar and an upscale dog salon. Gesturing for me to follow, she went inside. Lacking any better ideas, I trailed after her.

The aisles in your average New York bodega are narrow enough to inspire claustrophobia in circus acrobats. This bodega seemed to have been designed on the theory that all those other bodegas were wasting valuable shelf space. I wasn't sure anything even semi-human could have wedged its way into some of those aisles, which rendered the beer and chips effectively unreachable. That would be enough to keep the crowds away, even if they had the best prices in the city—which they clearly didn't. Every tag in sight showed a markup of at least thirty percent, and sometimes more.

Candy smirked as she caught me eyeing a two dollar pack of gum. "You'd be surprised how many tourists shop here for the 'authentic experience,'" she said. "Duane Reade would be a lot more 'authentic,' since there's one on every corner, but we're never going to sneer at profit. Come on." She wove her way between displays and down one of the wider aisles, moving toward the counter. A drop-dead gorgeous blonde was seated behind it, an expression of profound boredom on her face as she filed her already perfect nails.

The blonde glanced up as we approached, sky-colored eyes narrowing as she took in the disreputable state of my attire. "Is this the Price girl?" she asked, not taking her eyes off me.

"It is," said Candy. "We need the first aid kit."

Wordlessly, the other dragon princess—there was nothing else she could be, not with that complexion and that attitude; not unless she was working at *Vogue*, anyway—put down her file and produced a white box with a familiar red cross on top from behind the counter. She offered it to Candy, who took it and tucked it under her arm.

"Are they ready for us?"

"They are." The other dragon princess hesitated, glancing to Candy, and asked, "Is it true? What everyone's saying the Price girl found?"

"The Price girl has a name," I said.

Candy nodded, ignoring me. "It's true. I saw the servitors with my own eyes. They were new-made, and they understood me when I spoke to them in the old tongue. It's really true, Priscilla. It has to be."

Priscilla pressed a hand against her mouth, eyes growing bright. "Oh," she whispered. Clearing her throat, she added, "Go back. They're going to have a lot of questions."

"That's why I brought her," said Candy. Gesturing for me to follow again, she ducked around the counter and through the door to the employees-only part of the store. I was starting to feel a bit like a trained poodle, but I followed anyway. I'd come too far to turn back now, and I really wanted to know who "they" were.

The hallway was short, leading to an unlocked rear door. Candy pushed it open, and we exited into a perfect blind canyon that had probably been an alley, once, before construction sealed off the exits. I scanned as we walked across to the opposite wall, noting the places where the brick was uneven enough to let me get a foothold. If necessary, I could go up the wall to reach the fire escape and getting to the rooftops from there would be easy. Knowing that I could get away if I needed to made it easier to keep following.

Candy stopped with her hand on the door into the next building, giving me a hard look. "This used to be a slaughterhouse," she said. "We bought it back when there was nothing here *but* slaughterhouses, and it was invisible. Now it's blocked off by other buildings, and as long as we pay our property taxes, no one remembers that it's here. We've lived here for more than two hundred years." The underlying message in her voice was clear: *Don't screw this up for us.* Bringing me to the Nest meant risking everything. That said a lot about how dedicated they were to finding the dragon. It also said a lot about how important it was for me to keep track of my escape routes. If they changed their mind about the risk I posed . . . dragon princesses might not have any natural weaponry, but in today's world, guns level the playing field.

"I promise not to break the china," I said. "Why are you doing this?"

"Because we need to know what you know." Candy opened the door. The sound of distant voices and children laughing drifted into the alley. "What you found out is the first good news we've had in centuries, and we're not letting you run off and get slaughtered by servitors until we're sure we know everything."

"Mercenary to the last," I said dryly, and followed her inside.

The building had started life as a slaughterhouse, and didn't appear to have changed much since. The alley door led into what had once been the holding pen for sheep or cattle; the floor was concrete, with spilled-wine bloodstains worked deep into the stone. A few of the low holding walls were gone, replaced by empty space. Overhead, the walkways and management offices hung in the gloom like spiderwebs, gray and sterile. The light was uniformly low, and an air of decay hung over the entire place, like no one had been there for years.

Candy caught sight of my face and bit back what looked like laughter before taking hold of my wrist and tugging me after her. "Just because *we* can't do magic, that doesn't mean we can't *pay* for it," she said. "We have a good relationship with the hidebehinds. It helps."

"This is a glamour?" I asked, looking at my surroundings with renewed interest.

"And obviously a damn good one. I'll have to tell Betty we got our money's worth." She took one more step forward, still pulling me in her wake, and the gloom burst around us like a soap bubble.

Everything changed.

The basic architecture of the building only shifted slightly—it was still mostly one big open room—but the last of the slaughterhouse tools vanished, taking the animal pens and the suspicious stains with them. A well-worn carpet pieced together from scraps and sample sale rejects suddenly covered the concrete, looking like the world's largest quilting project. Lights came on in the rooms above and over the walkways, and the sound of voices was everywhere, coming from the dozens on dozens of women who filled the building. They were all unreasonably pretty. Most were blonde, but I saw a few redheads, brunettes, and even one with hair so black she could have made Goths weep.

And then there was the gold. There was no furniture; instead, there was gold. Where I would have expected chairs, beautiful women sat or lounged on heaps of piled-up jewelry, mixed coins, and even a few gold bars. Where I would have expected couches, more women did the same on larger heaps of precious metal. At the center of the room was a mound of gold that must have been nearly eighteen feet high and fifty feet around, covered in dragon princesses. Not all of them were adults, either. Golden-haired little girls chased each other in circles or sat quietly on the piles of gold, each of them as beautiful as their . . . what? Mothers, sisters, aunts? There was so much we didn't know about the biology of dragon princesses—where they came from, how they reproduced, how long they lived. I was going where no cryptozoologist had gone before, and I didn't even have a notebook.

"Dad's gonna kill me," I muttered.

"What?"

"Nothing."

Candy eyed me suspiciously. "Come on. Betty wants to see you as soon as possible."

"And Betty would be . . . ?" It was a little late to be asking questions, especially with more and more of the dragon princesses taking notice of our arrival. Better late than never.

"She's our Nest-mother," said Candy, like it should have been self-explanatory. "Come on."

I went.

Candy led me past the central mound of gold to the stairs leading to the overhead catwalks. We acquired a small procession as we walked, other dragon princesses stopping whatever they'd been doing before as they came to follow us. Most of them didn't look friendly. I was probably the first non-cryptid to set foot in their

Nest since it was established, and my presence represented a potential danger. Candy's face was set in an expression of resolute neutrality. Looking at her, I realized what a risk she was taking in believing me. If I'd been lying about the dragon, she could have been in serious trouble—and so could I. Good thing for both of us that I wasn't lying, even if it wasn't necessarily a good thing for the city as a whole.

A door labeled "Manager" in old-fashioned gilt lettering stood at the head of the stairs. "Behave," hissed Candy, and knocked.

"You may enter." The voice from behind the door managed to be ancient and alluring at the same time, like an aging Mae West turning on the sex appeal one last time before shuffling off to the retirement home.

Candy opened the door, and I followed her inside.

The downstairs had given me a pretty good idea of the dragon princess aesthetic where interior decorating was concerned: why waste money on furniture when it could be used to buy perfectly good gold? This room was no different. Gold in every possible form was mounded high against the walls, and flakes of gold leaf covered the floor, some of it still attached to pages ripped from antique books. It was a good thing my father wasn't there. Seeing books that old and valuable treated so poorly might have been enough to convince him that dragon princesses weren't harmless after all.

The décor only held my attention for a few seconds before I found more important things to focus on, like the woman in front of us, who had to be the oldest dragon princess I'd ever seen. She appeared to be a well-preserved seventy, the kind of seventy that had done everything—and every*one*—before retiring to a comfortable villa in the country. Her dress looked like it was made from real gold thread, and she was lying on a tangled pile of gold chains easily three feet tall. Time had bleached her hair white-gold, but it had done nothing to reduce the sharpness of her sapphire-colored eyes.

"So," she said, in that Mae West voice. "You must be the new Healy girl."

"We're Price girls now, actually," I said. "Have been for a couple of generations. I'm Verity Price. Nice to meet you."

"Betty Smith." She looked me appraisingly up and down. "I always forget about that little intermarriage. You do look frighteningly like your grandmother, you know, especially with all of that blood in your hair. There's never been a Healy girl who didn't look fabulous in red, which is a good thing; you spend so damn much time wearing it."

I couldn't decide whether she was trying to be insulting or not. I decided to go with the interpretation that was less likely to get me attacked by the cast of *America's Next Top Cryptid Model*. "I'd take it off if you'd give me a little time in the bathroom. I didn't exactly have a chance to clean up after Candy hauled me out of the sewer."

"She was fighting with servitors," said Candy.

Betty's eyes narrowed. "You're sure?"

"I spoke to them. They understood me, just like the stories said they would." Candy abruptly pointed at me, as accusing as the prosecuting attorney in a murder case. "She was there. She saw it happen."

"I saw something like that, yeah. I don't speak dragon, so I don't know exactly what Candy said, or how much of it they actually understood, but they stopped attacking me when she told them to play nice with the breakable children." I leaned over, plucking the first aid kit from under Candy's arm while she was distracted with pointing at me. "Look, I really, really want to know what's going on. I'd also really, really like to stop bleeding. Is there a place I can sit down and slap on some bandages while you explain? Please?"

"You truly are so much like your grandmother." Betty chuckled as she rose slowly from her pile of gold chains, sounding more like Mae West than ever. "She never had any patience either. Of course, most of the time she was impatient because your grandfather was watching my, ah, attributes when she wanted him to be watching her back, but no one ever claimed your family line was designed for patience. Sit down. My girls can take care of you."

"Do as you're told," hissed Candy, glaring daggers as she shoved me toward the spot Betty had vacated. Lacking any real grounds for argument, I sat. Three of the dragon princesses who had accompanied us upstairs moved to take the first aid kit and start tending my wounds. I was tired enough to let them. If it meant I stopped bleeding, it was fine by me.

"I'm assuming Candice has explained the basic nature of servitors to you," Betty said. "I do hope you haven't killed too many of them—the poor dears really don't have much control over themselves without the proper people to tell them what to do." Seeing my expression, she clucked her tongue, giving a small shake of her head. "That's what I was afraid of. Ah, well. It's not like they're a necessity, and really, they only serve to prove that you were telling the truth when you claimed there might be a male waiting somewhere in this fair city of ours. And you, my little rumpled darling, are going to find him for us."

"Wait—what?" It was difficult to sit up straight on a mound of slippery gold jewelry with several dragon princesses aggressively cleaning and bandaging my wounds. Somehow I managed. Blame it on the shock. "A male?"

"Oh, my dear innocent poppet." Betty smiled, Mae West turned pure predator. "Surely you didn't think that dragons were actually *extinct*?"

For a moment I just stared at her, with dragon princesses smirking at me from all directions. This was it: the big secret that they'd been keeping all this time, probably since the conflicts between the humans and dragons first began. Dragon princesses didn't exist. There were just . . . dragons. Big dragons and little dragons, but still dragons, regardless of whether they had scales or supermodel-quality skin. One species.

Betty smirked along with the others, clearly waiting for my expression of surprise and dismay. I settled back on the bed of gold, letting the dragon princesses around me go back to cleaning my wounds. "So what, you're saying is this is a case of extreme sexual dimorphism combined with parthenogenetic reproduction? That's a new one."

The dragon princesses stared at me.

I sighed. "Trained cryptozoologist, remember? God, it's like you put on one pair of five-inch heels and everyone forgets you have a brain. The tango is hard, people. It takes actual intelligence to do it right."

"Regardless," said Betty, recovering her equilibrium with admirable speed. She put a hand on her hip, taking a slinky step toward me. For a woman her age, she sure knew how to move. "You owe us, you and your family, and we don't take kindly to debts. This is your chance to pay them off. You're going to find us the male."

"That was already the goal." The dragon princesses who'd been working on bandaging my various scrapes and scratches were done, or close enough that I no longer felt like I was in danger of bleeding all over everything. I pulled away from them, tugging my shirt back into a semblance of order before I stood. "If there's a dragon in this city—sorry, a *male* dragon—then I need to find him before whoever's been sacrificing virgins in his name manages to wake him up. But since you've made it clear that you've got a pretty good reason to be interested in how this turns out, I'll make you a deal. Tell me everything you know that might help me find him without getting eaten."

"And what, you'll remember us in your prayers each

night? I'm sorry, but we prefer to work in more concrete coinage." Betty waved a hand, indicating the heaps of gold cluttering the room. "Interior décor this nice doesn't come cheap, sweetheart."

"And assuming I can find your dragon before his current keepers manage to kill him, I'll tell you where he is, *sweetheart*." I couldn't match her level of poisonous sweetness—I didn't have the practice—but I can be snide with the best of them. "Is that coinage concrete enough for you? I mean, sure, you can be a girl-band species forever, if that's what floats your boat, but wouldn't it be nice to shelve the parthenogenesis for a little while? I bet it's more *fun* when there's more than one person involved."

Betty squared her shoulders, glaring down her nose at me. It was easy enough for her to do, since she was easily five-eight and I wasn't wearing heels, but if it made her feel better, I wasn't going to make a big deal of it. I looked blithely back at her, and waited.

"Fine," she said, finally. "Candy will answer all your questions." Candy gave her an alarmed look, and Betty repeated, "*All* your questions."

"Actually, I have a question for you, if you don't mind," I said. "Did you really know my grandparents?"

Betty's smirk returned, expression going back to the languid Mae West look she'd been wearing when I first entered the room. "That strikes me as a question you ought to be asking your grandfather. Don't you agree?"

Before I could frame my response as something other than "He's in another dimension, so, uh, hell, no," she turned and sashayed out of the room, taking all the dragon princesses but Candy with her. Some people just aren't happy unless they're getting the last word.

There was nothing to sit on but the gold, so I moved to lean against the doorframe. Candy flounced over to the pile of gold where first Betty, and then I, had been stationed, and sat in a huffy heap. I raised my eyebrows.

"I didn't know anyone over the age of seventeen could pull that off," I said. "Congratulations."

"Shouldn't you be asking me personal questions and demanding blood samples by now?" Candy glowered at me. "I agreed to be your guide, not your specimen, and I only said I'd do that much because Betty was pretty sure you'd follow me. Since we're coworkers and everything."

"You've never actually been friendly enough for me to bank on that relationship, but I promise not to ask for any blood samples." I ran a hand through my hair, grimacing a little as flakes of blood came off on my fingers. "As for personal questions, I have plenty. First question: did you have any idea that there might be a dragon here in New York?"

"No." Candy shook her head. "We gave up believing that any of the Lost Ones were going to come back for us a long time ago." Catching the confusion in my face, she sighed and said, "The Covenant didn't kill all the males in one go. It took time. Some of them were fast enough to grab their wives and go into hiding for at least a little while. That's how our line got here, sometime in the sixteenth century. But even dragons die. The last male we know of passed away over three hundred years ago. We just assumed we'd have to make it on our own after that."

"But you kept collecting the gold."

"It's necessary if we want to stay healthy, especially when there aren't any males around."

Her expression challenged me to ask what the gold was used for. Since I wasn't looking for the cryptid Carmen Sandiego, I decided that it would be a lot kinder not to. Did I want to know? Absolutely. My father was going to give me hell when I called home and *couldn't* tell him exactly what purpose the gold served in dragon physiology. But Candy didn't deserve to be treated like some sort of specimen and, if we could just find the dragon, relations with the dragon princesses were certain to improve. "Here, I went into the tunnels and found you a boyfriend" was definitely one hell of a peace offering.

"Right," I said, nodding. I couldn't miss the relief in her eyes when she realized that I wasn't going to ask. Chalk one up to making the right decision. "What *can* you tell me about your biology, without going into anything too uncomfortable for you? You said that dragon blood is mutagenic—does that go for the females, too? Are there any other bodily fluids I need be watching out for?"

"You'd actually have to drink the blood for it to have any effect on you and, even then, it won't work if there's gold in your system," said Candy. "Just swallow some gold flakes before you go anywhere near where you think he is, and you'll be okay. Our blood doesn't work the way the males' blood does."

"Swallow gold. Got it." The idea of chugging an entire bottle of Goldschläger before I went back into the sewers was appealing, if somewhat impractical. "Can I, uh, get some gold before I go?"

Candy's lips tightened with obvious reluctance before she nodded. "I can get you a bottle of gold dust, but whatever you don't use, you'll have to give back."

"Deal."

"There's nothing you really need to be afraid of but the blood. Oh, and the fire-breathing—but he won't do that until he wakes up, so unless he thinks you're a threat, it shouldn't be a problem."

": . . right," I said. "Is he likely to wake up pissed off? And how do I keep him from perceiving me as a threat?"

"I don't know. I've never actually met a *boy* before." There was a wistful note in her voice.

That made me pause. What must it have been like to grow up as a member of a species that only had one gender? Worse, that only had one gender and knew that it was originally supposed to have two? "Are you mammals?" I blurted, summing up all the questions about loneliness and sexual frustration in three seemingly nonsensical words.

Candy seemed to understand the intent. She smiled a little, and said, "Not really. We think—I mean, the Nest-mothers think, after talking about it for a really long time—that we started out as a sort of dinosaur. We're warm-blooded, and we have a lot of mammalian traits, but most of them are window dressing."

"Like those praying mantises that look like flowers."

"Something like that, yes, only we're not insects. We think that the more we looked like people, the better our odds of surviving to breed were, and the more we bred, the more we all started to look like people."

"Protective coloration that doesn't even need a dye job. Remind me to introduce you to my cousin Sarah." They could form some sort of pseudo-human support group or something. "How long do your males live? The only records I could find about this area were from a good three or four hundred years back."

"Awake, about a hundred and thirty years. Asleep . . . it's all just stories, but some of them say that males can hibernate for hundreds and hundreds of years without getting any older. We can do it, too, but not for as long. Fifty or sixty years is about all we can manage, and even that takes a lot of preparation."

"Gold again," I guessed. She nodded. So much of the social behavior of dragon princesses was starting to make sense to me. "All right. Other than 'don't get mutated' and 'watch the morning breath,' is there anything I really need to know about dealing with the male of the species? Is there anything that can help me track him down?"

"If we had an easy way of finding him, you wouldn't be anywhere near here," said Candy, with calm matter-of-factness. "We have no idea where he is, except 'down.' The servitors are probably there to protect him, and are following the orders of whoever has him. He's going to be hard to wake up if he isn't finished hibernating. It isn't seasonal, but if he isn't prepared to be awake, he's going to be groggy and confused."

"How fun for me."

"No, how dangerous for you." She glanced down, not quite fast enough to hide the concern in her eyes. "I know you've been telling us for years that your family . . . wasn't like the rest of the Covenant anymore, but we've never really believed you. I'm still not sure I believe you except that I have to if I want to have any chance of meeting the male. We're not trained for the sort of things you are."

"Spelunking isn't one of my specialties," I said, slow horror dawning as I realized what she wasn't coming out and saying aloud. "He's going to think I'm Covenant, isn't he?"

"Probably." Candy sighed, looking up again. "If you don't talk fast, he'll probably kill you."

"Um, does he speak English?"

"I don't know."

"This gig just gets better and better," I muttered.

Candy shrugged. "It probably beats waiting tables," she offered. "At least this way you get to loot the bodies of the snake cultists."

"I'm not much of a looter, but thanks." I raked my fingers through my blood-stiff hair, and sighed. "Maybe I can find a really big tranquilizer gun. With armor-piercing darts."

"Just don't hurt him."

I offered her a wan smile. "Trust me, Candy, at this point? He's really not the one I'm worried about."

Twenty

"When all else fails, put on a fresh coat of
lip gloss and pretend you have no idea
what that horrible thing that just went running down Main Street was. A surprisingly
large number of people will believe you."
                                    –Frances Brown

Still in the Meatpacking District, well above street level

CANDY HAD BEEN ALMOST IRRITATINGLY EAGER to be rid
of me even though my departure meant giving me a
decently sized jar full of powdered gold. Dragon princesses watched me all the way to the door, none moving
to follow or attempting to say anything. I guess when
someone you view as your ancestral enemy winds up between you and your only shot at ever getting laid, you're
not overly inclined to be friendly.

"Can you find your way from here?" asked Candy,
once we were back in the blind canyon between the bodega and the former slaughterhouse. "I need to get
ready for my shift so I can start paying back the cost of
the gold you're taking."

"They're making you pay for this?"

"Yes, of course. It's not like *you* will."

"Right," I said slowly. "I'm good from here. I'll see
you at work."

Candy didn't say good-bye, just flipped her hair and

turned to stalk back into the building, letting the door slam shut behind her. I looked at the jar of gold powder in my hand, sighed, and shoved it into my pack. I was starting to think I would definitely have preferred the Goldschläger, especially with the little "fiery demise" rider on this particular adventure, but it's true what the sages say: you can't always get what you want.

I could, however, get the hell off the ground. I got a running start and threw myself at the far wall, where the bolts that once anchored the lowest ladder of a fire escape still protruded from the brick. Once I had hold of them, it was an easy matter to swing myself up to the remains of the actual fire escape and scramble up the creaking metal. In under a minute, my hands were hooked over the edge of the slaughterhouse roof, disturbing ancient grime and much more recent pigeon shit as I hoisted myself the rest of the way onto solid footing.

Seen from two stories up, the Meatpacking District was a strange patchwork of gentrified elegance and urban decay. Most of the less-attractive bits were hidden cunningly away, like the dragon princesses' Nest, tucked into spots where no one at street level would ever see them. Some were probably cryptid nests, hiding their own outcasts and secret societies. Others were no doubt slated for eventual destruction and replacement, clearing away the bones of the district one little bit at a time. New York is a city built upon the cannibalized remains of its own past, constantly changing, constantly the same.

Stepping back so that I wouldn't be visible from the street, I took a seat on the edge of a broken-off smokestack and pulled out my phone. According to the readout, I still had five percent of my battery charge remaining. That was enough to make both the calls that needed making.

Alex had clearly been waiting for my call; the phone didn't even have time to finish ringing once before he picked up, demanding, "Who is this?"

"Your sister. The one who isn't dead."

There was a long pause before he said warily, "Verity?"

"Um, yeah. What's Antimony up to today that you think she'd be the one making this call? Because seriously, I want to know."

"Chasing basilisks, remember?"

"Oh, right. My lizard is so much bigger than her lizard that I guess it just slipped my mind." I giggled, more from stress than actual amusement. "Hey, what do you know? Size *does* matter."

"Verity—"

"Only wait, it turns out that you were actually wrong about something. Dragons aren't lizards. They're sort of like dinosaurs that managed to hang after the big extinction parties, and evolved to fit a whole new niche. A weird, fucked-up niche, but still, you have to admire them for trying."

"Verity!" I heard Alex take a deep breath. "Can you please, please tell me what happened? I'm glad you're not dead. I wasn't relishing the idea of being called to the East Coast to fish your remains out of the sewer. Now explain."

"You really do care." I leaned against the crumbling brick of the next smokestack over. "Short form: I went down as carefully as I could. Piyusha was already dead when I found her. There were runes painted all over her body; I took pictures with my phone. I'll email them to you and Dad."

"Good. Why did it take you so long to call in?"

"Oh—I got jumped by draconic servitors." Silence. "Remember when I said I got in a fight with the Sleestaks?"

"I'm not in the habit of forgetting things like that."

"Well, see, dragon's blood is a mutagenic substance, and when people drink it or, I guess, get it fed to them, they turn into weird lizard-people. Hence the Sleestak attack. I don't know if there's a demutator, but I'd be willing to bet that there isn't. Evolution is generally pretty good about leaving things fucked up once it fucks them."

The sound of a heavy thump traveled through the phone as Alex sat down on his end. "You found the dragon."

"Not yet."

"So how do you know this?"

"Because it turns out the Covenant didn't wipe out all the dragons. Just the male ones. Think extreme sexual dimorphism, mimicry-based camouflage, and parthenogenesis. The dragon princesses are the female of the species, and they're sort of excited by the idea of getting their boyfriends back."

Alex swore quietly.

"Yeah," I agreed. "Like that, but louder."

Most people are familiar with the theory of sexual dimorphism. It's what gives peacocks those flashy tails while the peahens look like they've been dipped in boring, and what makes male lions so much bigger and lazier than the lionesses. Every gendered species is sexually dimorphic to one degree or another, even if it's as simple as "one of us has an innie, one of us has an outie." The female spotted hyena has what really looks like a penis from any sort of a distance. Lots of reptiles are visually sexless, which is why calling your tortoise "she" is silly if you're not a zookeeper. Other animals are *so* sexually dimorphic that they don't even look like the same species. We're talking anglerfish where the males have no digestive systems of their own, barnacles where the females are basically internal organs feeding off their male hosts, and stuff that's even weirder. Mother Nature is a freaky lady who probably created pot so she could spend all her time smoking it.

It's unusual to find really extreme sexual dimorphism in anything bigger than a skink, but it happens. The dragons were definitely on the high end of the weirdness scale, and the parthenogenesis just upped the crazy ante. If extreme sexual dimorphism is rare in bigger animals, parthenogenesis—reproduction without access to the male of the species—is practically unheard of. Komodo dragons can do it (although since they're Komodo dragons, they do it extra-freaky, and actually produce male offspring through what is essentially a method for self-cloning). Anything bigger than that? Not so much. But that explained why we'd never been able to figure out where the dragon princesses were coming from. They weren't pulling the tanuki trick and mating with anything that moved. They were mating with *themselves*, all in the name of making it through another generation. Parthenogenesis means never having your mother tell you to stop doing that or you'll go blind.

Anyone who thinks cryptozoology is the study of the impossible has never really taken a very good look at the so-called "natural world." Once you get past the megamouth sharks, naked mole rats, and spotted hyenas, then the basilisks, dragons, and cuckoos just don't seem that unreasonable. Unpleasant, yes, but unreasonable? Not really.

It took about ten minutes to finish explaining everything I'd learned from the dragon princesses, by which point the battery of my phone was on the brink of death. Emailing the pictures was going to need to wait until I got home to my charger. Alex agreed to call our parents and leave a message for them to pick up when they got back from the basilisk hunt, thus saving me from needing to go through the whole spiel twice in one afternoon. I was tired, I was sore, I still had to tell Piyusha's brothers that she was dead, and I really didn't want to deal with the risk that my parents were already home. The last thing I needed was to wind up getting grilled by Dad in full-on naturalist mode.

"You're sure you're okay?"

"Except for the cuts, contusions, bruises, damage to my pride, and slight dislocation of my worldview, I'm fine." I stood, feeling the muscles in my thighs protest. A little run would work out the majority of the stiffness, and some painkillers would have to do for the rest. It wasn't like I was going to be taking a hot bath and a nap any time soon. "I'm about to be unavailable for a little while, though—at least until I can charge my phone. I'll be checking email, or you can call Sarah."

"Doesn't she have class today?"

"She always checks her messages between classes, in case Artie mysteriously decided to fly to New York and wants to have lunch."

Alex snorted. "Yeah, like *that's* going to happen. I don't think he's left the basement in a month."

"Only a month this time? And you know Sarah. Hope springs eternal, especially when you're a socially awkward math geek from a species of dangerous telepathic psychopaths. At least she's fixating on the dork side, rather than the dark side. It could be worse."

"Charming as ever, Very. I'm going to go call Dad and let him know what's up on your end. Please try not to get killed before you can recharge your phone."

"Love you too, big brother." I hung up, tucking the phone into the pocket of my jeans before taking a step back and getting a running start toward the edge of the roof. If I got the trajectory right, I should be able to jump off, grab the fire escape on the building across the alley, and swing from there to the next roof over. It all depended on my building enough momentum before the first leap, but I had faith in my ability to clear the distance. I got one foot up onto the low concrete lip surrounding the roof, tensed to spring—

—and toppled backward as someone grabbed my arm.

I managed to avoid going into a full-out somersault as I yanked myself away, but I couldn't dump speed fast enough to keep from tumbling to the roof, absorbing the majority of the impact with my elbows. I've taken worse falls with less preparation, and all I left behind on the hard-pack gravel of the roof was a few layers of skin. I bounced back to my feet with knives already drawn, whirling to face my assailant. I was pissed, but not quite pissed enough to go straight for my guns. That sort of escalation never does anyone any good.

Dominic was still standing by the rim of the roof, looking faintly surprised, like he hadn't expected my interrupted leap to contain quite so much momentum. He was back in his duster and jeans, and there was fresh tape covering the wounds on his face. "Are you all right?"

"I'd be better if some asshole hadn't just stopped me from jumping off the roof." I straightened up, sliding my knives back into their sheaths. Sliding them into his sides would have been more satisfying, but not, in the long run, as productive. Stupid morals. "What are you doing here, De Luca?"

"I was concerned for your safety. You went into the sewers and didn't come back out."

I immediately regretted putting the knives away. "Wait, you were *following* me? Have you been following me all day? Because I could really have used some backup, if you were all that damn concerned."

"I haven't been following you *all* day." He sighed, stepping away from the edge of the roof. "How many weapons are you carrying? I'm beginning to think you have an entire armory in your bag."

"Don't start with the flattery. How long have you been following me?"

"Since your cousin called to ask if I'd abducted you."

"What? Sarah called you?" He nodded. I scowled. "I am going to *kill* that watery-blooded little—"

"Apparently, you were absent when she came back

from class and, given your accounting of our evening activities, she became concerned for your safety." Dominic's expression darkened. "What, exactly, did you tell her?"

"Are you actually asking me whether I told the telepath we had sex? Because she knew before we did. Seriously, you do *not* want to ask Sarah about your sex life, or anyone else's sex life, because she can draw you diagrams. She *will* draw you diagrams, with helpful labels, if you push her. I'd say she needs hobbies, but we sort of are her hobbies."

Confusion tinting his voice, Dominic asked, "So you didn't tell her?"

"Oh, the Covenant. What wonderful training programs they must be running." I crossed my arms. "Sarah called you and asked if you'd decided to run off with me, so you decided to track me down. Is that it?"

"Essentially, yes." He tucked his hands into the pockets of his duster, looking uncomfortable. "I managed to locate the sewer grate you descended through. I followed the blood trail from there to the PATH station. It took a while to figure out where you'd gone after that and, by the time I got to the appropriate district, you'd vanished again."

"I was getting the biology rundown from the dragon princesses, who do *not*," I raised a finger warningly, "need to be harassed right now. They're creepy and a little unpleasant, but they're still having a really hard week, and I think we just need to give them some time before we go prodding at them further."

"I wasn't going to harass them."

"Just kill them a little?"

Dominic cleared his throat. "Dragon princesses have long been filed as essentially harmless. I see no reason to adjust that designation. Unless you'd like to provide me with one . . . ?"

I gave him a measuring look. Either he'd arrived after I hung up on Alex, or he'd been listening to the whole conversation, and was just waiting to hear me tell him to his face. I liked Dominic, I really did, except for that superior "humans first" streak of his. That streak was the reason I had to at least try to lie to him.

"No, there's no reason to adjust the designation," I said blithely, with my best haughty Viennese waltz expression. It was the sort of face that implied that lemons would be too sweet for me. "They'd like the dragon under the city to be unharmed, since they're sort of fond of the idea of having an actual dragon around again, but they're pretty much harmless in and of themselves." *Not even technically a lie*, I thought. *Let's see you poke a hole in that.*

Dominic looked faintly disappointed, like he'd been expecting me to say something else. "I see. Well, then, may I ask what drove you into the sewers a second time? You already knew it wasn't safe down there—not that I don't think you can handle yourself in a fight," he added hurriedly. "It's just that even with two of us, we were hard-pressed to escape intact. I wouldn't have expected you to return to the depths alone."

"I . . . oh, crap, you really weren't following me for the entire day, were you?"

"I believe I just said that."

"Dominic . . ." I hesitated, unsure of how to continue. Would he even care about one more cryptid death? If he didn't, would I be able to resist the urge to shove him off the edge of the roof? I took a breath and said, "Piyusha's dead."

"What?" Dominic's shock didn't look feigned in the least.

I let out a breath I'd been only half aware of holding, and said, "I went to stay with Sarah last night after you left." His expression turned hurt. I raised my hands, palms outward, and lied, "I wasn't hiding from you. The mice went into full-out exultation mode, and I needed to get some sleep. This morning, I went to check on Piyusha at Gingerbread Pudding, and the place was closed.

Her brothers were waiting for one of us to show up. She went out to the store last night and never came back."

"And they thought we had something to do with it?" he asked darkly.

"Hey, you're Covenant and I'm an urban legend, remember? It was completely reasonable for them to think that we did it."

"We gave our word."

"They have no reason to consider it worth anything."

"I suppose," he said, not sounding at all happy about it. "Her trail led to the sewer?"

"Yeah. I found the body. I managed to take some pictures with my phone—not because I get my jollies from the corpses of innocent women; whoever killed her covered her with some sort of ritual symbols before they dumped her. I'd show you, but my battery's dead."

"What are you intending to do with the pictures?"

"I'm going to go home, plug my phone in, and mail them to my father so he can try to figure out what the hell they are." I sighed. "While I'm at it, I should call Sarah and tell her not to set Covenant assassins on my tail every time I fail to show up for roll call. And then I get to go and tell Piyusha's brothers that I found their sister, but not in the sense they were hoping I would."

"I'll come with you." Dominic smiled, very slightly. It wasn't a happy expression. "If she was targeted for talking to us, her death is my fault as much as it is yours. Oh, don't look so surprised, Verity—I can see that you're blaming yourself for what happened to her, and if you're to blame, so am I. I should be there."

"I . . . thanks, Dominic. That means a lot to me. Besides, you should probably see these pictures. I have a feeling your resources may be more useful than mine when it comes to figuring out what these symbols mean."

"True," he agreed. "I just have to request one favor, in exchange for access to whatever I can obtain from the Covenant records."

I blinked. "What's that?"

He hesitated before giving me an almost bashful look, and asking, "Can we please take a taxi?"

We were far enough from my apartment that a compromise wasn't really an option: if Dominic took a cab, he'd beat me home by at least twenty minutes and, even though I was substantially more beaten up than he was, he wasn't even willing to consider the overland route. It wasn't that he was uncomfortable on rooftops. He just really, really didn't like the idea of jumping off them on purpose. In the end, it was time to swallow my dislike of New York City cabs and descend to street level in order to get a ride home.

At least he picked up the tab without being asked. And he turned out to be a pretty decent tipper. Always an attractive trait in a man, even one who thinks half my friends and a large number of my relatives need to be exterminated.

The mice were nowhere in evidence when we got upstairs, although the signs of their bacchanal were everywhere, if you knew what to look for. Feathers, dried flowers, and brightly colored scraps of paper were scattered around the living room floor. A tidy pile of cheese rinds and Hostess Snack Cake wrappers surrounded the base of the kitchen trash can. Dominic raised his eyebrows when he saw that. I had to smile, if only because the reaction was so understandable.

"They try to make things easy on me when they have a big bash," I said. Taking the broom from behind the door, I swept the refuse into a dustpan and shook it into the trash. "See? All tidied up. If they weren't considerate about things, I'd be cleaning for hours before I could even get the vacuum."

"You are very strange," observed Dominic.

"You have no idea." I put the broom back where it belonged and crossed to the desk. My phone beeped with electronic satisfaction when I connected it to the charger. "Give me just a minute to send the pictures to myself, and I should be able to show you what Piyusha looked like when I found her."

"Would you be able to locate her body again if we returned to the sewer?"

I cast a look over my shoulder, replying, "I can find the place her body was; whether it's still going to be there is anybody's guess. I sort of got run out of there by servitors, and I don't know whether they were just passing through, protecting the body, or planning to treat it as some sort of all-you-can-eat buffet. Why?"

"I thought her brothers might appreciate her return. I'm not sure what, if any, funeral rites the Madhura practice, but most thinking creatures would find the opportunity to make the decision on their own . . . comforting." He shook his head. "I don't understand how you can be so relaxed about such things."

"What, you mean the idea of the servitors eating Piyusha's body?" I shrugged as I turned back to the desk. My phone was powered up, even though it was still charging; I hooked it to the USB transfer cable and started copying over the pictures. "I'm just as confused by your ability to be so relaxed about killing people like her, so I guess we're even. If the servitors eat her remains, it's because that's what they're designed to do. You can't blame them for doing what they're made for."

"What makes you so sure that humans weren't made to exterminate the cryptids from the face of this world?"

The question sounded entirely sincere. That didn't make it any less aggravating. Gritting my teeth, I continued copying pictures and asked, "How can you be so sure that we were? Maybe we're here to keep them from exterminating each other, provide some ecological balance to the place. You know. Mediate."

"I think you're being unrealistic."

"And I think you're being an asshole, and since we already had this fight once, can we *please* focus on what's important for a little while? A woman is dead, probably because she was seen talking to us. Somebody's turning innocent people into servitors for a dragon that isn't even awake enough to appreciate them. It's a fucking mess, okay? Just another big, fat, fucking mess." I wiped my eyes angrily with the back of my hand, glad that my back was to him. The last thing I needed was for a member of the Covenant to see me cry.

The pictures of Piyusha's body began popping up on my screen. They'd come out about as badly as I feared, managing to be overexposed and too dark at the same time, but the runes were sufficiently darker than her skin that they still stood out. Dominic hissed through his teeth as he moved to crouch next to my chair, tapping the screen with a fingertip.

"Can you expand this?"

"Sure." I moved the magnifier tool over the indicated area, clicking twice. "Artie made me learn how to do this when he got tired of updating my Facebook page. He'll be thrilled to hear that it had real-world applications that didn't have to do with airbrushing wardrobe malfunctions."

"Who's Artie?"

"My cousin," I replied thoughtlessly, and winced. "Crap. Can you not ask these things? I really don't want to explain to my parents how the Covenant got a full dossier on us again."

"The Covenant still doesn't know anything about you," said Dominic. Before I could ask what that meant, he tapped the screen again and said, "This symbol. Have you ever seen it before?"

I squinted. Between the picture quality and the magnification, it was difficult to make out any details. "I don't think so," I said finally. "I've always been more into the practical sides of the job. I never really did much research in the ritual symbolism."

"I'm reasonably sure that's a Burushaski symbol meaning 'control,' and I recognize a few of the others—

they all seem to mean the same things. 'Control' and 'wake' and 'obey.' This is a crazy mix of languages. I'm really not sure what you could hope to accomplish with this assortment."

"How about waking up something that no one's seen in a couple of hundred years?" I brought up another of the pictures, trying to focus on the symbols drawn across Piyusha's belly, rather than the angry red wound bisecting her chest. "This one, I do recognize. It's a standard piece of snake cult iconography. It means, essentially, 'feeding time.'"

"I thought you said you didn't handle ritual symbolism."

"I have an uncle." (Naga wouldn't mind being called an uncle under the circumstances, and he was the family go-to guy for anything involving snake cults, largely because he was frequently their target. It was just that explaining why I had an extradimensional professor of demonic studies as an honorary uncle would take too long—especially since the uncle in question was a giant snake from the waist down.) "Plus, my father talks a lot."

"For someone who dislikes talking about her family, you certainly do it a lot."

"What can I say? Corpses make me chatty, and not entirely in the good way. It's not like you're filling in the gaps, you know. What about your family? Dad says you're generational Covenant."

"My parents are dead." The statement was made without any real emotion. It was simply a fact, something that couldn't be changed. "They were hunting a hydra when I was young. They didn't return."

"I . . . I'm sorry."

"It was a very long time ago. I continued my training, so as to do what they had wanted of me. What was expected of me." He hesitated before adding, "I had never met a sentient cryptid before coming here."

A lot was starting to make sense. I pulled up my web-mail account, attaching the pictures and shooting them off to one of the family's blind accounts. Even if Dominic saw the address, he'd never be able to use it to backtrack anything important. Maybe I was being paranoid; I liked to think of it as being sensible. "Can I send you copies of these? I really do want you to check them against your records."

"Here; let me." He looked relieved at the change of topic, and leaned across me to type his email address into the "To" field. My cheeks flared red as his arms brushed against mine. I delivered a swift but firm internal slap to my hormones. No, Verity. Bad Verity. Giving in to the raw hotness of the Covenant boy once was bad enough. Doing it a second time would show a serious lack of judgment, as well as a definite failure of self-control.

Knowing exactly what he looked like under that shirt and duster wasn't helping matters. It says something about what passes for "normal" when I'm around that the pictures of the dead girl on my computer screen weren't doing anything to dampen my desire to jump his bones. They weren't helping it, either, but they weren't enough to kill the mood in and of themselves.

Dominic clicked the send button and pulled back. "There."

"Thanks," I said lamely. "You'll let me know if you find anything?"

"I will." He hesitated, eyes fixing on mine. "Verity—"

Someone started hammering on the front door of the apartment, about half a second before the telepathic static clicked on inside my head, telling me that "someone" was "my cousin," who I'd forgotten to call. "Crap, it's Sarah," I said, knocking Dominic to the side as I scrambled from my chair.

Sarah had her hand raised to start hammering again when I opened the door. At first, she didn't say anything. She just let her hand drop, and looked at me.

"Sarah, I'm sorry. I lost track of the time."

Her eyes narrowed, frostbite seeming to spread around the edges of her irises. I took an involuntary step backward. For Sarah's eyes to be whiting out like that, she had to be *pissed*. "I thought you were dead," she said, in a clipped, tightly controlled tone that was belied by the wave of telepathic fury that underscored it. "You disappear right after fucking a boy from the Covenant, you're not in any of the usual places, no one's seen you anywhere, and then one of the gargoyles tells me he saw you going back into the sewers *alone*. You couldn't even tell me where you were going?" *You scared the living shit out of me, and what is* he *doing here, anyway? I thought you were done with that asshole after he explained his platform on racial cleansing!*

The transition from spoken word to telepathic scolding was so smooth I barely noticed it at first, until I saw how much the white had spread across her eyes. "Sarah, you need to calm down. I'm fine. I'm sorry I scared you. I really didn't mean to."

You didn't think! You never think! She stormed into the apartment, which was something of a mixed blessing. On the one hand, it meant I could close the door, thus sparing the neighbors our little family drama. On the other hand, it meant I was shutting myself in the apartment with a pissed-off cuckoo and a man from the Covenant. Not the sort of combination that inspires many funny anecdotes. A few cautionary tales, maybe, but nothing you can really go repeating in mixed company.

"Miss Zellaby." Dominic straightened up, offering a shallow but impeccably polite bow in Sarah's direction. "A pleasure to see you again."

Sarah turned her narrow-eyed gaze on him, making me glad once more that Antimony's comic books got it wrong, and telepaths can't actually kill you with their brains. Give you a whopping headache and earworm you with annoying jingles, yes; kill you, no. (Although sometimes, when she's managed to stick "The Happy Banana Song" in my head for a week, I sort of wish she could kill people with her brain. It would be kinder.)

What are you doing *here?* she demanded.

He didn't respond. He couldn't. Without spending a lot more time around her, there was no way he'd be attuned enough to actually "hear" her when she thought at him like that.

The white rimming Sarah's eyes started to fade, replaced by a look of sheer frustration. "What are you doing here?" she repeated, out loud this time.

"You were the one that alerted me to your cousin's absence, if you'll take a moment to remember," he said mildly. "I went looking for her because I shared your concern, and assumed you'd like her returned to you with as many of her original limbs as possible."

The white fled Sarah's eyes completely, leaving her chagrined and a little embarrassed. "Oh," she said. "I did call you, didn't I?"

"Yes, you did."

"I shouldn't have had to." She stalked over and smacked me solidly on the shoulder.

I yelped. "Hey!"

"Don't you hey me! Why didn't you call? You know you're supposed to call before you go running off to your certain death!"

"I don't remember that rule." I rubbed my shoulder. Sarah doesn't hit hard, but she has an unerring gift for hitting squarely atop any preexisting bruises you might happen to have. "I'm pretty sure I'd need a better cell plan if that was actually a rule, because I'd be making a *lot* of phone calls. Besides, your note said you were going to class. I didn't want to interrupt you in the middle of algebra."

"Probability theory," corrected Sarah sharply, "and next time you'd damn well better interrupt me, or I'm telling."

"Who are you going to tell? Alex knew where I was going. Mom and Dad would've known, except they're off chasing basilisks, which is arguably even dumber than going into the sewers where the servitors are. I mean, all the servitors will do is bite me and maybe haul me back to the dragon for mutation. The basilisk will turn me into a piece of lousy garden statuary."

"I am oddly less reassured than I believe you intended me to be."

"And I find myself in the somewhat uncomfortable position of agreeing with a nonhuman," Dominic said, frowning. "Mutation does not strike me as being a desirable or laughable consequence."

"Oh! That reminds me." I dug the jar of gold dust out of my pocket and held it up, giving it a little shake to make the powder swirl like the world's most expensive snow globe. "The dragon princesses said that eating gold will keep us from being mutated."

". . . why does this statement not seem even slightly unreasonable or insane?" asked Dominic. "Something has gone terribly wrong with the world."

Sarah patted him reassuringly on the arm. "Welcome to life with Verity. Just wait. Soon she'll have you thinking that three-inch heels are suitable for combat situations."

"Unlikely," said Dominic.

"But funny," I added. "Besides, you have the legs to pull it off. Not many men do. Anyway, Dominic, I *know* you're planning to go down there again, and Sarah, I'm hitting the point of 'better safe than sorry.' So who wants a gold smoothie?"

"Can I have mine with ketchup?" asked Sarah.

Twenty-one

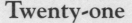

"Most of the time, there isn't time to adjust
to whatever's going on before you have to
deal with it. Life in our world is very sink
or swim, and that's for the best. If you can't
survive in the deep end, you should get out
before you drown."

–Alice Healy

*Drinking the world's most expensive milkshakes, the kitchen
of a semilegal sublet in Greenwich Village, soon to be late
for work*

THE PERFECT RECIPE FOR GOLD MILKSHAKES turns out to
be two tablespoons of gold dust to two scoops of
vanilla ice cream, a cup of vanilla soy milk, and either a
sizable quantity of Hershey's Syrup (if you're a reasonably normal human being) or a quarter-cup of leftover
chunky Prego with mushrooms (if you're a cuckoo).
Sarah was kind enough to let me make the human-style
milkshakes first, since past experience has taught us that
preparing one of her milkshakes leaves the blender
looking like the site of a particularly nasty massacre.
This time was no different. I could probably have
achieved a very similar effect by blending a human
hand, provided it was wearing a watch or a wedding ring,
or maybe just a lot of glitter.

Dominic watched me pour Sarah's milkshake, clearly

unsure as to whether he should be fascinated or utterly appalled. He settled for a combination of the two, demanding, "Why did you put spaghetti sauce into your cousin's drink?"

"Because I like it that way," said Sarah, taking the glass. "You have your chemical stimulants and I have mine, monkey."

"Monkey?" echoed Dominic, now sounding more puzzled than anything else.

"Not actually a mammal," said Sarah. She sipped her tomato-based milkshake before adding, "We're pretty sure cuckoos evolved from some sort of really big bug."

"Thanksgiving dinner with my family is *awesome*," I deadpanned. "Now drink your gold before somebody comes along and mutates you into a twisted parody of humanity." The milkshake tasted basically normal, if I was willing to ignore the gritty residue it left at the back of my throat. I'm willing to ignore a lot in the interest of avoiding mutation.

Dominic sipped his own shake, grimaced, and took a larger swallow. "Are you sure this will protect us?"

"Nope. But the dragon princesses said it would, and I don't have a good reason to think they're lying. Besides, they gave me the gold. Getting them to part with gold is sort of like getting Sarah to part with her laptop—it only happens under extreme duress, and it's something they'd really prefer to avoid if at all possible."

"I'm not that addicted to the Internet," said Sarah frostily.

"Sure you are. It's like telepathy you don't have to feel bad for using. Also you don't have to worry about stumbling over any sexual fetishes unless you're checking somebody's browser history, and I figure once was enough to teach you that lesson."

Dominic choked on his milkshake.

"I hate you." Sarah sipped her shake, expression mild.

"I know." I finished my own milkshake, putting the cup in the sink before I began digging in the junk drawer for plastic baggies. "I'm going to give you each a scoop of gold dust for later. I'd say wait about six hours and then swallow it. Mix it with something if you need to, but make sure it stays in your system."

"Are we even sure this stuff is going to work for me?" Sarah held up her glass. "It's tasty and all. I just don't want to take it away from the two of you if you're going to actually need it."

"Better safe than sorry." I started tipping gold dust into baggies, trying to distribute it in roughly equal portions. "We don't know that it'll work for you—we don't even know if dragon blood can mutate you the way it does humans, given your biology—but I'd rather not take the risk. The last thing we need is a snake cult with a cuckoo-lizard-hybrid doing its bidding. The servitors are problematic enough without adding telepathy."

"I'm afraid I would have to kill you at that point," said Dominic. He sounded apologetic, which was a bit of a surprise. I would've expected him to be happy about an excuse to kill a cryptid, even if the cryptid in question *was* a member of my family.

"It's okay, I get that," said Sarah.

"Touching as the threats of mayhem are, Dominic and I really do need to go and talk to Piyusha's family. What are your plans for the rest of today, Sarah?" I handed her a baggie of gold dust.

She tucked the baggie into her pocket, replying, "I'm going to hang out here, if it's okay with you. I promised the maid service I'd give them a few hours to clean my room before I locked them out again, and I'd like to catch up with the mice."

"That's cool." I handed Dominic his baggie. He promptly made it disappear into his coat. "Can you do me a favor before you go?"

"What's that?"

"Take Dominic on a Starbucks run? I'd kill for an iced coffee."

Sarah glanced from my empty milkshake glass to the

blood spiking up my hair. *You need a chance to shower?* she asked, as she said, out loud, "Your usual order is good?"

"Yes, exactly," I said.

"No problem. Come on, Covenant boy." She grabbed a startled-looking Dominic's elbow, tugging him toward the apartment door. "You can buy me a scone."

"Are you going to insist on covering it with ketchup?" he asked, glancing back at me with a question in his eyes. I nodded reassuringly. Either he was starting to trust me, or he could guess my real motives, because he didn't fight her as she guided him out of the kitchen.

"Don't be ridiculous; ketchup doesn't go on scones." Sarah stepped out into the hall, still pulling Dominic along. "Curry goes on maple scones, and steak sauce goes on blueberry scones."

"What about chocolate scones?"

The closing door cut Sarah off mid-"Ew." I smiled slightly, shaking my head, and turned to sprint for the bathroom. If I was going to tell Piyusha's family that I hadn't been fast enough to save her, I was at least going to do them the courtesy of doing it while not covered head to toe in gore.

Going by the clock, I was going to need to head straight to work after visiting Piyusha's brothers. Dave would probably let me get away with working a half-shift, given the whole "dragon under the city and snake cult killing people" situation, but if I didn't pick up some tips, I wasn't going to be paying the power bill. Protecting the human race should really come with a per diem, I swear.

At least knowing that I'd be changing into my work uniform soon made it easy to get dressed, since I didn't need to worry about looking good, just looking street-legal. By the time Sarah and Dominic made it back upstairs—both of them holding iced coffees, and Sarah gnawing on a sticky-looking maple scone—I was in the front room, emailing copies of the pictures to Auntie Jane and Antimony. I was wearing clean jeans, a dark gray tank top, and a pair of broken-in running shoes that would allow me to take my usual overland route to work without needing to worry about adding blisters to my existing collection. A little heavy-duty foundation was enough to hide most of my bruises, including the ones forming around my neck. Always an important consideration before a dance competition, or a night of cocktail waitressing. Covering the shiner would take more work, and I'd do that later.

"Here," said Sarah, thrusting the iced coffee she was holding at me. "Dominic insisted on buying it for you, so you can thank him."

"She was intending to walk out without paying!"

Sarah shrugged. "I left a tip."

"Let's not have the ethics of shoplifting coffee fight right now, okay, guys? Thanks for the coffee, Dominic. Sarah, the apartment's yours until I get back. Don't let the mice watch anything on Showtime or Animal Planet, feel free to eat anything you find in the kitchen and, if you're going to be playing with the computer, keep an eye on my inbox, okay?"

"I'll call if you get anything that looks important."

"I'll keep my phone on vibrate." I grabbed my backpack as I stood, slinging its reassuring weight over my shoulder. I was carrying a few dozen more weapons than I usually found necessary for casual city running, but with a snake cult making things complicated, I couldn't really be blamed for a little paranoia.

Dominic gave me a sidelong, half-amused look, commenting, "You're clanking."

"Damn straight." I waved to Sarah, who was already sitting down at the computer, and left the apartment without looking back.

Once again, Dominic insisted on taking a taxi, and once again, it just wasn't worth the trouble of fighting him. Besides, he probably had some sort of an expense account (thus explaining why I wasn't getting a per diem; the Covenant had all the ready cash). If the Covenant wanted to pay to move me around Manhattan, that was their problem, not mine.

Gingerbread Pudding was still closed. That made sense. If it was a family-owned business, they weren't going to open the doors until they knew what had happened to Piyusha. The researcher in me wanted to ask what their funereal observances were like, and whether they'd be willing to let me attend. The part of me that actually cares about being a decent person promptly punched my inner researcher in the jaw and stuffed her in a closet at the back of my head, to be retrieved later.

Dominic looked at the darkened storefront, frowning. "Are you sure they'll be here?"

"If you'd just sent a total stranger into the sewers to find your missing sister, would you run off before she came back with news?"

"No," he admitted. "But I also wouldn't send a stranger into the sewers to find my sister alone."

"Do you even have a sister?" I knocked on the window next to the door, peering into the gloom. I didn't see any movement. That didn't necessarily mean anything. "You know way too much about my family, and I don't know anything at all about yours."

"No. No siblings. No family of any kind." He continued watching the storefront, expression not changing. "I was an only child."

"That must have been nice. Nobody stealing your stuff while you slept, or setting snares on your bedroom floor, or digging pit traps in the front yard."

"Your siblings did all that?"

"My sister is special." That was putting things as mildly—and nicely—as possible. I knocked again, squinting into the dark. "I really thought they'd be here."

"Perhaps you could leave them a note?" I gave him a sharp look. Dominic winced. "Perhaps not. I'm really not sure of the etiquette here."

"Do you know what the etiquette would be if they were human?"

"Yes, of course."

"Well, assume that when Ms. Manners says 'human,' she really means 'sentient,' and run from there. It translates pretty well to everything but dining, dating, and divorce."

Dominic eyed me oddly. "Divorce?"

"Oh, yeah. Like when nue split up, the male generally gets sacrificed by the female and fed to the relatives to avoid creating bad blood between the two sides of the family." I shrugged. "People are weird."

"It will never cease to amaze me that you say these things in places where anyone could overhear you. What's to stop the populace from decrying you as a witch and rising against you?"

"I don't know. A couple hundred years of social evolution, combined with a general failure to believe in anything that doesn't have a Wikipedia entry? Except most cryptids have Wikipedia entries these days, so that's maybe not such a good measuring stick. You know, most of the edits on the Sasquatch entry are actually made *by* Sasquatch? They think it's hysterical watching the human editors argue about whether or not to let one of their corrections stand."

"That's something else that will never cease to amaze me. Your wealth of useless knowledge."

"Everybody needs a hobby." I knocked a third time. "I'm getting a little worried. The snake cult's only been taking girls before this, but if the dragon isn't waking up, they may have decided to mix it up a little. See if maybe the problem is that they're offering him the wrong kind of snack food."

"Should we break in?"

"Maybe." Something finally moved in the darkened

shop. I exhaled. "Okay, good, maybe not. Please be nice to them, okay?"

"I shall do my best."

Footsteps became audible as Rochak approached, undoing the deadbolt before opening the door. He looked worse than I felt. "You came back." It was almost an accusation.

"I told you I would." I gestured to Dominic. "This is Dominic De Luca. He was with me when I met your sister." I didn't offer Rochak's name. If he wanted to identify himself to a member of the Covenant, that was his choice, not mine.

At the moment, he didn't seem to be leaning in that particular direction. He stared at me like I'd just announced that I was standing on his doorstep with Jack the Ripper in tow, and demanded, in a low hiss, "And you brought him *back*? Are you trying to get us killed?"

"If I may," interjected Dominic, "I already know the location of your business, having been here once before, and I accompanied Miss Price with no intention of either harming you or notifying my associates of your presence. You have my word that I intend you no harm."

"See? He comes in peace." I looked at Rochak gravely. "May we please come in? I can guarantee Mr. De Luca's good behavior."

"It's true," said Dominic. "She'll shoot me if I misbehave."

"With pleasure," I added.

"I wouldn't want to miss that," said Rochak, and stepped backward. "Please, come inside. Sunil is upstairs."

Even with the lights off and the customers gone, Gingerbread Pudding smelled of sugar and honey and the sharp sweetness of candied ginger. Rochak didn't speak as he led us through the kitchen and past the employee break room to a set of stairs behind a door marked "Employees Only." His silence wasn't a surprise. He had to know what my showing up without Piyusha meant, and if he wanted to wait to hear for sure until we were in the presence of his brother, that was his decision. I try never to tell others how to grieve.

The stairs ended in an airy, well-lit hallway. Jars of honey sat on low shelves with candles burning beneath them, covered by mesh lids to keep out any errant flies. The heat was enough to spread the sugary sweetness through the air like incense, until the whole place smelled like the home of Willy Wonka's trendy older sister. The décor was a blend of traditional Indian and modern American, and the walls were covered with photographs of people who were clearly family. Pots of honeysuckle and live sugarcane lined the windowsills, all clearly thriving.

Dominic stuck close to my side, expression growing deeply uncomfortable as he looked around the upstairs hall. His training had probably prepared him for caves, dank lairs, and horror movie kitchens with bloodstains on the walls. Unless the Covenant had changed a lot more than he was letting on, it hadn't prepared him for polished hardwood floors and lumpy modeling clay "vases" of the type I recognized from Antimony's kindergarten year (before she moved on to homemade shrapnel grenades).

The room at the end of the hall seemed designed to serve as a combination kitchen and dining area, and was larger than the living room at my sublet. Sunil was at the stove, sautéing something in what smelled like more honey. He looked up when we entered. Seeing the look on Rochak's face, his own face fell, expression fading by inches from mere worry into something utterly empty of emotion.

"Piyusha's dead, isn't she?" he asked.

Unable to find the words to answer him, I nodded.

"What happened? Where is she?" His voice was even blanker than his expression, as flat as day-old soda.

"She's still underground where I found her," I said, once I could force myself to speak. It was hard to make myself look at him, rather than staring off at some point in the distance—some point that wouldn't look at me with accusing eyes. "I found her shortly after I went down. I'm . . . I'm sorry."

"You just *left* her there?" asked Rochak incredulously. "You found our sister, and then you just *left* her? What kind of a monster *are* you?"

"Rochak, be nice," said Sunil.

"Why? So they won't kill us, too?" Rochak glared, hands balling into fists as he looked from me to Dominic and back again. "How dare you leave her behind?"

"I left her behind because I thought you'd like to know what happened to her, instead of sitting here forever wondering if she was going to come home." I shook my head. "The people that took your sister, they're . . . they're not good people, and she wasn't the first."

"We knew that," snapped Rochak.

"Well, they apparently knew that somebody might come looking for her, because they left guards with her body." The two Madhura were silent. "Have either of you ever heard the dragon princesses mention something called a 'servitor'?"

"I . . . I don't believe so," said Sunil, a note of caution creeping into the emptiness of his voice. Rochak glanced at him with clear alarm. Sunil didn't acknowledge the look as he continued, slowly, "The term isn't familiar."

"Your brother seems to recognize it." I focused on Rochak. "What do you know?"

"Nothing! I—nothing." Rochak looked away. "It's not right to leave her down there. We need to recover her. See that she has a proper burial."

"Which will be easier if we know what's going to try to eat us when we go down to bring her back for you," I said. "What do you know?"

"I—"

"It wasn't the dragon princesses," said Sunil. All three of us turned in his direction, Rochak looking relieved by his brother's decision to speak up. "There were some men here about a week ago. Human men. Piyusha waited on their table; she said they were very dismissive of her service, called her a 'servitor.' At the time, we thought it was just general unpleasantness. I told her to pay it no heed. People have been casually nasty ever since we moved here."

"From India?" asked Dominic.

Sunil looked at him like he was an idiot. "From San Jose. Do we sound like we're from India?"

Dominic glanced in my direction, clearly startled. Apparently, the idea of cryptids being natural-born citizens of a country their species didn't originate in had never crossed his mind. "I see," he said.

I kept my attention focused on Sunil. "What did these men look like? And if they were just men, why so worried?"

"Like businessmen. They were middle-aged, they wore suits. They ordered gingerbread, but didn't eat it. As for my concern . . . they were here. They knew to come here, and we had no idea that we should be stopping them." He frowned slowly. "They were servitors?"

"No. But I think they may be controlling the servitors." If the men knew enough about cryptids to be trying to wake a dragon, they'd probably know how to identify the more common humanoid species. You can tell a Madhura by the sweet smell they use to mark their territory . . . or, if they're confusing their territory markers by working in a dessert café, by the taste of their baking. Relief washed over me. "They scouted out your sister a long time before Dominic and I showed up here."

"Wait." Sunil raised a hand. "This is the man from the Covenant?"

"She brought him with her, and vouched for his behavior," said Rochak.

"No harm will come from my hand to anyone in this house." Dominic's statement was as abrupt as it was unexpected. I jerked my head around, openly gaping at him. He met my eyes without flinching. "I have made no reports of your existence to the Covenant, and no such reports will be made. I am truly, deeply sorry for your loss. Your sister was a lovely woman. She deserved better."

You could have knocked me over with a feather. "So, uh," I said, trying to get my equilibrium back. "I'll go back down and try to get your sister's body from the servitors just as soon as I can. Please don't try to recover her on your own. It's not safe."

Just when I thought Dominic couldn't surprise me further, he managed it. "I'll bring her back here," he said. Now all three of us were staring at him. Looking faintly abashed, he said, "It is the least I can do for all the trouble that we have caused you."

Sunil was the first to recover. "That's very kind," he said. "Please don't feel the need to put yourself out on our account. Your offer is very generous, but my family's means are small. We can't afford to pay our debt to you."

"You misunderstand," said Dominic gravely. "This is my attempt to begin paying the Covenant's debt to you."

There wasn't anything to say after that. We just stared.

Sunil and Rochak escorted us from the café with a speed that would have been insulting, if they hadn't just lost a sibling and if I weren't traveling in the company of a man from the Covenant. They pressed sacks of fresh-baked gingerbread into our hands before closing the door behind us. The characteristic snap of the deadbolt clicking home made it plain that we weren't going to be invited back inside any time soon.

I shifted my gingerbread to my left hand and grabbed Dominic's elbow with my right, tugging him down the sidewalk to the alleyway behind the Chinese deli where I'd first caught Piyusha's scent. It wasn't a pleasant place to have a conversation, but that was sort of the point; it was disgusting enough to verge on private. There hadn't even been any homeless people there before, probably because they had a better class of alleys to hang around in.

Perhaps sensing my intent, Dominic allowed himself to be pulled along, shifting his own gingerbread to his off hand in order to make it easier for me. Once we were halfway down the alleyway—far enough from the street on either side that we weren't likely to be stumbled over—I let go and turned to face him, saying, "Pardon my French, but what the hell was that?"

He raised his eyebrows. "What the hell was what, exactly? There's been a great deal of 'that' today for you to be asking about, and it would be easier to explain if I knew which specific part you meant."

"The part where you just offered to help a cryptid family." And promised them, in so many words, that he wouldn't tell the Covenant about them. That was the part that was really giving me a headache.

"Is it so difficult to believe that I might have had a change of heart?" he asked quietly.

"After all that training you've been bragging about since you snared me? Yeah, it sort of is. It's like watching a classical ballroom dancer start clogging. You can see it, but that doesn't mean you can actually *believe* it."

"I . . . I'm sorry." The expression in his dark eyes made him look like the world's biggest, most heavily-armed puppy. "It's true that my training has been focused primarily on the more dangerous aspects of the cryptid world—"

"Exactly my point."

"—and I doubt I'll ever share your passion for preserving them without question or restraint, but Verity, I'm not *blind*. These people . . ." He hesitated, clearly at a loss for words before he continued, "These people are *people*. Those men were hurt by the death of their sister. When your cousin made me take her to get your coffee, she didn't remember to pay, but she remembered to tip, she smiled and was pleasant to the barista, she was *trying*. I'm not certain what these people are. It's become increasingly difficult to view them as monsters."

I blinked, twice, before doing something I'd expected never to do again. Stepping forward, I leaned up onto the toes of my sneakers, and kissed him. Dominic slipped his arm around my waist, providing the stability he needed to lean into me without toppling over. The alley around us smelled terrible. Rats rustled in the garbage lining the walls, and the scum on the pavement made the sewers look like a pleasant vacation spot. It was still one of the best kisses of my life, and when Dominic pulled away, it left me gasping.

"What was that for?" he asked, taking his arm from around my waist.

I smiled a little. "Having a learning curve."

"Your family still betrayed our sacred order."

"I can live with that."

"The servitors are still horrific perversions of nature."

"I can live with that, too. We'll have to agree to disagree on the dragon, but hey. Maybe the two of you will get along."

"I sincerely doubt that," said Dominic slowly.

"I guess we'll find out." I looked up, gauging the time by the narrow strip of sky visible between the buildings. "We're going to need to do our body recovery fast, or I'm going to be late for work."

"Your place of employment, is it . . . I mean, is that where you . . ." He gestured vaguely in the air, indicating either an impractically short skirt or the sudden uncontrollable need to make jazz hands.

"Yeah, that's where I got the uniform I was wearing the night you caught me." I shrugged. "It's a strip club—and no," I added, seeing his semi-stricken expression, "I don't strip. I'm generally a no-nudity zone."

A small smile tugged at the corners of his mouth. "Really."

"Unless the mice have a ritual that demands I get naked, really." His smile vanished, replaced by almost comic uncertainty. Even given the gravity of our overall situation, I had to laugh. "God, Dominic, I was kidding. The mice don't dictate my state of undress. The uniform is how all the cocktail waitresses have to dress. It helps us keep our tips up, and you'd be amazed by how many weapons I can fit under that skimpy little outfit."

"I look forward to performing a census, but you needn't worry about timeliness. I can retrieve Piyusha on my own."

I blinked. "Are you sure? There were a lot more servitors down there with her."

"I'm sure. You go and do what must be done. I'll return Piyusha to her family, and then—where should I meet you?"

"I'm not sure what time I'll be able to get out of my shift; feel free to just head back to the apartment. Sarah will either ignore you completely or kick your ass at chess, and either way, she'll be happy to keep you busy until I get home." I thrust my bag of gingerbread at him. "Take this with you. To the apartment, not into the sewers, if you can help it. The fastest way to the hearts of my mice is through their tiny, overactive stomachs."

"I'll take it to your apartment before I descend," he said. "You're sure you'll be all right?"

"I'm a Price girl, remember? We're like the antithesis of damsels in distress. Besides, I'm spending the evening at a strip club, waiting on drunk businessmen and frat boys who don't know how to pick a watering hole." I flashed a smile. "I'll not only be perfectly safe, I may get paid for breaking a few fingers."

"Good," he said, and kissed me again. It was a gesture that was becoming pleasantly familiar. He was getting seriously better at it, too. I'd be happy to help him get a lot more practice. "I intend to hold you to that."

"Don't worry about me," I said flippantly. "I'm the bad thing that happens to other people."

Sometimes I think the universe listens for lines like

that one, so that it can punish the people who use them. At that particular moment in time, standing in a smelly, deserted alley with a hot Covenant boy and two bags full of the world's best gingerbread, I found it difficult to care.

That was my first mistake.

Twenty-two

"Never tell anyone to be careful, never ask what that noise was, and for the love of God, never, ever say that you'll be right back."

        –Evelyn Baker

The roof of Dave's Fish and Strips, a club for discerning gentlemen, only ten minutes late for work

I HIT THE ROOF OF THE STRIP CLUB at a speed that probably qualified me for the free running Olympic trials. I slowed myself down by using the lip around the edge of the roof as a sort of high-speed balance beam, finally hopping down when I was sure I wouldn't twist an ankle doing it. All the muscles in my legs were complaining in that happy "feeling the burn" way that meant I'd be able to get through my shift without feeling the need to shove my foot up someone's ass, largely because I wouldn't feel like lifting my feet that far off the floor. The rooftop door was unlocked. I opened it and went inside.

Candy and Istas were in the locker room when I arrived. Istas stood in front of the mirror making the final adjustments to her coquettish pigtails. Watching a waheela try to play the Gothic Lolita is so wrong on so many levels that I immediately skipped to Candy, who was involved in the much less worrisome process of applying sparkly pink lip gloss. "Hey, guys," I said, heading for my locker. "Sorry I'm late."

"Don't worry about it," said Candy, flashing me a quick, stiff-looking smile. Guess Mae West told her to play nice.

Istas grunted. All things considered, that was probably the friendlier and more sincere of the greetings. Waheela are solitary creatures, coming into the company of others only when they absolutely have to, for things like reproduction and paying the cable bill. I've never been able to figure out what evolutionary advantage they got from being able to turn into humanoid bipeds, since their default big-ass wolf-bear shapes—or, as I like to call them, "please God don't eat me"—are a lot better suited to their natural habitat in Northern Canada. In her human form, Istas was a cute and curvy Inuit girl with slightly too-sharp teeth and a tendency to talk to people's jugulars. If she was just grunting, not attacking, she was in a good mood.

"Carol already on the floor?" I hooked open my locker, pulling out my uniform top before hauling my shirt off over my head.

"She called in sick," said Candy.

I paused in the process of unfastening my jeans. As far as I knew, Carol was unmarried, and lived alone. "Did she actually call in, or did she just not show up?"

Candy shrugged to show her total lack of concern for such nonfinancial niceties. Swearing under my breath, I went back to getting changed. Dave didn't like the waitresses to appear in the club out of uniform (he said it sent a mixed message; I was pretty sure he just hated not being able to see our tits), and I needed to go into the club if I wanted to find Ryan. He took his duties as bouncer and protector of us girls seriously. I was hoping that would extend to pulling Carol's emergency contact information and heading over to check on her. Just in case. If she was really sick, she'd probably appreciate some chicken soup and maybe some pinkie mice for her hair. If she wasn't . . .

I already felt lousy for going to work while Dominic—a man from the Covenant, for God's sake—retrieved Piyusha's body from its resting place beneath the city streets. If Carol had been taken because I didn't think to warn her about the goddamn snake cult, I was never going to forgive myself.

Twisting my hair roughly into a tangled bun, I secured it with a hair pick that could double as a stiletto and went stomping toward the front of the club. Time to dispatch the tanuki.

Ryan was exactly where I expected him to be this early in the evening: standing by the register chatting with Angel, who was wiping down the bar and trying to hear him over the thumping bass of the current dancer's personal soundtrack. She saw me coming before Ryan did. Tucking the rag into her pocket, she straightened up and looked at me anxiously. Once I was in earshot, she asked, "Well, Very? What's the news?"

"Verity!" Ryan smiled, displaying outsized canines. They were at half-mast; he was in good control of his therianthropy, which was a good thing if I was about to send him looking for Carol. "I wasn't sure you were going to come in tonight. Candy was saying you'd been out to visit the Nest today."

I paused to eye his expression. He looked sincere—no surprise there, Ryan always looked sincere—and like he had no idea that a dragon princess wouldn't just decide to have a Price girl over on a social call. Pushing my misgivings aside, I said, "It's been one hell of a week, and it's not getting any better. In the locker room, Candy said Carol was out sick tonight. Do you know if she actually called in to say she wouldn't be coming?"

"She didn't," said Angel. "Dave was *pissed* when she

didn't show, especially since we'd all been figuring you'd be out. Candy already gouged him for a promise of overtime."

"That's what I was afraid of." I turned to Ryan. "You need to go to Carol's apartment. You need to leave *right now*, and you need to go as fast as you can."

"What's going on?"

"You know how cryptid girls have been disappearing? Well, there's a snake cult under the city, and I'm pretty sure they're sacrificing them to a dragon in order to try waking it up. Not that it cares, since, well, dragons, not all that into the eating of sentient creatures and are you two even listening to me or are you too busy staring like I just grew a second head?" I touched my shoulder automatically. No extra head greeted me. After the week I'd been having, that was something of a relief.

"Dragons are extinct, Verity," said Ryan.

"And humans don't fraternize with cryptids, but there's Angel, and here I am, and somewhere under this city there are a bunch of assholes feeding cryptid girls to a sleeping dragon because they think it's the way to achieve ultimate cosmic power. Or something like that. I don't know—I haven't found the snake cult yet and, when I do, they can explain themselves to me during the pauses."

"The pauses?" asked Ryan. His canines were starting to get more pronounced. That was good. That meant that he was taking me seriously.

"I can't beat their heads against the wall constantly, now can I? So will you go, or do I have to start beating *your* head against the wall?"

"I'll drive," said Angel. I shot her a startled look. She met it without batting an eye. "Carol's my friend, too, and if she's in trouble, Ryan shouldn't be dealing with it alone."

"Won't Dave get pissed?"

"If we disappear together, he'll figure Ryan's instincts finally got the best of him, and he'll call it our lunch hour." Angel pulled the dishrag out of her pocket and dropped it on the bar. "Give me five minutes to get changed and I'll pick you up in front of the club."

"Got it," said Ryan. He watched Angel go before looking back to me. "Very, I really hope you're wrong about this."

"Trust me," I said grimly. "So do I."

L

Twenty minutes passed without word from Ryan and Angel. I worked five tables, avoided being kicked in the head by an overenthusiastic pole-dancer, and picked up about half my usual tips. Worry made it difficult to focus on flirting enough to get paid for it without crossing the line into coming off like I offered cocktails off a "special" menu. (Technically, Dave's had a special menu. It just involved slime, blood, and other unmentionable fluids, rather than cheap sex in the employee break room.)

I was making my fifth round with the cleanup tray when my phone started ringing. I promptly dug it out of my apron pocket, shifting the tray to my dominant hand as I wedged the phone between my ear and shoulder. "Hello?"

"Verity?" Ryan's voice was low and gravelly, and further distorted by the static of a bad connection. "Are you there?"

"Ryan!" I began beating a rapid retreat toward the bar, ignoring the people who were trying to flag me down. One of them flipped me off when I blew past his table without slowing. I made a mental note to fuck up his drink order at least once before the end of my shift. "Where are you? Is Carol okay?"

"She's shaken, but she's not really hurt. You were right about the snake cult coming to get her."

I sagged against the bar, dropping my tray atop it with a loud clatter. Angel's temporary replacement shot me a sour look. I showed him the gesture our beloved patron had so recently shown to me. "They came? But she's okay?"

"She is. Two of them aren't. Guess her hair really does bite."

"Oh, Jesus." I closed my eyes for a moment, letting my shoulders relax. "You should get her out of there. What's the address? I have someone I can send for the bodies." Gingerbread Pudding was in the phone book. If Piyusha's brothers wanted me to go bobbing for corpses, they could return the favor. Call it the first step toward justice: these were some of the men responsible for the death of their sister, after all.

"She's pretty damn rattled. I'll be back in about an hour; I'm going to get Carol and Angel set up at my place." Ryan's growl came through clearly, despite the static. "If any snake cultists want to try breaking into my home, they'll be sorry."

The defenses a pissed-off tanuki can throw up around his den rival the ones Antimony throws up around her bedroom. Ryan was right: Carol and Angel would be safe at his place, at least for the moment. "Just give me the address. I'll let Dave know that Angel won't be back tonight, and why."

"Great." Ryan rattled off an address uptown. It was reasonably close to Gingerbread Pudding, which was a relief; at least I wasn't going to be asking a pair of Madhura to tote the bodies very far.

"Thanks." I hung up, only to immediately dial Sarah's number.

The phone rang just long enough that I was beginning to worry about the fact that I'd run off and left my cousin alone with a member of the Covenant. Cuckoos are great hiders, but she didn't really have any natural defenses once she'd been spotted. I was starting to wonder what Artie would do to me if I'd managed to get Sarah killed when the phone was picked up, and she said, half-laughing, "Hi, Verity! We were just talking about you."

The mice were cheering in the background, probably because they'd just revealed some horribly embarrassing personal secret to Dominic. I let out a sigh of relief. "Sarah. Hi. Can you put Dominic on the phone?"

"You called me to talk to him? Way to make a girl feel loved, Very-Very."

"I'm serious. I don't have his number, and I need him to go look at a couple of corpses."

Sarah went quiet, leaving only the cheers of the mice to serve as counterpoint to the club's thumping bass line. "You're serious, aren't you?" she asked finally, voice hushed.

"Yeah, I am. The snake cult went after Carol from work." One of the passing bachelor party boys gave me a funny look. Given that he'd just been leering at a stripper with a tail, I really didn't see where he got off. I showed him my middle finger. He showed me his. Vital cultural exchange completed, he walked away.

"The gorgon?"

"That's the one. She's not hurt, but two of the cultists are dead, and I figure Dominic may be able to figure out some more about their MO by looking them over."

"I'll put him on," said Sarah, still hushed.

"I'll be here." I straightened up and started for the break room while I was waiting for her to pass the phone. If I could avoid any further "cultural exchanges" with our customers, I might also be able to avoid getting fired for another week.

I was halfway to the employee door when Dominic came on the line, asking, "Where are the bodies?"

"It's always business with you, isn't it?"

"As a rule, yes."

"Well, right now, that's a good thing. Do you have something to write with?"

"Yes."

I rattled off the address to Carol's place without hesitation. If the cultists knew where she lived, she was already compromised; one member of the Covenant of St. George wasn't going to make that much of a difference. "Call Gingerbread Pudding, get Sunil and Rochak to help you. You should probably take the bodies back to the café, since they have more room and probably a much bigger freezer. I'll be there as soon as I can."

"What are you going to do in the meantime?"

"I'm going to go and explain to my boss why he needs to shut down the club until we find the snake cult. This is the second cryptid woman I know of who's been attacked *and* has a job that brings her regularly into contact with the public. They may have started with the ones who lived outside human society, but they're getting more central, and Dave's . . ." I paused in the doorway, scanning the club floor. I could see half a dozen cryptids from where I stood without really making an effort, and that didn't include any of the staff. I shook my head. "Dave's is like an all-you-can-kill buffet."

The darks were on in Dave's office, spilling through the open door to fill the hall with an almost physical weight. Approaching the doorway was like wading into pools of tar that had no substance, only darkness deep enough to swallow all the light in the world. "Dave?" I called. "Are you in there?"

"Very, Very, quite contrary." His voice drifted from the dark, sounding more suited to an ancient tomb— curse optional—than the manager's office of a strip club. "How does your garden grow, I wonder? I wasn't sure we'd be seeing you around here again, given what the streets are saying."

"And what's that?" I held my position, not moving any closer to the too-solid darkness. I wasn't angry enough for that much bravado, and something about the sound of Dave's voice was putting my nerves more on edge than they already were. He liked his horror host turned pornographer routine, but he normally dropped it within the first few words.

"That you've changed sides, my pretty little dandelion flower. That you've been running the rooftops and searching the sewers with our intrepid young man from the Covenant of St. George, and that perhaps—just perhaps—your motives can't be trusted."

"Cut the crap, Dave," I snapped. "You were the one who didn't tell us he was in town, remember? I didn't invite him here, and you didn't send out the bulletin on his location until after he'd already caught me."

"But I'm not the one who took him into her home, Verity Price, nor the one who brought him to the home of an innocent family of Madhura. What *would* your mother say?" His voice hadn't moved once while he was speaking, but he was suddenly in front of me, gray-skinned face leering from the border of the blackness. It was a classic bogeyman trick; while they can't actually teleport or anything like that, they can control where their voices come from to a degree that any human ventriloquist would kill for. That's how they can be everywhere at once when they sneak into your bedroom in the middle of the night—vaudeville and chicanery.

I learned about the kind of crap bogeymen like to pull when I was still in elementary school. I should have been braced. But Dave, for all his asshole tendencies, had never done anything like that before, and I wasn't prepared. I jumped, taking a quick step backward and almost falling over my own feet in the process.

Dave smirked slowly. "Is that guilty conscience making you uneasy? Ashamed that someone finally found the purchase price for a Price?"

"Fuck you," I said flatly. "Are you done being a dick? I need to talk to you, and unless you fired me while I wasn't looking, I have the right to demand my manager's attention."

"Why in the world would I fire you when you're such

a source of amusement?" Dave's face vanished back into the shadows. A few seconds later the darks clicked off, filling the tiny office with dusty light. Dave was seated behind his desk, looking for all the world like he hadn't moved in days. His sunglasses were even in place. "Come in, Verity. Tell me what's so important that you had to leave the floor in the middle of your shift."

"Carol's been attacked."

It was hard to tell if Dave's expression changed at all. His tone certainly didn't. "Is that why she didn't come in this evening? I was wondering. Was it a mugging, or a home invasion?"

"Home invasion by snake cult, actually, and she's fine, thanks so much for asking." I slapped a hand down flat on his desk. "Cryptid girls have been disappearing all over this city—"

"I know."

"—and I know you know about it, because you . . . wait, what did you say?"

"I said I know. Given that you just accused me of exactly that, I don't understand quite why you look so surprised." Dave settled back in his chair. "Whatever's been going on hasn't been involving my staff, so I haven't really seen the need to concern myself with it."

"Did you not once think that I might have wanted to know?"

"Did you not once think that I might believe you were behind it?"

I stopped, gaping at him. "You're not serious."

"True enough, I'm not, but you should see the look on your face right now." Dave shook his head. "You don't pay me for information, Verity. You could have come to me at any point and offered an exchange. Money, gossip, you dancing on my stage, I would have taken any of those. You never offered, and so neither did I."

"You knew I was looking into the disappearances."

"Yes, and I also knew that you were laying traps for the Covenant boy, but you didn't feel the need to keep me updated on your progress, now, did you?" Scowling now, Dave leaned forward and drummed his simian fingers against the desk. "You can't go through life expecting something for nothing, whether or not you believe that you're on the 'right side.' The right side is the one that pays for the tools it needs."

The urge to punch him in the nose warred with the urge to punch myself. I knew he was a bogeyman when I took the job, and much as I hated to think it, he was at least partially right. The first question any bogeyman asks when you ask him for help is "What's in it for me?"

"Fine," I said, after taking a deep breath. "You want to trade information?"

"Why, my dear Verity," he said, scowl turning into an expression of predatory anticipation. "I was starting to think you'd never ask."

Trading information with a bogeyman is difficult under the best of circumstances. Since gossip is their primary currency, they'll not only try to get as much as possible while giving as little as they can get away with, they'll leave things out. Little things, like the number of wendigo reported in a neighborhood or the exact species of the basilisks in question. It's the little things that can get you killed.

Explaining how I was so sure there was a dragon under the city without telling him about Sarah was difficult, but not impossible. People mostly ignore the existence of cuckoos even when leaving them out of something causes it to stop making any actual sense. I just said I'd been "reasonably suspicious" after talking to Piyusha, and that I'd been able to find a write-up on the Sleestaks in one of Dad's bestiaries. I didn't tell him about the mutagenic properties of dragon blood, or that the servitors were originally humans. That was a piece of information that might be valuable, but was also dangerous; there were cryptids who would happily spike the city water supply and live off bottled water for a year if it meant turning the entire human population into lizards. As a part of the human population, I didn't feel it was my job to encourage that sort of thing.

I told him about finding Piyusha's body, and how the symbols confirmed that there was a snake cult trying to wake the dragon. After a momentary pause, I continued with an explanation of what had happened at Candy's. I left out everything I'd learned about the actual relationship between the dragon princesses and the dragons. It was a valuable piece of information. It was something everyone had been wondering for centuries. And it was none of his goddamn business.

When I finished, Dave looked at me thoughtfully, and asked, "You took pictures of the symbols on her body?"

"I did. I've been able to translate a few of them, and I mailed all the pictures to my family for further translation. I should know what kind of ritual they're trying to perform by tomorrow." How many cryptid girls was that going to be too late for? The thought was enough to turn my stomach, but there was no way to avoid it.

"I don't suppose you brought me copies."

"I didn't know it was your birthday."

"Ah, well; perhaps later." Dave drummed his fingers against the desk again. "I knew about the snake cult. They're largely human businessmen, with a few more gullible cryptids thrown in to make them seem more legitimate. I wasn't aware that their interests involved feeding my cocktail waitresses to a sleeping dragon. It seems like a rather frivolous waste of a cocktail waitress."

"I'm sure the cocktail waitresses would agree." Shaking him to get him to tell me what I needed to know would be satisfying, but it wouldn't help as much as I wanted it to. "What else do you know about the cult?"

"That they weren't trying to summon a snake god, despite being a snake cult, which struck me as odd when I first heard it. I assure you, this is the first time the word 'dragon' has come up in conjunction with their activities. Are you truly *sure*?"

"Dave, do you honestly think I'd be claiming something the size of Metallica's tour bus was under the city if I wasn't *sure*? Especially when it's something that's supposedly been extinct for centuries? It's a real dragon, I'm absolutely certain, and the assholes want it awake and doing their bidding. I want to stop them. Now, where are they?"

"I don't know." Catching the sudden darkness in my eyes, Dave raised his hands, palms out, and protested, "I don't! If I knew, I'd tell you. You've got enough credit, and hell, you think I want these people chopping up the staff? Kitty's going to be back from her tour any day now. I let my sister's kid get sliced and diced, I'm a dead man walking—and that doesn't get into the cost of training replacements for all my girls. I honestly don't know, Verity."

I could argue with him, or I could let it go. At the end of the day, arguing with him was just going to make him less likely to do what I was about to ask. "Fine. But since I just gave you a whole bunch of really good information, and you're not giving me anything I didn't already know, I get to ask you for a favor."

Dave's brief-lived smile faded, replaced by a wounded pout. "Confirmation wasn't good enough for you?"

"Not this time. I need you to close down for the night, and stay closed until we've managed to stop this snake cult. It shouldn't take long. We're closing in on the dragon's location, and now that I have copies of their runes, Dad should hopefully be able to tell me something useful about the rituals they're likely to be using to conceal themselves."

"What the hell do you want me to do that for?"

"Until you do, everyone here is basically just walking around with a giant target painted on top of the tacky uniform!" I pointed toward the door. "They already went after Carol. What's going to stop them from following the rest of the girls home? I need time to stop this, Dave, and I need to do it without being constantly worried that my coworkers are about to become Sacrifice McNuggets."

"Fine," said Dave, looking disgusted. "I'll close for the night, and we can discuss whether I'll be staying closed for the rest of the week. The week! No longer than that. I have a business to run here, and I'm not going to go bankrupt because of some stupid snake cult."

"Thanks, Dave." I flashed a quick smile in his direction. "Do you want me to help you clear the club?"

"I'll just have somebody pull the fire alarm. That'll clear things out fast enough, and it's better than giving people a reason to talk shit about the health inspector closing us down." Dave adjusted his sunglasses. "Now get out of here and go save the world, will you? All this talking with no nudity is giving me a headache."

"I'm on it." I turned and left the office. The darks clicked on before I was three steps down the hall, and shadows thick as tar pooled across the floor once more. I kept walking. That was my second mistake . . . and by that point, although I didn't really know it yet, I was just about out of leeway.

Twenty-three

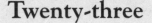

"There's no such thing as fighting dirty.
There's fighting like you want to live, and
fighting like you want to die. If you've got
anything to live for—anything at all—I
suggest you try the first way. The people
you love will thank you for it."

–Alice Healy

The dressing room of Dave's Fish and Strips, a club for discerning gentlemen

TRUE TO HIS WORD, Dave pulled the fire alarm about
five minutes after I reached my locker, sending the
sirens wailing through the building. It was loud even before the DJ killed the sound system, and then it became
practically deafening. I've known actual sirens who
would've been proud to make that kind of racket. (Not
all sirens are into the whole "sitting on rocky atolls luring sailors to their death" gig. At least one is making a
pretty good living as a pop singer. She calls herself "Emerald Green," pretends her hair is dyed that particular
shade of seaweed, and refuses to book gigs in coastal
cities unless they're purely acoustic. Nature isn't always
destiny.)

The other female members of the wait staff began
pouring into the dressing room. The uniforms Dave insisted on meant that they were already practically na-

ked, which you'd think would make the process of getting dressed go faster for them, but no such luck. Even with the fire alarm screaming bloody murder in the background, they mobbed the mirror, taking their time fixing their makeup, adjusting their assets, and, of course, bitching loudly about the sudden closure robbing them of half a shift's tips. Several glared at me while they gossiped, making it clear that they'd noticed how my visit to the manager ended conveniently right before the alarm went off.

I looked calmly back, making no effort to defend myself—or to hide the various weapons waiting to be concealed under my street clothes. One by one, the other waitresses looked away, and their preparations for departure got a lot faster after that. None of them had the guts to accuse me to my face, possibly out of fear that doing so would get their actual guts an introduction to the floor. I ducked my head and went back to adjusting my thigh holster, trying not to think about what that meant. Dave was right. I'd been seen too frequently with Dominic, and people were starting to question my loyalties.

I took my time changing out of my uniform, double and triple-checking the snaps on every holster and the placement of every knife as I pulled my street clothes on. I was dressing for war, and it was time I started taking that seriously. I needed to be on the move sooner, rather than later, but I didn't want to leave until Ryan got back to the bar, and that meant I had time to make sure that I was doing things right for a change. After this, it was going to be corpses and carnage until the snake cult was no longer a part of the picture. They'd killed too many girls. This needed to end.

The last of the waitresses teemed out of the room, moving in a cloud of hairspray, sticky glitter, and cheap perfume. A locker slammed. I looked up again, only to find Candy glaring at me much more openly than any of the others had dared.

"I hope you realize that I was planning to get *paid* tonight," she snarled.

"The snake cult went for Carol," I replied, too annoyed by the accusation in her tone to sugarcoat things. She recoiled, looking like I'd slapped her. I pulled my shirt on over my head, continuing, "Two of them got bitten by her hair. Dominic's getting the bodies now, so we can look them over to see if there's anything that tells us where they're operating. Unless you think your tips are more important than the lives of your coworkers, I suggest you drop the attitude."

"What is a 'snake cult'?" asked Istas, stepping around the bank of lockers. Waheela can move very quietly when they want to; I hadn't even realized she was there. "A species of religious serpents pulled the fire alarm?"

The look of honest puzzlement on her face was enough to make me crack a smile. "A snake cult is a bunch of idiots who think worshiping a snake god will get them unbelievable cosmic power, wealth beyond their wildest dreams, and all the chicks they could want."

"Ah." Istas nodded, opening her own locker. "Are they responsible for the ones who have gone missing?"

"Yeah, they are." I picked up my backpack. "I'm hoping I can stop them before anybody else gets hurt, but it took a long time to figure out who they *were*."

"I understand." Istas' street clothes kept up the Gothic Lolita look established by her pigtails: frilled faux-French maid's uniform with pastel pink petticoats, white tights, even a pair of antique-looking buttonhole shoes. She dressed with admirable speed, navigating the various buttons and snaps with an ease that appeared to impress even Candy. "Will there be rending and destruction in the name of protecting the territory?"

"Probably." I glanced to Candy. "You want to come with me? I'd like you to have a look at the bodies."

"If I don't go with you, Betty will have my head," Candy replied. "I'm not working, thanks to you, so I need to be doing *something* with my time."

"You are going to look at more bodies?" Istas frowned. "Were there insufficient bodies here?"

"Dead ones, Istas," I said.

"Ah. I will accompany you, then." She produced a ruffled lace parasol from her locker before swinging the door closed. She didn't bother to lock it. No one in their right mind would steal from a waheela. "I would like to see some dead bodies. I find them pleasurable."

Candy and I exchanged a look, for once united by our sheer bafflement. We know a lot about the biology and anatomy of the waheela. Their social behaviors, likes, and dislikes . . . not so much.

"Fine," I said. "We could use you, in case the whole 'rending and destruction' thing comes up."

Istas smiled.

The three of us finished getting ready just before the fire alarm stopped blaring. Dave probably shut it down to keep the fire department from showing up. The building was up to code as far as I knew, but the fire department in any given city is ninety percent human. The ten percent that aren't human—salamanders and afrits and the like—tend to get a little pissed off when they get called out for false emergencies. Dave wouldn't enjoy that, and he was too smart to risk it if he didn't have to.

"Bodies now?" asked Istas.

"Let's check the front of the club first," I said. "Ryan's supposed to be coming back after he gets Carol to a safe house, and I want to bring him along if he's willing to come. More muscle for the, ah, rending and destruction."

Istas looked pleased. Candy looked annoyed. Hanging out with a tanuki was probably beneath her dignity as a dragon princess. That, or she just didn't like the number of coworkers she was suddenly hanging out with. Dragon princesses aren't big on socializing outside their Nests, and the fact that I potentially had access to a male of her species was only going to buy me so much slack.

We stepped out into the main club, which looked even more like a deserted sideshow tent when there was no one in it. The British flags hanging from the walls were limp and listless without the air-conditioning to keep them moving, and the smells of sweat and alcohol were masked by a layer of hastily-applied bleach. Dave was closing for the night, if not for the week. That was a start.

"Ryan?" I moved toward the bar, craning my neck to search for signs of movement. "Hey, you back yet?"

No answer. Istas stiffened, a low growl rumbling from her throat before she said, "Something is not right here."

"What?" I looked back at her.

She popped open her parasol, twirling it in agitation. "Something is not right here," she repeated. Her canines were more pronounced than they'd been in the dressing room. "The bleach. This is not the brand Dave buys. This is cheaper, made to stink rather than clean. Everyone is gone. We should not be here."

"Crap." I turned. "Come on. Let's get back to the dressing room." From there, we'd have a clear shot on both the rooftop and cellar exits, in case Istas was right about something being wrong. Candy nodded quickly, and spun to power walk toward the hallway door.

The speed at which she was moving was the only thing that saved her. A servitor flowed out of the shadows surrounding one of the darkened stripper platforms, a lead pipe grasped firmly in its tail. Istas snarled, the sound conveying more shock than fear. Then the servitor's tail lashed forward, the pipe catching her in the jaw, and the waheela went down in a crumpled, incongruously lacy heap.

Candy screamed. Eight more servitors flowed out of the shadows between the two of us, hissing through bared teeth. So much for making it to the corpses any time soon.

Stop me if you've heard this one: so nine servitors, a dragon princess, a waheela, and a cranky ballroom dancer walk into a bar . . .

I started moving before the servitors could stop posturing and charge, running for the nearest stage as I shouted, "Candy! Tell them to stand down!"

Candy nodded and hissed out something in the sibilant language she'd used when we were in the sewers. The servitors ignored her, moving to form a sort of wedge before advancing toward me. She stomped her foot and tried again, louder, the note of command unmistakable in her voice. That got a reaction. The nearest of the servitors whipped around to face her, and snarled, tail lashing in her direction. Candy stepped quickly backward, eyes going wide in her suddenly-pale face.

"Okay, so *that's* not going to work," I muttered, and jumped up onto the stage, pulling a throwing knife from inside my shirt. I flung it at the lead servitor. It caught the knife with the tip of its tail and flung it back. I ducked, hearing the blade whistle over my head on its way to embed itself in the far wall. Oh, this was *so* not good.

The lead servitor leaped onto the table nearest the stage, grabbing a chair with its tail and whipping it twice over its head before launching it in my direction. I grabbed the pole and went into a one-woman deadfall, hooking an ankle around the pole's base to keep from toppling off the stage. The chair hit the wall just below my throwing knife. The servitor hissed in frustration, and then again in pain when I lashed out with one foot, catching it squarely in the kneecap.

Of the nine servitors in sight, seven were focusing on me, and two of them seemed intent on harrying Candy, who clearly had no idea how to deal with this. Istas still wasn't moving. The odds were so far from in our favor that it wasn't even funny.

I've dealt with lousy odds before. Taking advantage of the closest servitor's preoccupation with its bruised knee, I straightened up, yanked my iPod out of my backpack, and flung it overhand at Candy. Years of waiting tables had left her with the kind of reflexes many gymnasts would envy; she caught the flying MP3 player one-handed, shooting me a quizzical look.

"Sound system!" I shouted. "Track four!" The closest servitor seemed to be over his injury, because he lunged for me, taloned hands extended. I grabbed the pole again and dropped back into a bend, kicking forward at the same time. The side of my foot caught him in the chin with substantially more force than would have been possible in an unassisted kick. He dropped like a rock. That would teach him to go fucking with a trained ballroom dancer in a strip club.

"Then what?" shouted Candy, punctuating the question with a startled squeal. I stole a glance in her direction. She was running ahead of the servitors, eyes still huge and frightened.

Dragon princesses have no natural weapons, and only one real natural defense: they're completely fireproof. I grabbed the closest chair and smashed it down on the fallen servitor's head, just to be sure. Then I took off running for the bar. "Just get the music on!"

Out of the corner of my eye, I could see Candy stumbling up onto the DJ platform, the two servitors following behind her with the lazy grace of an apex predator. She wasn't fighting back; she was just running. There was no real reason for them to hurry. The seven servitors still "assigned" to me had clustered together again, and they looked *pissed*. Candy wasn't fighting, but I was apparently fighting substantially more than they wanted me to.

Tough titty. I vaulted onto the bar, grabbing a bottle

of the cheap-ass house vodka. "How's that music coming, Candy?"

"I think I've got it!" The speakers crackled on, hissing static white noise. Half a second later, the opening drone of the Tamperer's "Hammer to the Heart" blasted into the room.

"Catch!" I flung the vodka across to her as hard as I could, praying that the cap would stay on, and that I was still close enough to have any accuracy. Someone was listening, maybe for the only time that night, because the bottle spun end over end to smack into Candy's hand like the game-winning ball at the end of the ninth inning. "Now set yourself on fire!"

Her eyes went enormously wide. "*What*?!"

"Set yourself on fire!" I grabbed two more bottles of vodka, flinging them heedlessly at the lead servitors. They batted the bottles aside, but that didn't matter; taking the time to block had slowed them down, and that was all I really wanted. "They started human, remember?"

Candy's eyes remained wide, but the look in them was comprehension, not confusion. Dragon princesses were fireproof. For all I knew, dragon servitors were, too . . . but humans weren't, and these servitors started life as humans. They were likely to be afraid of fire on general principles, even if it couldn't actually hurt them.

Unscrewing the bottle, Candy emptied its contents over her head while I continued pitching everything I could get my hands on at the closest servitors. Her two started moving faster, apparently realizing that something was up. Then she produced a lighter from her pocket and hit the flint, sending a line of blue flame racing up her hand to her arm to her hair, until she finally went up like a Christmas candle. The servitors fell back, hissing furiously. Even my seven whipped around to face her, snarling and hissing with disbelief. The music was blasting, the beat thrumming through the bar and into the soles of my feet.

Dave always did want me to dance in his club. Grabbing the gun from my waistband, I launched myself off the bar again, and ran for the servitors.

They weren't expecting that. They also weren't expecting me to swerve off at the last minute, shooting enthusiastically but without particular concern for my aim as I ran for the nearest stage. Four of them broke off and chased after me, while the other three hung back, hissing in confusion. They must have been the smart ones.

The thing about dance—and by the same token, the thing about combat—is that it's all in the rhythm. If you can't find the beat, you can't possibly get the steps right. People who say they can't dance really mean that they have no idea how to get themselves synchronized to the beat of the music, and that screws them up. In a fight, the rhythm is generally set by the participants, rather than by any outside soundtrack . . . that is, unless you have a convenient sound system, and a dragon princess on hand to play DJ for you.

The other thing about dance and combat is that once you find the beat, it's borderline impossible to ignore it. I grabbed the pole and boosted myself onto the stage, testing out the four-four rhythm of the song as the servitors closed in. There were four of them approaching, but the shape of the stage restricted them to attacking two at a time. That was good. The fact that they were starting to move clumsily along with the music was better.

The first pair of servitors crowded up against the stage, one of them swinging a two-by-four at my calves. I grabbed the pole and spun myself out of reach, shooting it in the tail. It hissed and dropped the weapon, but didn't fall back as its companion grabbed a chair and slung it in my direction. I barely ducked in time. That's the trouble with bar fights: there's so damn much potential weaponry around. Even someone who doesn't have a clue what they're doing can find plenty of things to throw. Time to shut this party down.

Both servitors were moving, however unconsciously, with the beat of the music. I stopped spinning and leaned out to give them my best tango smile, one hand still clasping the pole. "Hey, boys," I said coquettishly. I wasn't even sure they'd originally been male, but regardless of gender, my behavior needed to be odd enough to throw them off their game. "You want to dance?"

The servitors looked puzzled. Then, snarling, they charged.

I grabbed the pole, dropping back and aiming squarely at the lead servitor's chest as I shouted, "Candy, track seven!" The flaming figure at the DJ stand gestured assent and began jabbing fingers at my iPod, which was hopefully fireproof. If it survived this experience, I'd be sure to send a nice note to Apple about the quality of their products.

The music changed abruptly, replacing the Tamperer with the high-speed frenzy of "Hey Ya!" by Outkast. The servitors kept charging—but they were off-balance now, thrown out of their comfort zone by the sudden change in the beat. I unloaded two bullets into the lead servitor's chest, dropping him, and swung myself hard around to slam my elbow into the second servitor's throat. It wasn't showing mercy; it was conserving bullets by hitting him while his equilibrium was off. He fell back, choking, and was promptly replaced by two more healthy lizard-men, both bent on ripping me to pieces.

I shot the first in the chest. The second lashed out with the lead pipe held in his tail, hitting my wrist and knocking the gun from my hand. I yelped and spun around the pole again, bringing my feet up and together to slam into the servitor's face. He rocked back, hissing ferociously, but didn't fall.

"Okay, time for plan B," I muttered, before shouting,

"Candy! Track eleven!" The poisonously bubbly sound of Aqua blasted from the speakers, the sudden addition of a bone-rattling bass line disorienting the servitors for the half second I needed to jump from the stage and take off running across the strip club. They followed. That was fine. I'd been looking for a reprieve, not an escape.

I spared a glance toward Candy as I ran for the wall. She was still burning brightly, her two harrying servitors hanging back and hissing at her. There was another update for the rapidly evolving file on the dragon princesses. They might not be able to create or control flame, but they could encourage it to last longer than it should have. She'd been burning long enough that the vodka should definitely have been gone. The flames didn't seem to mind the absence of an accelerant. They were perfectly content to leap and dance around her, consuming her clothing, and showing no signs of either dying out or spreading to the rest of the club.

I vaulted over Istas as I made my way across the room, not pausing to see whether she was breathing. With no backup in the building and no clear escape route that would work for all three of us, I just had to keep fighting until she either woke up or the fight was over, one way or the other.

When I reached the wall, I grabbed the nearest limply dangling flag and began pulling myself off the ground, scrambling upward with a speed that would have impressed my free running instructors. Most of the servitors were still in hot pursuit and, to make matters worse, the ones toward the rear of the pack were starting to get fuzzy around the edges. They didn't seem capable of staying camouflaged when they were actually attacking, but they could sneak up while I couldn't see them. This needed to end soon, or they were going to end it for me.

I stopped halfway up the flag, wrapping one leg tight

around the cloth and dangling like I was planning to audition for the next Cirque de Soleil show. I didn't even wait to be certain that I was secure before pulling the revolvers from under my shirt and started firing into the swarm of servitors. The thunderous echoes of the gunshots blended with the relentless cheer of the blaring pop music, making it sound like some sort of really badly thought-out remix.

Two servitors went down hard. I would have been pleased by the shift in the odds, if not for the two who'd been circling Candy suddenly deciding that I was a much more dangerous target. They turned from her to join the pack that was closing in on me, leaving me with fewer bullets and just as many targets in need of gunning down. I swore, firing twice more and felling a third servitor for my troubles. The one I'd kicked in the throat picked himself up off the ground and ran to join the fight.

"Fuck," I muttered, and took aim. This was looking bad. "Candy! Track two!" Aqua cut out, replaced by Pink. If I was going to get ripped apart, at least I wouldn't need to be embarrassed by the song I used for my last dance. "Now get out of here! *Run!*"

It was hard to make out any expression on her face, veiled as it was by the crackling flames. Still, I thought I saw her nod before she turned and fled for the hallway door, leaving me with the charging servitors and the screaming wail of electric guitars.

"All right, you motherfucking lizards," I snarled. "Let's dance."

I opened fire. They charged.

The thing about waheela is that they're like the Timex watch of subarctic cryptids: they can take a licking and keep on ticking. Right about the time the remaining servitors reached the wall, driving me farther up the flag as they grabbed for my ankles with their whipcord tails, Istas sat up.

First she rubbed her jaw. Then she looked around the room, clearly bewildered. And then she saw her parasol, which had not only fallen to the floor when she did, but had landed in the path of several servitors. The lace was ripped. A large footprint marred its previously pristine surface. Istas, seeing her property treated with such an obvious lack of respect, began to growl. And then she unbuttoned her shoes.

It was almost possible to feel sorry for the servitors after that. Sure, they were creepy lizard-men trying to kill me, but they weren't doing it voluntarily. They were men when all this craziness started—and as men, they probably never even *heard* of waheela, much less learned what a bad idea it was to piss one off. I shot one of them in the shoulder, and another in the tail. Then Istas stood up, balancing on the toes of her feet, and roared.

It wasn't a sound that should ever come from a human throat, which made sense, since Istas didn't technically *have* a human throat anymore. What she had was a neck that was rapidly swelling like an inner tube as her musculature tripled in mass and density. Sort of like the Incredible Hulk if Bruce Banner were a cocktail waitress instead of a rocket scientist. Several of the servitors whipped around to hiss at her. Istas roared again and then, while the echoes of her challenge were still ringing through the club, she charged.

For the servitors, it must have seemed odd in the extreme when the cute little chick in the frilly maid uniform started running toward them, howling challenge all the way. It just got odder from there. By the second step she took, she had doubled in size, shredding her stockings and splitting the seams all up and down the sides of her cute little uniform. By the third step, her clothing was falling away like so much debris, but it didn't really matter, since her pelt was coming in, covering her body with a thick, protective layer of red-black hair. By the fourth step, she was only technically bipedal. The changes accelerated after that, as did Istas, and she slammed into the servitors in full animal form: a wolf the size of a grizzly bear, with a grizzly's flexible paws and the furious mind of a pissed-off Gothic Lolita.

The servitors didn't stand a chance. She slapped two of them aside like they were bowling pins, and I dropped back to the floor, putting three bullets in the head of the last one standing. Istas pursued her two across the floor, hitting them every chance she got, until they went down and didn't get up again.

"I think they're dead," I said, breathing shallowly to keep from hyperventilating. One of the servitors closer to me twitched. I shot him twice in the spine. He stopped twitching. I amended, "I think they're dead *now*."

Istas growled deep in her throat, smacking a fallen servitor one last time before she turned to do a slow survey of the room. The hair along her shoulders and spine was standing on end, making her look even larger. As if she needed the help. She finished her circuit, snarled, and trotted over to me, claws audibly scratching the club floor.

"You okay?" I asked her. She shot me what could only be called an amused look. "Sorry. Reflex. Come on; let's go find Candy. She's not safe here on her own."

"She's not on her own," said a voice from behind us.

I turned toward the hallway door, blinking in confusion. "Dave? I thought you left with the rest of the—oh, God, Dave, I am *so* sorry about the damages. In our defense, they were trying to kill us—wait, what?" I stopped talking as his words sank in. "Where's Candy?"

Dave looked awkwardly at the pair of us, his long-fingered hands tucked deep into the pockets of his cheap polyester slacks. "She's not alone," he said. "I really am sorry about this, Verity, but business is business, and you never would have danced for me anyway."

I took a step back, my hip brushing Istas' shoulder. "Dave?" I said uncertainly.

"Good night, Miss Price." He pulled his hands from his pockets and blew their contents—a sparkly white powder that I recognized from the Tooth Fairy arsenal—in our direction.

We were both unconscious before we hit the floor.

Twenty-four

"Well, crap."

–Frances Brown

Some distance beneath the streets of Manhattan, being held captive by a snake cult

TOOTH FAIRY DUST IS MEANT TO BE ADMINISTERED to sleeping children to make sure they *stay* asleep while the Tooth Fairy feeds. (The specific dietary needs of Tooth Fairies are irrelevant and a little bit disgusting, so I'm not going to talk about them. Even I have limits.) The standard dose, according to Grandpa Thomas' *Field Guide to Pixies, Sprites, and Other Household Pests*, is a small pinch. A small pinch, as measured against the hand of something a little bit bigger than a Barbie doll. Dave had blown two full handfuls on me and Istas. At that kind of dosage, it was no wonder that when I finally stumbled back toward consciousness, I felt like I'd been shot full of curare, chloroform, and cockatrice venom.

I groaned, trying to lift a hand and wipe the residual grittiness from my eyes. My arm wouldn't move. I couldn't actually feel my arm. That realization snapped me the rest of the way out of my fugue damn quick, and I opened my eyes to find myself staring up at a distant ceiling that looked like poured concrete shot through with massive brass pipes. The sewers. I was somewhere in the sewers, only this time, I was either paralyzed or tied down. This definitely wasn't an improvement over my earlier descents.

I tried moving various parts of my body. Nothing responded, but at least I was able to feel my hands and feet when I really focused on it. All my bits were still attached; they just weren't speaking to me at the moment. I started hurriedly reviewing everything I knew about Tooth Fairy dust, trying to remember whether it had a known overdose point.

"I see one of our guests is awake," said a jovial voice. I turned my head toward it—or tried to, anyway. All I was able to manage was the faintest twitch of the muscles in my neck. That was better than I'd been able to accomplish a few seconds before. I'd take it. "I'm sorry about the way you had to be brought here, dear. It was unnecessarily violent, and I apologize."

I made a strangled squeaking noise in the back of my throat. Not the most effective comeback I'd ever managed. This paralysis thing was getting old fast.

"Oh, I'm sorry again—I didn't think. Here." Meaty hands grasped the sides of my head, turning it to face the speaker: a big, ruddy-faced man with thinning hair and a Brooks Brothers suit that definitely didn't come off the rack. Whoever my apologetic kidnapper was, he came from money. "Is that better?"

I made the strangled squeaking noise again.

He nodded like I'd just said something brilliant. "I thought it might be. I do apologize that we had to meet under these circumstances, Miss Price. I've been a big fan of your work. Oh, don't look so surprised—we've been keeping an eye on you since your arrival on the East Coast. It's admirable, the way your family has pursued an accord with the unnatural races that battle humanity for rulership of our fair planet. Idiotic, but still admirable."

If I could look surprised, I could also glare. I did, wishing looks could actually kill as I stared at the asshole who was apparently responsible for my current situation. The asshole who was, unless my instincts had gone totally haywire, part of the snake cult that killed Piyusha.

Chuckling, he leaned over and ruffled my hair. "Has anyone ever told you that you're adorable when you're angry? The sedative our operative administered should be wearing off soon, and then we can begin. I'm afraid you can't be anesthetized during the ritual. It might disrupt things, and we're dealing with too many variables as it is. As a scientist of sorts, I'm sure you understand why we can't risk such contamination."

I kept glaring at him. There are only two good reasons for a villain to monologue: either they're stalling for time, or they're sure there's no possible way for you to escape. This asshole was apparently combining the two. He needed to stall until I was no longer a danger to his dragon's delicate constitution, and he clearly wasn't worried about me getting away any time soon.

The tingling in my hands and feet was getting stronger. If he'd just continue his monologue for a little while longer, there was a good chance I could surprise him. His easy dismissal of the city's cryptid community meant that, while he might work with them, he probably wasn't inclined to *listen* to them. That was too bad for him, because if there was one thing they could all have agreed on, it was that you never mess with a Price girl. Not unless we're already gut-shot and bleeding out . . . and frankly, not always then.

"There's nothing to be worried about. You're doing a great favor for the human race. Your service will be remembered long after the actions of your traitorous family have been stricken from the record of history."

I squeaked again, glaring. If I hadn't already known that he couldn't be working alone, his speech would have confirmed it; no one who couldn't *say* "sacrifice" would be capable of *performing* one.

"I *am* sorry that it will hurt. I wish there were another way. Sadly, the situation is delicate . . ." My captor continued rambling for another few minutes, using vague and bloodless euphemisms for what he and the rest of his freaky snake cult friends were planning to do with me. I kept squeaking. Eventually, my responses stopped amusing him, and he returned my head to its original position with a jovial, "Well, I'll just give you a little time to get your head in order," before walking briskly away.

I listened closely to the way his footsteps echoed. I hadn't heard any other voices while he was talking to me, and nothing interrupted the clack-clack-clack of his expensive dress shoes against the concrete. Another sign that he had to be working with a full cult: no one who had a clue what they were doing would be stupid enough to go into the sewer wearing shoes like that. They'd give him no traction at all if the place flooded.

I counted to ten, waiting for the sound of footsteps coming back in my direction. When that didn't happen, I started trying to flex my fingers and toes, feeling very much like I'd just been cast in an unnecessary remake of *Kill Bill*. The tingling was getting stronger. It didn't take long before my toes twitched in answer to my command, followed by my fingers, and then my hands. Sensation began rushing back into my skin so rapidly that it bordered on painful. I gritted my teeth, just glad that I *could* grit my teeth, and kept trying to get my body to respond.

The return of physical connection brought a host of information in its wake. I was definitely strapped down, not tied, since whatever was holding me in place was leathery-smooth (and given the suit my captor had been wearing, possibly real leather). I was also naked, or close enough as to make no difference, because the leather straps were pressing down directly against my skin. Three straps for my legs, one for my waist, one for my torso, and another for my shoulders. I had to give the snake cult this much, if nothing else; whoever was in charge of securing the sacrifices definitely did a bang-up job.

Someone groaned to my right. I turned toward the

sound—abstractly pleased to realize that I *could* turn toward the sound—and saw Istas. She was strapped to a metal gurney, naked, with arcane symbols drawn in Sharpie all up and down the length of her body. The same symbols I'd found on Piyusha. Her hair was back in its sleek little girl pigtails, making the sight of her even more surreal.

She groaned again before licking her lips and whispering, eyes still closed, "Did we lose because of improper tactical behavior?"

"No." I was trying to speak softly, but my voice came out as a whisper even fainter than Istas'. Lingering paralysis of the vocal cords, most likely. "We lost because that asshole we work for decided to sell us out."

"Oh, good." Istas' shoulders tensed as she tried to move. The tension passed quickly, with no real visible effect. "I will enjoy removing his insides and displaying them to him as a part of his outsides." She paused, considering, before she added, "I believe I will wear his liver as a hat."

"Okay, well, good, that's a goal," I agreed slowly. "First we need to get loose. Then we can think about internal organ haberdashery. Can you change shapes?"

"I do not know." Istas tensed again, the muscles in her neck visibly bulging as they twisted into a new formation. Then the skin smoothed out again as she sagged, chest moving in rapid, if shallow, heaves. ". . . no. I cannot."

"Okay. Well, thanks for trying." I could feel my shoulders again. I pulled them upward, feeling the drag as the leather straps caught my wrists. I was still feeling weak and disconnected from my body, but I could move it, and that was enough.

Growing up in my family meant ambushes on your birthday, crossbows for Christmas, and games of dodge ball where the balls were occasionally rigged to explode. It also meant learning how to work your way out of a wide variety of death traps. Failure to get loose on your own could lead to missing dinner, or worse, being forced to admit that you missed dinner because your baby sister had tied you to the couch. Again.

The leather straps were probably intended to keep us from bruising ourselves. Maybe sacrifices are like apples—they go bad when they're bruised. Whatever the reason, leather was better than rope, since it wasn't as likely to rip my skin off when I started squirming. I went as limp as I could, letting the remains of the Tooth Fairy dust do the majority of the work for me. By breathing out until my lungs ached, I was able to get almost a half an inch of give between myself and the leather. With this accomplished, I pointed my toes and began to pull.

I had to stop twice to breathe. The second time, I caught Istas with her head canted to the side, watching me intently. I offered her a wan smile and kept working.

Ballroom dancing teaches strength, stamina, and above all, flexibility. I gave my left leg one last firm tug and pulled my calf free of the two lower leather straps. After a pause to take a deeper breath I repeated the trick, this time pulling my right calf free. Most of me was still pinned, but now that I'd managed to get things started—

"Well, aren't you the industrious one?" A hand slapped down on my shoulder. I tilted my head back, unsurprised to see that the well-dressed snake cultist was back. He beamed at me like a demented Santa Claus, giving a small shake of his head as he said, "My dear, you really are astonishing. It's a pity someone with your training and potential has to . . . well, you can stop fighting now. It was a lovely try, but it simply wasn't lovely enough. Boys!"

The hissing that greeted his call told me what was coming even before the first servitor came into view. It was limping, and the look it was directing toward me seemed to have more than the usual dose of reptilian menace. "I think we've met," I said.

"Oh, you've met several of the boys," said evil Santa, pulling his hand away from my shoulder. "It's good to have the family together like this, isn't it? Boys, take them to the Chamber of the Dragon."

The servitors made sure to strap my legs down tight before they moved the gurney. The muscles in Istas' neck bulged again when they began pushing her toward the door. That was the only visible change in her anatomy, and it passed quickly. Tooth Fairy dust must have a more incapacitating effect on waheela physiology, because I felt almost back to normal. Still a little shaky, and doubly naked without my weapons, but still, almost back to normal.

The servitors pushed our gurneys down a sewer tunnel that looked like it had been constructed and abandoned sometime in the early 1800s. The clacking of their claws and the rattle of the gurney wheels echoed off the rounded walls until it was impossible to estimate how many servitors there were. It could have been the six I'd managed to count; it could have been sixty. Not that it really mattered with Istas and me both strapped down, but miracles have happened before, and as Mom always says, no miracle has ever come off without assistance.

The room at the end of the tunnel made the chamber we'd woken up in seem small. The walls were natural stone, carved out of the rock by time and erosion, rather than by human intervention. People in long brown robes stood in a loose cluster up ahead of us, clearly waiting for our arrival. And behind them, with his massive head resting on his crossed forelimbs, slept the last of the male dragons.

My breath caught in my throat, all thoughts of captivity and impending sacrifice replaced by awe. Since the dragons supposedly went extinct before photography was a factor, none of the books or field guides came with anything other than drawings of dragons, and half the time those drawings couldn't agree with each other, much less present a reliable picture of what dragons were really like. The number of limbs, the number of wings, even the number of heads was a subject for debate. At least one early Covenant bestiary showed the dragon as some sort of super-sized naga, with the dragon princess being nothing but a lure growing out of its tail. So it's not a surprise that I was unprepared for the reality of what was in front of me. There was no way I *could* have been prepared.

The dragon's head was shaped like a raptor-type dinosaur's, assuming you like your Velociraptors super-sized; it was easily the size of a small car, covered in pearly green scales that managed to look delicate, despite being the size of dinner plates. His eyes were closed, but judging by the size of his eyelids, they were each somewhat larger than a bowling ball. He had hands—huge hands, covered in scales and ending in talons, but hands all the same—and a long, serpentine neck that led to the immense bulk of his body. His wings were furled like broken umbrellas along the length of his spine. There was no possible way they could have supported him . . . but maybe that was part of what got the dragons killed. Maybe the males were only mobile when they were young, before they outgrew the potential span of their own wings. They couldn't start off *too* big, or the dragon princesses would never have been able to bear them.

His breath was slow and easy. Whatever the snake cult had been doing to try to wake him up, it clearly wasn't working. That was almost a pity. I might not be able to sweet-talk my way around snake cultists, but I was pretty sure "I know where you can get some girls" would have been a bargaining chip worth having.

One of the servitors pushing Istas suddenly snarled and jumped away from her gurney. I looked over, and smirked as I saw the blood running down her chin. "Get a little close, did you?" I called. He turned and hissed at me.

"Now, now," said evil Santa. "There's no call for that sort of behavior. You're both about to assist us with a great undertaking."

"Um, not so much, really. Snake cults are pretty passé. Couldn't you have joined a swing dance club or something? Not to get overly personal or anything, but you could stand to lose a few pounds, and it would be a way to meet women that doesn't involve stripping them naked and drawing on them."

Santa scowled. "I see that you're not going to be reasonable. Well, I suppose we can take care of that by letting you be the first one to leave us today. Marcus! Claude! Prepare the ritual circle."

Me and my big mouth. Two of the men in brown ropes stepped forward to my gurney and wheeled me away from Istas, toward the slumbering dragon.

I estimated the ritual circle as about twelve feet in diameter when they wheeled me into it. It was drawn onto the rough stone floor with Sharpie, and looked like it had been retraced at least once in blood; the lines were rust-brown and irregular around the edges, like they'd been working with an uncooperative medium. It smelled like a half-dozen different kinds of blood—the sharp copper-iron of human, the slightly acidic bite of harpy, and the maple-sugar sweetness of Madhura. A bubble of fury rose in my chest, making me buck involuntarily against my restraints. I wanted to kill these people. I wanted to kill them all.

All I had to do was break through a bunch of institutional-strength leather straps and kick all their asses, naked, without a weapon. Somehow, I didn't think this was going to be as easy as it sounded—a thought that was only reinforced when one of the figures in brown stepped forward, holding a bowl of deep ruby blood between her outstretched hands. I gaped at her.

"*Betty*?"

The dragon princess matriarch smiled her smug little Mae West smile as she asked, "You were expecting someone else?"

"But—"

"If I helped them, they left my girls alone. I'm sure you understand the importance of family in matters like this one." She leaned over me, setting her bowl down on my stomach and dipping her fingers into the liquid. "Besides, I have a—shall we say, vested—interest in their success. Once that beautiful boy in there wakes up, everything will change."

"Even if he's being controlled by a snake cult?" I spat. "I thought we were on the same side here."

"I'm on the side of whatever wakes the male," she said, and began using her fingertips to trace over the symbols on my body in what was now indisputably blood. Leaning closer, she whispered, "Why else would I have given you the gold? You just had to go and tell Candice that this lovely buck was down here, and she told the Nest, because she didn't know any better. I had to do *something* to show them I was serious about finding him—and giving you the gold meant you couldn't be changed, only killed. You aren't worthy of such a transmutation. What the Covenant stole from us will be restored, and you won't have any part in it."

I bit back the urge to scream. There it was again: the belief that we were still Covenant, that nothing my family had done since leaving could change the fact that once upon a time, we stayed. "You bitch."

"Yes, dear, and I've had a very long time to practice." She stroked bloody fingertips along my cheeks before moving down to work on my stomach and legs. Voice back to a normal conversational volume, she said, "This one will be ready in a moment."

"Good," declared another of the cultists. "We've

never had a double sacrifice before, and I need to get up early tomorrow."

"So sorry my death is going to inconvenience you, asshole," I said.

He glared at me. "We've never had a human sacrifice before, either. Are we sure this won't set us back?"

"Oh, no," said evil Santa, while Betty painted arcane symbols along my thighs. "Her family was instrumental in the slaughter of the great dragons back when they still ruled the skies. Her death will be a signal that we truly mean our assurances of renewed dominion—that even as the dragon serves our interests, we shall serve the dragon's."

"Killing me won't wake him up!" I snarled. "Dragons don't run on the human sacrifice alarm clock model!"

Evil Santa cast a glance at Betty, who shook her head. "She's lying," she said.

"Even if it would wake him, do you people have, like, no concept of how mass works?" I asked. "How are you planning to get the dragon out from under the city? A forklift? Dig a really big pit in midtown and hope nobody notices the super-mega-size lizard before you're ready? In case you've never seen a Godzilla movie, let me remind you that one fire-breathing monster versus a major metropolitan area never ends well for anybody."

"We have more than 'one fire-breathing monster,'" said evil Santa, and waved a hand to indicate the servitors. "We have an army of the blessed."

"Stop arguing with the little bitch and kill her already," snapped Betty, picking up her bowl of blood and stepping back from the gurney. "I'm going to develop a migraine if I have to listen to her much longer."

"Know your place, you unnatural whore," said Santa, in a mild, almost reasonable tone. Betty took another step backward, expression furious—but not, I realized, particularly surprised. When she got into bed with these people, she knew what she was doing.

"My apologies, master," she said, her Mae West voice dripping with loathing.

"Don't forget again." Evil Santa stepped back, gesturing for the others to come closer. "The virgin is prepared to make her glorious journey into the abyss, to carry news of our faith and earnest plea for the dragon's support! Soon, she —"

"Wait, wait," I interrupted, involuntarily straining against the straps as I attempted to sit up. "You think I'm a *what*?"

The snake cultists turned to stare at me with expressions ranging from sheer bafflement to anger. Several of them produced long, wicked-looking knives from inside their robes. The combination was just too much. Sagging back against the gurney, I burst out laughing.

The snake cultists had apparently never tried to deal with a sacrifice who laughed at them before, because my hysterical laughter threw them into utter chaos. Cultists swarmed around me, demanding to know what I was laughing about, demanding to know what I knew that they didn't, and most of all, demanding I cut that out *right now*. Evil Santa seemed to get the picture, because he wheeled on Betty, cheeks going red with fury as he shouted, "You said she'd be a virgin! You assured us that she was a viable offering!"

"Just look at her!" said Betty, pointing a finger in my direction as she backpedaled rapidly away from him. "She looks just like her grandmother, and I know this family! There's no way she's not eligible!"

"Grandma *did* have sex eventually, or I wouldn't *be* here," I said, between gusts of laughter. "That's what 'grandparents' means!"

Verity, are you there?

Sarah's query came half a second before the static hiss of "telepath in range" kicked in at the back of my mind. I was startled enough to stop laughing for half a second before resuming, even more loudly than before. The cultists kept arguing. Only one of them seemed to have the presence of mind to realize that a laughing sacrifice would probably stop laughing if you killed her. The man with an early morning ahead of him started toward me, knife held in front of him at chest level. If I wasn't going to be a cooperative sacrifice, I could at least be a cooperative corpse.

Istas' front paws slammed into his chest when he was still four feet from me, carrying him to the stone floor. The sound of her snarls was almost loud enough to drown out the sound of tearing flesh, although nothing could have blocked his shrieks. The rest of the cultists stopped arguing, and there was a moment of stunned silence before most of them started screaming and ran for the exit. The servitors reacted better, maybe because the servitors were created, on some level, to fight; they produced weapons from inside their tattered clothing and fell into a defensive formation around evil Santa, all hissing viciously. If Istas was intimidated, she wasn't intimidated enough to make her stop shredding the fallen cultist.

Betty backed up until her hip hit the gurney. It rocked a few inches to the side, wheels screeching, and she jumped with a small shriek. Whirling on me, she grabbed the top strap and demanded, "If I release you, will you protect me? For old times' sake?" Her attempt at a smile looked more like a grimace of sheer terror. I couldn't say that it was a bad look for her. "For everything I've been to your family?"

The man Istas knocked down wasn't screaming anymore, although the sounds of tearing flesh continued. I wondered how long it would take her to realize that he was dead and go for a more interesting target.

"If you'd made that offer five minutes ago, I might have been a hell of a lot more interested," I said. "How about this offer: you let me go, and I don't call Istas over to rip your face off? She may do it anyway, but you'll stand a better chance of running if she isn't directly after you."

Betty stared at me, face contorted with rage. "Why you little—"

"Offer's not forever, Betty. Take it now, or run like hell, and hope I don't send her after you." Istas' massive, shaggy head appeared behind her, almost level with Betty's shoulder. A deep rumble started in the waheela's throat. "Looks like the offer's just about expired. Let me go, or Istas eats you."

Istas kept growling, voice taking on a lilt I could only interpret as agreement.

"All right—all right. Just don't kill me." Betty moved her shaking hands toward the buckle on the first strap. Then she spun away, producing a pistol from inside her brown cultist robe and emptying the clip into Istas' chest. Istas howled, and fell. Betty turned back to me, snapping a new clip into place. "You stupid little bitch," she snarled, leveling the muzzle on my forehead. "I've been waiting to kill a member of your family for fifty years. And after you're dead, every cryptid in this city is going to know that it was *you* who sold us out, *you* who told the cultists where to find us. Be proud. You've finally killed your family name." She cocked back the hammer. A gun went off.

It just wasn't the gun in her hand.

Betty wobbled, raising her hand to the bullet hole in her throat. The shot had gone clean through, missing the major arteries . . . but really, when you shoot someone in the throat, the major arteries are sort of extra credit. With blood running through her fingers and an expression of utter perplexity on her aging Mae West face, Betty fell, revealing her shooter. Candy stood behind her with soot marks on her face and throat, wearing nothing but a cheap cotton slip, the kind that doesn't really need to fit to render you decent. She had both hands wrapped around the pistol grip, and their shaking was visible, even from a distance.

"I didn't know you could shoot," I said inanely. Candy forced a wavering smile, which fled as several of the servitors went for her, blocking her—and that entire side of the cavern—from my view.

I tried bucking against the straps holding me down, to no avail. The telepathic static was still there, and getting louder. "Sarah?" I shouted, trying to think it as hard as I could at the same time. "A little help?"

We're on our way, Sarah replied. *Candy ran ahead. Are you hurt?*

"Not yet!"

We're almost there. Try not to die.

"Wait, 'we'?" I bucked against the straps again, trying to get a look at Istas, who hadn't moved since Betty shot her. "Sarah, what do you mean 'we'?"

There was no response from my cuckoo cousin. Whatever was standing between us, it was distracting enough that she wasn't bothering to talk to me anymore. Cultists were running everywhere, and Candy was shouting in the sibilant language of the dragons. It was impossible from my position to tell whether it was doing her any good—but since she was still shouting, rather than screaming while they ripped her to pieces, I was willing to say that it wasn't doing her any harm.

Shouts rang down the corridor connecting the dragon's chamber to the room where Istas and I had been brought first, and several of the cultists that fled in that direction came running back like their robes were on fire. I bucked against my straps . . . and actually slipped upward about an inch. All the blood Betty poured on me before Candy shot her was working like a lubricant, making my skin slippery and making it easier to move against the leather. No one seemed to be coming after me for the moment; I guess with Candy shooting at people and a couple of corpses on the floor, I seemed like

the least of their worries. Flexing my feet as hard as I
could, I began pulling my legs free.

Working my legs out of the straps was surprisingly easy,
now that I was covered in gore and no longer actively
worried about being sliced up and offered to a sleeping
dragon. I yanked them loose, paused to take a breath,
and dug my heels into the base of the gurney, starting to
pull myself downward. The blood-slick metal beneath
me offered little resistance to the movement. "Amateurs," I muttered, and twisted my head to the side, slipping it under the strap that had been fastened originally
across my shoulders.

With my head free, things got much easier. The band
across my chest was loose enough to let me get my hands
unpinned, and then it was just a matter of fighting the
blood-soaked buckles on the sides of the straps until
they came loose. Any inmate in an eighteenth-century
asylum would have been able to do it easily. I had a bit
more trouble, but compared to what I'd already done, it
was a cakewalk.

I slid off the gurney, almost stepping on Betty before
I managed to get my balance back. The fight was still
staying mostly on the other side of the cavern, so I
paused to do the sensible thing: looting the dead. Between Betty's unfashionable brown robe, the gun she'd
been carrying, and the knife originally held by the cultist
Istas took down, I was slightly better prepared to fight
my way out of the sewers.

Betty's gun still had three bullets. If I needed them,
that would have to be enough.

Istas was sprawled where she'd fallen, still in her
hulking canine shape. I crouched next to her, feeling the
side of her neck for a pulse. It was steady. I slid my hand
down to her chest, where the bullets had hit her; there
was very little blood. She might be in shock, but thanks

to her physiology, she wasn't in danger of dying. "I am *so* asking you to let me give you a physical when we both get out of here alive," I said. Istas didn't answer.

I stood, scanning the room for an idea of the direction we'd need to flee in. There were several tunnels leading in and out; presumably, at least one of them would lead to the surface. The servitors were focusing their attentions on Candy. Wiping the worst of the blood from the soles of my feet onto the dead cultist's robe, I took off running in her direction.

"Verity! On the left!"

I spun without hesitating, shooting the cultist who'd been charging me squarely in the chest. Two bullets left. His eyes widened in surprise, and he fell, momentum carrying him past me to land in a crumpled heap on the floor. It wasn't until after he'd stopped moving that I realized who'd warned me—Sarah—and that the warning had been verbal, not telepathic. Eyes wide, I turned.

Dominic De Luca was standing at the entrance to the room, flinging knives at cultists with clinical precision. Those he wasn't impaling had problems of their own, in the form of Ryan, who'd abandoned his human shape for something a hell of a lot more intimidating: a seven-foot-tall raccoon-man with talons longer than most kitchen knives, really sharp teeth, and the ability to block attacks by turning parts of his body into stone. Those were some cultists who were having a seriously lousy day.

Sarah was standing behind Dominic, her eyes so white that at this distance they seemed to glow. One of the servitors charged at the pair while Dominic was throwing a knife in the opposite direction, and she raised her hand, palm-out. The servitor promptly froze.

"What the—"

He can't remember how his muscles work. I can't hold him for long. Now go help Candy!

"On it," I said, and took off running, slowing only to shoot a servitor before he could smash a lead pipe into the side of Ryan's head. Candy was still shouting, her commands starting to take on a pleading, terrified note. I kept running toward her, elbowing a cultist in the throat and vaulting over two bodies before plunging into the knot of servitors surrounding her. Several of them were on the ground, bleeding from a variety of inexpertly placed bullet wounds. Three had moved to stand between Candy and the others, hissing and clicking furiously. Those had to be the ones she'd talked around to her side. Four others were trying to claw past them to get to her.

"I am *so* fucking tired of fighting with Sleestaks," I grumbled. I only had one bullet left. I aimed at the nearest servitor, fired, threw the gun aside, and charged.

We were making a lot of noise. Between the screaming, the shooting, the rending, and the tearing, we were getting close to loud enough to wake the dead. Since that isn't actually possible without some very complicated ritual magic, we managed to achieve the next best thing. One of the servitors went down with a final, earsplitting shriek after I stabbed it in the neck, and then the Voice of God—or at least the Voice of James Earl Jones *as* God—came rumbling out of the darkness, so deep it seemed to shake the ground beneath our feet:

"*What* is going *on* here?"

The servitor that had been attacking me hissed and cringed back, posture turning subservient. Candy stopped shouting, the gun slipping from her hand to clatter to the ground as she stared with wide eyes into the space behind me. I turned.

The dragon looked at me.

"Oh," I said faintly. "Hey, Candy, guess what? I found the dragon, and he speaks English."

Candy whimpered.

Twenty-five

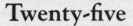

"The greatest joy is the joy of discovery.
Followed closely by the joy of a discovery
that doesn't kill you."

–Enid Healy

*Somewhere below the streets of Manhattan, hoping dragons
don't usually wake up cranky*

THE DRAGON'S EYES WERE a luminous pumpkin orange, like giant jack-o-lanterns burning in the face
of the largest lizard the world has ever seen. He was still
mostly prone, but his head was raised like the head of a
snake getting ready to strike. The few remaining cultists
cheered, apparently thinking he'd finally woken up at
their command, and would now be happy to do their
bidding. I wasn't completely sure they were wrong.

"You!" One of the cultists ran forward, pointing im-
periously toward me and Candy as she addressed the
dragon. "Destroy these infidels!"

The dragon looked down at the cultist before turning
those jack-o-lantern eyes back on the two of us. Sarah
and Dominic were still near the door, and Ryan was
kneeling next to Istas, trying to get her to wake up. As a
fellow therianthrope, he probably had a better idea of
what she needed than anybody else in the room. No one
moved to attack anyone else; all of us were waiting to
see what the dragon would do.

The dragon lifted one enormous hand and slammed it down on the cultist, smashing her the way I might squash a bug. There was a long pause as everyone considered this. Then the remaining cultists went back to screaming and running away. Candy stepped around me and broke into a run of her own—but unlike the cultists, she was running *toward* the dragon. The servitors stayed frozen where they were. I ran after Candy, but more slowly. I was, after all, covered in blood and dressed like a cultist; I wanted the dragon nicely distracted by the female of his species before I started bothering him.

Dominic and Sarah started moving when I did. We met at the center of the room. Dominic grabbed my arm, pulling me to a halt, and then—before I could protest that I was trying to get to the giant lizard—pulling me into a hug. "You frightened the life from us," he said, without letting go.

"I'm sorry I got captured by a snake cult." I hugged him back. It seemed like the easiest course of action, and it wasn't an unpleasant position to be in. He hugged solidly, without crossing the line into hugging too hard.

"This is sweet and all, but dragon? Remember, dragon?" Sarah tugged on the sleeve of my borrowed robe. "It's really big, and it's really confused right now, so this would be the time to tell it that you come in peace."

"How do you know?" asked Dominic, pulling back and giving her a wary look.

"Telepath, remember? Now come on." She grabbed my arm, pulling me out of his embrace and starting toward the dragon. I didn't put up any resistance. This was, after all, a real live *dragon* we were talking about. That's not the sort of thing a cryptozoologist gets the opportunity to meet every day.

Candy beat us to the dragon by a considerable margin. She wasn't actually saying anything when we got there; just standing with her hands pressed against her mouth, looking up at the dragon and crying silently. I shook my arm free of Sarah's grasp and put a hand on Candy's shoulder, looking up at the dragon.

"This wasn't in the manual," I murmured to Sarah, before saying, more loudly, "Um, hello, Mr. Dragon. I'm Verity Price. This is Candice. She's a dragon, too." Dominic and Sarah both gave me startled looks. Candy kept crying. The dragon wasn't saying anything, and so I added, "It's nice to meet you."

"Who are these others?" asked the dragon, lowering his head to what passed for eye level. He had an accent, faintly British, that made me think of period dramas about the American Revolution on PBS. "Who has sent you? What is going on here?"

"Um, no one sent us, and what's going on is sort of a long story. This is my cousin, Sarah Zellaby."

"Hi," said Sarah.

"And this is our friend Dominic De Luca."

Looking unsure as to whether or not he was doing the right thing, Dominic bowed to the dragon. "Sir," he said.

Candy took her hands away from her mouth and pointed at Dominic. "He's from the Covenant," she announced. Catching my expression, she added, "But he came to help save you from the snake cult."

"Is that what these noisy little people were on about?" The dragon lifted his left hand, studying it. "My fingers are quite sore."

"The, um, 'noisy little people' have been trying to wake you up, and while you were still sleeping, they were taking blood and using it to turn people into servitors," I said. "I'm sorry I don't have any bandages."

"I am sure I will recover without them, but I appreciate the offer." The dragon transferred his orange gaze to Dominic. "The Covenant of St. George is here? I have never seen one of your kind so poorly armored, or so alone. What do you think you can do against me, small one?"

"Nothing, sir," said Dominic. I'd never heard him

sound so respectful. "I came here to assist my friends, not to bring challenge. This is not my city to defend." He nodded toward me. "It's hers. I, and by extension, the Covenant, will stand by her decisions in this matter."

I stared at him.

The dragon seemed to take this much more in stride. Maybe he was used to humans being insane. Turning back to me, he asked gravely, "And what are your decisions in this matter, Miss Price?"

"I promised the dragon princesses I'd find you for them, and I promised the cryptids of the city that I'd make the snake cult stop sacrificing virgins to you. I think both of those are pretty much done. Candy? What do you think?"

Candy nodded, still crying.

The dragon tilted his head to study her before looking to the servitors clustered at the back of the cave. A deep sadness seemed to fall over him like a burial shroud, and his voice was very soft as he said, "None of the others survived. After all that we did to flee, none of the others survived. Oh, you poor dearest one." He placed one fingertip on Candy's shoulder. She grabbed hold and cried even harder. "So long without us to protect you." He looked toward me. "How long?"

"It's been about three hundred years since you went to sleep," I said. "There haven't been any reports of dragons in that time. Everyone thinks you're extinct."

"Everyone except you." He studied us thoughtfully. "What stops me from destroying you all, and keeping myself secret?"

"I have a family, and Dominic has the Covenant," I said. "They'd come looking if we disappeared. Besides, we came here to help, and you're going to need allies if you're going to restart your species. Candy isn't the only dragon princess left."

The scaly ridges over the dragon's eyes—what would have been his eyebrows, if he'd had any hair—rose. "Truly?" He turned a quizzical eye on Candy. "We always knew the females could survive without us for a little time, but everyone assumed there was a limit to the number of generations."

"If there is, it hasn't been reached," I said. "There are more than a few women waiting eagerly to meet you right now."

Candy sniffled, still holding onto the dragon's fingertip. "We prayed and prayed that somewhere, somehow, one of the males had survived. I never thought I'd still be alive when we found you."

"Poor dearest ones, waiting so long. I would have woken long ago, if I had realized." The dragon tugged his fingertip gently, leading Candy closer to him. Turning his eyes back to the rest of us, he said, "I was hunted. I was hurt, and I was weak. I asked my sisters to guard me while I slept and healed. I thought I would wake . . . sooner than I did."

"The local settlers found your sisters, and took them," I said. "No one thought you might still be alive down here. I'm so sorry."

"Perhaps it was better this way. The Covenant seems to have changed—at least enough that one dragon may be left in peace with his family." His jack-o-lantern eyes blazed. "Is that not so?"

"Unless you directly threaten the human population of this city, I will not tell the Covenant you are here," said Dominic. "You have my word that I will not take away your peace . . . as long as you do not take away ours."

"The Covenant *has* changed." The dragon sounded somewhere between amused and amazed. Looking past us to the servitors, he added, "But humanity has not. You say this 'snake cult' made them of its own?"

"I think they probably made them of the city's homeless and a few mysterious tourist disappearances, but yes, it was humans that did this. One of your females—" I glanced at Candy. "One of your females sort of lost sight of what it means to keep other people's best interests at heart, and she told them how to do it. She was trying to help them wake you up."

The dragon narrowed his eyes. "Where is she?"

"I killed her." Candy's voice was very small. "She was going to shoot Verity. She was dressed like all the others. She was saying things . . . and she lied to us. She didn't tell us you were here. She knew, and she wasn't going to tell us."

"Shhh, my little dearest one. You did nothing wrong. If you hadn't, I would have." The dragon bent his head, blowing gently on Candy's cheek. Sparks danced along her cheek like firefly kisses, leaving more soot marks in their wake. "You are more beautiful in my eyes than you could ever know."

Ryan stepped up next to us, back in his human form, with a semiconscious Istas lying sprawled in his arms like a starlet on a bad B-movie poster. *Tanuki Terror*, coming soon to a theater near you. At least he'd managed to coax her back into her own human shape, which was probably easier to carry. "Hey, Very."

"Hey."

"That's a dragon."

"Yup. That's two dragons, actually. Candy, and . . ." I paused. "Excuse me, Mr. Dragon? What's your name?"

"William," replied the dragon, with immense gravity.

". . . okay," I said. If the dragon wanted to be named "William," I wasn't going to argue. "William, this is Ryan—he works with Candy and me—and the naked, unconscious one is Istas."

"Hi," said Ryan.

"Hello," said William.

"I'm talking to a dragon. Cool." Ryan looked at me. "Istas is in a pretty bad way. I need to get her to a first aid kit."

My eyes widened. "How bad?"

"She's alive, but she could use some stitches and some britches." He smiled, showing teeth that were still longer than the human norm. "Get it? 'Stitches and britches'?"

"You're a riot, Ryan. Can you get her to someplace safe?"

He nodded. "I can, if you're sure you're going to be safe with a dragon, a murderer," he wrinkled his nose at Dominic, "and some chick who called saying she was your cousin."

I smiled a little. "I'll be fine. You go on—and if Istas wakes up, tell her she's not allowed to kill Dave until I get there. He isn't getting off that easy."

"Dave?" asked William.

"It's a long story." Catching the looks that Sarah and Dominic were giving me, I amended, "But I'm happy to tell it. See, Candy and I have been working as waitresses—that would be serving girls to you, I guess—in this place called Dave's Fish and Strips, and the owner's a real asshole—"

The servitors crept over to huddle against William's side as I provided a summary of everything that had gone down since my arrival at Dave's earlier that night. Sarah and Dominic broke in a few times to add details I hadn't been present for, like what happened after Candy showed up at Gingerbread Pudding, hysterical and with her clothes burned half off, having barely evaded the snake cult goons Dave sent to grab her. Sarah called Ryan, and between my telepathic cousin and his tanuki tracking powers, they'd found their way down into the sewers and into the cult's secret sacrifice cave in no time. Not the way any of us had been planning to spend our evening, but it beat being sacrificed hands down.

When the story was finished, I glanced at the servitors, and asked, "What are you going to do about them?"

"Done is done, I'm afraid; what they are now is what they'll be the rest of their lives." William sounded honestly regretful. "We'll care for them. There are ways to bring them closer to intelligence, if properly looked after."

"And you'll make no more," said Dominic. It could have been a question. It wasn't.

"The properties of our blood are not a weapon," said William, in the sort of tone an adult might use when speaking to a small child. "They are a defense. I will not promise not to protect myself and my family if someone comes to trouble us, but I will not be seeking out humans to claim. It was only ever a necessity when the females became rare, usually due to humans 'rescuing' them from their mates."

"Good," said Dominic. "I appreciate your candor."

Candy stepped away from William, looking up at him. "I don't want to go," she said regretfully, "but I have sisters, and they'll want to know that we've found you. Can we . . . can we come back? Can we come to you?"

William blew on her face again, this time igniting the tips of her hair. They burned for only a moment. When they went out, her hair looked even better than it had before. "I will wait more eagerly than you can imagine for your return."

None of the fallen cultists had shoes even remotely near my size, and while they'd kept my weapons in the antechamber—thank God—my clothes were nowhere to be found. Dominic solved the problem by picking me up and toting me toward the exit. I considered protesting, but decided that having fully functional feet was more important than my pride. Besides, anything that gave him something to focus on beyond changing his mind about killing William was probably a good thing.

Candy walked at the front of our little group, looking as lovesick as a teen who'd just met her Disney Channel idol for the first time. Sarah brought up the rear, and smirked every time I looked at her over Dominic's shoulder.

So I guess you've converted him through the power of your naughtiness and flexibility. What are you going to do with him?

"Shut up," I hissed.

Dominic cast a startled look my way, then looked back to see where my attention was. Seeing the smug look on Sarah's face, he chuckled. "Whatever she's saying to you, it can't possibly be as bad as the argument we're going to have when we get back to your apartment."

"What argument is that?"

"The 'never run off to get kidnapped by another snake cult' argument." He sounded completely serious. I raised an eyebrow. "I'm quite serious. I think I aged six years tonight."

"Wasn't he *beautiful*?" asked Candy.

There was a pause while the rest of us tried to make sense of this apparent non sequitur. "Yeah, Candy, he was gorgeous," I said carefully.

"If you like 'em tall, dark, and scaly," added Sarah.

Candy sighed dreamily. "Yeah," she agreed.

Okay, that was weird, thought Sarah.

Lay off, I replied. *She just met her first boy. She's allowed to be a little weird.*

You mean that *was the male of her species?* Sarah's expression mirrored her mental "voice," all shock and awe. *Wow. Talk about size really mattering...*

My laughter lasted for the rest of our trip back up into the light.

Dominic and I reached Dave's Fish and Strips an hour later, fully dressed and ready to kick some bogeyman ass. Ryan and Istas met us there, the latter looking even grumpier than usual. Both of them glared at Dominic. I put my hands up, relishing the feel of having sleeves again. "Back down, both of you. He wanted to come, and after the little stunt Dave pulled last time, I didn't think it would be bad to have the backup."

"If you're sure," said Ryan, still eyeing Dominic with suspicion.

Istas was more direct. "If you interfere in any manner with our continued survival, I will play skipping games with your intestines while wearing your lungs as a hat."

"That's fair," Dominic agreed.

"Enough," I said. "Let's go kill a bogeyman in the most painful way we can think of."

"Works for me," said Ryan.

The main club hadn't been cleaned up at all—even the bodies of the fallen servitors were still there. I paused to retrieve several of my knives. "Poor bastards," I said, and pulled a knife from a servitor's shoulder. "They deserved better."

"So did we," said Istas. I followed her gaze to the white smear of Tooth Fairy dust on the bar floor. Her parasol was next to it, more battered than ever. She stooped to retrieve it, hugging it to her chest. "Mayhem now, please."

"Right this way." I picked up my last knife and started for the manager's office.

Dave's darks were on, turned higher than I'd ever seen them. They filled the hall for three feet on either side of the door, making it impossible to tell what was in the actual office. I stopped at the edge of the darkness, shouting, "Dave! Come out here right now and I won't let Istas have you!"

Istas shot me a hurt look. I mouthed "I'm lying," and she calmed, returning her attention to the wall of shadows between us and our target.

There was no answer from the office. "This is a limited time offer, Dave. We'll come in there if you make us."

There was still no answer from the office. We waited a

few minutes, until I was absolutely certain Dave wasn't going to come out. Istas started to growl.

"Oh, fuck it," I said, and strode into the blackness.

Finding the office door was a matter of finding the wall and feeling my way along. I kept a knife in one hand, groping along the wall next to the door for a light switch with the other. I kept waiting for Dave to grab me and yank me away from the safety of the walls, but it didn't happen. My fingers found the switch, and the lights came on, leaving me first blinking and then staring at the scene in front of me.

"Verity! Do you—" Dominic rushed into the room with Ryan and Istas close behind him. All three of them stopped, joining me in staring at the ransacked office. The filing cabinets were open and empty, and Dave's computer was missing from the desk.

"He's gone," I said. "The bastard pulled a runner."

"Well, fuck," said Ryan.

Epilogue

"All's well that ends with only minor lacerations."

–Alice Healy

The dinosaur wing of the Museum of Natural History

Six weeks later

THE SKELETAL TYRANNOSAURUS LOOMED OVER ME like
something out of a horror movie, showing teeth longer than throwing knives and claws capable of gutting a
human in less than a second. I looked thoughtfully up at
it, wondering what it must have been like when it was
ruler of the world. Did it think? Was the Tyrannosaurus
one of the first intelligent cryptids, here and gone before
the planet even thought of hairless apes?

"I'm sorry I'm late."

"It's okay. I've been bonding with the dinosaurs." I
gestured toward the skeleton. "Sort of makes you feel
small, doesn't it?"

Dominic gave me a look, half-amused, half-
exasperated. "You remain the strangest woman I have
ever met. How can this impress you, given what we've
seen?"

"Hey, Bill's a lot friendlier than this guy ever was."
William was also likely a lot happier, since he was now
being pampered and cosseted by no fewer than forty-
eight buxom representatives of the female of his species.
Candy had taken over leadership of the Nest, thanks to

her defeat of Betty and her early bond with William, who called her the sweetest of his "dearest ones." She'd actually started smiling after that. It was a little creepy, but better than being scowled at all the time.

"True enough." Folding his hands behind his back, Dominic joined me in contemplation of the Tyrannosaurus. Finally: "I take it things have continued well in my absence?"

"Pretty well, yeah. I've had a few auditions, nothing serious, and James has mostly forgiven me for letting him get stuffed into a closet. I had to promise him it would never happen again."

Dominic grimaced. "It won't. Not at my hands, anyway."

"Good. As for work, Kitty's running the club—Dave was her uncle, and he either left her the place or her boyfriend is a really good counterfeiter. Either way, she says we're getting new uniforms, and that makes her okay by me."

"Excellent. And your cousin?"

"She changed hotels again, and she's added some physics courses. She seems happy. I don't have a clue what she's talking about most of the time. That's always a good sign with Sarah. How was your trip?"

"It was . . . interesting." Dominic glanced my way, measuring my expression. "My superiors were quite skeptical of my report at first, until I showed them a tail from one of the deceased servitors. They now believe that the disappearances were due to giant alligators in the sewer, which I fought alone. I made no mention of dragons or cultists . . . or of you. You remain a cryptid in your own right, so far as the Covenant is concerned."

"And to think, once that would have been an insult coming from you. Are they keeping you in Manhattan?"

"For now. I take it you will also be remaining?"

"Are you kidding? My family has been waiting for this opportunity for longer than I've been alive." They'd come back from the basilisk hunt the day after things got bad, and Antimony was still sulking about not getting to kill any snake cultists. Mom and Dad, on the other hand, had a seemingly inexhaustible font of questions, all of them centering on the dragons. Big surprise, that.

"I see." He paused before saying, delicately, "My superiors wish me to continue my assessment of the need for a purge."

"How are you leaning so far?"

Dominic's smile was strained, but it was there. "This has been very educational so far. I look forward to seeing what else this city has to teach."

"It'll be an adventure." I took a step closer to him, leaning up onto my toes, and kissed his cheek. "Call me." Turning on my heel, I walked toward the museum exit, leaving Dominic standing alone beneath the skeleton of a prehistoric killer. The past isn't the future. Dinosaurs can become dragons, and that meant there was hope for Dominic, if he wanted to take advantage of it. Either way, I needed to go home and call my father to let him know that Dominic kept his word—the Covenant still didn't know we were alive, and we were free to continue as we were.

There are times when I really love my job.

Price Family Field Guide to the Cryptids of North America

Aeslin mice (Apodemus sapiens). Sapient, rodentlike cryptids that present as nearly identical to noncryptid field mice. Aeslin mice crave religion, and will attach themselves to "divine figures" selected virtually at random when a new colony is created. They possess perfect recall; each colony maintains a detailed oral history going back to its inception. Origins unknown.

Ahool (Acerodon ahool). Large, batlike cryptids with monkeylike heads. The ahool are cooperative hunters, and host toxic bacterial colonies similar to those found in Komodo dragons. An adult ahool can be the size of a large dog. They are territorial, vicious, and always prepared to attack.

Basilisk (Procompsognathus basilisk). Venomous, feathered saurians approximately the size of a large chicken. This would be bad enough, but thanks to a quirk of evolution, the gaze of a basilisk causes petrification, turning living flesh to stone. Basilisks are not native to North America, but were imported as game animals. By idiots.

Bogeyman (Vestiarium sapiens). The thing in your closet is probably a very pleasant individual who simply has issues with direct sunlight. Probably. Bogeymen are close relatives of the human race; they just happen to be almost purely nocturnal, with excellent night vision, and a fondness for enclosed spaces. They rarely grab the ankles of small children, unless it's funny.

Chupacabra (Chupacabra sapiens). True to folklore, chupacabra are bloodsuckers, with stomachs that do not handle solids well. They are also therianthrope shape-shifters, capable of transforming themselves into human form, which explains why they have never been captured. When cornered, most chupacabra will assume their bipedal shape in self-defense.

Dragon Princess (Homo draconem). The dragon princesses are humanoid cryptids believed to have evolved alongside the now-extinct great dragons. They have no special powers, save their ability to withstand extremes of heat, and their unerring ability to make money. There are no males of their species. We don't know how that works, either.

Ghoul (Herophilus sapiens). The ghoul is an obligate carnivore, incapable of digesting any but the simplest vegetable solids, and prefers humans because of their wide selection of dietary nutrients. Most ghouls are carrion eaters. Ghouls can be easily identified by their teeth, which will be shed and replaced repeatedly over the course of a lifetime.

Johrlac (Johrlac psychidolos). Colloquially known as "cuckoos," the Johrlac are telepathic hunters. They appear human, but are internally very different, being cold-blooded and possessing a decentralized circulatory system. This quirk of biology means they can be shot repeatedly in the chest without being killed. Extremely dangerous. Origins unknown; possibly insect in nature.

Lamia (Python lamia). Semihominid cryptids with the upper bodies of humans and the lower bodies of snakes. Lamia are members of order synapsedia, the mammal-like reptiles, and are considered responsible for many of the "great snake" sightings of legend. The sightings not attributed to actual great snakes, that is.

Lesser gorgon (Gorgos euryale). One of three known subspecies of gorgon, the lesser gorgon's gaze causes short-term paralysis followed by death in anything under five pounds. The bite of the snakes atop their heads will cause paralysis followed by death in anything smaller than an elephant if not treated with the appropriate antivenin. Lesser gorgons tend to be very polite, especially to people who like snakes.

Madhura (Homo madhurata). Humanoid cryptids with an affinity for sugar in all forms. Vegetarian. Their presence slows the decay of organic matter, and is usually viewed as lucky by everyone except the local dentist. Madhura are very family-oriented, and are rarely found living on their own. Originally from the Indian subcontinent.

Oread (Nymphae silica). Humanoid cryptids with the approximate skin density of granite. Their actual biological composition is unknown, as no one has ever been able to successfully dissect one. Oreads are extremely strong, and can be dangerous when angered. They seem to have evolved independently across the globe; their common name is from the Greek.

Sasquatch (Gigantopithecus sesquac). These massive native denizens of North America have learned to embrace depilatories and mail-order shoe catalogs. A surprising number make their living as Bigfoot hunters (Bigfeet and Sasquatches are close relatives, and enjoy tormenting each other). They are predominantly vegetarian, and enjoy Canadian television.

Tanuki (Nyctereutes sapiens). Therianthrope shapeshifters from Japan, the tanuki are critically endangered due to the efforts of the Covenant. Despite this, they remain friendly, helpful people, with a naturally gregarious nature that makes it virtually impossible for them to avoid human settlements. Tanuki possess three primary forms—human, raccoon dog, and big-ass scary monster. Pray you never see the third form of the tanuki.

Tooth fairy (Pyske dentin). Tooth fairies are small—no taller than the length of a tall man's hand—and possess dual-lobed wings. Their dietary habits are unpleasant, and best left undiscussed. Do not leave unsupervised near children.

Waheela (Waheela sapiens). Therianthrope shapeshifters from the upper portion of North America, the waheela are a solitary race, usually claiming large swaths of territory and defending it to the death from others of their species. Waheela mating season is best described with the term "bloodbath." Waheela transform into something that looks like a dire bear on steroids. They're usually not hostile, but it's best not to push it.

PLAYLIST:

Here are a few songs to rock you through Verity's adventures.

"Just Dance"	Lady Gaga
"Kids With Guns"	Gorillaz
"We Are Mice"	Azure Ray
"Manic Monday"	The Bangles
"Whipped Cream"	Ludo
"U+UR Hand"	Pink
"Fingerprints"	Katy Perry
"America"	Bree Sharp
"Nobody Move, Nobody Get Hurt"	We Are Scientists
"Secrets"	One Republic
"Snakes and Ladders"	Basia Bulat
"Corrupt"	Karissa Noel
"House of Wolves"	My Chemical Romance
"Dead is the New Alive"	Emilie Autumn
"Bad Moon Rising"	Rasputina
"Beauty Has Her Way"	The Lost Boys Soundtrack
"Maps"	Yeah Yeah Yeahs
"Susan"	Aimee Mann
"Rumor Has It"	Adele
"Do You Recall"	Royal Wood
"Sugar"	Thea Gilmore

"Oisin, My Bastard Brother"..........The High Dials
"Hammer to the Heart"...................Tamperer
"Ramalama (Bang Bang)"............Roisin Murphy
"Back Against the Wall" ....Alan Parsons Project
"Cowards in a Brave New World" ....Kim Richey

ACKNOWLEDGMENTS:

Discount Armageddon marks the beginning of my second urban fantasy series, and my greatest thanks are extended to Phil Ames, without whom this series would not exist. Betsy Tinney endured my endless questions about the world of professional ballroom dance, while Kate Secor put up with my insistence on watching every single episode of *So You Think You Can Dance* (sometimes twice).

The tireless machete squad provided proofreading and editorial services, with yeoman labors being performed by Will Frank, Ryan Nutick, and Priscilla Spencer. Amy Mebberson and Bill Mudron supplied incredible artistic interpretations of my characters. Meanwhile, back on the ranch, Chris Mangum and Tara O'Shea made sure my website and graphic needs were met with sleep and élan. I couldn't do this without them.

My agent, Diana Fox, never lost faith in me, even when I explained that my latest project involved fighting evil through the power of ballroom dance, while Sheila Gilbert and the entire team at DAW worked to make this book a thousand times better than it was to start. My cover artist, Aly Fell, was a dream come true. I am so blessed.

Thanks to Kate Secor and Michelle Dockrey for

sharing my time with fictional people, to my mother, for cat-sitting during convention season, and to Jude Feldman and the staff at Borderlands Books, for everything. Any errors in this book are entirely my own. The errors that aren't here are the ones that all these people helped me fix.

Seanan McGuire
The October Daye Novels

"...will surely appeal to readers who enjoy my books, or those of Patricia Briggs." —*Charlaine Harris*

"I am so invested in the world building and the characters now.... Of all the 'Faerie' urban fantasy series out there, I enjoy this one the most."—*Felicia Day*

To Order Call: 1-800-788-6262
www.dawbooks.com

DAW 142

Diana Rowland

The Kara Gillian Novels

"Rowland's hot streak continues as she gives her fans another big helping of urban fantasy goodness! The plot twists are plentiful and the action is hard-edged. Another great entry in this compelling series." —*RT Book Review*

"Rowland's world of arcane magic and demons is fresh and original [and her] characters are well-developed and distinct.... Dark, fast-paced, and gripping." —*SciFiChick*

Secrets of the Demon
978-0-7564-0652-3

Sins of the Demon
978-0-7564-0705-6

Touch of the Demon
978-0-7564-0775-9

Fury of the Demon
978-0-7564-0830-5

To Order Call: 1-800-788-6262
www.dawbooks.com

DAW 176

Tanya Huff

"The Gales are an amazing family, the aunts will strike fear into your heart, and the characters Allie meets are both charming and terrifying."

—#1 *New York Times* bestselling author
Charlaine Harris

"Thoughtful and leisurely, this fresh urban fantasy from Canadian author Huff features an ensemble cast of nuanced characters in Calgary, Alberta.... Fantasy buffs will find plenty of humor, thrills and original mythology to chew on, along with refreshingly three-dimensional women in an original, fully realized world."   —*Publishers Weekly*

The Enchantment Emporium
978-0-7564-0605-9

The Wild Ways
978-0-7564-0763-6

and now...
The Future Falls
978-0-7564-0753-7

To Order Call: 1-800-788-6262
www.dawbooks.com

DAW 200

Diana Rowland

"Rowland's delightful novel jumps genre lines with a little something for everyone—mystery, horror, humor, and even a smattering of romance. Not to be missed—all that's required is a high tolerance for gray matter. For true zombiephiles, of course, that's a no brainer."

—Library Journal

"An intriguing mystery and a hilarious mix of the horrific and mundane...Humor and gore are balanced by surprisingly touching moments as Angel tries to turn her (un)life around." *—Publishers Weekly*

My Life as a White Trash Zombie
978-0-7564-0675-2

Even White Trash Zombies Get the Blues
978-0-7564-0750-6

White Trash Zombie Apocalypse
978-0-7564-0803-9

How the White Trash Zombie Got Her Groove Back
978-0-7564-0822-0

To Order Call: 1-800-788-6262
www.dawbooks.com

Gini Koch
The Alien *Novels*

"Gini Koch's Kitty Katt series is a great example of the lighter side of science fiction. Told with clever wit and non-stop pacing, this series follows the exploits of the country's top alien exterminators in the American Centaurion Diplomatic Corps. It blends diplomacy, action, and sense of humor into a memorable reading experience."　　—*Kirkus*

"Amusing and interesting...a hilarious romp in the vein of 'Men in Black' or 'Ghostbusters'."　　　　　—*VOYA*

(coming December 2014)

To Order Call: 1-800-788-6262

www.dawbooks.com

DAW 160

Katharine Kerr

The Nola O'Grady Novels

"Breakneck plotting, punning, and romance make for a
mostly fast, fun read."　　　—*Publishers Weekly*

"This is an entertaining investigative urban fantasy that sub-
genre readers will enjoy...fans will enjoy the streets of San
Francisco as seen through an otherworldly lens."
　　　　　　　　　　　　　—*Midwest Book Review*

LICENSE TO ENSORCELL
978-0-7564-0656-1

WATER TO BURN
978-0-7564-0691-2

APOCALYPSE TO GO
978-0-7564-0709-4

LOVE ON THE RUN
978-0-7564-0762-9

To Order Call: 1-800-788-6262
www.dawbooks.com

DAW 180